Advance praise for

ᴛʜᴇ
SEALWOMAN'S
GIFT

'A remarkable feat of imagination: from the first, it leaps from the page. Its richly vivid sense of time and place recall Jessie Burton's *The Miniaturist* and the novels of Cecilia Ekback, and there is a particular pleasure in its highly original choice of subject matter. Magnusson writes with an infectious verve, so that I found myself absolutely persuaded by Ásta's extraordinary journey from the harsh Icelandic coast to the strange and splendid palaces of Algiers. Nor is this a novel afraid to inform: at each reading I came away feeling enriched by Magnusson's use of Icelandic myth, and her absolute authority over her subject. It's enormous fun to read – I enjoyed and admired it in equal measure'
Sarah Perry, author of *The Essex Serpent*

'Icelandic history has been brought to extraordinary life. I was swept up in the story and the vivid plight of people taken away from everything they knew and understood. Transported to a time long ago, I was completely enthralled by Sally Magnusson's skilful story-telling. An accomplished and intelligent novel – highly recommended'
Yrsa Sigurðardóttir, author of *Why Did You Lie?*

'Sally Magnusson has taken a little-known historical event – the Barbary corsair raid on Iceland in 1627 – and produced a moving story of suffering and redemption. Her tale of Ásta, the Reverend's wife, indomitable survivor of tragedy and heartbreak, is vivid and compelling'
Adam Nichols, co-editor and translator of
The Travels of Reverend Ólafur Egilsson

THE
SEALWOMAN'S
GIFT

TWO ROADS

www.tworoadsbooks.com

First published in Great Britain in 2018 by Two Roads
An imprint of John Murray Press
An Hachette UK company

1

Copyright © Sally Magnusson 2018

The right of Sally Magnusson to be identified as the Author of the
Work has been asserted by her in accordance with the
Copyright, Designs and Patents Act 1988.

A CIP catalogue record for this title is available from the British Library

Hardback ISBN 978 1 473 63895 2
Trade Paperback ISBN 978 1 473 63896 9
Ebook ISBN 978 1 473 63897 6
Audio Digital Download ISBN 978 1 473 66259 9

Typeset by Palimpsest Book Production Limited,
Falkirk, Stirlingshire
Printed and bound by Clays Ltd, St Ives plc

Hodder & Stoughton policy is to use papers that are natural, renewable
and recyclable products and made from wood grown in sustainable forests.
The logging and manufacturing processes are expected to conform to
the environmental regulations of the country of origin.

Hodder & Stoughton Ltd
Carmelite House
50 Victoria Embankment
London EC4Y 0DZ

www.hodder.co.uk

To Vigdís Finnbogadóttir

A Note About Icelandic

For the ease of non-Icelandic readers, the letter ð (pronounced as a voiced th) is transcribed throughout as an English d, the letter þ as th and the dipthong æ as ae. Accents alter the way vowels are pronounced. For instance, á is the sound in owl, é as in yet, í and ý as in seen, ó as in note, ú as in soon, ö as in the French fleur, ae as in life, and ei and ey as in tray.

Some Icelandic Words

Badstofa *[bath-stova]*	Communal living and sleeping room
Mín kaera *[meen kyra]*	My loved one (to a female)
Minn kaeri *[minn kyri]*	My loved one (to a male)
Kvöldvaka *[kveuld-vaka]*	Storytelling time, literally 'evening awakening'
Skyr *[skeer]*	Dairy product similar to yoghurt
Vestmannaeyjar *[Vestmanna-ayyar]*	Westman Islands
Jökull *[yeu-kutl]*	Glacier
Eyjafjallajökull *[Ayya-fjatla-yeu-kutl]*	Literally 'Islands'-Mountains'-Glacier'

Characters (in alphabetical order)

Icelanders

A fisherman

Agnes — Mother of Magnús Birgisson

Anna Jasparsdóttir — Newly married Westman
[Anna Yaspars-dohtir] — islander

Ásta Thorsteinsdóttir — Wife of Rev Ólafur Egilsson
[Owsta Thorstayns-dohtir]

Ásta and Ólafur's children:
  Helga
  Egill
  [Ay-yitl]
  Marta
  Jón
  [Yone]

Einar Loftsson — Westman islander
[Aynar Lopt-son]

Erlendur Runólfsson — Slain Westman islander
[Erlendur Runohlfs-son]

Eyjólfur Sölmundarson — Husband of Gudrídur
[Ay-yohlvur Seul-moondar-son] — Símonardóttir

Finnur Gudmundsson — Husband of Helga Ólafsdóttir
[Finnur Gveuth-munds-son]

Gísli Oddsson — Bishop of southern Iceland,
[Geesli Odds-son] — based at Skálholt

Gísli Thorvardsson — Priest married to Thorgerdur
[Geesli Thorvarth-son] — Ólafsdóttir

viii

Gudbrandur Thorláksson	Northern bishop who printed
[Gveuth-brandur Thor-lowks-son]	the Bible in Icelandic
Gudrídur Símonardóttir	Wife of Eyjólfur Sölmundarson
[Gveuth-reethur Seemonar-dohtir]	
Gunnhildur Hermannsdóttir	Captured from Djúpivogur in
[Goon-hildur Hermanns-dohtir]	the east of Iceland
Halldóra Jónsdóttir	Elderly Icelandic woman
[Hatl-dohra Yones-dohtir]	
Hallgrímur Pétursson	Trainee priest
[Hatl-greemur Pi-eturs-son]	
Inga	Serving girl at Ofanleiti
Jaspar Kristjánsson	Danish father of Anna
[Yaspar Krist-jowns-son]	Jasparsdóttir
Jón Jónsson	Son of Margrét and Jón (later
[Yone Yone-son]	the Westman)
Jón Oddsson	First husband of Anna
[Yone Odds-son]	Jasparsdóttir
Jón Thorsteinsson	Island priest at Kirkjubaer
[Yone Thor-stayn-son]	
Kristín	Friend of Ásta
Magnús Birgisson	Westman islander, friend of Egill
[Magnoos Birgis-son]	
Margrét Jónsdóttir	Wife of Rev Jón Thorsteinsson
[Margri-et Yones-dohtir]	
Oddrún Pálsdóttir	A sealwoman (possibly)
[Oddroon Powls-dohtir]	
Ólafur Egilsson	Island priest, husband of Ásta
[Ohlavur Ay-yils-son]	Thorsteinsdóttir
Thorgerdur Ólafsdóttir	Ólafur's daughter by his first
[Thor-gerthur Ohlafs-dohtir]	wife

Thorlákur Skúlason	Succeeded Gudbrandur as
[Thor-lowkur Skoola-son]	Bishop of Hólar
Thorsteinn Einarson	Ásta's father, priest at Mosfell
[Thor-stayn Aynar-son]	in south Iceland

Corsairs

Murat Reis	Corsair admiral, born Jan Janszoon
Sa'id Suleiman	Ottoman janissary
Wahid Fleming	Dutch-born corsair captain

Citizens of Algiers

Ali Pitterling Cilleby	Slave-owner and member of the ruling council
Alimah	Cilleby's first wife
Flower	Servant in Cilleby's house
Husna	Cilleby's second wife
Jón Ásbjarnarson	Former Icelandic slave in the civil service
Jus Hamet	Second husband of Anna Jasparsdóttir
Zafir Chitour	Servant to Captain Fleming

Diplomat

Paul de Willem	Agent of King Christian
Wilhelm Kifft	Denmark's emissary to Algiers

Monarchs

Christian IV	King of Denmark, Norway and Iceland

THE SEALWOMAN'S GIFT

Murad IV	Sultan of the Ottoman Empire

Saga folk

Egill Skallagrímsson	Warrior poet and protagonist of
[Ay-yitl Skatla-greems-son]	Egil's saga
Gudrún Ósvífursdóttir	Beautiful protagonist of Laxdaela
[Gveuth-roon Ohs-vivurs-dohtir]	saga
Kjartan Ólafsson	Disappointed suitor of Gudrún
[Kyartan Ohlafs-son]	
Bolli Thorleiksson	Gudrún's third husband, Kjartan's
	foster-brother
[Botli Thorlayks-son]	
Bolli Bollason	Son of Gudrún and Bolli
[Botli Botla-son]	

Contents

17th CENTURY EUROPE

ONCE UPON A TIME God Almighty came to visit Adam and Eve. They welcomed him in and showed him around. They also showed him their children, whom he found most promising. Then he asked Eve if she had any others. She said she had not. But it so happened that she had not finished washing some of her children and, being ashamed to let God see them in this state, had concealed them from him. This God knew full well. He said: 'Whatever has to be hidden from me will henceforth be hidden from man.' Then these unwashed children became invisible to human eyes and took up their abode in mounds and rocky heights, in hillocks and great stones. From them are the elves descended, while humans come from those of Eve's children who were shown to God. Elves can see human beings, but they can never be seen by them, unless they so will it.

Traditional legend

1638

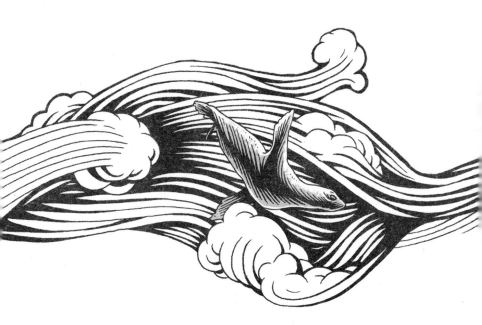

The rain has freshened the air again, leaving one of the soft springtime evenings she used to love best, the clouds harried on their way by an eager breeze, a spangle of late sunshine on the water. Behind her a snipe has begun a humming circuit of the heath and she has to force herself not to turn and search the sky for it. No, straight down the wall of the cliff is where she must look, nowhere else, and only pay attention to the waves bellowing up for company. She steps closer to the edge, smoothing her skirts against the flurries of wind. The stones are slippy with damp moss.

Here is a point to consider. If the wind were to take her before she made another move, or if, say, her chilled toes should lose their grip, it wouldn't be so bad a sin, would it? Hardly her fault at all, really, if you look at it that way, although that is not to say God would. Certainly it would be better received at her funeral. On this matter at least people would be sure to give her the benefit of the doubt. Poor soul, she must have forgotten how easily the April gusts can seize you. God be praised, she won't be able to corrupt anyone now.

The patrolling snipe is distracting her, like one of those dozy black flies that insists on buzzing when you want peace to think. *Go away, please. I am trying to imagine my funeral.* The whirring stops, then starts up again, somewhere high in the sky but nearer now. She tries to guess which direction it will come from next; imagines the flash of white breast behind her as it swoops, silvery in the sun.

3

SALLY MAGNUSSON

Oh, this is no good. The emotion that drove her from the house has started to ebb, all that furious despair giving way, now that she is truly on the edge, to a numb misery she can feel draining the power of action. So perhaps she will just turn and permit herself one look at the bird circling in its lovely blue vault, and let it be her last sight on earth before she closes her eyes.

She turns and her hand flies to her mouth.

The man is little more than an arm's length away. His face, what can be seen of it under an unruly beard that makes him look very different, is white with alarm. The arm he has reached out to grab her is frozen in mid-air.

'Oh,' she says. 'It's you.'

GREY

July – August 1627

The pirates rushed with violent speed across the island, like hunting hounds . . . Some of my neighbours managed to escape quickly into the caves or down the cliffs, but many were seized or bound . . . I and my poor wife were amongst the first to be captured.

Reverend Ólafur Egilsson

I

There is nothing to be said for giving birth in the bowels of a sailing ship with your stomach heaving and hundreds of people listening. Really there is not, no matter how many blessings Ólafur insists on counting. In fact, Ásta is some way from persuaded that he is entitled to a view at all. During her last confinement he was so long at the harbour bidding the Danish governor *skál* over a brandy consignment from Copenhagen that there was no one to fetch the midwife.

Ólafur says she should be grateful for the tent. Tent? It's a couple of lengths of damp sail hung from a beam, which arrived with the compliments of the big pirate captain with the pink face and blond eyelashes with whom her husband has struck up an inexplicable camaraderie. Ólafur has a knack for friendship: he will swallow the most flagrant offence to see what he might learn from another mind. Well, much pleasure may he take from that man's mind. Today Ólafur is pleased to report that the length of cloth required to construct a Turkish turban is three yards and the sash around the long jackets they wear over those ridiculous trousers is even longer: 'More than seven yards, my dear. Can you believe it?'

It is bad enough to be penned inside the hold of a galleon on

7

the high seas, the first twinges of labour upon you and the panic growing, without being exhorted to be grateful for a sail and excited about the length of a silken sash.

He is probably trying to help.

Ásta heaves her belly to the right and stretches the cramp out of her left leg, trying not to prod old Oddrún Pálsdóttir, whose curled back is pressed against the other side of the sail. More neighbours, dozen upon dozen of them, are sprawled to the gunwales beyond the old woman, trying to sleep. Ásta can hear her fellow prisoners, and smell them. She can feel the weight of their torpid misery pressing in on her. Stockfish tossed together end to end and skin to skin for selling is hardly packed more tight than this wretched human cargo. But at least she and her family are largely out of sight. To that extent the sail does afford a modicum of privacy, which in fairness (*mark this concession in your sleep, Ólafur*) she should probably be gracious enough to admit.

Ólafur is forever urging her to be fair: 'Pray consider rising less quickly to the boil, Ásta *mín*, and judge more calmly.' He would do well to remember that fairness and coolness are just as quick to desert him when he mounts the pulpit. His zest for admonishing the congregation is by common consent a model of intemperance. It is true, all the same, that when everyone else inclines to hysteria Ólafur will reliably be at his most reasonable. This she must also acknowledge. Being fair.

'Don't be afraid to look in their eyes,' he said that first day, as she lumbered over the side of the ship and turned to look back at the fire leaping through the wooden church of Landakirkja. 'You will see they are men like any other.'

He took her arm then, trying to nudge her from the sight of the flames. 'See, my love, no tails. No knives growing out of their elbows, no sulphur pouring from their mouths. So much for the rumours. Some of them don't even look particularly wicked up close, do they?'

She felt the tremble of his hand, though. His voice was brittle, the way it goes when he is hurt and trying not to show it. His face, always thin, was taut with the emotion he was holding in. Even the English had not gone so far as to raze God's house to ashes.

The dark young corsair who came to attach the sail did not look much like a devil either, for all that his eyes were black. As he hoisted it over a joist, the sleeves of his tunic fell back and Ásta was disconcerted to find herself admiring the cormorant sheen of his arms. When he caught her glance and saw how close she was to her time, he smiled down at her. That was too much. Ólafur said later he thought it was a kind smile, kind enough at least, but she was seized only by the most ferocious desire to strike the man on his cheerful mouth.

How pleasantly did they smile, this handsome corsair and his fellows, when they murdered her uncle Jón in a cave by the sea? Or chased Kristín, merriest of neighbours, until she could run no more and bled to death on the hill, her skirts about her waist and the dead baby hanging from its cord? Or drove young Erlendur Runólfsson to the edge of a cliff, stripped him to the waist and fired their muskets until he toppled backwards into the waves?

How can Ólafur talk to these people? How can someone who spends his days down here consoling the frightened and the heartbroken take even a moment to weigh the kindly intent behind a pirate's smile? Ásta seethes every time she thinks of it.

Ólafur is doing his best to stay reasonable and raise spirits. She cannot deny it, although in her present state of weepy exhaustion even his consolations are obscurely annoying. Day after day he squeezes around the hold, trying to avoid stepping on his flock as he reminds them they are only being tested, that suffering is what all people must endure in this world and they should look to the life beyond and not be discouraged.

'Ólafur,' she is fit to erupt, 'may God above forgive me, but we are completely and utterly discouraged. How could it not be so?'

If Ásta were dwelling on her discomforts (which she is trying so hard not to that she is dwelling on nothing else), she might enumerate surging nausea, tightening belly, cramping leg, fisting baby and the mounting urge to pee when there is no pail to hand and no prospect of one for hours, if then. To say nothing of the grind of bare wood on her spine, the tickle of coiled rope at her neck or the fleabite on her left ankle that is impossible to reach without disturbing at least four people. Unless she can find something else to think about, that itch is going to be what shakes the ship with her roaring before the labour ever does.

But what is there else to think about that will not tear her with grief?

The smell? The dark, unspeakable stench of human beings oozing distress? Worse. She must not on any account think about the smell. (But still – might it actually be possible to die of a smell? How long would it take?) No, try concentrating on the night noises. Not the slow creak of the timbers and the sea slap – not those noises – but the sounds of the people: the lone sob, trembling away to nothing; the snores (no mistaking Oddrún's high-pitched whistle, and that can only be Einar Loftsson's volcanic rumble dominating many lesser efforts); somewhere nearby a grunt of furtive pleasure; further away a fart so stirring (as Ásta reflects, blinking) that it would have proved its mettle in the Battle of Jericho. The sigh of murmuring voices rises and falls. A woman is retching. A child won't stop moaning. A man, perhaps in sleep, lets out a cry of naked sorrow. These sudden cries are the worst. All the weeping down here Ásta can tolerate: hear enough of it, do enough yourself, and you hardly notice after a while. But the howls of anguish in the night still make her heart pound with terror.

Here comes another of the tightenings, harder and harder until her belly feels like a stone you could beat and flake a dried cod on, then relaxing. They don't hurt much yet, but nor do they make sleeping any easier. The floor undulates beneath her, making her stomach lurch and bringing bile again and again to her throat. She has never been a good sailor: even being rowed out to the Westman Islands as a girl had her hanging over the side, to the amusement of the fishermen at the oars.

It is becoming difficult to judge how many days they have been at sea. Ólafur says nine. But when the only light is from lamps swinging and clattering in the swell, it can be a struggle to tell day and night apart. Some communal instinct below has established a night-time, but it is one that Ásta's body remains reluctant to observe.

Tentatively she stretches another leg, this time provoking a muffled yelp from the other side of the sail. Poor Oddrún. She hardly deserves to have her miseries compounded by the restless foot of a woman whose baby is past its time. The island's greatest talker has hardly said a word since the voyage began. Day and night she lies still and forlorn, with her face turned away and her cap holding on by a thread, paying no heed to the mockers who torment her still. 'Oddrún will be all right, seeing she's a seal,' they taunt, too loud, too close. 'Lend us a flipper, Oddrún, will you, if we go down.' But the old woman has only sunk further into herself and kept her eyes closed.

Ásta shifts again, disturbing a rat. It streaks across her fanned hair and back into the darkness beyond the lamplight. Shadows leap across the sail as the vessel dips and climbs. Ólafur's face is buried in her back. Egill lies with his head next to hers, one arm reaching across little Marta to touch his mother's hand. She wishes the boy would weep. When the pirates put Ofanleiti to the flame, he saw sights that no child should. He is also tormented by the thought that he was not as brave as his best friend. 'After we were captured, Magnús managed to creep away,' he has told her, looking at his hands and refusing to meet her gaze. 'He asked me to come and hide on our secret gannet ledge, but I didn't dare.'

And what can a mother say? That a part of her is glad he was not brave the way Magnús was, because otherwise she would not have him here at her side, her firstborn son, the pool from which her heart drinks? At eleven Egill is too nearly a man to want to hear this. He has never been one to speak his own heart aloud; but in the night, when no one is looking, he slips his hand in hers.

Marta is curled, neat as a mouse, in the space between Ásta's chin and her protruding belly. By day she sits more or less calmly by her mother's side, as if sensing there is no point in making a fuss. Ásta used to find her composure at not yet three years unsettling, especially after the bawling tantrums from Helga at the same age, but in their present calamity her stillness is a comfort.

Helga is not here. She left for the mainland earlier this summer and is surely safe. The pirates raided parts of the coast, but Torfastadir is well inland. Has Helga heard yet that her family has been seized by Turkish corsairs and carried off in a ship with great white sails to a place beyond imagining? The news must have been carried across the water by now, although it will have taken time for the remaining islanders to work out who is taken, who escaped and whose bloated body might yet be discovered on some desolate strand. Is her eldest daughter at this moment crying herself to sleep in the priesthouse at Torfastadir, wondering what will become of her? Dear, fiery Helga, so eager to get away from an island where they talked of nothing – 'nothing at all, Mamma' – but fish, who begged to go and keep house for her stepsister because (may God forgive the child) nothing interesting ever happened at home. The conversation in the home of Thorgerdur and Gísli will not have proved for one minute more stimulating: Ólafur's daughter by his first wife is exceedingly dull and her husband nearly always drunk. But when Ásta said as much, Helga tossed the auburn curls of which she has always been more proud than she should be and retorted huffily, 'You came to the island when you were not much older than me, Mamma, and wasn't it because you were just as glad to be offered something more? Isn't that what you told us?'

Something more. The ship rolls and bucks and Ásta fights

down another wave of nausea. One child she may never see again; two with a future she dare not contemplate; another agitating to be born in a reeking prison-ship on a voyage into slavery. Dear God, how did it come to this?

2

It was a fine morning. That she will always remember – how lovely dawned the seventeenth day of July in the year 1627, the day the pirates came. It was one of those mornings when the wind breathes the scent of cut grass and the sea wrinkles like an old man's hand. When you can see nearly all the islands dozing for miles around in the clear light. When your fingers fly so lightly to the plucking that you forget the pile still waiting. When you raise your face to the sun and it warms you and you realise – so Ásta did, tossing a feather in the air for Marta to catch – that the dread hanging over the island for weeks has gone and you are happy.

The panic the previous day when three ships were spotted off the mainland, tacking back and forth in the lee of the Eyjafjalla glacier, was over. When it drew nearer, the lead galleon had turned out to be flying a Danish flag, bringing not terror but protection at last. The pirates who had ravaged parts of the mainland and shocked the whole of Iceland to the core were gone. The Westman Islands could breathe again.

Lined up before Ásta were her beloved Small Isles. There stood neat, round Haena, jagged Hrauney and Hani, with that look of a seal in a cap that always reminded her so delightfully of someone she knew. 'Hello, Oddrún,' she would nod to the bulky isle of a morning. 'What story have you for me today?' Ásta has never told Oddrún about her nickname for the island: the old woman has strong feelings about being a seal and tires of jests. Long ago her sealskin was lost under the midnight sun. She is emphatic about this, her oyster eyes liquid with sincerity. She and the other sealfolk swam ashore to dance on Heimaey's black summer sands, and there they took their skins off and laid them on the warm rocks to dry. All night long they span and they sang, their bodies lithe and golden under the unsleeping sun, until it was time to slip back into their skins and return to the sea. Oddrún made to go with them, but when she looked for hers it was gone. Stolen, she is sure. 'Come back, come back, don't leave me here,' she called to the retreating sealfolk as they plunged into the waves' bosomy embrace. But one by one they disappeared, and Oddrún was left without her skin to make a life on Heimaey, never feeling quite herself. She was young then, she insists, and her body firm and slender; but if the thief were to return the pelt now, it would no longer fit a waddling old woman. This is her particular grief. This is the point in the story when she always starts to weep fat, despairing tears.

Ásta's sharp-tongued aunt Margrét used to explode with exasperation. 'Oddrún,' she cried once, 'half the folk on this island knew your father.'

But Margrét (may God protect her wherever she is now) has never been one to look much further than her own pointed nose. She would be the last person to wonder whether Oddrún Pálsdóttir has been weeping all her life for something else.

It was not long before Oddrún arrived in person that sparkling morning, labouring up the Ofanleiti slope with her broad face pouring sweat and her cap askew. By the time she reached Ásta, she was panting so much she could hardly speak.

'I . . . have . . . news, Ásta dear.'

Any news borne by Oddrún repays caution, having normally arrived by way of a dream, but Ásta was grateful for an excuse to let the puffin drop to her lap and stretch her stiff fingers. She straightened her back with a grunt, brushed a couple of feathers from her face and thought about trying to stand up. No, too much effort. Oddrún could join her on the grass.

'Take a minute to get your breath, Oddrún mín. Then sit down here beside me and tell me your news.'

Egill had gone with his friend Magnús to hunt birds and Marta was serenely inspecting the vein of her feather and rubbing its softness against her cheek. Ólafur had disappeared inside the house to write.

Oddrún remained resolutely on her feet. 'We must call Ólafur at once,' she urged, eyeing the closed door. 'Ásta mín, this is urgent!'

Oddrún's news is invariably urgent. After her last dream she had come thumping at their door in the early hours to say she had seen the mountain behind Ofanleiti erupting along its eastern flank: 'Fire pouring from one side, my friends, and the earth opening, just opening before my very eyes, in a line of flame'. Ólafur dragged himself out of bed and Oddrún stumbled over her skirts after him, and they both stood in the dawn mist taking in the sight of the implacably serene Helgafell doing nothing at all. Ólafur marched back inside in a silence that Ásta could tell was costing him dear. He has always been astonishingly patient with Oddrún, whose convictions do not accord with his own at any point. But every man has his limits, and Ásta knew he would not thank either of them for being disturbed this morning for another dream. She, on the other hand, has rarely minded listening to any story the old woman might produce. She has long been intrigued by a quality in Oddrún that is not so risible – a secret, serious, elusive thing not entirely of this world. It touches a yearning in herself that she has never been quite able to define.

'Tell your tidings to me instead,' she said, patting the grass.

With another wistful look at the door, Oddrún flopped down and shoved her iron curls back under the cap. And then the words came tumbling. A dream. So real. So urgent.

'Hundreds of men, Ásta, in clothes with more colours than a puffin's beak. They were jumping out of small boats near Brimurd. I'm sure it was there, because I recognised the surf. They were running across the island with red banners flying behind them. We have to tell Ólafur at once. They're coming for us.'

She gazed at Ásta, her eyes huge in their pools of fat, willing the younger woman to believe her. Two strands of hair had re-emerged from the cap.

'Brimurd?' Ásta sat back on her heels. A small foot, or perhaps a knuckle, jabbed her in the side and she put a hand there to feel it. Brimurd was an inhospitable bay down the east coast, where the surf blasts the boulders and no fisherman would dream of hauling in a boat.

'Nobody ever lands down there – you know that. Come, Oddrún, you mustn't frighten us like this when we're just starting to feel better.'

'I'm telling you what I saw. There was a big ship in the background, with huge square sails like a Danish one, and the boats were past the rocks and these men were just pouring on to land and —'

'Well, it probably *was* a Danish warship you were dreaming about then. We saw three of them yesterday, remember, come to protect Iceland at long last.'

'If they *were* Danish ships,' Oddrún said sulkily.

Oddrún was not famed for her maritime insights. Ásta, who had been scared out of her wits by the appearance of those ships, laughed easily. 'Well, the men are all sure they were Danish galleons. They sailed right past, didn't they?'

Oddrún was beginning to look mulish and Ásta patted her knee. 'Look, you know the pirates are gone from Iceland. Everyone says so. And if they ever happened to show their faces in the harbour, the Danes have cannons at the ready, don't they?'

Oddrún started to say, 'But this ship wasn't at the harbour . . .' and then gave up. Ásta will long remember the look on her face, the not-quite-resigned sadness of it, her mouth opening as if to speak and from long practice closing again; the way she rested her whiskery chin in her hand and finally looked away, defeated. She hauled herself to her feet and Ásta watched her cap bobbing back down the slope until it was out of sight.

She finished the bird and laid its carcass on the heap next to the orange flippers and rainbow beaks that Egill had severed and piled before he left for the cliffs, grumbling that it was women's work and Helga should be here to do it. Trying a new position on the grass, Ásta stretched her legs out (oh, to be able to do that now), smoothed her dress to the ankles and began on the next one. She had barely started when she spied Kristín

plodding up the slope to collect water from the Ofanleiti well.
They had grown big together these months past, she and Kristín,
laughing at how long an arm they both needed to stir their pots
over the kitchen fire.

Kristín came to stand a moment beside her to get her breath
back. Picking a couple of feathers out of Ásta's hair, she remarked
conversationally, 'I poured Siggi's ale into the piss-pot during
the night.'

Or was it his piss into the ale-mug? Ásta keeps trying to
remember. Not because it matters – not in the slightest – but
because it is nearly the last thing Kristín said to her and so
perfectly typical: it was a point of agreement between them that
her husband was a boor. What she does recall now, chasing sleep
in the ship's hold, is how Kristín laughed at the thought of what
she had done, her curly dark head thrown back in a gust of
merriment and a hand on her great belly. Then she winced and
muttered something about that one being a bit sharp.

Ásta shooed her away with a laugh. 'You'd better hurry up
with that pail or you'll be having the child here.'

Then she turned over another puffin and began on its breast,
blowing Marta a whirr of white feathers now and then to keep
her dancing. As her fingers found their rhythm again, she became
aware of a distant noise and stopped again to listen. The sea was
muttering beyond the heath and that must be a couple of plovers
piping in the long grass near the elf-stone. Somewhere over by
the wall she could hear a redshank – yes, there it was, flashing
its orange knees in the long grass. But something else was being
carried on the soft summer air, louder now, and coming closer.
Dogs perhaps. But there were not enough of them on the island
to make that kind of din. Not dogs.

It was only when she turned to see a gang of vividly attired men exploding over the brow of the hill behind her in a glitter of raised swords, that Ásta thought about Oddrún and knew who they were. Lying here on the bucking timbers, she is chilled again by that cold wash of panic. It was the moment everything changed, the moment that will divide her life – she knows it for a certainty – into before and after the Turkish raid.

3

Much exercised by the whereabouts of Spanish privateers, Captain Wahid Fleming is keeping a nervous eye on the horizon. A dozen extra captives are being manhandled into his ship from the smaller one swaying next to his in the empty ocean. He has already reprimanded his fellow captain with some energy for not sorting out his numbers before they left Iceland. The last thing Fleming wants is to be surprised on the high seas grappled to another vessel, his topsail furled and a cargo worth a fortune in the hold.

He slaps another palmful of brine over his face and under the lip of his turban, wincing as it trickles down the back of his suppurating pink neck. This sun will be the death of him.

'Put some elbow into that whip, Sa'id,' he roars to the janissary in charge of the arrivals. 'Nobody asked you to welcome them to our happy home. Just get them over the side and down to the hold fast.'

A tiny, sharp-featured woman looks up. She is trying to straddle the side of the new ship, her skirts making it hard to grip, the janissary flustering her with threats. But at the sound of that voice she freezes.

'Come on, Mamma,' urges a blond, broad-shouldered lad who

has leaped to the deck before her. 'Take my hand. It's not far to jump.'

The captain watches idly as Sa'id flicks a desultory whip across the woman's shoulders. There is something familiar about her, although it's hard to say what. They all look the same, these Icelanders. Grey clothes, grey faces.

Surely there can't be many more to come: his own hold is bursting with prisoners already. One swell at the wrong moment and he'll have the hulls knocking and the yardarms and riggings entangled and a pretty mess to unpick. The captain helps himself to another dollop of water from the barrel and is essaying a gingerly pat on the back of his neck when he is disturbed by a piercing screech.

The woman is down and flying across the deck towards him, screaming at the top of her voice with the janissary at her heels. The captain waves Sa'id back and folds his arms calmly, awaiting the onslaught of Margrét from Kirkjubaer, who has recognised the man who murdered her husband. She halts in front of him and squints up to release a torrent of Icelandic. After which she throws her head back, juts it forward again and fires a missile of spit. It only just clears the captain's waist, striking above the red sash in which are secured his two daggers, scimitar and a musket of polished black walnut. With an effort he keeps his hand from straying there.

'Think you can wash yourself clean, do you?' Margrét is shrieking in a voice that has always compensated generously for what she lacks in size. 'Well, let me tell you, you can wash from now till the coming of the kingdom and you will never be clean.'

The captain makes a show of laughing off both the tirade and the spit, staying the impulse to knock every tooth out of the small woman's head. On-board handling of captives who will require to be sold whole and in decent health at the other end requires a lighter touch than the raid itself. Get your planning right and the raid is the easy part. The lads race ashore and perform their wild Turk display with plenty of flags and barking and waving scimitars around. Then you deal with any resistance in time-honoured fashion and bundle up the rest. Tried and tested method. But it's different when you've got them at sea: you have to keep things calm.

Gesturing for Sa'id to remove the tiny harridan, the captain watches while she is marched below. He has an idea now where he has seen her: she's the one who crawled over and tried to batter his knees with her fists when he took a sword to the priest – not the talkative priest (God knows, he would be only too glad to take a swipe at that one), but the insolent fellow in the cave. Well, no regrets there. The whole household trooped along like lambs afterwards. As he told the men, that is exactly the kind of example you want to make, cool and deliberate, choosing your target. Not – he had to speak to Sa'id severely about this – not going around chasing women about to give birth. Yes, she should have known better than to run, but that was just wasteful. You have to remember they sell well, the mothers with infants.

Shouting for the ropes to be untied and the grappling irons released, Captain Fleming stomps off to the quarterdeck, gingerly feeling the back of his neck. One of these days he really must think about going home. A well-appointed house in Rotterdam, maybe. Nice wet climate. And no having to get on his knees to pray every five minutes either. It would mean licking the Prince of Orange's arse and a tricky religious shift again, but he wouldn't be the first renegade corsair to pull that one off.

Fleming lobs a wandering sheep out of the way with his foot and returns his wary attention to the horizon, as the two galleons begin to strain apart.

'And what did he do when you spat in his eye?'

Ásta is propped against her rope-pillow, stroking Marta's hair and longing for the labour to proceed with more conviction. As she well knows, this wish for brisker pains will be succeeded in short order by the most fervent prayers for them to cease at once – but that can't be helped. All she wants now is for this child to be born.

Margrét shrugs. The spittle, she admits, did fall marginally short of the captain's eye. 'But I spoke my mind. In the cave there was nothing I could do. I held Jón's head, that's all, and then they pulled me away. Today I did something.'

'Jón would have been proud of you.' Ásta squeezes her hand. It is still hard to believe that her big, booming uncle is dead.

Fresh arrived from the smaller ship, Margrét has managed to insert behind the sail not only her own diminutive person but her strapping son. Never one to favour consultation, she is busy trying to tug the front wing aside. 'Plenty of time for us to suffocate inside this thing when you're properly on your way, my girl.'

Ásta is too relieved to have her aunt back among them to care that she has lost even the veneer of a tent and must now look forward to fifteen-year-old Jón Jónsson's feet up her nose in the night. With Margrét in charge she feels better able to face this birth. It's like being back at Kirkjubaer before she married Ólafur, when Margrét ran her life.

Margrét takes a good look at her niece. She notes the tired eyes, the matted fair hair, the slim frame that has made previous deliveries a challenge. The sweat is dripping off her in the heat down here and she looks exhausted, poor girl, before she even starts. Margrét lifts a beaker to Ásta's lips, holding it steady in one hand and leaning for balance with the other against the swaying floor. The water is warm and brackish.

Ásta grimaces. 'Do you remember, Margrét, when I came to you and Jón at first, and I got such a shock that the Westman Islands had no mountain water?'

How young she was then. She assumed that everywhere in Iceland had leaking glaciers and white rivers carrying ice-cold sweetness from the hills. But not a stream could she find anywhere on Heimaey. No water at all, in fact, except for a slimy pond in the Herjólfs valley, a couple of wells and whatever household pot or dip in the lava would hold some rain. Of which, of course, there was always plenty.

'Oh, you were put out all right.' Margrét manages a spectral smile. 'You asked Jón most stridently, "Where is the water, Uncle? I want to wash." And he said, "Take this pail, young woman, and go and fetch it for us, but you'll be lucky if there's enough left to splash on your face. The animals are thirsty."'

'And I walked from Kirkjubaer across to Herjólfsdalur, and there was almost nothing in the pond. Then when I got some into the pail at last it was all shiny and warm and swimming with insects.'

It was nothing like her lovely Leirvogsá river back home in Mosfell, where the water ran between slopes of tumbling scree fast and clear, and cold as winter ice, and horses idled along its stony banks.

'And I wanted to run away, didn't I, Margrét, and beg someone
to row me to the mainland and give me a horse to ride home.
It was such a shock.'

'Not as big a shock as when you said you would just go for a
ride to calm yourself down. Do you remember? And Jón had to
point out that we didn't actually have a horse.' Margrét puts on
a piping, querulous voice: '"But Uncle, don't be silly, everyone
has a horse." And Jón sat you down and explained that hardly
anyone except the Danish merchants owned horses on the
island. You were in such a temper that day.'

She was, she was. Ásta had been told she was coming to the
pearl of Iceland. Everybody said how rich these islands were,
with so much food swimming in the sea and shrieking around
the cliffs that the Crown of Denmark itself had set them in a
league of their own and talked of ruling Iceland 'together with
the Westman Islands'. It was all she heard about: a dozen tongues
at the harbour; ships flying the flags of far lands; the trading
station grown into what some even boasted was Iceland's only
town. Nobody mentioned they had no rivers and drank from
puddles, or thought to warn her there was so little land for
grazing that old horses were pushed over a cliff into the sea with
their throats slit.

And what would she have done if she had known? Just the
same, no doubt. Rushed at the opportunity her uncle offered
when he arrived in Mosfell with his news, throwing open their
door with a blast of rain and conviviality and planting warm,
brandy-laced kisses around the room. Jón was her mother's
brother – their father, like hers, a Thorsteinn – and the house
swelled to receive him. Both men were priests in the Lutheran
church, Jón as big, full-haired and expansive as her father was

small, neat, balding and punctilious. Thorsteinn was a scholar, Jón a poet with visionary leanings on a full stomach.

Jón had come to tell them he had been appointed one of the two priests on Heimaey, biggest of the Vestmannaeyjar, the scattering of islands and skerries off the south coast named (somewhat ingloriously, her peaceable father always opined) after ten westmen slaves from Ireland who were slaughtered there by ninth-century settlers in revenge for a murderous mutiny of their own. Ásta served her uncle his mutton. She can see him wolfing it down now, chewing and talking and pointing his knife and waving those huge hands of his around, all at the same time. He had something else to say, too.

'Thorsteinn *minn*, I also bring a word from Margrét.' He had winked at his niece then, hugging her knees at their feet. 'She asks if you might consider sending Ásta to help with the housekeeping at Kirkjubaer. There will be a lot to be done on the croft there.'

Her father raised an eyebrow. 'How Margrét thinks she will get any work out of this one, I dread to think. She will have to drag her out of your books.'

'Oh, I think we can rely on Margrét,' Jón beamed.

And so it was decided.

The stone-and-turf-house at Kirkjubaer proved to be more cramped than the one at Mosfell, and Jón's knees reached almost to the other side of the *badstofa* in which they all lived and slept. But there were indeed books. Her uncle's prized possession was a hymnal compiled by Gudbrandur Thorláksson, the bishop who barely twenty years earlier had printed the whole Bible in Icelandic on his press at Hólar in the north.

'Think of it,' Jón said reverently. 'God's own word in the tongue of the Icelander.'

'Have you got a copy, Uncle?'

He roared with laughter. 'Have you three cows spare to purchase the great *Gudbrands biblía*? I've seen it, though, and wondered at its beauty. But look.'

He picked up a small printed book, bound in stained calfskin, and ran a pudgy finger across the title page.

'What do you think of his new psalm-book? Bishop Gudbrandur, may God be praised, has not rested in his efforts to reform the taste of our fellow men, whose enthusiasm, may I remind you, for bawdy rhymes and foolish folk stories is much to be deplored.' He glanced at her suspiciously. 'Much to be deplored, Ásta.'

Jón leafed through the hymnal, reading out verses here and there. He showed her how most of the hymns were no more than crude translations from the German, Danish or Latin, but there were a few that had been composed in a native Icelandic style. He declaimed one or two of these with much feeling and waving of arms.

'The diction is not perhaps the finest, but can you hear the difference in the craft, in the way the sounds repeat and the structure of the lines? These ones sound much more Icelandic, do they not?'

Ásta turned the words over on her own tongue and heard the syllables answer and speak to one another. She felt the flowing tide of the lines and fancied she could discern a dim shadow of the gnarled workmanship that had so moved her at home when her father recited the poetry of the mighty saga skald Egill Skallagrímsson. And she wondered then what it would feel like to make a poem from words, as you might make a stitching needle from a sheep's bone, or a vest from woven wool, or a rope bound so strong from slender horse hair that it could swing a man through the air across a cliff face. To tie one word to another and one line to the next and with it let one person enter the mind and heart of another – would that not be a fine thing to do?

Jón had begun writing hymns himself. He would rise before the rest of the household, when barely enough light to see by seeped through the cloudy sheep's uterus stretched across the window space, and pour himself around a small table. They would awaken to the scrape of his feather or a groan as he struggled for rhythm. In the winter evenings, when flame burned in the fulmar oil and she and Margrét were hard at their knitting, Jón would turn his paw of a hand to translating the psalms of David into Icelandic verse. That too occasioned much groaning, but the labour was a sacred duty.

However, he did have a sheaf of epic *rímur* in his chest, written in many hands and stored from earlier times. For all that he disapproved of the narrative poems' frivolous subjects and jaunty forms, he had not cast them away, and if Margrét had only let her, Ásta would have spent every day immersed in courtly poems about knights and lovelorn swains in foreign lands. She did nothing of the kind, of course. Margrét prodded her out to the cow, in to help with the weaving, out to gut the fish, or hang it for drying, or soak the heads, or stone the bone-hard carcasses until they were tender enough to eat with a smear of liver oil, away for water, back for plucking, out to rake hay with their toddling son in tow, a white-blond child named Jón for his father, in to melt the suet or heat the milk or boil the sheep's blood or feed puffin bones to the kitchen fire.

'Do you remember, Margrét, how you had to keep dragging

me out of that chest of Uncle's?' she says, shuffling against the rope at her back.

Margrét sniffs. 'I soon had you in shape, though, didn't I? You would have been no use as a wife to Ólafur if you hadn't known how to soften a cod's head in whey.'

Margrét is near as anxious as Ásta for the labour to take hold and give her something to do. Idleness has no merit at the best of times, but to be doing nothing when her head is pounding with agonies is hard to bear. She is desperate to scour something, to sweep and scrub and straighten and clean, to hurl herself into an assault on the vomit and every other kind of filth that have assailed her afresh in this new ship's hold. Ásta, in her exasperating way, has always embraced idleness like a puffin-down pillow. She could dream any number of hours away, that one. The Lord only knows how she is going to cope when they reach wherever they are going. She's never been in the slightest degree resourceful – head always stuffed with more stories than sense. Ólafur was a brave man to take her on. 'She's captivating, Ólafur,' Margrét remembers sighing, 'but she'll argue you to death and makes the worst butter in Heimaey [which – she might have added – is the least of it: you should taste her liver pudding] and you had better hide your books at once.' Jón adored her, of course. Ásta could wind her uncle around her finger easier than she ever managed with a skein of wool.

Jón.

In the cave Margrét had cradled him in her lap (this same lap, this dress, brown still with his blood and smeared with other nameless bits of him), rocking him to and fro and thinking in her daze that he could be kissed back to her, that her husband might survive with half a head. (*But he has no hair*, she thought as she rocked him. *He'll need his hair*.) For how could such a man as Jón Thorsteinsson, so large and full of life, have gone like that in an instant? One minute he was reading aloud from his psalm-book, intoning words of hope and salvation as calm and steady in that dripping cave as if the household had merely thought to gather for prayers on the shore because the weather was fine. Nobody could have told from his demeanour that they had all rushed there in a fever of panic when word came of the invasion: servants, children, anyone passing Kirkjubaer that morning. Not for a second did he falter as the whoops and shouts came nearer. She is proud of that. Jón would say pride is a sin, but so, she used to tell him, is gluttony. 'You eat all you can, Jón *minn*,' she would say, 'and I'll have pride enough for both of us.'

Not even when a shot from above had the rest of them clutching each other did he pause in his reading. The next minute the pirates had leaped down to the beach and were there. The huge one in front paused to adjust his eyes to the gloom, so that there was that moment when Margrét saw him framed at the mouth of the cave like a vision from hell, dressed in flaming reds and yellows with a sickle sword in his hand. He took a second or two to assess what he saw, which was a man as big as himself, not cowering like the rest but striding forward to meet him with a book held aloft. And then he took just one step towards Jón and slashed at his head. When he fell, the man struck again, and then again. And there was the crown of Jón's head, whipped off and discarded like a hat, and she with her shawl wrapped around him, dementedly trying to rock him back to life.

Margrét closes her eyes, sways a little and straight away opens them. She must not think about the cave now or the flies will be back inside her eyeballs. Those flies, the bold, long-winged kind that arrive from nowhere to sniff out a mess of brains on a hot July day. She will be seeing them until the day she meets her maker herself.

Ásta's belly tightens again and relaxes. Even while giving minute consideration to whether that one hurt more than the last, which she rather fears it did not, Margrét's gust of anguish is not lost on her. Her aunt's features were always sharp – a nose like her tongue, Ólafur used to say – but her face is now shockingly thin and pecked with grief. Ásta can tell she is seeing over and over what she saw in the cave.

Ásta's own household at Ofanleiti had no time to escape to a cave or anywhere else. The pirates reached the farm so swiftly that there was no warning other than poor, ignored Oddrún's, nor anyone murdered before her eyes, although she passed bodies enough later. Nor did Ólafur stride forth brandishing a prayer-book, but merely opened the door to see where the noise was coming from and was soon doubled over with a blow to the gut. Ásta does not even recall wanting to flee. In those seconds of throat-closing panic when the man in billowing yellow trousers came bounding towards her, all she can remember is a frenzied checking of the register of her heart. The names roared through her. *Marta . . . here. Ólafur . . . there. Helga . . . away. Egill . . . where is Egill? Which cliff did he choose today? Is he caught? Is he hurt? Dear God, where is he?*

The man grabbed her, scattering flippers and crunching beaks

underfoot. She aimed an armful of feathers at him, and then a
volley of beaks, but was quickly hauled to her feet. She was
sticky with puffin blood and he, perhaps, with something worse,
for when the feathers floated down again they settled on them
both.

They went after Kristín next. She could easily be spied in the
distance, plodding homewards across the heath with her pail.
Four or five of them broke away to pound after her. She saw
them coming and began to run, but they gained on her quickly
because she was slow, her legs barely supporting her and the
labour pains upon her. Ásta cannot bear to think of her terror.
And then she went down. Ásta saw her crumple and the men
gather around, but she was too far away to see what they saw.
She only found out later that her beloved, light-spirited friend
had died on the grass in front of them, her infant parted from
her in an angry rush of blood. Ásta strokes her own belly now,
feeling for the life within. She imagines Kristín's pursuers
standing around her like a gang of boys who have harried a
wounded pigeon until it can flap no further and who watch,
curious but without pity, the lifeblood seeping into the grass
and the eyes clouding over at the last.

She and Ólafur, with Marta in his arms, were marched to the
harbour and thrust into one of the wooden warehouses that the
Danish merchants used for trading. Egill was captured later and
thrown in to join them, his face white as death, but alive, alive.
He said the pirates had set Ofanleiti on fire. He had seen them
push a crippled woman into the flames. She had screamed to
God for help and her body made a popping noise as she melted.

More and more captives joined them as the day wore on. The
squeeze was such that nimble young Magnús Birgisson saw his

chance to crawl between their legs and slip away. Ásta sank to the floor in exhaustion. There was no food or drink all day.

Drawn back to scenes neither wishes to visit, Ásta and Margrét look at each other in wordless understanding.

Captain Fleming is relishing the cooler afternoon air on his skin, his temper much improved by the successful transfer of prisoners and a spry revival of the wind. As long as the Spanish keep out of the way, this expedition is set fair to be a triumph. The moment of purest pleasure will be telling Murat Reis about the trick that won the Icelandic island. From what he hears, Murat's own advance role in the invasion could have gone better, although that won't stop him claiming all the glory as usual.

Fleming strolls around the quarterdeck musing cheerfully on how much he loathes the Barbary's fêted admiral, before pausing to check on the westering sun. Hell's teeth, it will be time for prayers again soon.

His own manoeuvres really did go beautifully. After roaming up and down the fjords in the east *very* productively (he will lay emphasis on this point when he sees Murat), he went on to capture the island with a perfect piece of subterfuge. Of course it stood to reason that the harbour would be fortified after the mainland raids: it's a valuable trading post and the Danes had cannon. So, fly a Danish flag, sail on past with confidence, land the boats somewhere the locals would never think of and storm the harbour from inland. Fucking brilliant plan, even if it did have its perils. He thought his last moment had come trying to land on that promontory. Never seen surf like it.

After that he divided the men into three groups and sent

them to cover the island east, west and through the middle, with orders to search every hovel, every cavern, every hollow, every dip, ledge, crevice or damn puffin-hole they came across and take the prisoners to the harbour, where the ships would sail back to meet them.

It worked like a dream. By evening the warehouses were full of captives and his ship was back, sweetly anchored outside the harbour to receive them. Sa'id had the job of harrying the prisoners to the boats, while he himself ran a last eye over them as they passed: no point in taking anyone he wouldn't be able to sell. That's when he had his next idea. He spied a thin, elderly-looking character in a black coat moving past. This was not the sort of man you could imagine pulling a plough with his teeth, so he shouted an order and jerked his head for him to come over and wait behind. The man turned. He had a wife with him, gross with child, who then started screaming something at the top of her voice. The husband looked at her and then turned back. Flatly disobeyed the order. Made it plain he meant to stay with her.

'I'll get him,' Sa'id muttered. He looked like a fucking canary with those feathers stuck to his backside.

But there was something that made the captain hesitate. He's glad now that he did, even if the priest is testing his patience. He watched the man resume the shepherding of his family towards the boat. Noted the easy way he swung the young child into his arms, the quick smile of encouragement for the older boy, the calming touch on that hysterical woman's arm. There and then the captain saw there could be other uses for a man like that.

'Leave him be, Sa'id. If he's that keen, he might as well come.'

The idea remains a good one. If he can pull it off at the other end, it will be something else to rub in Murat's face. Mind you, if he is interrogated by that priest one more time about the length of his sash or, God help him, how the future tense is conjugated in the common tongue, the man is going straight over the side.

Around him, with a silent instinct that has remained beyond him, the crew are beginning to drop to their knees. The captain groans.

4

Oddrún's eyes flutter open as Ólafur bends to offer his swaying ministrations. She has scarcely raised her head since they set sail, refusing food and accepting only a sip of mead each day, but for Ólafur's sake the old woman is making an effort.

Ásta watches the pair until the next pain diverts her. Here it comes – peaking, passing. The grip is tightening as the hours wear on, but the intervals are still so lengthy that Margrét has suggested she might try speeding the process with some light scrubbing. This is Margrét's idea of a joke.

Oddrún is listening earnestly to Ólafur, her big eyes fixed on his. Ásta doubts if Oddrún has attended so well to anything he has had to say in all their years of ill-matched friendship. Their habit has been to speak comfortably past each other, she assenting with good cheer to every spiritual admonishment while he has tolerated a more lurid weight of dreams, visions, omens, warnings and tales of life among the sealfolk than any man of Christian conviction might be expected to shoulder. So rarely successful have her predictions been that Ólafur has spent half a lifetime caught between sympathy and irritation.

Oddrún's most celebrated triumph was in the summer of 1614, when she came hammering at their door with a breathless report of a huge black raven flapping away with the bell of Landakirkja hanging from its beak. Ólafur packed her straight home to bed, assuring her he would keep a close eye on any passing raven and take whatever action he judged best. A few days later a band of English pirates landed on Heimaey, led by a brigand called Gentleman John. They pillaged houses and livestock and kept everyone awake for days while they caroused loudly on Danish ale stocks. After a week or so the Englishmen sailed off, carrying with them – to Oddrún's abiding gratification – the great church bell. It has long been agreed (her most recent success having gone largely unremarked in the general misery) that this was Oddrún Pálsdóttir's finest hour.

While Ólafur's attitude to Oddrún is touching in its way, Ásta is not above finding her husband's tolerance exasperating. She has frequently been stung by his readiness to offer more forbearance to an old woman's ramblings than to any suggestion of her own that cannot be firmly located in the Lutheran catechism. Oddrún is suffered to blather on about being a seal until the cows come home – or at least until Ólafur recalls his responsibilities and invites her to ponder the pronounced absence of sealwomen in holy scripture. But one word about elves, one shudder over the ghosts that brush your face with frost in the night, and Ásta is required to submit to a very long lecture.

Her father had just as little sympathy when she was growing up at Mosfell. Lot's wife could transform without comment into a pillar of salt, but it was ridiculous to think a night troll crossing the lava might turn to stone when the sun rises. In the Mosfell priesthouse there was scant patience for a child who looked for signs of the hidden people living invisible lives just like theirs in the ravines and grassy mounds around them, and who shivered to think she might have perched on an elven window unawares.

Her father's own affections belonged with stories of a different kind. Although his enthusiasm was not (as he sometimes remembered to point out) uncritical, Thorsteinn had a deep partiality for the sagas about Icelandic men and women in the days long past when the country was young. The eagerness with which people in the sagas slayed each other was of course regrettable, and superstitions from the days of darkness before the country knew the truth of Christ must self-evidently be understood in their context, but his respect for the sagas could not be denied. Ásta often smiled to hear him. A roistering pagan like Egill Skallagrímsson, who in old age had also lived in the Mosfell valley, was as different a character as could be imagined from her fastidious father, who would rather leave the breaking of a cockerel's neck to his wife and was no more inclined to roister than serve his own dinner. But Thorsteinn was never done telling stories about this Egill, and in the winter nights when the wind growled outside she would sit at his feet with hammering heart to hear what happened next. Heavy-browed and ugly, with a temper too spiteful for a discriminating girl to admire, Egill Skallagrímsson was hardly the stuff of romantic dreams. But you never knew what he would do next – that's what young Ásta liked. This was a man you could not pin down, a man who surprised you at every turn, fighting and roaring one minute and composing strange, sensitive poetry the next to make pictures grow and argue in your head.

Over and over she would ask to hear how King Athelstan of England had gifted Egill two chests of treasure and how he buried them at Hrísbrú, where the old Mosfell church had stood before it was moved to the hill where her father now had his living. For years Ásta kept an eye open for the glint of silver. She would ride along the valley on her dark, shaggy-maned colt, Skími, looking for Egill's treasure. Her plan, once she had found it, was to slip out one night and hide it again herself, just as old Egill did, and if any asked where it was she meant to shake her head with an enchanting air of mystery, taking care not to dislodge the jewel-encrusted headdress she would be borrowing from another saga.

As she grew older, Ásta began to suspect that her father was more drawn to the sagas than he felt to be entirely proper for a Lutheran priest. He had been born in 1550, the year Iceland's last Roman Catholic bishop was summarily parted from his head for defying the reformed faith brought from Denmark, and had grown up with the country's religious life in all sorts of turmoil. He had hymns by the fiery reformer Martin Luther in a small printed book translated from the German, and by his own hand he had copied some poems by Ólafur Jónsson of Sandur, a priest in the west fjords whose work, he noted approvingly, was thoroughly based on scripture. But it seemed to Ásta that, try as he might, Pabbi could never muster the same ardour for the devotional readings with which he solemnly ended the evening as for the sagas that were in his blood, passed through many generations, and which he told by heart with a gleam in his eyes.

Perhaps he detected a similar failing in his daughter. Perhaps he felt responsible for the way her own eyes misted more dreamily than he thought appropriate at the passions of the Laxdaela saga's beautiful Gudrún, whose love for the impossibly handsome Kjartan went so badly wrong. At any rate he announced his intention one day to teach her the letters of the alphabet.

If she was quick to learn, he might even show her the principles of Latin.

'In this way, Ásta *mín*, you will be able to study the religious works for yourself and rein in the wilder excesses of your imagination as you ponder the joys awaiting us in the kingdom of heaven.' Saga romances and hidden folk alike (she could practically hear him thinking) would be firmly assigned their place.

His stratagem succeeded to the extent that she was immediately ravished in a different way by the pleasure of working out how an Icelandic or a Latin word changed as it played its part in a sentence and how one fitted with the next to make sense. She could have spent hours at the books if she had not been constantly chivvied to work.

Her mother shook her head. No good could possibly come of a girl learning to read and write when her life was to be spent rubbing kitchen smoke from her eyes and hauling on a loom.

'Ásta *mín*,' she said, as they sat together sewing the stomachs of two newly slaughtered sheep into bags, a task requiring patience that Ásta particularly hated, 'it is not wise to know too much. If you get a dull husband you are storing up great unhappiness.'

'Then to be safe I will have no husband, Mamma.' After all, the saga's manly Kjartan Ólafsson (with whom she had lately initiated a number of chaste embraces in the privacy of an imaginary bed) was a long time gone.

'Believe me, you will,' Mamma said, shaking her head in the infuriating way of mothers who have forgotten what it is to dream for more and for better. 'And whoever it is, may the good Lord help him.'

'Amen,' Ólafur whispers, giving Oddrún's cap a brisk pat. Picking his way onwards between the tight-packed bodies, he answers every hungering glance with the same reassurance: suffering of any kind, even violent abduction and every indignity of their present plight, is what they are put on earth for, but they can look forward to the most wondrous happiness, to joys they cannot begin to imagine, in the next world. Pretty Anna Jasparsdóttir, who only last month secured the fond heart and well-appointed croft of Jón Oddsson, the island's wealthiest farmer, pouts back that a little happiness in this world would not go amiss. Ólafur shakes his head wearily: Anna never did pay attention in church.

As he eases himself to his feet again, the swell throws him off balance and he sits down hard on someone else's legs. Apologising, he hauls himself to his feet and rubs the small of his back.

Focussed as she is on contractions that have at last assumed an air of purpose, Ásta can still spare a gush of tenderness for the husband making his dogged way around the hold. It has only lately occurred to her that Ólafur must have passed sixty years. Surviving winters is more important than counting them so she cannot be sure, but at least a quarter of a century separates their births and she will have reached five and thirty herself by now, perhaps more. Yet Ólafur has never appeared old to her. The brown hair trailing over his collar is only lightly flecked with silver and he still has the lithe physique that made her uncle Jón look like a mountain beside him. Jón used to grumble about how fast Ólafur walked on their rambles between Ofanleiti and Kirkjubaer, and the wearying energy of his friend's mind. 'He tires me out in every way,' Jón lamented once. 'Do you know he spent our entire walk yesterday practising German on me?'

Only when the huge captain made to keep Ólafur behind on the first evening of the raid did it strike her, with a sickening lurch, that others might view him differently. As they were lining up to enter the boats, he was ordered to join a small group of islanders being held to one side. Every man in that group was old. In the agony of realising it, she screamed at him, 'Don't go, Ólafur. For God's sake, don't leave us alone!' Afterwards she was so ashamed of herself. Overwhelmed by the prospect of having to do all this on her own, she had called her own husband, her own *elderly* husband, into captivity. Even as they were being rowed out to the great ship, the guilt of forcing Ólafur to share a fate he might have escaped was beginning to gnaw at her.

They found a large group of Icelandic men already on board. Captured days earlier in the raid on the mainland's east fjords, they were shackled to one another on the deck. 'Prepare yourself, Ásta,' Ólafur muttered, placing a hand on her arm as they both reeled at the sight of their countrymen in neck-irons. 'We must expect to be next.' But nobody else was put in fetters, and shortly afterwards the other prisoners were released from theirs. They were all given bread and bad water, and as they ate they watched the flames of their ransacked church searing the island sky. Then they were shoved below to the hold. All the next day more islanders were caught, brought on board and thrust down to join the crush, until it came to the second evening. That was when the pirates, preparing to leave on the morning tide, set the tradehouses alight. Ásta could smell the burning from where she lay. She could taste it on her tongue.

Those who had just joined them on board could hardly speak for weeping. There had been old people still inside those buildings, they said.

44

'I don't know if the pirates knew they were there or cared,' one woman sobbed, 'but they're burning. There was nobody to get them out.'

And then it was that Ólafur leaned over and whispered, 'If I had stayed behind, I might have burned with them. You know that, don't you, *mín kæra?*'

Slumped there on the splintered wood, her head cradled awkwardly in his lap and the two children squeezed beside them, Ásta wept then too. But not for those who had perished. She felt a little guilty when she realised her tears were not for them, but that she was crying with a sort of wondering gratitude that Ólafur should know her so well. He had understood the shame she felt at her own weakness in calling him back and looked for a way to comfort her. She remembers that now, watching him with his flock and bracing for the next pain.

The ships weighed anchor the following morning. Ten days ago, that must be. The prisoners never even saw what they were leaving: those familiar cliffs topped by grassy crowns of midsummer green and streaked white with waste, the incurious fowl peering from every pock. Ásta listened for crying gulls, but all she could hear was the tumult of wood and sail. Then somebody began to wail, an eerie, unearthly cry of abandonment. It was picked up by one person and then another, until suddenly they were all doing it and the whole of the dark space swelled with the sound. Marta sat with her small hands flat over her ears and Ásta put an arm around her and held her tight. Then Ásta too opened her mouth and joined in the keening of her exiled people.

As the wind filled the sails of the departing ships, those islanders who had not been discovered began to creep from their hiding places, parched and staggering, into the light. Panic ensued among the gannets high on the cliffs as Magnús Birgisson, squinting doubtfully at the beating waves below, tested first one leg and then another and decided to attempt the climb.

Far down on the shore, farmer Jón Oddsson heaved himself over the protruding stone lip that had kept him covered between two crushed shelves of granite. With leaden feet he managed to pull himself high enough to watch the course of the ships as they rounded the island of Ellidaey to head south. Which of them held Anna, the bride he had barely had time to bed? He thought he could hear over the water a great crying in the wind that was bearing her away, and for a moment he wondered – so shaken was he and dizzy, such an ache for her in his chest – if the sound had come perhaps from him.

Meanwhile, in a puddled cave near Kirkjubaer, a contented mass of full-bodied flies was feasting on both parts of Jón Thorsteinsson's head.

5

Dear Lord, will this never end? The pain grows and tightens and takes a long time to die. Two or three minutes later it begins again. Ólafur has taken Marta away and the sail is back in place. Ásta's head is resting on the rope and Margrét is stroking her hair. She is soaking with sweat. The ship is rolling and she has retched on the floor until there is nothing left.

Margrét makes her take a sip of the horrible water. She brings it straight back up.

'You know what I need, Margrét? Some of that potion the elfman gave to the girl in the shieling. You remember the story?'

Margrét sniffs. 'What you need is a bed in a nice empty *badstofa* and some water boiling on the kitchen fire. And you won't be getting that either.'

'Tell me the story instead, then. That will be help enough.'

'It's unsuitable. What would Ólafur say? No, don't try and tell me. Is that another one? Just breathe slowly then. That's it. Slowly, slowly. There you go. Is that better?'

'Please, Margrét. A story.'

Margrét rolls her eyes. Jón would turn in his grave. *Oh God, oh God, is he even in a grave yet?*

'Very well, then. We could both do with a distraction. There

47

was once a priest – just like your father, Ásta – and he had a daughter he loved more than all the world. Just as yours did you. She used to go up to the shieling in summer to milk the cattle in the high pasturelands and make the *skyr* and keep house for the herdsmen. She was a girl of great beauty and skill and considered the best match in all the world.'

'Just as I was?'

'I think not. I imagine it's safe to assume this girl did not overfill her liver-pudding bag so that it kept bursting and every meal was ruined.'

'Oh, hurry up, Margrét. Before the next one.'

'Well, in the autumn the girl returned from the shieling, and soon everyone began to notice that she was putting on weight. Her father was convinced she must be expecting a child, and he urged her not to go back to the shieling at the end of spring, since it was no place to give birth. But the girl insisted she was not with child and would return as normal. Her father let her go back. I think we can agree that your own father would not have been so obliging. But he ordered his herdsmen not to let her out of their sight up there for a single moment. Are you still all right?'

A nod.

'They did as he asked and she was never left alone – except for just one evening when all the sheep and cows mysteriously went missing. Everyone hurried into the hills to look for them except the girl, who was left behind in the shieling. When the men returned with the animals in the morning, she was busy at her work as usual, but they did think she seemed lighter on her feet. As the weeks passed, the men noticed she had lost her plumpness, but you know how men are – the matter was soon forgotten.'

Here it comes. Ásta closes her eyes and fights the urge to yell. Margrét offers a skinny arm for clutching and waits for the tightening to ease.

'Then, the following winter a neighbouring farmer asked for the girl's hand in marriage. He was a fine man and everyone thought well of him. No heed was paid to the girl's objections. 'At last the wedding day arrived. Just before they were married, the girl went to her betrothed and said, straight out, "I have no desire to marry you. But since I must, I insist that you promise never to allow strangers to lodge with us during the winter without first telling me, otherwise things will go badly for you."'

Margrét selects another sniff from her large store. 'He was a tolerant man, this husband, considering the girl was trouble from beginning to end. Far too easygoing. I would have sorted her out in no time. His mother was also a kindly soul. She found her new daughter-in-law sullen and unhappy, but she tried to cheer her up by entertaining her with stories as they sat together carding the wool. One day, the old woman's storytelling flagged and she begged the girl to tell her a tale instead. The girl said she knew only one story, but she would tell it. And here – are you all right, Ásta? – here is the story she told.'

'Wait, Margrét. Give me your arm.'

Ásta clenches her teeth and fights to the top of the pain. On it goes, and on.

'Well done, Ásta *mín*. A few more of these and we'll be nearly there. Now where was I?'

Stop talking, Margrét. Leave me alone. Be kind enough to let me die.

'Ah yes. The story the girl told her mother-in-law. It was really her own story, of course. And this is what she said:

'There was once a farm girl who had worked at the shieling all the summer long. Near the bothy were rocky cliffs where she loved to go for quiet walks. A man, one of the hidden folk, lived inside one of those rocks. He appeared to the girl one day and they became extremely attached to one another. Some time later the girl discovered she was bearing a child.

'Early the following summer she returned to the shieling. One night all the animals went missing and her companions went out to look for them. While everyone was gone the girl went into labour. Really, Ásta, are you sure this story is wise?'

'It's . . . fine. Give me . . . a minute.' They are coming fast.

'Take it steady then. That's it now. Try not to panic. I said don't panic, Ásta. That's better. Good. Let me dab your forehead again. Now, just think about this before the next one. All of a sudden the elfman appeared at this girl's side and he helped her through the birth. He gave the girl a delicious drink to sip and it stole all her pain away. Imagine it, Ásta. Imagine this drink slipping through you, cool and sweet as mountain water, and the pain tumbling away with it. There it goes, rushing far, far away to the sea beyond. See, I've made you smile.

'Well, he cut the cord, this elfman (so the girl told in her tale), washed the child and wrapped it in a warm blanket. Then he slipped away, carrying their child with him, and the girl was left to get on with her life. But after that – this is what she told her mother-in-law very coldly – she was compelled to marry another man. And she has grieved bitterly for her child and her lost lover ever since.'

When the next pounding arrives, Ásta closes her eyes and tries to picture the pain being doused by a drink, carried off by a cool river, tumbling away on the foaming mane of the Leirvogsá to the sea. It is not the slightest help. A cry bursts through her gritted teeth and she clutches Margrét for dear life. Margrét strokes the hand on her arm while making a surreptitious movement to ease it off.

'It did not end well for the girl,' she continues at last. 'Many years later two strangers arrived at the farm, one tall and the other shorter, requesting lodging for the winter in return for work. The farmer agreed, but without consulting his wife. A mistake, of course, as you will recall from his wedding-day promise. The men lodged in an outbuilding and the wife made every effort to avoid meeting them. But at last the farmer forced the issue, asking how she could be so rude as not to greet these strangers with a hospitable kiss. His wife went wild with rage.'

Margrét puts on a flouncy voice. '"First you take in these men without consulting me and now you force me to kiss them. Fine. I will obey you. But let me tell you, you'll regret . . ." Ásta *mín*, you're panicking again. You need to calm down. That's it. There you are. Good girl. That's it.'

This one is too long. She can't climb to the top of it. She can't do this.

Margrét wipes her cheeks with a filthy apron. 'Shall I stop now?'

Yes. No. Yes. Make it all stop.

'Well, it's nearly done. The wife stormed out and was gone a long time. At length the farmer went to look for her in the lodgers' room. And there he found her and the tall stranger lying on the bed, wrapped in each other's arms, dead. They had died of grief, supposedly. Nonsense, if you ask me. Who dies of grief? You get on with it. Anyway, the younger man was standing over the two of them, weeping. When the farmer entered the room, the boy disappeared and was never seen again.

'The farmer's mother decided this was the moment to share the story that her daughter-in-law had recounted many years before. It was then that everyone realised that the older man had been her elfman lover from the shieling and the younger one their son.'

Margrét leans over to dab Ásta's face again. 'There now. That has passed the time nicely, hasn't it? I dare say the good Lord will forgive us the indulgence in the circumstances.'

Her niece has only the briefest moment to reflect that the most down-to-earth woman in Iceland is not the person to bring out the full pathos of the elfman lover, the lost child and the disregarded husband who had not (really, when you think about it) been so very much at fault, before she is grabbing at Margrét's arm again.

Someone is making a monstrous grunting noise. Through a red haze of pain, Ásta is dimly aware that it might be her. The long drawn-out shriek that follows hushes every voice in the hold, reaches a group of pirates dozing in the crew quarters directly above and trails thinly to the upper deck, where Ólafur is slumped beside a parakeet with Marta by his side.

But still the effort is not enough. 'Come on, Ásta, you've done this before.' Alarm is making Margrét testy. This is taking too long. 'Hold back and pant some more.'

'Can't do any more. Too tired.'

'Wheesht and hold my arm. No, the other one. Now try again. Now!'

Ásta has no idea of herself any longer. The haze is enveloping her, the screams tearing out of a throat far away.

Margrét peers again between the slender white thighs. She is so narrow, Ásta. Same figure she had as a girl. The Lord alone knows how she got the others out. And this one's big. That last push was too weak. At this rate she won't make it.

'Ásta, listen to me. Look at me.'

A glassy gaze finds her.

'You have to come back to me and try harder. Do you hear me? You have to jut that chin of yours out. The way you did when you were going to run away from our house back to Mosfell, remember? Do this for me. Do it for Ólafur. Do it for Kristín. Here it comes. One big push again. Are you listening, Ásta? WE HAVE LOST ENOUGH.'

Ásta's eyes close. Her chin shifts. Her mouth opens in a great, animal roar. Muscles bulge and tear. The baby slides out in a cascade of blood.

Margrét grabs him, peers closely and gives him a stern shake. Holding him upside down by the ankles, she smacks and cajoles him. She blows into his nose. She runs a finger inside his little red mouth. But there comes not a sound nor a tremor. A blue tinge is creeping over his face, dusting the pearly skin with violet.

'Breathe!' Margrét mutters, glaring at the limp child.

The hold quivers with uneasy silence. In the gun-deck Sa'id turns in his hammock. Thanks be to Allah, the caterwauling is over and he can get some sleep before the night shift. He is annoyed to find himself tensing for the sound that should have come next. Ólafur, straining to hear from the deck, grabs the parakeet and flings it away in an indignant flurry of feathers. Someone is hammering to his left. The captain is roaring his usual spleen from the stern. Even the slap of halyard against mast is suddenly deafening. Can he have missed it?

Ólafur forces himself to count slowly to twenty, flinching at a sudden rumble of chain across the deck as the ship swings on a shifting wind. *Ten, eleven, twelve.* No, he can't stand it. *Thirteen.* He pulls Marta to her feet and bolts for the hold.

The shock of it makes him stagger. There is blood on the timbers, blood spattered across the sail, blood on Margrét and blood all over his wife, who is lying limp and ashen with wild hair stuck to her forehead and a bundle on her chest wrapped in what looks like Margrét's grimy apron.

Margrét waves him in impatiently. 'Come on, man, don't look so appalled. You have a son. And a wife, come to that, though I had my doubts for a while.'

Collecting himself with a few long breaths, Ólafur squats at Ásta's side. Her eyes begin to flicker.

'He took his time deciding to stay, but there he is,' Margrét goes on, nodding to the bundle. Her hands are full of some liverish mess, plainly just delivered, from which Ólafur queasily averts his eyes.

He lifts the apron cautiously and peers underneath. 'And what a world we have brought him to,' he mumbles, more to himself than Margrét. The shock is fast succumbing to a powerful attack of gloom.

He is relieved to find them both safe. Of course he is. There was a moment when he thought . . . But to see the infant in this hideous, stinking place without so much as a decent swaddling cloth brings him suddenly very low. Here walks the priest of Ofanleiti, unable to dress his own child. He is also suffering from an emotion that might in another life have been described as embarrassment. When every privacy and all of life's dignities are gone, the notion has little meaning, but Margrét sees it in him, tight behind the eyes: a tormented awareness of how publicly unclean the priest's wife has become before all.

He reaches his long fingers to touch the stained head of his son and belatedly remembers an encouraging smile for Ásta, who has swum back far enough to return a watery one of her own.

'We'll christen him Jón,' he says, 'after our departed friend.'

'Jón Ólafsson,' Ásta whispers, trying it on her tongue.

Margrét looks up briefly, then away.

6

On the evening of the thirtieth of July, the day of his son's birth, Ólafur Egilsson is standing on the deck of the slave-ship, looking out at the sinking orange sun. His spirits are still low. Jón Thorsteinsson used to tell him he had never known a man so excitable one minute and so cast down the next. Is it any wonder that Jón is the one the Almighty in his infinite wisdom chose for martyrdom? Always so calm, Jón, always so sure of himself. Ólafur sometimes suspects that the people take more comfort from the report of his fellow priest's devout dying, prayer-book in hand, than they do from his own bumbling efforts below deck. The thought makes him feel even worse.

Unnoticed, three corsairs are loitering behind him. After a brief whispered dispute, one of their number is appointed to tap the priest on the shoulder. Ólafur wheels around with an off-target fist.

He is surprised to be presented with nothing more alarming than a pair of wide-shouldered men's shirts, pale as bleached wood. Even while gazing at the men in mute astonishment, Ólafur cannot help running the cloth through his fingers and rubbing the weave with his thumb. The shirts are thinner and lighter than any woven with Icelandic wool, and clean. So very clean. Fresh as the wild air. He can smell the wind on them.

What is this? A gift? Ólafur becomes daily more confused by the pirates and what to make of them. One day they are treating people with a savagery no Icelander ever witnessed before, and the next he catches them tickling children's chins and whiling away the voyage teaching ever more intricate sailors' knots to Jón's big lad and his own Egill. One day their captain is slicing a man's head in two and the next sending down a tent for Ásta's confinement and offering Ólafur the freedom of the deck. Adequate food and drink arrive in the hold each morning for everyone, and the captives are at last being allowed a spell of fresh air each day. Now this.

They are manifestly evil, these men. They bow to false gods and steal innocent Christians from their homes. And God will punish them, no doubt about that, just as he will glorify those who bear witness to him in their present agony. Still – Ólafur's sense of fairness has rarely proved more inconvenient – some of the subtler shades of wickedness are perplexing. As Ásta said when one of them came to put up the tent, how can evil smile? It was a pleasant smile. That's what had bothered Ólafur. He has not been able to dismiss the thought that a black heart producing a kind smile might, in all fairness, tend to a shade of blackness somewhat less than pitch. Or is he a fool to believe it? God's fool, he thinks, suddenly bitter – the priest who couldn't even get himself martyred.

He fondles the soft shirts and buries his nose in the sweetness of them. The three young corsairs are watching him cheerfully, pleased with themselves. Two have dark faces and the third's is freckled to his turban. They had heard the child's cry and thought of it, the freckled lad explains, and Ólafur is gratified to discover that his conversations with a grumbling Cornish mariner forced to winter on Heimaey the year before last stand him in good stead. With no idea any longer on which side of expediency any act of humanity on this ship might lie, Ólafur jerks his head.

'I thank you,' he replies in English, and rushes off to show Ásta.

She is lying on her side with one arm around the baby. Little Jón is curled on her chest, plump and bare and shiny clean. Margrét must have begged some brine for washing. She also seems to have scoured some of the timbers and drawn aside the bloodstained sail. Ásta too looks fresher, her hair smoothed back, eyes bright. She has the air of exhausted elation he recognises from previous births. It looks to him, even here, even now, like happiness.

Easing himself down beside her, he is confident of bringing more. 'Look, my dearest. Two shirts to cover the baby.'

He leans over and slips one of them under the child, tucking it around his yielding chin like a shawl and gently setting Ásta's hand aside so that he can wrap the rest of it around him. The shirt spreads out like a christening gown. The long wide arms hang loose down her soiled dress. The baby snuffles in his sleep.

'Some pirates handed me these. They must have guessed the child would lack covering.'

Ásta flares up at once. A long labour and a difficult birth have done nothing to dampen her feelings about their captors.

'I won't thank them, Ólafur, so don't expect it. I won't be grateful.'

He nods soothingly. 'We'll be grateful to our heavenly father instead, then, who sends us all good things. And here' – he touches the baby's furred cheek, marvelling that there can exist anything in the world so soft – 'is one of them.'

Ásta presses her lips to the small, linen-clad back, drinking in the scent of salt air. Then they look at each other in the swinging lamplight. Shadows are playing across her eyes, these eyes Ólafur has loved since he watched them studying his map the day she first came to Ofanleiti. He has delighted ever since in trying to describe to himself their colour, which is not quite grey, or not always grey, but a shade closer to the hue of the sea when the sun catches it by surprise some days. There are gulls whose wings become exactly so in their second autumn: you could study them for an hour without deciding whether they are grey or blue.

He remembers the way these eyes appraised him as he showed her around that day. Here was Jón's slip of a niece, nervous as a foal and daunted by just one glance at the loom, yet he was the one who felt he was being assessed. An opinion was being formed. Almost immediately he found himself showing off.

It was Jón who had decided he needed a housekeeper. Ólafur's formidable young daughter Thorgerdur, who had more or less managed the house since she was twelve, was bound for the mainland to keep the priest's house in Torfastadir.

'It's time for Ásta to move on,' Jón had said. They were returning from one of their shared services at Landakirkja, where the two island priests took it in turns to preach and sing by the altar. 'She's eighteen now – some years older than your Thorgerdur. I confess that Margrét has occasionally had to take issue with . . . how shall I put this? . . . her dedication, but my dear wife can be difficult to impress. She assures me she has taught Ásta well.'

The men's habit on a Sunday was to walk awhile on the hill behind the church, enjoyably dissecting the shortcomings of the congregation, before the one headed east to Kirkjubaer and the other west to Ofanleiti. Sometimes they stopped to enjoy a libation from Jón's capacious pocket at the sentinel rock dubbed the Priest Stone, from where the whole island could see them perched like a couple of ravens in their flapping ministerial coats. It was there that Jón made his offer. Whether he suspected that Ólafur, many years on his own since his wife died, was lonely, and had it in mind from the start that he needed more than a housekeeper, was never made clear.

'You need have no worry that you are depriving us,' Jón added gaily. This was a point that had not occurred to Ólafur. 'Margrét has plenty of other help now.'

Jón was not giving a convincing impression of a man who believed his niece would be any loss to the housekeeping arrangements at Kirkjubaer and Ólafur was sceptical. (As well he might have been, he smiles to himself now, watching Ásta put the baby's wrinkled fingers to her lips.) But Jón had made up his mind. He slapped Ólafur heartily on the shoulder.

'I believe you will enjoy her company, my friend. She'll keep you on your toes. Trust me on this matter.'

When Ásta arrived – small, sharp-chinned, with thick fair hair and those disconcerting grey eyes – Ólafur showed her around the house. It was arranged much like any other, only somewhat bigger, as he could not resist pointing out. He darted up and down the passageway from the kitchen, where meats were smoking above the fire for winter, to the pantry and the dairy, then up a rickety stair into the communal *badstofa*, lined with the usual wooden beds. When the cold began to bite, she would find this room warmed by the beasts wintering below, he heard himself boasting, knowing it was still a novelty on Heimaey to have your living and sleeping area in the loft and that Jón did not. Sensing her examination, Ólafur fairly bounced from room to room, expanding his chest a fraction as he passed through a shaft of light, quite unnecessarily lifting the edge of the loom with one hand to demonstrate how heavy it was. He must have been well past forty years by then, but every priest in Iceland had to be as much farmer as pastor and he knew he was strong. He still took his turn to swing from cliff to cliff to capture the spring eggs and – God preserve him from vanity – could shear a sheep as fast as any.

He showed her his writing paper. He showed her his books. Her amber hair was pulled back, plaited and fixed under her cap, and when she bent to look he could not help noticing a shapely neck. There was a tinge of red in her hair – no, more like gold, really; a hint of sunset, anyway – that you would need to see unpinned to judge. May the Lord forgive him, what was he thinking of? By the time he came to show Ásta his map, Ólafur Egilsson was in love.

The baby stirs and Ásta puts him to her breast, sucking in her breath at the sting of it, flooded with the love for this child that pours out of her faster than any milk. Ólafur, sitting on the floor at her side, turns courteously the other way, and she is touched by the civility of the gesture in the midst of so much chaos. He has always been polite, her Ólafur.

'Do you remember, *mín kaera*,' he says, still facing away, 'the day you came to Ofanleiti? I shudder to think how I began prancing around the moment I met you.'

She laughs. 'You knew me from the very first,' she says to his back. 'I was so appalled to see Thorgerdur's big loom with those dread stone weights and realise that I was to be in charge of the weaving, not to mention everything else. And somehow you understood. You were different from the man I had seen in the pulpit.'

'Was I? In what way?'

She can't see his face and hopes he is not offended. Ólafur can be defensive about his priestly status.

'You waved your hands a great deal and had plenty to say for yourself, which I would have expected. But you also became quite still and watchful and, you know, thoughtful. And not so sure of yourself. That was a different side. And you laughed – there was the real surprise.'

He says nothing. Now she is sure he is smiling.

She remembers noticing, as she followed him from room to room, how slender his shoulders were, and that he did not blunder about like her uncle or bash his head on every lintel, but was quick and graceful. She noticed the wiry arms and the long hair, brown as a nut, which hung often across his eyes and begged for the services of a sharp knife. She noticed him noticing how she nearly burst into tears when she saw that loom. The prospect of taking over from efficient young Thorgerdur Ólafsdóttir in the home of such a notoriously censorious preacher terrified her. She had begged Jón not to send her.

And then – she drops a kiss on the baby's head and thinks back – didn't he ask what was troubling her and didn't she mumble something about fearing she would fail him in the tasks ahead? Yes, that's how it went. And he smiled, his eyes crinkling in a nice way, and said he was sure she would not fail him – although he assumed she knew they must eat. 'We have old people and labourers to feed here and I must confess to being partial to a meal myself from time to time.'

She gave him a wobbly smile.

'And we will be hard put to clothe ourselves if the loom is not made to rattle now and then, won't we?'

She nodded uncertainly.

'But we might also have a look at a book together when the summer work is past and we can award ourselves some winter lamplight in here. Your uncle tells me you like to read, do you not?'

This is the moment she remembers best: the strange fluttery feeling at the mention of books. She probably gaped a bit. Ólafur was looking at her very directly, slightly amused at her reaction, as if trying to work out the nature of this package he had been sent.

'I have something of which I'm very fond that I will show you. You've heard of Bishop Gudbrandur Thorláksson perhaps?'

'You don't have his Bible?' she squeaked.

'Sadly not. Every church in Iceland is supposed to buy one, although God knows how. Perhaps one day. But I've got something else. There's hardly enough light to see properly, but look here.'

From under one of the beds he pulled out a wooden box, simply carved, and withdrew from it a piece of parchment. He sat down on the bed and patted the space next to him for her to join him. Then he spread the parchment on his knee, gently smoothed the creases and nudged it towards her. She gazed at it with heart-pounding awe. Never had she seen a thing of such beauty. Around the edges there swam great fish in an ocean of waves. She made out sea-creatures with gaping maws and curved horns, cattle frisking in the shallows, giant birds. They all cavorted around a large shape, strangely formed with bulbous noses and fat fingers. What monster was depicted here? There were words all over in a flowing hand, but none she could decipher easily in the dimness except one alone, there at the top in capital letters: ISLANDIA.

She looked at him for guidance, feeling stupid.

'It's a map, Ásta. A map of Iceland. A copy of one that Gudbrandur drew and a good enough likeness to his, I'm told. Can you see how it works? Imagine that this line here, see, is the southern coastline. Above it is drawn the volcano Hekla and further along we see the glaciers Eyjafjallajökull and Mýrdalsjökull with – look just here – birds below.'

She stared at the birds with delight, bending close to study the lines.

'And you can follow the coast all the way around – in and out of the east fjords, see, and up and around the north. Here is Hólar, the northern bishopric where Gudbrandur has his seat. And then come with me further along. This big fistful of fingers up here is the west fjords and then down we come again to the southwest.'

He was tracing a bony index finger round the knobbly lines of the map as he talked, his voice becoming ever more excited and his speech faster. A hank of hair kept falling into his eye and he pushed it away impatiently.

'See, we can hop inland a little just here and we're in the valley of Mosfell, with a red sign to show a church and houses there. That's you, although I think you were not born when this was drawn. Or perhaps there you were, newly arrived on God's earth and looking about you in your mother's arms with just such a solemn expression as you wear now.'

He laughed a little sheepishly, and she wondered at the way this man only encountered before in confident pulpit diatribe seemed so suddenly ill at ease. He returned his gaze to the map immediately.

'Just a little further over to the east is the southern bishopric of Skálholt, where I went to school, and your uncle Jón also. It has a much bigger red symbol, because the church there is large and there are farms all around.' His finger moved south. 'And look down here, Ásta. What do you think these great rocks are in the middle of the sea, surrounded by such mighty fish? Can you read what it says?'

'VEST . . . MANNA . . . EIAR,' she sounded out carefully. 'Our Westman Islands are here!' She laughed out loud for the joy of it. 'And these words in the corner, they're Latin, aren't they?'

'Yes they are,' he said quietly, giving her another long look. She supposed he had not known a girl before who knew Latin. 'Ponder what this means, Ásta. Here we sit in a house in Ofanleiti, without so much as a plank of driftwood to line the walls and spare us a few draughts, and yet here we also are on the map of Iceland.'

She gazed at it, beguiled.

'Think of it. Maps mean our poor nation is known not just to God and the Danes and a few English rogues and squabbling German merchants, but to the whole world. Can you imagine that there are countries with white sands that stretch forever and fruits that would sate you with sweetness? I have heard of these places and if my map went far enough south they would be just about . . . here.'

He ran his finger past the Westman Isles to the bottom of

the map and let it drift on through the air until it dropped on the bed between them like a pouncing gull and stabbed within an inch of her dress. Then he removed his hand hurriedly and began to tidy the map away.

'They are places you and I will never see, but I hear stories at the harbour every day. Perhaps you will like to hear them too.' He smiled again. 'Once you have mastered the loom.'

'I would like that very much,' she said, setting the loom firmly aside and hugging to herself the thought of maps and stories and a *badstofa* warmed by animal heat in winter. She was beginning to think she might be happy at Ofanleiti.

The baby is asleep again. She lifts him to her shoulder and the pirate shirt fans out around him.

'You can turn back now.'

Ólafur shuffles around and they look at each other again, mellow with memories, their newborn son between them.

7

Getting up is painful, but so is sitting so it might be as well to try. The delivery has left Ásta torn and bruised, and after reclining in the same position for so long, there exists scarcely another part of her that is not also aching. She is entitled to a turn on the deck and longs for it, but rope ladders are still beyond her. All she can do is hold on to Margrét for support and essay an old woman's totter about the confined area that has been her home for two weeks, each clutching at the other as the ship pitches. Two steps forwards to where Oddrún is still clamped to the floor, two back, turn, two forwards, two back, feeling herself ripped again with every step. Then she sinks back to the wood and yelps on to her side, wondering if her body will ever feel normal again.

Around her, life in the hold has arranged itself into a kind of routine. People have found themselves tasks: some hand out bread and mead; some are appointed to collect waste where they may and throw it to the waves; others organise the allotted excursions on deck at such times as the wind is light, the sea clear and the captain in reasonable temper. The interminable hours below are occupied by reciting sagas or *rímur*. Egill Skallgrímsson's kennings boom out of the shadows to make more hearts than Ásta's contract with longing. She strains to catch each saga telling, exulting to see in her mind's eye the breaths of horses over the lava plains and their tails streaming in the wind. Even Oddrún has been persuaded to suck on a biscuit soaked in ale and give voice to some quavery dream that takes her listeners from where they are to a land where ravens beat their tattered wings and slumbering volcanoes wake.

Margrét has done her best to rub the excretions of childbirth from both their dresses and, emboldened to demand yet more water, embarked on a frenzy of scrubbing. She shoves her bucket between listless neighbours with a sarcastic retort for anyone who protests. Her efforts have done little for the stench and less for anyone's peace of mind, but they keep the flies out of her head.

From time to time Anna Jasparsdóttir slips over for a chat. Ásta watches her twisting a stump of rope for Marta, a crescent of pink tongue just visible as she concentrates. How lovely the girl is, with her even teeth and neat nose and blue-green eyes. No wonder half the men on Heimaey were after her before doting Jón Oddsson swept her off to the farmhouse at Stakkagerdi with the promise of a blue dress from Copenhagen. He is not on board. Escaped, Anna believes, although Ásta finds it hard to imagine stout Jón Oddsson flitting down a cliff. Her father Jaspar, a slow-talking Dane with too many teeth, is thought to be on one of the other ships.

'I've come to a decision,' Anna says, offering Marta the rope-doll and smiling as the child takes it in her arms and begins to croon.

'What have you decided, Anna *mín*?'

'I've made up my mind that whatever awaits us when we land, I am going to make the best of it.'

Ásta glances at her again, this time with a flicker of admiration. For all the softness of her looks, this is not a woman you would catch howling for her husband at the water's edge or enquiring after elven elixirs when life becomes painful. Anna's spirit reminds her of Margrét, scrubbing away invincibly over there, refusing to be cowed. Personally Ásta is looking ahead with nothing but the most gut-wrenching dread.

Ólafur continues to keep her supplied with information gathered from around the ship. Now that he has persuaded one of the pirates to teach him the rudiments of the common tongue used by the crew (a source of the frankest fascination), his news has advanced from the composition of turbans. He reports that the janissary soldiers are mainly Turkish but others among the corsairs are from countries like England, the Low Countries and France. Some of those, he has learned to his distress, have chosen to recant their Christian faith to become renegade privateers, while others, captive themselves, are forced into piracy. Ásta is still at a loss to understand how Ólafur can bring himself to exchange a friendly word with any of them.

She is on her knees removing a strip of lavishly stained cloth from under the baby, who is making a firm protest, when she looks up to see her husband navigating his usual hazardous course across the hold.

'Hear what I've learned today,' he begins with an air of high drama, casting around for a space to sit. 'I know how they carried out the invasion of Iceland.'

A sudden roll of the ship throws him forward against Oddrún, who grunts and stirs. He rights himself hurriedly.

'Dear lady, forgive me.' Used to the company of a well-padded

Oddrún, he is shocked at how thin she feels to his flailing hand, how sharp the bones in her spine.

'Anyway, Ásta, here is what I've discovered. It seems that after making free around the Mediterranean for years and years, the Turks had an eye on the northern lands. But they could only venture there once Dutch and English and Venetian renegades had taught them how to build sailing ships. Their oared galleys would never have made it so far. This is most interesting, don't you think?'

Ásta, wiping away more yellow curds, agrees that it is, indeed, interesting.

'It turns out the raid was not planned by the captain of our ship but by another Dutch renegade who goes by the name Murat Reis. His real name is Jan Janszoon from Haarlem. Remember this name, Ásta. He is the man who brought us to this. The two of them operate from different parts of the Barbary, but this Murat seems to have commanded the whole fleet and . . . Are you still with me, Ásta?'

'Ólafur, the first time you take it upon yourself to wipe a child's backside on a rolling ship with your most intimate parts on fire, you can tell me how easy it is to attend to the finer points of privateering.' She scoops the mewling baby to her shoulder. 'Pray go on.'

'Yes, well, Murat went first. He took the southwest. So it must have been he who captured our people from Grindavík in June and then got chased away when he tried to attack the Danish governor at Bessastadir. Apparently it was Fleming's role to follow on and invade the east of Iceland and then come for us. Murat is based in Salé in Morocco and Fleming in the port of Algiers.'

He leans closer. 'Which means, dearest, that Algiers is where we're going. I have it confirmed.' Receiving no encouragement, he trails off damply. 'I thought you would wish to know.'

Ásta, not sure that she does want to know, gives the baby's back a bleak rub. Ólafur revels so in finding out. Despite himself he is excited: she sees it in his eyes. He is probably remembering the tales he used to bring home from foreign traders, thinking about all those countries he has always longed to see. Not she. Her forebodings are only deepening as the weeks at sea pass. To put a name to where they are sailing is not exciting at all.

On the day that Ásta finally makes it up the ladder, Captain Fleming is inspecting the rigging, his thumbs hooked on his armed sash. Not that she notices him, so dazzled is she by the light, so exhilarated to escape the shadows and the stench. Walking is painful, but her cheeks are soon tingling with the slap of the wind, her starved skin sucking up the sun with the purest delight. Her head has lightened so pleasingly with the rush of crystal air that, leaning on Ólafur's arm, she feels a little drunk.

Fleming turns his back as soon as he sees them. God's blood, he can't face another question from that priest. He is on the point of heading swiftly in the opposite direction when the thought occurs that it might, after all, be wise to inspect the wife. This is his first opportunity since her outburst at the harbour. If he is to persuade the Moor when they reach Algiers, he will need a thorough understanding of all the assets. Cilleby can be difficult.

He makes up his mind and strolls, paddle hands behind his back, towards the couple making careful progress across the deck.

'So this is your wife, Reverend?'

The woman turns quickly. Small. Full-breasted. Smells, but so do they all. Eyes – now that's interesting – eyes glaring up at him very hard.

'*Ja, sie heisst Ásta Thorsteinsdóttir*,' Ólafur replies in his best German, the nearest he can manage to Dutch. 'You may not be aware, Captain, that husbands and wives have different surnames in Iceland. I am the son of Egill and my wife here is the daughter of Thorsteinn. *Ja*. Each taking the first name of the father. An old custom.'

Ólafur knows he is gabbling. This is the man who murdered Ásta's uncle and here she is, standing right next to him in a state it would be fair to describe as intoxicated. He is really very nervous. There is nothing she can say that the captain will understand (*is there?*), but even the way she is staring at him like that is dangerous. It feels provocative.

Ásta does not move. She keeps her eyes raised to the captain's face, which is some way above hers. Is this what wickedness looks like? Can it be that evil, so far from waving a devil's tail and breathing fumes of sulphur, manifests itself in a pair of drooping blond mustachios and a peeling nose?

Fleming scowls. Why is the woman looking at him like that? There is not a trace of fear in her. Not even the wary loathing you get from them all. And nothing like the uncontained fury of that madwoman the other day. He registers the searching in the look and the challenge. Challenging him to what? Moistening his bottom lip with his tongue, he studies her face. Wide-spaced eyes, frown, chin jutted up. Temper there? He knows how to deal with that in a woman. Those eyes, though – blazing away at him. A man could look at them, and look.

The captain makes himself turn towards Ólafur, whose German is being increasingly challenged by the Icelandic patronymic system. When he looks back, the woman is still staring. At which point the captain disregards Ólafur entirely and returns the stare. Ásta sees the tongue flicking over the cracked lips. She sees the glitter as it enters the pale eyes. She senses – too late she senses it – the insipid menace that has suddenly charged the air.

Still without making a sound, she turns and walks away as quickly as her bruises allow. Her fists are clenched. She thought she could search out the pip of evil in the core of a man just by looking. She is a fool.

With a hasty '*Guten Tag*', Ólafur rushes after her.

The captain watches the grey skirts until they are out of sight.

8

As the ship blusters through the straits of Gibraltar, the corsairs jumpy because the Spanish have caught them here before and Margrét declaring darkly that if a sea-battle finishes them off now it can only be for the best, Oddrún Pálsdóttir is dying.

She has been hovering for days now, drifting in and out of dreams, never sure if she is awake or asleep. From the murky deeps she has seen her sister beckoning. She has heard the sealman with the soft voice, the one she loved, calling back to her to hurry as he sinks into the midnight waves. She has felt the tides wrap her in seaweed and embrace her with kindness. So safe she feels then, she wants never to wake up. But there are other dreams, too, important things she must tell the others if she can only pull herself above the water.

From somewhere near at hand she hears Ólafur giving the artificial cough that means he has an announcement to make. Dear Ólafur. Not once has he paid attention to a word she has said, but he understands loneliness and she has adored him. He stands up now, planting a leg on either side of his son Egill for balance, and adopts his most stentorian pulpit voice. Their captors have told him, he declares, that nobody is to be allowed out of the hold from now on because they are nearing the destination where they will be sold into slavery in whatever form this takes. He urges them not to be afraid because Jesus Christ, who knows their pain, will be with them and will bring blessings upon every one of them, even in the adversity to come.

The dear man, Oddrún thinks dreamily. Isn't she the one who is supposed to have lived her life on a wish and a story?

'I want you to know that I have spoken to a French crewman,' Ólafur continues, 'a Christian yet, who was taken captive himself at sea. You need not be long where you're going, he told me. Your king will pay the Turks and then – as he said – *pouf*, you will be back home.'

This report excites a rising murmur. It is interrupted by an ear-piercing aside from Margrét to the effect that the Frenchman's own monarch has obviously not produced such a ransom or else, *pouf*, he would not be here either. Einar Loftsson, half lying between a pallid wife and two drooping children, begins speculating loudly about the chances of the Danish state reaching into its pocket – 'never mind that it's a pocket bulging with the profits on Icelandic fish' – to rescue anyone. It is then that Oddrún raises her head and makes an attempt to speak. The flesh is loose on her face and her eyes, deep sunk in her head, appear to Ólafur bigger than ever. The long, grey hair lies tangled around her shoulders and her cap must have been dislodged at last because he sees no sign of it. Probably swept into Margrét's bucket.

'I have a word, my friends.' Oddrún's voice is too weak to carry far, but the audience nudges and shushes itself to attention. 'I have seen Ólafur in a great palace. He is kneeling before the king.'

This occasions a pleasing intake of breath among those

closest. Ólafur gives Oddrún a look that Ásta, nursing the baby on her other side, recognises from the night he was dragged from his bed to inspect Helgafell as it failed to erupt.

'Hush,' someone hisses further back. 'Listen to Oddrún.'

These are not words Oddrún has heard before and she revives further.

'In my dream' – Ólafur's eyes meet Ásta's and roll faintly upwards – 'in my dream the king, a most distinguished gentleman, was dressed in a red coat with rows of fine gold buttons, and a pair of boots shiny as a black stone polished by the sea. He indicated to our Reverend Ólafur that he should rise, just as I do here.'

A hand trails out from the mound of fetid clothing and twirls regally in Ólafur's direction. '"Sire, I beg you give me money that I may save my people," spake Ólafur to the king.'

Everyone waits. Hardly a breath is drawn as, with great effort, Oddrún drags herself into a sitting position, the better to fix her moist gaze upon them.

'And the king said . . .' She hesitates. 'The king said . . .'

She stops again. Relishing the attention as she does, Oddrún has also realised the effect her word may have on people too full of fear and sorrow to want truth. They have never wanted her truth. She opens her mouth and then closes it again. She begins to cry. Some of her sprawled audience turn away, guessing what is to come.

'Hear me.' She raises her voice through her tears. 'I cannot keep this from you. You all must know it. You must know that the king said no.'

There is an uncomfortable silence. Oddrún has heard uncomfortable silences before but nobody breaks this one with a snigger. Ólafur moves to comfort her, but before he can squeeze to her side, she has fallen back again and turned her face to the floor.

Egill Ólafsson is sitting with his legs crossed, attempting to twist two pieces of rope into a complicated knot he thought he had mastered. He is trying to imagine what being a slave will feel like. What will be expected of him? Will the torture hurt very much? If he is quick to his tasks and obedient, might he be able to work out what his tormentor likes best and avoid the worst? At home his father could be deflected from most beatings with a promise of keener attention to his catechism and a dewy request to hear more about Jacob's ladder. Ólafur is no tormentor, but the principle may be sound.

'Whatever befalls us when we get there, hold fast to your faith, son,' Ólafur whispered last night, lying tight by his side, sensing the dread that will not let him sleep, the fear he cannot confess to his mother. Perhaps this is the answer. Egill must keep the Christ in a secret part of himself, as his father advises, and whatever is asked of him be the perfect slave.

Ásta, the baby snug in her neck, watches her older son studying the ends of rope, trying this loop and that. His hair is so stiff with sea-salt that it is standing up by itself. What is going through his mind there as he concentrates with the slightly ethereal expression that has always caught at her heart?

She wonders if Ólafur, whose thin, untidy bones Egill has inherited, ever looked that delicate and otherworldly as a child, before the priesthood brought him to earth. She smiles into little Jón's cheek at the thought. Nobody could be less ethereal than Ólafur. How sternly unimpressed he was when he came upon her gazing at the Ofanleiti elf-stone soon after they were married, chin in hand and lost in imaginings about the hidden folk inside. She has lost count of the admonishments since. There are no trolls in the Bible. Grotesque shapes in the lava are the way the Almighty once instructed a volcano to behave and not frozen giantesses awaiting the sun's caress. Believing there are invisible people born of Eve who live in rocks and crags all over Iceland is a scandalous blasphemy and not to be indulged for one second – especially not by the wife, daughter and niece of three reputable priests, carriers of the light of Jesus Christ, battling against ignorance . . . and so on.

No, if Egill's expression is rapt and faraway sometimes, it is certainly not his father he takes it from. Where he has gone to now, though, as he weaves his rope with those nervy fingers, she has no idea. Egill keeps his feelings close.

She remembers once Helga rushing in to complain that Egill had pushed her over and smashed every egg she carried home. Ásta stormed outside and struck him about the ear. He received it quite still and merely looked at her without speaking, letting only his brimming eyes do the accusing. A trifling moment, but one she has not forgotten. Helga, who could never hold to a lie for long, confessed later that she had dropped the eggs herself.

'Ásta,' Ólafur is calling to her. 'Come now. Leave the child.'

She places Jón between Egill's knees and steps across Margrét's pail and around two pairs of outstretched legs to where her husband is sitting with Oddrún's grey head in his lap. The social proprieties are so far behind them now that no one raises an eyebrow to see the priest of Ofanleiti's arms about the island madwoman.

'Our poor friend is not long for this world. She wants to speak to you.'

Ólafur bends low to Oddrún's ear, and his hair trails across her closed eyes.

'Come, Oddrún *mín*. Open your eyes and see who's here.'

The old woman takes a few moments to focus. Her face is so gaunt that her eyes seem all that is left in it. They gaze up at Ásta with the pleading look that she and Ólafur have always recognised as a sign of danger.

'Ásta,' she croaks, 'I have a word for you. It came as I slept.'

Ásta is horrified to feel a tickle of laughter at her throat. All her life she has struggled with this impulse to laugh at the wrong time. Ólafur has never quite forgiven her for giggling uncontrollably the day he roared from the pulpit, 'Suddenly there came from heaven a sound like a mighty rushing wind', just as a large farmer at the front shifted his buttock and blasted the congregation. The worst of it was that Ólafur heard her and had to swallow twice himself. He said afterwards that he had never been so mortified and refused to speak to her for the rest of the day.

She dares not look at him now, just in case he is so far gone in manners himself as to wink. As long as no offence to the Holy Spirit is involved, this is quite possible: it is why she loves him. But Oddrún is dying and this is not the time.

'Tell me, Oddrún,' she says, stroking a tangle of hair from the worn forehead. 'Tell me your dream.'

'Not a dream exactly.' The words come in little, effortful gasps.

'It's all right. You can tell me later.'

'No.' Her hand reaches blindly for Ásta's arm. 'It's time for me to return to the sea.' Ólafur twitches. 'I must give you this word at once. Lean closer.'

Ásta moves so close that she can smell Oddrún's sour breath and count the black teeth.

'You remember Gudrún from the Laxdaela saga?'

Of course she does. The Mosfell story evenings celebrated no more compelling heroine.

'She came to me here, this Gudrún, as I was lying in and out of sleep, thinking about the sealfolk and everything I have missed out on in this life. I never knew the love of a man, Ásta. Not in this world anyway. And I never learned how to love in return. I left all my charms behind with my youthful skin under the midnight sun.'

Her clutch tightens. 'But hear this. Gudrún had every chance with men, though luck fell badly for her more than once. Don't do as she did. That is my word to you, Ásta, as you face what is to come. Do not do as Gudrún did.'

And what is that supposed to mean? Ásta stares at her in bewilderment. *Really, Oddrún, must you always be so dramatic?*

Gudrún Ósvífursdóttir, most beautiful and haughty of heroines. She wed the closest friend of the man she really wanted and then – in a fit of jealousy that never failed to make young Ásta tremble – talked this husband into slaying his friend. Is that what she is to avoid? *Oddrún mín, you have excelled yourself this time.* The dearest friend of her own husband has already been slain in a cave – and that friend, by the by, was her uncle.

No, either Oddrún at the end of her life is as muddled as she ever was (could anything be more likely?) or there is something Ásta is missing.

'Oddrún, tell me what it is about that story you want me to remember.'

But the old woman's eyes are fast shut and her hand has become limp. Ásta looks a question at Ólafur. He shrugs back.

Trying to work out what Oddrún means about anything is a labour he gave up long ago.

They sit by her as the hours pass, her head resting on Ólafur's lap. When the last breath has gone with a sigh, Ásta places a farewell kiss on top of her head, watching out for lice. She has not the faintest idea what she is not to do.

Ólafur and Einar Loftsson take down Ásta's sail and roll it around the emaciated body. With the help of Margrét's strapping son Jón Jónsson, they shuffle it up to the main deck. Ólafur and Jón push the body up each of the rope ladders and Einar hauls from above. They are not unpractised: others have gone this way before.

They lay Oddrún down on the upper deck and Ólafur, casting aside one or two theological reservations, prays that God will take their Christian sister home. Then the men raise her over the side. With one push Oddrún Pálsdóttir, tight wrapped in grey, is sent headfirst into the deep where she longed to be. The sea closes over her, taking into itself an old woman's hopes and dreams, and the mysteries no one will ever know.

Next day the ship arrives in the North African port of Algiers. It is the seventeenth day of August, 1627.

WHITE

August 1627 – June 1636

His first choice amongst the boys was my own poor son, eleven years old, whom I will never forget as long as I live because of the depth of his understanding.

Reverend Ólafur Egilsson

9

The Moor strides across the courtyard, pausing only to admire his new fountain. An extravagance, perhaps, but the gush and fall of the water are pleasing. He plunges into the jostling streets and makes his way briskly downwards. It is always sensible to be early for the slave-market, especially when in possession of such precise instructions as Alimah has felt moved to issue this time.

Long before he reaches the base of the city he can see the great galleon docked at the end of the mole. No doubt the usual crowd will be rushing to gape and celebrate: nobody could have missed those cannons. It's good for the city, a big fresh cargo like this. Puts a spring in everyone's step.

He swings left towards the slave-market, which is beginning to fill with buyers, and arranges himself languorously on a stone bench shiny with wear. This is his usual place. The pillared arcade is cool and commands a decent view of the sales. It is also well placed for slipping up the hill when he has had enough. You never do get quite used to the screaming of the mothers.

Patting out the dust from the hem of his cream-white burnous, he picks idly at a wisp of thread that has worked itself free. Alimah was unusually insistent this morning when she noticed the thread.

'Make sure you get someone who can sew,' she said, eyeing him from between half-closed lids. 'Never mind breasts like pomegranates this time, if you please. A skilled hand will do.'

Cilleby sits back to wait.

10

The captives stumble up from the hold in a daze, shaken by the blast of celebratory cannon-fire and choking with gunpowder fumes. For several minutes the sky remains dimmed with smoke. But as they watch, the saltpetre haze begins to disperse and the most astonishing view reveals itself. A white city. A completely white city. In the shards of returning radiance the sight stuns Ásta as nothing else since she rode out with her father one cornflower day in Iceland and saw in the west, the beauty of it making her chest hurt, the Snaefells glacier glittering in the sunshine.

Here is another angel-bright cone of ice. It lies broad and flat along the seafront and rises, narrowing sharply, to a citadel at the tip. It is enclosed by a gated wall, within which a dense jumble of chalky buildings clings to the mountainside. The roofs are flat – she notices this from the ship with amazement – and between them rise strangely sculpted domes, rounded to a point. From the sea the effect is of a white gemstone in a frame of emerald hills.

A festive reception appears to be awaiting them. As they stagger along the mole that forms a long causeway down one side of the harbour, a mass of people surges forward to meet them. They are in every kind of attire, from bright robes to sackcloth, with some wearing next to nothing at all. One or two are wrapped from nose to toe in a capacious cloth that Ólafur, longing to touch it, thinks might be of the same linen as the pirates' shirts. Everyone is pushing to get a better look at the arrivals. Ásta has peered just as curiously herself at the cargo offloaded from the first spring ship into Heimaey, although salt and nails and an occasional length of Norwegian wood for Jón Oddsson hardly stand comparison to a galleon-load of bewildered slaves.

From the harbour the Icelanders are paraded in groups, men and women separately, through a maze of streets so narrow they quickly lose sight of the sky. Vendors shout their wares from hollows in blank white walls and animal drivers yell at small, oddly shaped horses with mangy coats and ears so large they look set for flight.

'Donkeys,' Ólafur will tell Ásta in the pasha's prison. 'And that other beast, the huge one with the lips like a bull, that was a camel, I believe.' Not that either of them will care by then.

After their bare, solemn island and a subdued month in the ship's hold, the babble of the streets makes their heads ache. At one point an unearthly music wails out above them and they hear a man's voice holding first one note then another, high and long. Margrét pokes Ásta in the back to hiss that someone must be having a tooth pulled.

The slave-market is a wide square full of men. Away from the shade of the high buildings, the broiling sun burns their cheeks and makes everyone feel dizzy; the cobblestones roast their bare feet. Ásta pulls the pirate shirt further over the baby's head and tries to shade Marta, who is clinging to her leg, within the filthy folds of her dress. Anna Jasparsdóttir begins to sway and Margrét offers her a sharp shoulder to lean on. The girl even swoons prettily, Ásta thinks distractedly.

She looks over to where Ólafur and Egill have been herded with the other men. They are being arranged in a circle. Egill looks very small between Ólafur and the burly Einar Loftsson. From above the square comes a blast of trumpets. A dignitary of some kind, accompanied by a retinue of armed guards, is making his way down the hill. Ásta glimpses a flash of green turban and a white feather bobbing nearer.

Cilleby watches the pasha making his way across the square with the usual pomp and trumpetry to size up the first batch of male captives. They look as half dead as they always do when they have just stepped off a ship. Hot, too. Every one of them is as pale-skinned as that boor Fleming over there, who never ceases complaining about the heat.

The pasha is strolling from man to man, two armed janissaries with unsheathed blades stepping around the circle with him. He peers into dull eyes, feels hands and arms and prises open several mouths. Occasionally he pats a buttock or cups a horri-fied groin.

Cilleby is close enough to make out the fleshy nose, the small eyes screwed so tight in the sun they are hardly there. Constantinople sends the regency all kinds of pashas, but this one particularly revolts him. There is a flutter of red silk as the Ottoman governor of Algiers, exercising his historical right to choose for himself an eighth of every group of new slaves, pads from one man to another, considering his options. Cilleby feels faintly sick.

The white feather stops, moves on, stops again. Ásta, peering over from the female group, begins to understand that the fleshy dignitary is making a choice. The feather hovers a moment beside the shaggy blond head of Margrét's son Jón, who stands nearly as high as its tip. Then it glides on and Margrét clutches Ásta with relief. Neither of them knows who the man is or what this choosing means, but every watching mother's instinct is shrieking. The feather passes over a scowling Einar and reaches Egill. He looks so small that Ásta has almost convinced herself that the man will not notice him at all. Then the feather halts and a hand reaches out to ruffle Egill's red hair.

When Ásta thinks back on this day – waking to latticed shadow on a white wall, too muddled with sleep to fend off the memory – she will see again that scarlet sleeve, rising first to toy with her boy's hair and then in peremptory summons. She will listen for the click of bejewelled fingers, thinking she really did hear the sound they made, like the soft snap of a puffin's neck. She will see a baggy-trousered soldier jerk Egill forward. She will stop breathing. She will stop breathing all over again, lying there in the harem, because that is what happened: she stopped breathing. She will watch as Ólafur makes to follow and is halted by a curved sword to his throat. She will hear him calling in Icelandic, 'Don't, in God's name, forget your faith, my son.' She will hear Egill answer in a high, wobbly voice, 'I won't, Pabbi,' and feel her throat close, just as it did then. And the sweat will pour from her and she will struggle all over again to make a shout when there is no breath to give it voice. She'll *will* Egill – will him again with the titanic force of the love in her – to turn and look across to where the women captives are. And she will remember how he did turn, and the fright on his face. She will remember his eyes finding hers, the same eyes he turned on her when she struck him for smashing the eggs. She won't be able to look at them for long, though – not afterwards – because she can't bear the silent pleading in them; she cannot bear it. Then she will make herself watch the soldier yanking him away. And she will remember how, when the scream left her throat at last, she saw his step falter. Sometimes she will cry out again, and Marta, lying at her side, will pat her hand.

Captain Fleming has spotted his man. He raises a large sandalled foot to the stone bench and leans across his knee until he is level with the Moor's hooded face. Cilleby receives a waft of sardines and inches away.

'I've got a proposition for you.'

The renewed blare of trumpets interrupts the captain's train of thought. He glances over at the ostrich feather drifting back up the hill towards the white palace at the head of an enlarged retinue. 'That's the pasha made his choices, poor buggers. About time. I can get on with selling the rest now.'

'Make this quick, though, Fleming.' They are speaking in the *lingua franca* of the Ottoman ports that proves so useful for every sort of commerce. 'You're blocking my view.'

The remaining captives are being hustled into groups of ten. Buyers stroll among them, pointing and stroking their chins. A leather-faced man with twig legs and a grubby tunic has begun plucking the men forward one by one, whacking their flanks with his staff to make them trot in a circle. Ólafur's mouth is wrenched open to have his teeth inspected. Jón Jónsson, feeling a rough hand measure his back, tries to hunch his shoulders.

'Easy to catch as spiders, these Icelanders,' confides the captain. 'That's why it's such a big market today. We'll have to see how they perform in the heat, but most of the men seem strong enough. Spent their lives on ropes and pulling in nets, far as I can gather.'

'And your proposition, Captain?' The women are being paraded now. Will this buffoon get to the point?

'Right. Just wanted to give you the general picture. By the way, some of the women are worth a good price, too.' An unbidden image offers itself of Ásta's eyes raking his. 'They seem to do a lot of the work back home, outdoors and in, so you'll get plenty of wear out of them. They'll think they've landed in heaven here.'

Cilleby shifts impatiently.

'Anyway, you'll make your own mind up as usual. But today I am also pleased to offer a special deal.'

The women are being examined now. The captain's brokers are jabbing at them and everyone is shouting at once. Numbly Ásta registers Fleming himself leaning over a seated figure in a pale cloak with a hood. Next to her Anna has a gross hand put up her skirt to feel if she has been with a man. Spared by the child in her arms, Ásta's overflowing breasts are prodded instead. Margrét, lost in her own silent agony at seeing her handsome Jón led away by a thug with thick arms, bites the finger that tries to test her teeth and receives a slap so hard that one of them shakes loose. She spits it out on the cobbles (which in another life she might have admired for their spotless shine) with furious contempt.

Resisting the temptation to detach a hank of peeling skin from the captain's nose, Cilleby tells him to hurry up or he knows where he can put his deal, special or not.

'Right then. Icelandic family. Eldest boy's gone to the pasha now, but that leaves one male (ageing but fit), one female worker (thirty years, maybe more, nice shape for her age and smart, I'd say).' He swallows, rolls his tongue between his lips. 'One female child (two or three years), one healthy infant, male, born on board.'

Cilleby frowns. 'I don't buy families, Fleming – you know that. Nobody does. Too much trouble. And what am I supposed to do with an old man?'

'Don't give me that, Cilleby. You've got so many houses, you could put them in one each and they would never see each other from one year's end to the next. But that's not the point. The old man is a priest in their church. No money, but educated. I put some effort into engaging him on the ship, let me tell you. His people seem to respect him.'

'I believe you mentioned a point, Captain?' Cilleby strains past him to see over to the women. Alimah will sulk if he doesn't get this right. 'And since you are taking so long about it, I'd be grateful if you could move aside and let me attend to the reason I came – which is to buy, if I may enumerate, a sewing woman, a few labourers so that I can trade up some of my skilled ones, and perhaps some men to replenish the galley if I see any muscle. Which I'm not likely to do with your backside in the way.'

The captain flushes. 'The point, Cilleby, if you'll do me the honour of listening one minute longer, is that I've got a couple of hundred of these Icelanders here, and there will be as many again sold by others, but they're dirt-poor. Not a wealthy relative back home among them, according to this priest.'

'You'd have been better sticking to Venice then,' Cilleby growls, pulling irritably at the gold thread. 'Plenty of rich families there.'

'But the point is they're a colony of Denmark, and the Danish king could be a different ransom proposition if we can only make contact. Which the city council has not yet been able to do, if I may remind you, in regard to the subjects of his we've already taken at sea. Look, Cilleby, you'll get all the labour you want from this consignment, but I don't need to tell you the business works best if countries pay to get their people back.'

'What are you suggesting?'

'I'm offering a way of getting directly to Christian of Denmark. You know how long that damned council of yours has been looking for a diplomatic route to Copenhagen. So, send the priest to Denmark to appeal to the king to ransom his family – that's my proposition.'

The captain folds his arms. That's got the Moor thinking.

'It should also force the old rogue's attention on to the rest of them. Four hundred subjects is a lot to lose at once. There's a tidy ransom to play for here.'

'And the price?'

'High, obviously. But think of what you'll get back. I tell you, Cilleby, this city needs a way through to Denmark, and that priest is the man to do it. Believe me, he can talk. Christian will hand over the Danish mint just to close his mouth.'

'And what's to stop him running off and never going near Copenhagen?'

'Ah, that's the beauty of it. He's fond of his family – that's what gave me the idea. I've watched this fellow very carefully. He's not the sort to set up home with a brothel owner on the way through Livorno.'

The captain, who enjoys a similar arrangement in Marseilles, leans in so close that Cilleby is awash in sardine. 'And in the meantime you've got a woman for work and whatever else takes your fancy. And of course the children will be worth their weight in silver in the fullness of time.'

Cilleby eyes him with distaste. 'All right, I'll take the family. It's worth a try. But, Fleming' – he glances over to where the women are being crudely inspected – 'make sure you check her fingers. I need a woman who can sew.'

II

The state prison is entered through a convivial courtyard full of men eating and drinking at wooden tables in the shade, laughing loudly or staring gloomily into a diminishing flagon. The air is laden with the aroma of frying meat. Inside there is less cheer. As Ásta and Ólafur are being led to their cell, the state-owned slaves are returning to their hammocks from the quarries or construction sites where they spend their days. The dank passageways resound to the dismal clang of chain on stone.

The couple are surprised to be still together, since every one of their compatriots was taken from the slave-market alone, with mothers allowed to keep only their youngest children. But Ólafur has been warned that they are to go to different houses tomorrow. The Norwegian guard says their purchaser is a private citizen, and assures them that a private owner of any cast is a better fate than to be bought for municipal labouring like the fettered wretches who live here. Ólafur is glad to have found a blessing for which he can make a genuine attempt to be grateful. Ásta listens to the faceless men clattering their desolation through the prison and thinks about the many ways in which people can be made to suffer.

With Marta and Jón in their arms, they sit against the cell's

96

wet wall and talk of Egill and where he might be lying tonight and what use the pasha could have of him, being so small and slight. Ólafur says there is bound to be a lot to administer in a land with so many captives and ships bringing more all the time. 'Egill reads well, remember, and you can see his intelligence at a glance.'

Ásta sees the pooled tears and turns away.

Ólafur had hoped Egill would become a priest. In fact, the matter was settled. He would go to study at Skálholt and perhaps spend some time assisting afterwards in the church at Torfastadir, as Ólafur had done himself.

'He would have liked Torfastadir,' he says.

'If he could have put up with Helga tormenting him,' she says.

And each wishes the other would stop torturing them both.

'You would like Torfastadir too,' Ólafur tries next. 'The church is on a hill and you can look over the heath to the broad mountain of Vördufell. Shut your eyes, Ásta. Let's forget where we are and I'll take you there.'

Ólafur has always liked to take her places. 'Come with me, my dear,' he used to say, eyeing the mangled knitting. 'Tonight we'll visit a place where the winds blow warm and orange trees bloom in winter.' And she would listen, rapt, while the real wind beat on the door.

He takes her hand. 'See, it's springtime and we're standing on the hill, you and I. Are you with me? Over there is Hekla, our lovely volcano, and she's dusted in snow because it's still just April. Do you see her? Below us we can spy the Hvítá river winding across the plain and down to the sea. And across that sea are the islands.'

Ásta closes her eyes. *Please stop. Please go on.*

97

'If we listen we can hear Helga and Egill arguing in the drowsy meadow. About nothing, of course. Helga will be insisting she's right and tossing her hair, and Egill will madden her by letting it be understood that he knows better but doesn't care to explain why.'

Ólafur, spare me this.

'Imagine just for the moment,' he flounders on, 'that . . .' But in the tremble of his voice is so much of their pain expressed and not expressed that Ásta can bear it no longer. She cries, 'Stop, Ólafur. Telling stories won't help this time,' so sharp that the baby stirs. And he falls silent, bending to hide his face in Marta's knotted curls. They cannot comfort each other.

The smell of cooking meat through the high window is making Ásta's stomach ache. She shifts the baby to the other arm, scratches a few bites and lays her head against Ólafur's. The tang of salt is still on his hair, along with much else. He shuffles closer. They have always fitted together, the two of them: she understood it from the first. From the day she arrived at Ofanleiti she had liked the way he looked at her. True, it was not quite like being ravished with one sizzling glance by, say, the gorgeous Kjartan of saga fame, but it made her feel warm and special. She liked the way he spoke to her, most of the time. She knew she annoyed him by arguing so much, by speculating mischievously about the hidden people when she knew exactly the shade of red his face would turn to hear it. ('When they dip their silver oars in the sea, Ólafur – just supposing – would we see the waves *actually* parting?') But she could soothe him too, and make him laugh. She liked the way irritation and a grudging admiration would struggle behind his eyes for mastery. It was as if he grasped, even while thoroughly infuriated, that although she was a woman there was as much going on in her head as his.

She remembers how she would run across the lava heath to meet him on his return from sorting out some problem at the harbour or among the farmers, so that they could walk back to Ofanleiti together. He would tell her about the people he had met that day, what new quarrels the English and the Danes were involved in, how long he had spent listening to Oddrún Pálsdóttir's latest dream.

She has a sudden image of him nuzzling her hair one evening as dusk was gathering. Oh, the sweetness of letting this come back to her, the beautiful bite of the frosted air.

She had rushed headlong down the slope to greet him and could tell from his wayward stride and the suspiciously moist brightness of his eye that he had overdone it on the Danish ale. Also that he was agitated. He explained that her uncle Jón was saying that Gentleman John's terrifying invasion of Heimaey had been divinely ordered as a punishment for the wickedness of the Westman Islanders. (It must have been 1614: she and Ólafur would have been married by then.) As if there was no debate about the matter, Ólafur said indignantly, with the hint of a sway. He lapsed into silence and stared moodily at the islands.

As usual she had rushed out without her shawl. Folding her arms against the wind, she watched a stream of purple clouds chasing each other across the sky and waited for him to speak. She was becoming colder and colder.

'Sometimes,' he said at last, blown, no doubt, into sobriety, 'I cannot see God's face. I know his word but I can't tell his mind. It troubles me, Ásta. There, I've said it. And Jón, he just goes to sleep and wakes with a vision and it's all quite clear to him.'

Her uncle was famous for his visions. This time he had dreamed of a bleeding sun over the island and a man dressed in red riding across the sky. ('Too much mutton and beer in his belly before he turned to sleep,' Margrét had muttered under her breath.) He insisted that Gentleman John's English pirates had been sent to punish the islanders for their sloth and complacency and that his dream was the clearest possible warning (though not in the smallest degree clear to Ólafur) of worse punishment to come if they did not mend their ways.

Later people would remember that dream. Many on the ship blamed the entire Turkish raid, including Jón's martyrdom, on themselves, as if they had not woes enough to face. Even Ólafur felt by then that his friend must have been right. But that evening, looking to the islands, he was perplexed.

'We are punished so that we are not lost eternally. This is clear from scripture and I am not shy of proclaiming it, as you know. We must fear God's wrath. But are our Westman Islanders really so much more sinful than the next Icelander that this English scourge should be visited so cruelly upon them? Why one and not another?'

Ásta scanned his face gravely for a moment and decided to risk making him laugh. 'When next you dream of finding yourself in church without your breeches on, Ólafur' – she well knew he had dreamed nothing in his life more interesting – 'you must put it in a sermon, too, and scare us all.'

Ólafur looked as if he felt more like crying.

'My uncle is the finest of men,' she added lightly, 'but he does not climb the mountains of the mind as you do. You and I both know he spends all his time scoffing mutton in the foothills.'

Ólafur had smiled then, as she meant him to, bent his head

to hers and buried his face in her hair. Arm in arm they walked together up the hill. And she laid her head against his shoulder as they went, just like this.

He is asleep now, his snores irregularly spaced in the annoying way that always makes her hold her breath for the next one. A lick of hair has spilled over one eye, and she can see dozens of threads of silver in it, gleaming in the barred moonlight. There are surely more than a month ago. She strokes the hair back over his forehead, giving the rumbling chest a nudge with her elbow while she is at it.

Another image. That louring afternoon when her uncle Jón clumped into the house with the news that Ólafur had written to her father to ask for her hand in marriage. The matter was settled, Jón breezed, and he knew she would be pleased. She remembers how Ólafur winked at her. After Jón left he opened his arms, and she flew in. But something was nagging at her. Now that the betrothal was real, there was a feeling she could not define; a feeling, better to say, that was not there. Assuring Ólafur she wouldn't be long, she had hurried out into the draining light to clear her head.

Ásta closes her eyes. She has never told Ólafur what happened on the shore that afternoon. Not once has she spoken of meeting the stranger, or of what she did, the weight of her finger on his lips. Well, obviously not. There are some places it is not wise for a wife to go, and mentioning how close you came to disappearing with an elfman is surely one of them.

They got married, she and Ólafur, and made children, and together they struggled through the winters and told stories in the dark. They were like a couple of nesting gulls, perched on a windy ledge with their backs to the world. And now they are here, about to be lost to each other. And Egill, her heart's delight, is gone to the pasha.

Their diffident Norwegian guard was a mariner before his ship was seized by Algerine corsairs. He explains this to Ólafur in halting Danish as they leave the prison. Now he too is a slave, hoping for ransom one day.

Carrying a child each, they follow him high into the city. Ásta scans the teeming streets for signs of Egill, half expecting to spot him waving shyly from a sculptor's dusty workshop, white to the roots of his hair, or emerging from behind the baker's honeyed stall to say, 'Don't worry, Mamma, I'm here. Try some cake, won't you?' And really why not, she tells herself, pausing to peer over a hookful of sheep's intestines in case the butcher has a small apprentice on the other side. It is the most likely thing in the world that she will come upon Egill about the town.

The streets are narrowing as they climb, so that the teetering buildings on each side almost touch each other at the top. Looking up you can see vines strung between the flat roofs, but no more than a slit of sky. Ólafur stares at the featureless white facades of what he takes to be houses opening straight into the alleys, pondering how little you can tell from their wooden doors of what lies within. For all the clues on the outside, they might open to the grandest mansion or any number of mean dwellings. The row of chalky sea captains' villas along the front, which Fleming had pointed out yesterday from the ship, hoarded the secrets of their character in just the same way.

But novelty has always raised Ólafur's spirits. When they halt at an entrance promising access to one of these blank buildings, a rush of excitement banishes the tiredness from his legs and the weight of Marta from his arms. To reach it the guard has swung to the right along a walled alleyway set with a small number of high, square windows. Squinting up, Ólafur notices that the copper fretwork in them is moulded with flowers, quite exquisite, where the metal is joined. The alley ends in front of a great wooden door adorned with rows of iron studs and framed by an archway of stone sculpted with more flowers, each with a disc at its centre and a fan of petals. Like the rays of the sun, Ólafur decides. (Ásta, miserable with heat and the hungry squalling at her breast, sees only a door to get through and the prospect of sitting down.) Best of all – Ólafur's eyes sparkle with zest – is the pulley around the door, which will remain for him the city's foremost wonder until the moment he sees limestone being boiled in four enormous kettles and understands why the buildings are white. The door closes behind them entirely by itself on a rope running along the top of the frame and attached to the latch. He nudges Ásta to show her the cleverness of it, and wishes he could open the door again and see it close. But now they are inside, in a courtyard open to the heavens.

And at once Ólafur sees what he missed from outside. Here are the marks of status: cool marble floors, a fountain, twisting pillars, stairwells glowing with ceramic colour. Here are the gardens: trailing from earthenware tubs and pots. Here is the sky at last: right inside the house, tipping light into the courtyard past three galleried floors. An *atrium*. Isn't that the Latin word? Ólafur gazes around him in awe. Is it possible that the Romans, the race of Pontius Pilate, were once on these shores and showed men how to build? Of course nobody would need to live under grass like Icelanders in heat like this. They wouldn't need sheep and cows huddled beneath to make them warm in this land (do they even *have* a winter here?) but only shade and cool.

His eyes scuttle everywhere, but there is little time to absorb it before a shaven-headed manservant is gesturing for him to place his daughter on her feet. Ásta is beckoned upstairs by a girl with a violet blossom in her hair. She is wearing wide trousers tied at the ankle. *Extraordinary*, Ólafur thinks, in the instant before worry about where she is leading his wife and children takes over.

With the baby in one arm and Marta by the hand, Ásta drags herself up the marble staircase. She looks back as it curves around on itself and for a second – resigned, infinitely weary – holds Ólafur's gaze. Then she continues out of sight.

A boy serves Ólafur bread and grapes in a plain room off the pillared arcade, before he is unceremoniously hurried out again. Crossing the courtyard he looks up to the gallery. There is no sign of his family. On his way out he does not even notice the pulley.

12

The house where Ólafur will spend one unsettling month in the white city is not (he is just a little pained to discover) as grand as the one in which he left Ásta. The courtyard is too small and the height of the building too tall to admit much sky. The pillars are of rough stone, and the tiling sparse. He is made to sleep on the bare floor of a narrow room and is never offered a covering. The natives also sleep on the floor, but it is not lost on him that they do so between thick blankets. Ólafur knows that envy is a sin and is careful not to indulge it, but he cannot deny that they look snug.

After two or three weeks a resident Frenchman takes pity on him and gives him a length of homespun woollen cloth, a litre of brandy and – joy of joys – a pair of shoes. Ólafur is so moved by this kindness that he weeps. Afterwards he muses on the oddity of tears, that they should pour down his face for a stranger's kindness but never come to relieve the mind's agony he wakes to every day. He is especially grateful to have a cloth to cover him because he is ill by then, tossing night and day with feverish sweats and sickness. The Frenchman brings little cheer when he reports that Icelanders are dying everywhere.

'Not all have your strength to meet the bad diseases in this city, *mon ami*,' he says, keeping his distance. He has counted thirty-one of Ólafur's compatriots in the Christian cemetery already.

When Ólafur recovers, he has to admit he is not being treated badly, despite being given no fresh clothes to wear, which means he is still in the shirt and breeches in which he left Iceland. For company he has his old friend Jaspar Kristjánsson, who arrived aboard a different ship but has been purchased by the same man, a staggeringly rich Moor whom they have never met by the name of Ali Pitterling Cilleby. Jaspar is frantic with worry about his daughter Anna, of whom nothing has been seen since the slave-market.

Ólafur cannot puzzle out what is expected of him. He is given the freedom of the house and in time allowed to roam the streets, as long as he goes nowhere near Ásta's house, which he would be hard put to discover anyway, since he could find his way around a maze of puffin burrows easier than this warren of a city. But he is given no labour, no occupation. Jaspar is taken out each day, along with an Icelandic carpenter who has joined them, to work on the construction of a new house, but Ólafur's days are empty.

His life is not materially unpleasant. The food is good: bread warm from the oven morning and evening, tasty porridge oats and as much fruit as he can eat. Any bread left at night is fed to the horses in the morning, while porridge dregs go straight over the wall or down the privy (another marvel). To a man schooled in Iceland's poverty to lick every bowl clean and suck every fishbone dry, the abundance is amazing. It seems to him that all the fruits of the earth are here, bestowed on a people who don't deserve it and will surely be punished some day for the evil they have brought upon others, although in which life he cannot offhand be sure.

He misses Ásta and the babies, and tries not to imagine what might be happening to them, because he can't do anything about it and is very easily brought low. He longs to see Egill and prays for him night and day. He wishes he had paper on which to make notes, in case he ever has the chance to write about this one day: it is much on his mind that Icelanders in generations to come should know what happened to their people when the Turks came to Iceland in the summer of 1627. Ólafur constructs instead a shelf of impressions inside his head and adds a few every day. He commits to memory the shapes of the copper dishes and washbasins, the sheen on the clay drinking cups, the way people eat with their legs straight out on the floor and don't use a knife. He notes, wondering if it is just this house or every-where, that there are no tables, or benches, or even storage chests. People seem to be much attached to the floor and he never does discover where they put everything. He is fascinated by the women's dresses, which are surely of the finest silk weave in the world (not that he has seen the world, but really he can't imagine finer). He has studied with especially beady attention the linen trousers that reach right down to their shoes, with one cuff attached to the instep and the other to the heel, blushing to think he might be accused of a prurient interest in ankles.

To be fair, many of the Turkish people look rather fine on the lives they live here. Which actually does not seem that fair at all, when he thinks about it, until he remembers that paradise on earth counts for nothing beside what is to come, and reminds himself that it is not his place to question the inscrutable but always merciful ordering of events by his loving Father in heaven, who wills all things for good and answers every prayer, even if not always in the way his children ask.

He looks and he listens and he has plenty of time to notice all that he notices, because Ólafur Egilsson has nothing else to do. Nothing. He has been stolen from his homeland and separated from his loved ones and fed better bread than he has tasted in his life (apples too, and grapes that smell of summer). And for what purpose he has not the slightest idea.

On the twentieth day of September, 1627, two janissary soldiers enter Ólafur's house and order him, none too gently, to accompany them.

He is marched to another street, another anonymous house, a small, shaded room, in which he is astounded to be issued with a document that he is given to understand will ensure his safe conduct on the high seas. When he looks around for enlightenment, there steps from behind the seated official another man, a Moor by his appearance. The dimness of the room and the white hood pulled low over his turban keep the man's face in shadow. Ólafur cannot make out his features.

The Moor explains with a few curt words in the common tongue that Ólafur is being sent as an envoy to Christian of Denmark to raise a ransom for his family and as many others as the king might wish to see returned. He will set sail today and should endeavour to reach Copenhagen with all speed. He is strongly advised to show his pass to any ship in the Ottoman fleet that might trouble his journey. Holding out an elegant hand to be kissed, the Moor dismisses him with the lofty assurance that Ólafur will be permitted to say a brief farewell to his wife and children on the way to the harbour.

Hours later Ólafur is on board an Italian barque bound for Livorno. For every one of his years left on this earth it will haunt him that he never saw the face of Ali Pitterling Cilleby.

13

September 1630

My dear husband,

It is three years since you left for Denmark. Three years. How can we have been parted so long?

All this time I have been having conversations with you in my head, in which you will be glad to hear you give very sensible answers, but writing is much better. Husna, the second wife (yes, there are two of them), has brought me – after much pleading – a piece of bamboo cane, shaved to a point, and a small pot of burnt wool mixed with water. Also some paper. Unfortunately it is quite difficult to write with a stick. As you see, the letters I make are like hen-scratchings and it takes such a long time to form each word that I may be at it for weeks. Especially since I must also do this in secret from Alimah, my chief mistress, who would rather I sewed.

I have no idea if this letter will reach you. I hear of no Icelander who has received a letter back. But it is good to speak to you all the same. This morning I am writing in the harem before the other women wake. It is pretty here at first light, when the sun spills criss-cross patterns from the window on to the wall opposite. But it is also the time I feel most the heaviness of our situation. Sometimes, even now, I awake believing I am back under our draughty pane at Ofanleiti, with you beside me and the children around, and I am winded all over again to realise I am not.

Do you remember our parting at that summer's end? How could you not – pushed in the door by the soldiers, allowed just a moment to tell me your news and then thrust so roughly out again? Could they not have given us five minutes? But what news! Released to beg a ransom from King Christian! I was so happy and sad and fearful all at once. I tried to be brave for you, though I wept after you were gone. I think I was crying from hopefulness, and also perhaps from something that is not hopeful at all, because I suddenly recalled Oddrún's word about the king, which she seemed so sure about. Then I reminded myself of how often she used to be wrong. (I do miss Oddrún and all the dreams and warnings we used to smile over.) After that I began to worry about the long journey ahead of you, and whether you would be shipwrecked, or murdered by another set of pirates, or set about by thugs, or struck down by plague, or discovered only years hence, starved to death behind some mouldering wall in a foreign land with your bones picked clean. Oh, what a range of misfortunes I lined up for you, my husband, on your way to Copenhagen. I pray without ceasing that nothing of the sort has befallen you, but as the months have passed, and then the years, without word of a ransom, the imaginings creep back and it is every day harder to keep them at bay.

We had so little time to talk at the last, you and I. You did try to be cheerful and tell me how lovely it was to see me dressed so fine – and you still, my poor husband, in the clothes you were in when the pirates streamed into Ofanleiti. Indeed I still shiver with pleasure to *recall how it felt to drop my own soiled rags on the floor the day I arrived in this house. A servant girl whom I call Flower, for the blossom always pinned to her hair, took me upstairs to the women's area, which is called here* 'haram'. *(Observe the Arabic I am learning!) She washed me and the little ones all over with water from a blue jug, and gave us fresh clothes and even a cradle for Jón. It took some time to become accustomed to wearing pantaloons, but I cannot deny they are cool and comfortable and make hastening up and down the stairs much easier.*

My job here is mostly to sew. Yes, Ólafur, there is no need to fall to the floor as you read this. Margrét did teach me one or two skills, and although I am sure I am not the seamstress Alimah hoped for, I have learned to pass a needle through a tunic tolerably enough. I also have the task of attending the wives as they bathe once a week. You would love *the public bathhouse. Water gushes into the basin from two brass taps, hot and cold, and with the steam and the heady scents and the tinkle of water on marble, we all become very pleasantly drowsy. I scrub their skin with pumice stones and rub it with cloves and ginger. Then I spread a burning paste all over and scrape the hairs off with a mussel shell. I must say it is the most peculiar way to spend time, but I cannot pretend it is arduous. In fact, if I could be sure – absolutely sure, Ólafur – that you were in the mood to receive a joke, I would say that if this is slavery I will expect more of it when I get home!*

That really was a joke, dearest husband, to show you I can still make one. The serious point of it is that the work of women captives in this city is probably no worse than anywhere, kitchens being (as I now suspect) kitchens the world over, and it is certainly a boon to have the laundry dried in minutes. My own place in the household is privileged compared to some: I can understand that a captive with a price on her head and an envoy sent to retrieve it is not one it makes sense to mistreat. But I am afraid there are bad tidings concerning Margrét, who bit the finger of a buyer at the slave-market. She has been seen carrying water with her ankles bound in iron, and it grieves me very much to think of it. Please have particular regard to her in your prayers.

The burdens I carry myself are of a different kind, and I will not, indeed I must not, dwell on them in this letter, for they are yours too. I offer them daily to the Lord, along with the blessings for which I need no reminder to give thanks, not least the continued presence by my side of our two youngest children. How I rejoice to imagine the smile breaking across your face as you read this, the relief, the joy. I will tell you more of Marta and Jón anon. Of Egill, our darling boy, I will say only this: that he is not found. Sometimes I slip out to look for him when I will not be missed. I have lost count of the number of reddish-haired lads I have almost accosted. Then they turn around and pierce me to the core with a stranger's face.

Picture me, Ólafur, as dawn filters through the high window and the children slumber by my side. I am on my knees again with the paper on the floor before me, bent over double to scratch upon it. (It never struck me before how useful a table can be.) Today I thought I would tell you something of the household. The two wives are Alimah and Husna. Alimah is about the same age as me, to make a guess, although more rounded and graceful. She has very dark eyes that are difficult to read, and a relatively easy disposition for which I have reason to be grateful. Husna looks barely older than our Helga. She is strained and nervy all the time. The way her eyes dart about makes me think of one of our soot-headed Arctic terns scanning the grassland for an intruder. At any moment I feel she might open

113

her crimson beak and screech her unhappiness across the roofs of Algiers.

They both have hair that falls below their waists and shines like a raven's head when I brush it out and sew it with jewels, or gather it into a knot at the nape and bind the tresses into bands of gold to make a headdress so heavy I am heartily glad not to have to wear it myself. They both make me feel extremely plain. I never thought of it before, since who owns a glass in Iceland and of what use would it be anyway to pamper a face that will only be streaked by smoke and flayed by gales the next minute? I have sometimes helped Alimah to dress or painted kohl on her lids and marvelled, truly marvelled, at the beauty to be savoured in the artful outline of an almond eye and the cool loveliness of silk. I never knew this before.

Both wives, along with their daughters and a pair of aged aunts, sleep in rooms off the first-floor gallery, with slavewomen and servants like Flower and me nearby. This floor belongs entirely to the women, except for one room with the most delicate ornamentation of diamond shapes and trailing roses on the door, which is the master's. Nobody is allowed to enter it unless invited. I do not see much of the menfolk (male servants and the like) except on the stairs or passing across the courtyard. Their business is on the second floor.

I see that Jón, curled warm and soft at my side, is awakening. I must lay aside the letter and sit up straight, before he decides it would make a fine start to the day to leap on to my back (as he did yesterday) and instruct me to trot.

Today, Ólafur, I am stealing a few minutes to write on the rooftop while Alimah is out. I often sit here sewing, far above the street and washed by a breeze from the sea. On a day like this, when the horizon has separated itself into layers of silver, I can look out and

*pretend it is the Icelandic mainland. Over there is Helga, I will say
to myself. What is she up to today?*

*Well, that is only a foolish dream. Better I tell you about Jón
and Marta, who are here before my eyes. They have both managed
to overcome the illnesses that afflicted us all in this city at first
and, thanks be to God, are thriving. There are one or two difficult
matters with regard to them, with which I will not burden you.
Let me tell you instead that Jón is still allowed to be among the
women all day and runs about with ceaseless energy. Does this
remind you of anyone? And he prattles as loud and long in Icelandic
as a young man from a distinguished line of preachers might be
expected to.*

*Marta sometimes takes my breath away with her cleverness. She
speaks Arabic as well as Icelandic, and also has a good grasp of the
common tongue. Her fingers are the nimblest I have seen. In fact, I
live in fear that one of these days Alimah will notice that she sews
a neater hem at the age of six than I do myself. Such a great
comfort she is when I am sad. 'Mamma,' she will say, 'let us go
inside a story and shut the door' – and I will tell her a saga or a
VERY harmless story about the hidden people and she will sit and
listen, perfectly still. You remember how Helga could never stay at
peace for two minutes at a time? Marta is quite different. You
should see her now, Ólafur, this very minute. Her face is vanished
into an orange as big as her head. Now she is daintily and very
precisely licking the juice from her fingers. Looking at her I am
thinking of how you and I would have given anything (so we
thought in our terrible innocence) to taste an orange. Now our children suck them like guillemot eggs.*

*Let me tell you what I know of other Icelanders. It is little
enough, because although I am not chained to the house, there are*

115

few opportunities to be out hearing news and I depend on Anna Jasparsdóttir for most of it.

I do know that Einar Loftsson has fared badly. He was thrown into prison for fetching water from a well that Christians are forbidden to use, though nobody had told him, and for punishment his nose and ears were cut off and strung around his neck. Can you imagine such a barbarous thing? I have not seen him myself, but I hear he was bandaged by a doctor and is feeling well enough again to have started making his own brennivín *brandy from local herbs to sell. You recall how Einar was always resourceful. Apparently he is declaring to all and sundry that he intends to earn his own ransom.*

Anna visits me here from time to time, more blooming than ever. I fear you will be upset by what has become of her, so let me merely tell you she is happy, although Jón Oddsson must expect trouble. It might be kinder not to mention this if you see him. Did Jaspar ever arrive home?

Margrét and Jón's boy was bought by a seafarer and made to row on a galley carrying cloth shipments to the east. The galleys are much feared because so many die at the oar, but the word is that he learned so fast that he is now trusted to command one himself.

It seems that most Icelandic men find the work harder than anything they were used to. Some have been put to dragging a plough in the fields outside the city and others labour in quarries or mills. I hear of men being beaten like camels and driven harder than a horse, and I myself have seen some (though no Icelander yet) being led through the street on a chain, just like a bullock. Others do better, especially if their owner is not harsh. Unlike the miserable souls who passed by our cell in the state prison, men working for private owners are generally at liberty to go about the city, and some masters even pay a little.

Many Icelanders have died from disease and heat, and I am sorry to tell you that Einar's wife is one. There have also been a number of religious conversions among some wishing to improve their conditions and thoughtless of how they will be judged at the last day. I know how it must pain you to hear this. I will say no more, and conclude my thoughts for now.

I awoke this morning thinking I should tell you something of this master of ours, but I hardly know what to say. He is the only man allowed into the harem, but his visits are not frequent and they are very *formal. Honestly, you would think the King of Denmark himself had swept into Ofanleiti on a visit. He sits cross-legged on a rug and smokes a big curly wooden pipe, in silence more or less, while the women flutter nervously around him. Sometimes he will sip a cup of coffee, and then he departs with a dark gaze around the room, whereupon everyone begins to talk and act normally again. You may not be surprised to learn that I have not yet been entrusted with making or serving the coffee. This leaves me nothing to do during the royal visits but watch from my own rug against the wall, remembering now and then to make a stitch.*

Cilleby has once or twice looked across at me – not at all improperly, you may rest assured, but as if trying to work out what I am. How strange to buy something and not know what it is. I have lately decided that his puzzlement is because I have on occasion looked out of curiosity at him, sitting there with his vermilion waistcoat and a yellow turban with a red cap at its centre a tenth the size of the pasha's that still invades my dreams. When one of the wives speaks to him, she addresses a point nearer his chest than his eyes and he in turn speaks into the air above her head. This seems to me as astounding as any of the customs of this land. No doubt Cilleby feels at liberty to make a frank appraisal of me because he owes a slave-woman none of the respect accorded to a wife.

I must record in his favour, however, that he appears to be a not ungentle father. I notice such things because I am aware each day of my children growing up without theirs. The other day one of the smallest of his daughters perched on his knee and stroked his chin with an artfulness as captivating as Helga's when she was preparing to confess a misdemeanour to you. But forgive me: my pledge to write nothing that will make either of us sad is too easily broken. It was just the way Cilleby patted her head absently. It brought tears to my eyes.

I must conclude this letter soon, Ólafur, else I will be at it for ever, but there is one last thing I must tell you. I have learned to speak another tongue!

Can you guess how many captured people there are in this city, all trying to make themselves understood to one another? As many as TWENTY THOUSAND, according to Anna, who seems to know most things. Here are the countries they come from: Portugal, Holland, Scotland, England, Denmark, Norway, Ireland, Hungary, Spain, France, Italy, Syria, China, Japan, Egypt, Ethiopia. And Iceland, of course. I dare say I have forgotten some. Half of these countries I had not even heard of before.

Now, do you remember the language you began to learn on the ship? They speak it here. Masters give their orders in it and slaves speak it to one another. It has just occurred to me that you must know this already because you were here for those four weeks, but what you do not know is that your wife now speaks it very well. Note this, Ólafur. You are no longer the only linguist in the family. In fact, it is not so difficult to speak or to understand. I recognise many words from Latin, which I think are Spanish or Italian (you would be able to tell me at once), and there are others from local languages, all mixed up together. But it is not nearly as complicated to learn as Latin, because there is less heed paid to how a word ends, only to its root. The women of the family speak only Arabic, which is much harder, but we do well enough with nods and signs and I am beginning to understand more.

I have also found out that the people we were wont to call Turks are by no means all Turks. It is true that the highest people are most often from Turkey – they are also called Ottomans – but others, like the family of our high and mighty Ali Pitterling Cilleby, are Moors from Spain. Then there are Berbers, native to this land, and Jews. And besides the slaves, there are the European renegades with their new Arabic names who are here to make money and stride about as if they own the place, which many of them do.

So, my dear husband, I like to think of you reading this letter as my heart has spoken it, but if you should not, it has given me joy to talk to you. It must be near a month now since I began writing. The heat here is losing its fiery strength and is not, I will confide to you, unpleasant at this time of year. But how much, how very much, do I ache to be at home, with the bite of winter returning to the air and the birds starting to answer the call of the south. I think of it, and of you, all the time.

If it proves possible, I will take this letter to the harbour tomorrow and wish it God speed to Iceland. I pray it will find you safely back on the island after completing your mission in Denmark.

I will mention to you only lightly in closing that I am not alone in waiting anxiously to hear word of your audience with the king. We had expected news before now. I am told that a group of

SALLY MAGNUSSON

Icelandic men have sent a petition to his majesty King Christian to remind him that his subject people, so long hidden from sight in the Barbary, begin to feel forgotten.

I am not forgotten, Ólafur. I know that. I know you will have done your best.

Your loving wife, who wishes upon you every Christian blessing,

Ásta Thorsteinsdóttir

14

Scurrying down the steep alleyways of the white city to despatch her letter, Ásta is pleased with the craft that went into those stolen hours with the bamboo stick and the burnt wool ink, and the thought devoted to what not to say. She has been measured and relatively candid, so she assures herself, but also careful of her husband's feelings. She has not shrieked her desperation to know where the ransom is. She has given no hint of how often she wakes in the dawn to Egill's white face as he is pulled away, torn from her very ribs, and how she cries then and cannot stop. She has not told him about Marta.

If this paper survives the perilous journey to Iceland, Ólafur will be smiling a few months hence to know that his wife can make a joke in captivity and his children are eating oranges. Of the things that would most deeply distress him he will remain in ignorance. Not a whisper will he hear of how Flower took her aside one day and urged her to prepare herself.

'Alimah has decided it's time,' Flower said.

'Time? Time for what?'

'Time that Marta learns to pray.'

Flower was a slave once herself. She has forgotten the name

of the land she was snatched from as a child. Free now, she will remain a servant of the household until she marries.

'Ásta, you must know that all enslaved children in Algiers grow up as Muslims, wherever they come from.'

Ásta did not know.

Now Marta has been taught to pray five times a day to the east, pressing her forehead to the floor on a specially woven mat. She chants words that stop Ásta's blood with ice and would bring such agony to Ólafur as can scarce be imagined. She does it with solemn attention, but also with a touching sensitivity to her mother's pain.

'Marta *mín*,' Ásta whispered one night when they were cuddled on their blanket in the darkness, waiting for sleep. 'What do you think about when you pray with Flower?'

The child took a moment to consider. 'I think a little bit about the words I'm saying. That Allah is great, the most . . . I'm not sure how to say it in Icelandic.'

Ásta could feel her daughter's eyes on her, sensed her pondering the right answer.

'But then I think about a new stitch, Mamma. Or I think about the stone I found, the blue one that I keep beside me here, and how well the sea has polished it. Look, here it is.'

She reached below the blanket, and Ásta felt a cool pebble pressed against her lips in the dark.

'Feel how shiny it is. Let's make up a story about it, Mamma, and we can tell Jón in the morning.'

Ásta kissed the stone and stroked Marta's downy cheek, smiling fondly at her daughter's artlessness, before she remembered that Marta, even at six, was never artless. Then she prayed over the girl and her slumbering brother and tried to quell the dread, never far from the surface, that she would lose them both one day, not only in this life but, worse by far, the next.

Nothing, but nothing, is to be gained by Ólafur knowing this.

Nor is it her place to tell him about Anna Jasparsdóttir, who wasted little time before converting to the infidel faith herself and marrying the man who bought her. Ásta hardly dares conceive of how this news would go down in Iceland, where adultery is deplored by Church and state with a zeal she remembers Ólafur's sermons reflecting only too energetically. It is hard to imagine the category of sinfulness in which a captive Christian wife voluntarily marrying her Muslim owner might belong.

Anna protests that she is only making the best of the life forced upon her and has married, by the way, a good man. See how quickly her new husband, a Moor by the name of Jus Hamet, settled the ransom on her dear father, enabling Jaspar to be released to make his way home. But Anna's swift overlooking of the husband awaiting her in the croft at Stakkagerdi still takes Ásta's breath away. If Anna has given a moment's thought to ardent, red-faced Jón Oddsson, there is no sign of it. And if she has suffered a moment's doubt over placing her soul in immortal danger, Ásta is yet to discern it.

'She's pretty, your little Marta,' Anna said the other day, watching the child hum quietly to herself as she sewed on the roof garden while Jón scampered around their feet, pretending to be a horse. Now that she is a free woman Anna can pay visits as she chooses, and Ásta is permitted to receive her as long as her own less than indefatigable hemming is not interrupted.

'I know you get distressed to watch her at prayer, but only think how easy it would be for you to take the step that I did,' Anna said, patting the belly that has begun to swell beneath the folds and pleats of silk about her waist. 'As a Muslim you could hold on to her and little Jón forever, honoured one day in the families they will make here in time. You must know there is little chance of children being released. I have never heard of it.'

'Hold them forever?' Ásta cried. It was clear that Anna had never attended to a word she had heard in church. '*Forever* is separation from God and burning in the fires of hell. *Forever* is seeing none of them again in the life that comes, a life that will be better than this one, Anna, let me assure you.'

Anna's clear, blue-green eyes studied her thoughtfully. Ásta always became prim when the conversation turned to faith: it was only to be expected, being married to a priest. 'You sound like Ólafur, Ásta *mín*. Not,' she added hastily, 'that there is anything wrong with that. Only I've come to wonder myself if it is always so simple and whether God himself has no discretion in the matter of who goes to dwell with him.'

'Of course he has discretion. God asks only that we believe in him through Jesus Christ and judges us accordingly,' Ásta snapped, sounding to her own vague annoyance even more like Ólafur. 'Do you not believe in heaven?'

'I do. And you would be amazed at how many Moors and Turks and Berbers believe they are going there too, and pray to that effect. Of course I don't understand exactly what they pray, but I have to admit' – she gave Ásta one of her enchanting smiles – 'that I never understood Ólafur's prayers much either.'

All in all, there is much that has not gone into the letter that Ásta is holding as tightly as if it might somehow gust from her grasp in the airless streets. But there is much of herself that it does carry. She skips down the last of the cobbled steps with a feeling that might even be happiness to think that one of those ships in the harbour, their masts pricking the hazy morning mist, will bear her heart to Ólafur.

On the quayside an unsmiling sailor is accepting coins to have letters thrust into his hand. A cluster of men have handed theirs over already, all slaves by their rough attire and no Icelander among them. The sailor glances at her coin, begged from Anna who has plenty.

'Others have paid better,' he grumbles in the common tongue.

She ignores him. 'Livorno?' The Italian port is only a week's sail away, and it is from there that letters have their best chance of being carried north.

'Thereabouts,' he replies, sneering a little.

With a dozen papers stuffed under his shirt the sailor strides up the mole, at the end of which a double-masted ship is preparing to take breath. The group watch every footstep.

As the wind catches the sails, a flock of white birds flies upwards, rising from the deck and then fluttering one by one to the water. Surprise ripples through Ásta's companions on the quayside. One man points, babbling to himself in his agitation. Another shouts, then starts to run uselessly up the mole, hurling foreign curses across the water. Very quietly, without realising she is doing it, Ásta begins to weep.

She is the last of the group to turn away. All those words lost, and with them the imagining. If the wretched sailor had only waited until the ship was out of sight before he opened his jacket into the sea, she could have feasted for months and months. How it would have sustained her, deciding which port her letter lay in now, making a story of who carried it next, picturing Ólafur's expressions as he read.

Without sea and masts to guide her, finding the way back
proves harder than it was to reach the harbour. The city is flat
along the front before it begins its steep rise, but even here the
streets are full of confusing twists. She is hurrying now, although
her head-to-toe covering makes for ungainly progress. The outer
cloth is fastened under her chin and beneath one arm, then
tugged over her hair and down her forehead. Her lower half is
so amplified by the voluminous trousers beneath that she feels
as awkward as an earthbound gannet. In her haste to be there
and back before Alimah notices, she has pulled the muslin veil
too tight across her nose and around her ears. It is now half
covering one eye.

Frustratingly, the first street she tries brings her out near the
sea again, only further along this time, on the other side of the
mole. Ahead of her is a row of five large white villas curving
along the water's edge. They are blank-walled at the back, with
barely a window between them, but on the side facing the sea
each has an arched opening into which the water is lapping.
From where she stands, it looks as if the sea is swirling inside
the houses themselves.

As she tries to get her bearings, the prow of a small boat
noses out from the nearest villa into the misty sunshine. A pale,
heavyset man is at the oars, rowing powerfully. She feels instantly
sick. That tongue on the cracked lips, the sudden glint of lust:
she has not forgotten. The man is looking over at her now,
rowing parallel to the mole, his back to the open sea.

Surely he cannot recognise her. Her hair is well tucked – she
puts a hand up to check, dashing a couple of escaped strands
back under wraps – and with her veil askew there must barely
be two eyes visible. Ridiculous to think anyone could guess who

she is. She turns away and rushes back the way she came, skin crawling. The man rests up his oars.

In the vestibule of Cilleby's house she leans against the cool tiles to catch her breath, fiery-faced and panting from taking the hill too fast. The panicky sense of pursuit is ebbing and she is ready to laugh at herself for imagining it. Her attention is already adjusting to the pile of punishment waistcoats she must expect upstairs. As the door creaks behind her on its clever pulley she thinks, with a swift stab of longing, of Ólafur. Tugging off her veil, Ásta steps into the courtyard.

Cilleby is half leaning against a pillar, arms folded. His burnous is hanging open, the hood loose about his shoulders. A plain, white cloak is the mark of the Moor in this peacock city, so Anna says, although she has also been at pains to assure Ásta that Ali Pitterling Cilleby, while regrettably richer than her own husband and boasting his own fountain, is not a real Moor. 'My Jus Hamet can trace his family on both sides straight back to Spain, but Cilleby has the blood of the renegade in him,' she confided once, lowering her voice so conspiratorially you would have thought the whole roof garden spoke Icelandic. 'His father was an Englishman or a Dutchman or some such. Probably the owner of a corsair ship, because that's where they make all their money. Or was it, let me see, his grandfather? He has a Moorish lineage – but not as pure as some, I can tell you, for all that he strides around in white.'

Ásta lowers her eyes and makes to scuttle past.

'I would talk to you,' he says. The common tongue sounds strange and formal on his lips; she has heard only Arabic from Cilleby in the harem.

He takes a step towards where she is rooted to the floor. It is so long since a man of any kind has addressed her directly about anything, unless you count today's scoundrel sailor and the garlic seller round the corner, that she feels all of a sudden girlish and fluttery.

The moment does not last.

'Come to my chamber before sunset,' he orders, addressing her chin.

15

The day that Ásta watches her letter drown dawns sharp and blue on the Westman Isles. It is just the sort of bright day on the cusp of winter that she used to love, which is why Ólafur has placed himself outside Ofanleiti with his hands clasped behind his back and is picturing her enjoying it. Ásta would be out without her shawl, of course, heedless of the chill in the air. She would be gazing around to see if any more of the migrant birds were on their way south today or if the first flock of Iceland gulls had gusted in yet from the north. She would be listening for the autumn-pale golden plover fluting among the tussocks, and would rejoice (as he does now, for her, although he would hardly have paid attention on his own account) to find it here yet, still dashing about for the last worm while the earth is soft, still seeking out trembling spiders' webs to invade before it is time to leave. And then – Ólafur smiles to himself ruefully – she would run back inside because another pot was sure to be burning dry.

There are no burned pots at Ofanleiti any more. Thorgerdur's meals are sparing but never ruined. Ólafur's firstborn daughter has done her best to keep three children, a feckless husband and listless father in a house that is a poor shadow of the old Ofanleiti.

She is fond of her father but would be glad to see some of his old energy again. Back more than two years now, he does little but stare at the islands or sit inside using up the oil to write. There has hardly been a decent hour's work from him around the croft since he returned and Gísli is still supervising much of the church business on his own. Not that there *is* a church any more, with the ashes of Landakirkja long scattered to the sea.

Thorgerdur bustles to his side now, a big-boned woman with a face that was not made to express joy and a life that rarely supplies it.

'Father, you've been standing there an hour. Will you not at least look to the cattle?'

'I was thinking of Ásta,' he says, exhaling in a manner that strikes Thorgerdur as indulgently mournful. 'It is three years since we parted – just a little over – and today I have been feeling it keenly. Forgive me, daughter. I am no longer the man I was.'

With a sniff intended to convey that whatever man he might be the cows will not attend to themselves, Thorgerdur stomps off to do it. Her father's grief is wearing.

Thorgerdur and her husband have been back at Ofanleiti since the spring of 1628, when the Reverend Gísli Thorvardsson, a Heimaey boy himself originally, was despatched from the church at Torfastadir to take over religious duties on an island that had lost both its priests. Gísli had been a charming, floppy-haired youth in his time, popular with women and quick to take up with young Thorgerdur Ólafsdóttir when she arrived on the mainland to do battle with the grime in Torfastadir. Ólafur had given the marriage his blessing with some reluctance: everyone knew the rumours that Gísli had fathered a child out of wedlock. But the young man was a trained priest, well enough educated if inclined to be casual with his responsibilities, and Thorgerdur could be forceful.

On their return to the crushed island Thorgerdur and Gísli set about rebuilding Ofanleiti. It was poorly done and she knew it. Yet how could it have been otherwise, with hardly a soul to help cut the turf and every piece of wood that drifted ashore fought over for a new frame or rafter? They struggled for food, as did everyone with so many men gone. Few parishioners had fish spare to pay the priest and they lived on what Gísli, never a practical man, could catch himself. Ólafur returned later that summer to find Thorgerdur whisking around a diminished croft with desperate vigour and Gísli more prone than ever to gulp down his troubles too fast.

Ólafur sighs and waves a hand to young Magnús Birgisson, passing on his way to climb Helgafell. The lad is on watch duty today. He will join another man up there, and the pair will scan the sea for pirate ships and build a cairn to show the island they have not fallen asleep. The men who come tomorrow will pull down that cairn and build another, and people will look to Helgafell to see the stones rise and fall with the tides and thank God to be safe another day.

Magnús waves back. He is hoping the reverend will be waiting for him with a hunk of dried fish when he comes down at sunset, and a story or two from his travels. Bonded in a way that neither has found it necessary to express, they have formed the habit of sharing the last of the light together at the end of these fast-shortening days. Ólafur looks forward to the boy's undemanding company. Sometimes he can almost imagine him to be Egill, sitting there in the gloaming with his eyes wide and the soft suspicion of hair on his lip.

They have sought each other out often, these two, since Ólafur's return from Algiers. When he was rowed ashore from the Danish ship two summers ago, Magnús's was the face at the harbour that told Ólafur he was really home. That day was the sixth of July, 1628, a year after the Turkish raid. It was the end of a journey that had taken him more than nine gruelling months by sea and by foot. When he thinks back on his humiliating struggles in one port after another to raise the fare for onward passage, the days without food, the roads so dangerous he walked in fear of his life and finally – finally – at the end of his two months in Denmark a full thirty-one days on the North Sea with barely a breath of wind, Ólafur still thanks God in genuine wonderment that he made it here at all.

Everyone rushed to see him of course, shouting the news from house to house and from cliff to cliff that their lost priest had returned. Ólafur dreaded having to face them. Bouncing through the waves towards the quayside with the rain slicing his cheeks, he could not decide whether what he did know or what he did not would burden these people more. What were the names of the thirty-one in the Algiers cemetery, and surely by this time more? He couldn't say. How were their loved ones being treated in Algiers? He didn't know. What should he tell Jón Oddsson, lumbering down from Stakkagerdi to inspect some piece he had ordered from Copenhagen, about his wife Anna? That Ólafur had last seen her being led away from market by a heathen, black-skinned Moor? And as if all that were not difficult enough, what (may the Lord give him wisdom) was he supposed to tell them about the king?

He stepped from the boat, conscious of the poor, gaunt figure he must cut. The shirt he got from that blessed man who had taken pity on him in Kronborg was too short in the arms, and the frayed priestly collar, another gift, had been made for a plumper neck. Ólafur swallowed nervously when he saw how expectantly people were gazing at him. More and more were arriving to join the throng, shouting questions as they approached.

'Why are you alone, Ólafur?'

'Where are the others?'

'What news of my son?'

'Do you have letters?'

The weight of hope pressing on him was too much. Ólafur passed a hand over his eyes and cleared his throat. 'My friends, I intend to travel tomorrow to the mainland, where I will visit the bishop at Skálholt.' The plan had just that minute come to him. 'It is right that I should speak to him first.'

'Have you been ransomed?' called a farmer at the back. A hush fell. Everyone looked avidly at Ólafur.

He was not to know that the island considered itself an expert on ransoms. There was hardly a merchant of Lübeck or seaman from Leith who had been allowed to drink his ale in peace this last year without being badgered for gossip by anyone who could dredge up a foreign phrase and make sense of the reply. Before long the depleted island had been discussing with airy authority which countries paid best to bring their people back from the Barbary. England, it was confidently asserted, would pay no ransom on principle in case this encouraged more piracy, while both Church and Crown in France had organised the return of thousands of their people. All year it had not been the weather or the price of a codfish that the islanders had debated as they tried to order their lives again, but which way the wind might be blowing in Copenhagen for the Icelandic captives.

Ólafur tried to raise his voice and found it no longer carried.

'I was set free by my captors in order to secure a ransom from the king,' he shouted hoarsely. 'To this end I sought an audience with our gracious majesty King Christian. My friends, the situation is complicated. I beg you are patient until I have explained it to the bishop. In the meantime let us thank God for his many mercies.'

With that he began to walk forward and the crowd parted for him with a quiet sympathy that nearly unmanned him. Magnús Birgisson came over to speak then, offering to walk him home.

'Thank you,' Ólafur said. 'You've grown tall this last year, Magnús.'

'I'm thirteen now,' the boy said shyly. 'Egill too in a few months. When will he get here, Ólafur?'

Ólafur said nothing. He took Magnús by the arm and they trudged off up the heath towards Ofanleiti in silence.

The light is dimming by the time Magnús bounds down the mountain. He is soon settling himself on a roughly assembled wall to gnaw on hard cod and a smear of butter smuggled from Thorgerdur's dairy.

'Have I ever told you,' Ólafur says, leaning against the wall and watching him eat, 'that there is so much food in the land I was in that they give what is left each day to the horses?'

Magnús nods and carries on chewing. He has heard most of Ólafur's tales by now, but they are none the worse for the repeating and there is nearly always a new detail.

Ólafur himself finds it soothing to be with the lad at the end of the day like this. There are no tearful questions of the kind he has faced interminably these two years past, no expectations of a slick explanation of God's role in this sorry saga, no pleas for reassurances about loved ones that he cannot give. Just a generous ear for the adventures he had on his way home, the countries he walked through, the dangers he met, the sights he saw. It is a relief to be able to talk as he used to. The jaunty confidence of old is mostly gone: lost with his son in the slave-market, lost along the lonely, dangerous byways of Europe, the last of it ground underfoot in the court of King Christian. But Ólafur has never been averse to the sound of his own voice.

'Did I ever show you my pirate pass?'

Twice, Magnús could answer, but does not.

When he and Egill were small, Ólafur used to sit them both on these very stones, point to the islands one by one and see which boy could remember more names; it was usually Egill. Sometimes Ólafur would wave towards a pretend dot on the horizon and tell them it was Snorrastadir on the mainland, where he had grown up and dreamed of being a priest, or Skálholt, where he went to school and learned a language called Latin. There is a comfort in being with Magnús in this place.

Out from his pocket comes the safe conduct pass issued before he boarded the Italian ship. The paper is dog-eared with fingering and soakings.

'I sailed in many ships, Magnús *minn*, and it was this piece of paper alone that would have saved me if we were attacked by Barbary corsairs, although I am glad to say it was never put to the test.'

'Tell me about your travels,' Magnús urges, sucking his fingers for butter.

135

Ólafur smiles. 'Which part would you like today, then? The time when a Turkish ship chased our Italian one for two whole days and I held tighter to that pass than my hat (which flew overboard, did I tell you)? Or shall I remind you what it was like having to beg for food and money? Or being stripped to the buttocks and inspected for pestilence? Being helped by strangers (as I've told you often, there was much of that also, may God be thanked)? Walking all the way into Germany with the thought of making it to Hamburg, only to learn that soldiers of the Emperor were murdering travellers on the road ahead, which meant (have I told you this?) that I had to turn and walk four days back to Livorno and try a different route? Sleeping in the very first bed since before I was captured sixteen weeks before – that was when I got to Marseilles – and able to take my clothes off for the first time too?'

Ólafur smiles. 'Or the sights, Magnús *minn*, the sights. Seeing a city on a distant hill aglow with lights that seemed to hang higher in the sky than the stars themselves. Gazing up for the first time at a stained-glass window and feeling a catch in my throat as the sun poured through and lit the colours. Watching a ship's anchor being forged in a smithy where the hammers were driven – think of it – by the wind. Wondering at the clothes people wore. Do you know that in Livorno even the porters and the soldiers wore silk and velvet, and their jerkins were cut in five strings at the shoulders and their garters alone must have been worth more than anything you or I have ever worn.'

Ólafur loves to look on the lad's eager face and watch his eyes catching light. Sometimes he thinks he might have found with these anecdotes a way of redeeming the months of penniless misery and degradation. Not in a sacred way of course – not that kind of redemption – but by forming them into a new shape, still truthful, that brings pleasure and insight to others, just as the stained-glass artist did with his scenes from the Bible. Might this also be why he has been so anxious to commit his experiences to paper: so that he can tidy the fearful disorder in his own mind of all that has happened since the pirates arrived on Heimaey? Is that what he is doing? Hoping he will be better able to convince others of divine orderliness if he can first convince himself?

'Or perhaps, my boy, you would rather hear again about the tamed bear in Genoa, the one that walked on its hind-legs. Or the time I was so thirsty I had to drink water that a lion, an ostrich and a fair number of monkeys had drunk from and befouled before my very eyes. What do you say?'

Magnús is grinning broadly. 'Anything you like.'

Ólafur considers a moment. 'I don't think I've ever told you about something I saw in Livorno. It shocked me very much. Every morning I saw at least a hundred people, maybe more, being driven about the streets in chains, shackled together two by two like horses. Every one of them was near naked, with only a cloth about the waist. I understood then that slavery and demeaning cruelty exist in Christendom too. I am still pondering this.'

Ólafur lapses into silence and Magnús, wiping his nose on a cuff, hopes any immediate pondering will not take long. The last tendrils of pink in the west have left with the setting sun and the sky has all but joined the sea. It will be a clear, cold night. There are stars out and a sliver of moon, and the verdigris lichen on the stones is already twinkling with frost. Ólafur's long, angular face is deep in shadow.

'Here is another thing that struck me. When I came by ship to Marseilles – that's a great port in France – I watched fisher families in small boats working in the harbour. The wife would row while the husband stood in the bow and reached to the seabed with a corded net at the end of a long pole. He was scratching in the mud for flatfish. The wife would then let go of the oars and help him draw up the net and rinse the dirt. And what would they find in it? One flatfish. Sometimes two or three, but just as often none at all. I found it humbling to see how hard they worked for so little. I tell you, Magnús, there are poor folk in more places than Iceland. Remember this.

'By the February of that year I was in Holland, and there I saw windmills that work night and day when the wind blows. I've told you of them before. Then I had passage to Denmark and by the end of March came to Kronborg, where I had a look at an immense stronghold built to see off the Swedes. I cannot tell you what a relief it was to arrive in Denmark. After so long in so many strange places, it almost felt as if I had come to Iceland.'

Magnús is turning over the names of cities and countries in his head, seeing windmills dipping and fisherfolk in a faraway town scrabbling in the mud for a paltry dab. He steals a quick glance at Ólafur. Magnús is not one to romanticise, but neither is he too young to wonder at how far and how long a man who has lived well past sixty summers could be driven by his love.

'And the king, Ólafur?' he asks diffidently. The reverend has never been very forthcoming about his audience and people have drawn their own conclusions. 'What happened when you went to see the king?'

Ólafur blows out a long puff of air and stares past him to

where the islands have smudged to grey and the sky beyond has begun playing with wisps of ice-green light. Wraiths, Ásta would call these, the way they swirl about and trail their fingers like smoke. Forgetting that he once lectured Ásta for a full ten minutes on the ancient phenomenon of the northern lights, Ólafur stands like this for a long time. Magnús, practising rings with his breath and shuffling a bit, hopes the old man isn't about to cry. He should have asked him about the tame bear.

'It's late,' Ólafur says at last. 'My daughter will be opening that door any minute and demanding to know if it's my intention to die of cold. Go on, Magnús, while you can see your way home.'

The boy slips off the wall and lays an awkward hand on Ólafur's shoulder. He feels himself blushing as he does, because this is the priest of Ofanleiti and what does Magnús know? Then he starts off down the slope and Ólafur watches as the shadows absorb him. The eerie green lights shift and stretch across the sky. Wraiths, Ólafur thinks. They look like wraiths.

16

Before sunset, he said. What does that mean? Five minutes before? An hour? Ásta tries to remember the point at which other women have left the roof garden of an evening, flitting from the honey cakes and the stories to the chamber behind the flowered door.

More to the point, what does the command signify? Ásta well knows that slave-women are violated throughout the city: why else the shaming inspections at auction? Nor is she blind to the ways of this household. Yet it is one thing to have noticed some pretty slave-woman who is not a wife returning to the harem in the morning, flushed or sad, and to have revelled in despising Cilleby's appetites as heartily as the way he makes his money, but it is quite another to enter the picture herself. She assumed . . . well, what exactly? That she was bought for ransom before service? That in any case he has the choice of others younger than her and more beautiful? That after three years she is safe?

With thumping heart Ásta joins the rest of the women around the low table and keeps an eye on the sun's progress towards the sea. Might she even, reviewing the matter, have misunderstood? Perhaps she is only required to serve the man his Turkish coffee.

Normally this is her favourite time of the day. Unless it is raining or the turning season has cooled the air too fast, the harem gathers on the roof, enfolded in the drowsy perfume of evening jasmine, to tell its tales. Sometimes the stories go on by starlight.

When she first arrived, Ásta was content to listen to the murmur of voices and guess how each story went by how the audience rolled their eyes or grabbed each other in fright. She quickly recognised that Alimah had neither the art nor the energy to tell a story well: she could never be bothered to spin out a web to draw the others in, and they soon began to fidget. Equally, the plump aunt with the drooping nose would have the younger girls nudging each other, as if to say, 'Not this again'; even Ásta could tell that her quavery stories were going on for a very long time. On the other hand, the other aunt, with skin like paper and little to say at other times, revealed herself to have the gift of making everyone chuckle. Flower laughed so much one evening that she choked on a vine leaf. But it was Husna, usually so serious and withdrawn, who proved the greatest revelation. Ásta saw at once how the subordinate wife came into her own here and made her audience glassy-eyed with imagining. When it was Husna's turn to speak, the women would lean forward and lay their chins in their hands, and she would look around them one by one, fixing them with her intense stare and drawing them in.

It began to bother Ásta that she could not share these stories. She could pick out phrases she recognised in Arabic, but it was never enough to let her grasp the plot or join the enchanted circle. One evening she became so frustrated that she shuffled closer to Flower and whispered, 'Tell me what she's saying.'

Flower, as eager to wrap herself in a story as Ásta, did not welcome the request. Without taking her eyes off Husna, she whispered back tersely, 'It's about a nightingale who loves a rose.'

Ásta had no idea about this word 'nightingale' in the common tongue. But she realised it must be a bird and thought of the golden plover piping its heart out in the tufted grass. As Husna told her tale, Flower listened for a while and then turned to Ásta with a rapid translation.

'The rose was white,' she whispered. 'All roses were white long ago. And when the rose heard the nightingale's song, she trembled. Like this, Ásta.' Flower made her arms shiver. Her bracelets clattered and Husna shot her a warning look.

'One night the nightingale came closer to the trembling rose and sang, "I love you, rose. I love you. I love you." And when the rose heard it, she blushed pink. And in that moment were pink roses born.'

She forgot to report for a while after that. Ásta nudged her.

'Pardon, Ásta. The nightingale, he came closer and closer, until one night the rose opened its petals and . . . Actually I don't have the words for what happened. But in the cool morning the rose turned red with shame. And that is why we have red roses. Ever since then the nightingale comes to ask for love, but always the rose refuses, for Allah never meant flower and bird to mate. The rose still trembles at the voice of the nightingale, but her petals stay closed.' She sighed. 'Isn't it a beautiful story?'

Ásta thought she might have missed something in the telling, which had taken Husna considerably longer than Flower and occasioned many gasps and groans from the audience. She did think the rose might have fought harder for her honour. But really she was away dreaming about the plover, and how she used to ache for its return: the first lone peep that meant winter would soon be behind them, the golden flurry of new beginnings in the puddled snow.

Mostly, though, the roof is an escape. Here she can leave behind the curling fear about Egill, the anxieties for the souls of her little ones, the never-blunted longing for Helga and Ólafur, for the frenzied bawling of an Icelandic wind, for ice in the air and decently cold rain and a draught in the *badstofa*. With Flower's translations and her own smattering of Arabic, she can bury her woes under tales of magic and adventure from times as far past as the sagas and lands more exotic than any conjured in the *kvöldvaka* at home. There are bawdy romps (those told, to her astonishment, by the papery aunt with unblushing verve) and poems and riddles and impossible romances. Stories wind themselves inside other stories. Sometimes a tale is held up for nights while a character within it begins on another at such length that she forgets the first. There are ghouls and sorcerers and magicians and scoundrels. There are kings and princesses and supernatural creatures called *jinns*, who can be good or evil, just like humans, and which she is particularly glad not to have to explain to Ólafur. The *jinns* are supposed to live in an unseen world beyond this one, of which Ásta feels she has some experience.

Lately Husna has been enthralling the harem with a character called Scheherazade, who volunteers to spend the night with a murderous king called Shahryar. Ásta floundered for several nights before feeling in command of this plot. Betrayed by his wife, Shahryar has decided to lie each night with a different virgin (a word that caused Flower some difficulty) and to kill her the next morning before she has a chance to dishonour him (more puzzling circumlocutions from Flower). The slaughter goes on for some time, until the chief adviser eventually runs out of virgins to send to the king.

Really, the stories her father worried about Ásta hearing at Mosfell seem decidedly tame these days.

Now the adviser's own daughter, Scheherazade, offers herself as the next bride. She has a plan. She has studied all sorts of books and histories and memorised every kind of story. She enters the king's bedchamber and offers to tell him one. Shahryar settles down to listen and becomes so engrossed that when Scheherazade stops before the end of the tale, he graciously announces that she can stay alive for one more night and finish it next time. Off she goes. The next night she brings that story to an end but starts another, which – here is the genius – she also leaves at an exciting point, thus earning herself another stay of execution. And so it goes on, as Flower whispers, for one thousand and one nights in all.

Well, may it please God that Ásta is not around to hear the end of this one. The loss could, she feels, be borne. Husna does make a compelling Scheherazade, though. She knows just when to stop a story and make her audience beg for more.

But even a tale from the lips of Scheherazade herself would struggle to hold Ásta's attention this evening. Especially now that the sun is beginning to dip to the sea and the light is turning to gold. She gets up and makes for the staircase. Alimah watches her go with a long stare, impossible to see behind, and the curling of a shapely eyebrow.

Outside the door Ásta smoothes her hair back nervously, realises what she is doing and runs her fingers through it from the back instead, returning it to what Helga once described as seeded grass. Appalled to think she almost preened for this man, she knocks on his door.

The chamber is glowing with the last of the evening sun and the expensive wall ceramics facing the window are ablaze. Mellow light is flooding the mattress of golden yellow satin that dominates the room.

At the foot of this mattress Cilleby, in a long cream kaftan, is sitting with his legs crossed, having second thoughts. What was he thinking of? The woman looks like a beggar. Is there a chance – he prickles slightly – that she has messed her hair like that deliberately?

Ásta, standing just inside the door and determined not to look at his face, is concentrating on his hands. They are clean and slim, rather lighter of skin than she has noticed before, with neatly pared fingernails. There is a whiff of rosewater in the air.

Cilleby beckons her forward with a jerk of his chin and she drags her feet in his direction like a naughty child. She has an image of standing before her father in a similarly reluctant pose the day she pulled six feathers off the cockerel. And suddenly she wants to laugh. It's nerves, of course, but the tiniest snort does escape her, and this only makes her worse. Gaily she adjusts her gaze upwards. All of this – the satin quilt, the rosewater, the man with the shapely nails and polished head in an embroidered dress like a woman's – all of it is ridiculous. *Look at me*, she feels like saying. *I am Ásta Thorsteinsdóttir from Iceland. I'm a mother of four with freckles and I ought to be getting home.*

Cilleby holds his gaze to a point around her knees. This was definitely a mistake. When she piqued his attention in the harem, coolly studying him from the other side of the room as if she had the right to look, she was not chuckling to herself and snorting like a madwoman. Could she be deranged? Alimah has never suggested she is mad. The worst seamstress he could have brought home if he had trawled the slave-markets for a year, but not mad.

'I wish to lie with you,' he says, patting the bed, thinking, *Do I?*

Ásta notes again how formal the common tongue sounds on his lips. It gives the words a politeness he may not intend. She does not move.

His eyes flicker to her face and then swiftly down again. 'Pray come here.'

Ásta takes a careful breath. 'I have a husband,' she says slowly, anxious to speak the words correctly and make her meaning clear. 'I do not lie with other men.'

'It is of no concern to me how many husbands you have. I—'

'Just the one.'

'Pardon?'

'I said I have only one husband. And you have two wives, sir.' She was not sure if 'sir' was quite appropriate, but thought a *signor* would do no harm. 'What do you want with the wife of another?'

'Ásta – that is your name, I believe – you must know it is permitted in law for me to have four wives and as many concubines as I wish.' Cilleby has an uneasy sense of being drawn into an explanation he is under no obligation to give. One day he will look back on this as the beginning. 'Do you know what a concubine is?'

Ásta has not met the word in this language, but can guess. 'I believe there was one in the Laxdaela saga. She was the daughter of the King of Ireland. A slave, like me.'

She sees it. She catches the exact moment that interest kindles in his eye and he forgets to look at her knees.

'Sit down, would you,' he says, less harshly than he meant to.

She takes a couple of steps backwards and sinks to the floor on the furthest extremity of a lavish rug, clasping her hands coyly. Strange to admit, she is almost enjoying this. There is the same bubbling of excitement, impossible to distinguish from fear, that used to come upon her in Mosfell as she picked her way, stone by slippery stone, across the river when it was wild in spate. It was truly terrifying. She could fall at any moment and expect no mercy from the foaming water horses, but she had never felt more alive and on her mettle.

He is openly studying her face now, so she studies his: the shaven head and haughty nose; the black hair trained downwards from his lip to meet a neatly clipped beard running under his chin and up to his ears. She marks with grudging approval the absence of the more twiddling kind of moustaches that always make her think of the captain. His most marked feature is a pair of thick black brows that overhang his eyes like a gannet ledge and make him look fierce.

'It is my understanding,' she says, feeling it time to take the initiative, 'that I was not purchased as a concubine.'

'No, you were not.' There, he has done it again – justifying himself when there is no need. He has a sense of having been carried up the beach on an unexpected wave.

She catches the hesitation and waits. Really, a whole family of gannets could nest in those eyebrows.

'What is that word?'

'Which word?'

'Saga.'

'It's a story. Just an Icelandic word for a story. Would you like me to tell you one?'

He stares again. Then he shakes his head, as if batting off an irritating fly, and to her astonishment lets out a rumble of laughter. 'Who do you think you are, woman? Scheherazade?' He folds his arms. 'I'm right, am I not? You've been listening to Husna.'

She can't think what to say. Is this a crime?

'Persian nonsense. Pay no attention. There are better stories by far.'

'Indeed there are. And it's Icelanders who tell them.'

A light collision of brows. He is beginning to look annoyed. Ásta is afraid the novelty of having a slave-woman answer back might be wearing thin. As indeed it is. This game, he is thinking, is going too far.

'Look, *signor*,' she says quietly, 'you have left me in peace thus far. Why have you called for me now? You know my husband has gone for a ransom.'

'Well now, that is precisely the point.' Cilleby relaxes. The wave has retreated and he is on firm sand again. 'I see no ransom. Three years since your husband was sent for it, free pass and all, and I have received no word from Denmark, not one. This is not a business for impatient men, but I would have expected an approach by now. Three years is a long time to wait, you must agree.'

Oh, she agrees. With that she can certainly agree. She closes her eyes for a moment. Her hands are damp. Cilleby presses home his advantage.

'In fact, one might conclude that either your husband or your king has forgotten you.'

'My husband has not forgotten me.'

'And your king? Whose wars, I may inform you, are long over.'

Ásta knows nothing about any wars. And anything she has heard of the king came, unhelpfully, from Oddrún Pálsdóttir.

'My king . . .' She fights to steady her voice. He is watching her carefully. 'My king must do as he sees fit. But I will not lie with you.'

He glares at her. 'You will do exactly as I command. I paid a great deal of money for you and your children. You sit there in my harem, looking at me as you should not, while I am expected to receive nothing back from my investment?'

She lifts her chin high and glares back. 'If I have ever looked at you' – she is furious to feel herself blushing – 'it's only that I am ignorant of the customs of this land and curious. It will not happen again.'

They eye each other balefully. Cilleby is wondering when he was last challenged so cheekily in his own house and why it is not bothering him as much as it should. Making up his mind, he returns his gaze to a point near her feet.

'I will give the king more time,' he says, and waves her out with a resigned hand.

Anna's hand flies to her mouth.

'Ásta *mín*, you have such nerve. He could have taken you in a second and had you killed afterwards for impudence. I hear such things of the Turks. Though of course' – she looks thoughtful – 'he is a Moor, *of sorts*, and they're more interesting. But a man is a man, and the wealthy ones can get away with anything in this city.'

Ásta picks in a desultory way at her sewing and lets the younger woman chatter on. Anna's lustrous eyes in their kohl frame are full of shine and vim. She tears into gossip like a juicy fruit.

'But then, he has plenty of others to pleasure him, if he so chooses. In fact, Ásta *mín*, I know you won't mind my saying that it's difficult to see quite why he wanted to add you to them.'

'You mean because I have no art to make my eyes into windows like yours,' Ásta snaps, feeling needled, and at once annoyed that she should.

Anna touches a finger to an artfully shaped brow. 'Well, it's a comparison any man might make. You should be glad of it, Ásta. It may protect you yet.'

17

When the next summons comes, Cilleby is awaiting her not on the gold mattress but at a square table so low it is practically sweeping the floor. He is also wearing more clothes. Trousers under the tunic at least, which is encouraging. Smiling thinly at her relief, he waves her over.

Through the lattice window above them the muezzin at the mosque on the corner can be heard calling the faithful to prayer. Inclining her head that way, Ásta raises an enquiring eyebrow. The impudence of the look takes them both by surprise. Ásta can hardly believe she has done it: if Helga had made a face like that, she would have issued a stern reprimand for cheek. And Cilleby might have done the same if he had not instead heard himself muttering, 'I've prayed already,' and been aghast to realise he had just explained himself again.

So it is possible, Ásta reflects, to discomfit him. And without even trying.

Since the formalities of the below-chin gaze seem to have been abandoned on this occasion and they are a mere table's width apart, Ásta has the opportunity to study his eyes. They are a very dark blue. How strange. Even serving coffee in the harem, a role to which she has lately been promoted, she has never noticed this. Well, how could she? She has counted the black hairs on the hand curled around the beaker but not once raised her gaze. Really, though – a blue-eyed Moor. Extraordinary. Perhaps she is gaping a little, because it is his turn to raise a fulsome eyebrow. With as little design as he a moment before, she bursts out, 'But your eyes are blue.'

'My father,' he says shortly. How in the world have they advanced to a footing where a slave-woman feels free to comment on his appearance?

Yet there is something in Ásta's capacity to surprise him that Cilleby is once again finding indefinably exhilarating. It is as if the floor has shifted a fraction and he might at any moment find himself flying. Inspecting his motives (not a skill in which Cilleby is practised), he wonders if this is precisely the reason he has summoned her back at all, on the pretext of hearing a saga. A saga. What interest does he have in stories from a country nobody had even heard of before Murat Reis had his great idea? No interest at all. More interest than he could ever have imagined.

Cilleby inspects his perfectly manicured nails and says politely, 'Tell me this story of yours about the concubine.' Then he lights his pipe and sits back in a haze of smoke to listen.

So she tells him about fifteen-year-old Melkorka in the saga of the Laxdaela folk. She was the daughter of the King of Ireland, captured from her home and carried north by an Icelander who made her his concubine. The baby she gave birth to became known as Ólafur the Peacock – and would later (Ásta feels compelled to mention) become the father of Kjartan Ólafsson, the most handsome man in Iceland.

'And how handsome was that?'

'Oh, very.' She is a girl again at her father's knee. 'He had beautiful eyes, as the saga tells, and his hair was long and curly and fine as silk. He was a good swimmer, too.'

'So did Icelanders make a habit of sailing off to wrest maidens from foreign shores?' he asks smoothly.

She looks at him suspiciously.

'And when this Peacock fellow arrived in Ireland to visit his grandfather the king – have I got this right? – in the terrifying longships you have described for me so vividly, with their shields overlapping all round the sides and a spearhead jutting out from below every rim (I think that's what you said), how did the Irish feel about it?'

'What do you mean?'

'I merely wondered.'

How dare he question her sagas? 'I don't recall any saga-teller making mention of what the Irish thought. I believe they, er, fell back at once, or something like that.'

Gracious, she has never thought about this. She can see exactly what he is driving at, but there is no way this man is going to be allowed to claim the moral high ground for the slavemasters of Algiers and their filthy trade.

'I dare say not everything in Iceland's past was conducted as it ought to have been,' she says, wishing she knew more about it, 'but I was only telling a story, as you asked.'

'I thought so,' he says, with irritating mildness, enjoying her confusion.

'And really it's a very long saga and there is too much to tell you tonight anyway.' She is now the one feeling discomposed and wondering how it happened. 'If you are of a mind to let me depart, I could tell you more next time.'

At that, Cilleby puts both hands on the table and roars with laughter. 'Ásta, you really do think you are Scheherazade.'

'Well, perhaps just a little.' This is a good idea: she has sagas to last till the coming of the Lord's kingdom, never mind the arrival of a ransom. 'As long as you are not Shahryar and plan an execution in the morning.'

'I will not execute you, Ásta, daughter of Iceland and descendent of slave-owners,' he says, looking at her very straight and thinking that he might on the other hand do something else, yet to be decided. 'We will talk more.'

18

The seasons turn and return without any sign of a ransom. As the years pass Ásta comes to appreciate them in an exact reversal of the way she used to. She longs not for spring but for the autumns that herald an end to the onslaught of the sun and the hot wind blowing fine Sahara sand into eyes and ears and over every unprotected surface of the house. She relishes the winter rains when they cascade down through the house, freshening the air and draining from the courtyard into the reservoir below to replenish their underground water supply. She loves – yes, she may in truth say she has come to love this – to look over the jumbled rooftops after a night of warm rain to the scaly palm tree that rises tall and straight from the square below and see the tasselled leaves glistening. In January and February, the months when the sun will be losing its way back to Iceland, she sometimes places her arms on the wall facing the glassy sea and watches the dawn stealing away and forgets, quite forgets, to wish for home. She will look at the hills on either side of the city then, bright with lemon and orange groves even in the middle of winter, and forget to be angry that countrymen of hers are slaving there to harvest them. After six years in Algiers she can hear the empty cry of a gull and not be instantly transported to Ofanleiti. She can go for days without thinking of Ólafur.

The children bring her joy. Marta is her golden-skinned shadow and sturdy Jón is still permitted to trot around the harem, although not for much longer. Soon Jón will go to live upstairs with the men, and have his head shaved, and learn to pray at the mosque. Ásta is prepared for that. It is a surprise to find she can contemplate the religious life awaiting her youngest child with, if not exactly equanimity then a less visceral horror than she would once have believed possible. Over the years she has become used to Marta's devotions. In her most honest moments she will acknowledge, as the women kneel to chant their prayers, that there is at least as much reverence on show here as in the fidgety evening worship at Ofanleiti or Kirkjubaer or Mosfell. She has even had to scold herself for lavishing more tears on little Jón's hair than his soul. It is the same nut-brown as Ólafur's when they married, finer in texture than Egill's curls and silky to stroke, and she has kissed it so often and so urgently of late that she begins to worry that she will make him as anxious about losing it as she is. But Jón is not easily made anxious. He skips away with a grin, as buoyantly different as might be imagined from Egill at six, who even then had an air of being weighed down by thinking. Jón is tall for his age, lively and light of heart, and never happier than when running errands around the house or carrying small jugs of water, precipitously balanced, from the well in the courtyard to the rooms on the second floor where the male slaves and servants dwell. This house is all the life he has known, and Ásta has observed with both relief and sadness – never quite able to separate the two – the way he has come to sense his place within it and is beginning to strain away from the women, like a flower seeking out the sun. He is proud and eager to be moving upstairs, excited that he will have his head shaved like the older boys and a job to do, and Ásta has readied her mind. She will still see him: that is what matters. She will know how he lives and whether he lives, and at her side she will still have Marta.

At almost nine, Marta has retained the precocious composure that was unnerving when she was younger but on which Ásta more and more relies. It is not only that she will lean over and quietly point out a mistake in Ásta's embroidery, nor that her quick hands can press pastry faster than her mother and so thin that the edges fray as they are supposed to, like lace, which Ásta's never have. What Ásta finds so deeply restful about being with her daughter is that Marta senses her emotions with uncanny intuition. She knows when Ásta is thinking of Egill and will lay a cool hand on her arm to say, 'Tell me again the poem that the hero Egill Skallagrímsson made about his son who died.' And Ásta will close her eyes and say:

> *A storm-bowed maple,*
> *I sorrow for my son,*
> *My boy, who has bent*
> *His body to earth.*

Ásta will think then of the breeze dribbling through the palm tree's wet leaves. She will remember that the old warrior knew, all those centuries ago, that grief is not a rough stone the tides will polish in time but a storm that may abate but always returns, fiercer and angrier for the lull. And then Marta will repeat after her some of the verses and Ásta will be comforted to hear them.

'Tell me about *our* Egill,' Marta might say next. 'I hardly remember him.' And Ásta will tell her about how he used to squabble with Helga, and how long and white his arms were, and how he and his friend Magnús reckoned they were the best fowlers on the island. 'Without much evidence, I have to say,' she will smile.

She still looks for Egill. Whenever there is an excuse to leave the house, she is off down the winding way to the pasha's white palace, enquiring at the stalls and vegetable markets on the way. Sometimes she has stood at the street corner opposite that faceless block for as much as an hour, boring her gaze into the studded door like a poised hawk and rehearsing the story she has trained her mind to believe.

Egill is inside the palace, carefully writing up the regency accounts. She can see him as clearly as if she were in the room beside him. He is being rewarded with a big red apple and a kind smile from the pasha's thick lips, which are not as repugnant as they looked from a distance but merely fat and jovial like her uncle Jón's. Egill has made friends in the palace, and they have taught him to ride a horse as he always wanted. It's black, a mighty steed and twice the size of Skími. He keeps the other boys awake in their room at night telling tales of his valour as a fowler, when he used to swing from thin ropes above the surging sea on an island far away. His companions' eyes shine with admiration and his with shy pride. He looks happy. He thinks of his family sometimes (well, naturally) but really he is very happy. He has not given up his faith, even if he has had to adopt rituals in which he does not believe, because he will never forget his father's last despairing words to him. He has forgiven his mother for not lunging towards the pasha that day and throttling him with her bare hands, and thinks only of how she loves him and how well everything has worked out, all things considered.

The details of this story vary, but any version will do when she is staring at that great wooden door, willing it to open and a thin-armed boy to stroll out – tall, perhaps, like Ólafur. Yes, at seventeen he will be tall, with a straggly beard perhaps; yes, definitely a beard. And he will look across and catch sight of her, and his eyes will light up – she'll see the light from here, so radiant and lovely it will be – and he will bound over and take her in his arms and she will crush the breath from him with hers.

Only, she has never seen him. One day she was in time to catch the pasha himself processing up the hill to the palace, feather aloft, and was able to inspect every member of his retinue from her vantage point, but Egill was not among them. Not one word has she heard of her elder son in six years. She asked Cilleby once if he knew anything, confident enough in his company by then to hazard a hint that he might care to find out. But he only replied irritably that he could hardly be expected to know the fate of every slave in the city. He gave her a look as he said it that she found hard to read. Impenetrable expressions are the currency of their discourse, but the look made one thing clear: he does not care much for the pasha.

Marta has begun entertaining the women with Icelandic stories in Arabic. Perhaps recognising a fellow talent, Husna invited the child one night to speak.

'What shall I tell them, Mamma?' Marta whispered, not flustered in the least by the expectant eyes upon her in the gloaming.

'Tell them about the girl at the shieling who was loved by an elfman,' Ásta whispered back, feeling there was nothing in the story that devotees of *One Thousand and One Nights* would not take in their stride.

Then Marta folded her hands and in her high voice took the women to a land of lava fields and elf-mounds that she cannot remember and they delight to imagine.

Jón has an altogether grosser taste in stories. 'Tell me about Gunnlaugur,' he will say when it is time to sleep. And Ásta tells him again about Gunnlaugur Adder Tongue, the Icelander who was visiting a Norwegian earl and had such a sore foot that he trailed pus over the earl's grand floor.

'Yeuch.'

'In fact, his foot looked so very sore that the earl asked him why he wasn't limping. And what did he say, our friend Gunnlaugur?'

Jón always giggles here and pretends to be Gunnlaugur addressing the earl in a deep voice: 'Men do not limp while their legs are the same length, sire.'

The night before he leaves her Ásta adds on a whim. 'If life ever becomes in the smallest way hard, Jón *minn*, remember Gunnlaugur.' She keeps her voice light. 'There might come times when you must just walk forward and make yourself forget you should be limping.'

'I'll remember, Mamma,' he says, inspecting his legs and feet solemnly. 'I've got strong legs. See.' He hops to his feet and marches about the room until the sleepers begin to stir and she tugs him to her side for the last time.

When he is fetched next day to go and live upstairs, Ásta refuses to be sad. Nothing, but nothing, is going to persuade her to cry about losing a child to a well-fed life only one floor above, separated by a curved staircase on which she is bound to meet him as she passes up to the roof garden or down to the kitchen, and in the courtyard too if she keeps a close watch. There are worse sorrows.

'Go on with you,' she smiles gaily, with a flick of his hair. 'I'll look out for you tomorrow.'

He trots up the stairs behind the manservant, waving cheerfully before it bends out of sight. That night Ásta sobs herself to sleep.

19

Could it be, could it possibly be, that a man with too many women likes nothing better than to relax with a pipe and an Icelandic saga? Considering the matter, as Ásta not infrequently does, it is a challenge to think of another reason for this bemusing man's continuing pleasure (although that hardly seems the right word, since she manages so often to annoy him) in their chaste encounters. With wives to serve twice a week by law and others besides, perhaps Cilleby finds it all exhausting at times.

What the rest of the harem thinks of this arrangement can only be guessed. Sometimes she wonders if Alimah, watching her slip away with the usual half-smile, knows how little goes on behind the forbidden door, or if she ever asks Cilleby why this one woman always returns so early. And then Ásta wonders what he tells her, and whether they laugh about it, and how much he loves his number one wife anyway. And what kind of question is that?

Three years or more they have been meeting whenever it suits him. Sometimes she might be required for an evening two or three weeks in succession, a demand she would gladly put down to her captivating flair for telling a story, were it not that she may then wait so many weeks to be called again that they have both forgotten where they were. She is perplexed to realise that waiting is precisely what she is doing much of the time, as if she did not have more important things to wait for, and she deeply resents every minute spent wondering when the next summons, usually by way of some insolent manservant, will arrive. Looking forward to these sporadic encounters is not, Ásta tells herself, wholly surprising in a life without event.

She has retained her early knack of pressing Cilleby to the edge of his tolerance and he of sending her close to the precipice on which her own temper rests. Dangerously close, in fact, because her tendency to erupt is as unpredictable as Hekla's and his power to hurt her remains a constant undercurrent of their exchanges. They are on relatively safe ground with the sagas, of which her supply remains plentiful, but it is becoming ever easier to stray.

One evening Cilleby mentions that he is proud – proud! – of the opportunities that exist for young male slaves who have converted and proved their worth to advance in the city. He boasts that a leading official on the ruling council has taken as his personal adviser a youth who started life as a farmhand in Iceland.

Ásta knows of this boy from Anna. His name is Jón Ásbjarnarson, an amiable, sharp-witted lad from the east fjords who kept company with Egill on the ship. Since arriving in Algiers he has risen in such favour with his master that he has been able to ransom the farmer who once employed him in Iceland.

'And how does that justify you people stealing Christians from their own country to bring them here in the first place?' she demands, infuriated by his self-satisfied air.

'*You people*,' he repeats mockingly. 'Can you be so ignorant, Ásta, as to think it's only Muslims who do this? Well, yes, I suppose you are.'

He sighs in a heavy, obvious way that makes her teeth grate. 'I take it you haven't been to Trieste or Livorno, which open their markets to slaves of any colour? You haven't heard of the Knights of Malta, who have plundered people all along our coast? The names of Marseilles, Madeira, Genoa, Gibraltar, Villefranche, Nice, Saint-Malo mean nothing to you either, I assume? You can take it from me there is hardly a Mediterranean state that doesn't have privateers operating out of it and galleys manned by captured Muslims and Christians alike. Really, I think you can hardly blame the Algerines for learning the seamanship and construction skills to do it on a bigger scale.'

'Strange to say,' she retorts, wondering how she should make sense of all this, 'I have not had the opportunity to see the sights of the Mediterranean. I was otherwise engaged in the hold when I crossed that particular sea.' He listens impassively. 'But whoever else is doing it – and don't talk to me about the early Icelanders: that was hundreds of years ago – ruffians licensed by *your* state, *your* council, slaughtered innocent people in my country. They broke up families and carted hundreds of us off like sacks of sugar, things to be weighed and measured and kept or discarded. All to keep your houses in fountains and your wives in silk.'

She sees her mistake at once. She has made this personal. The brows collide and she waits for the explosion. But she also sees, or thinks she does, signs of a tussle behind those eyes. (Really, the rainy blue of them never ceases to startle. Where has she seen a colour like that before? The bilberry, perhaps? The darkening sky on a clear northern evening?)

Cilleby is indeed angry. But he is also conscious of the competing impulse to justify himself that in Ásta's company is his particular weakness.

'Do you know who the Moors are?'

'I know you're one,' she mutters gracelessly.

'Well, next time I'll tell you a story.'

She is at Ofanleiti. Egill is swinging his legs on the wall and Ólafur is talking to him and pointing to the islands. She sees a man creeping up behind them with a curved sword and tries to shout out to warn them. But she can't get the words out because there is another man's hand over her mouth. She can't breathe. She struggles and struggles to pull the hand away, until at last it begins to loosen its grip. She seizes the hand. The back of it is lightly covered with black hair. She pulls it to her lips and begins to kiss it. Over and over.

In the morning she cannot think of the dream without nearly expiring with shame.

'A long time ago,' he begins, 'an army of Berbers from North Africa crossed the Mediterranean and conquered Spain. They created a civilisation that would last there for more than seven centuries. It was Islamic, which is what we call the Muslim religion, but also Spanish. The people became known as Moors and their land was Al-Andalus.'

Ásta shuffles on her side of the table. All these years and still not comfortable on the floor. He is sitting straight-backed across from her. She can smell the rosewater on his skin.

'Cordoba was the capital. Jews and Christians lived under the Moors there in harmony – a measure of harmony, at least – and were able to practise their own religions. Out of this mix came a great flowering of Islamic and Jewish culture. I was taught to think of this as our golden age. Poetry blossomed, and philosophy, and medicine, and the study of numbers and the stars. Our holy Koran was translated into Latin there.'

Latin. Perhaps she can read this book one day and learn from it what her children are being trained to believe.

'But the Christian kingdoms of Europe would not rest until we were gone. The Moors were expelled from Spain, and the Jews too. The last order to convert or depart came little more than twenty years ago. Over that time many hundreds of thousands of my people had to flee their homes. Some trekked across the mountains into France, and others poured back to the lands from which their Berber ancestors had first set sail all those centuries ago.

'My ancestors came to Algiers as refugees with nothing but their skills of hand and brain. They made silver jewellery. They found ways of leading water from the mountain streams straight into their houses, and from there they looked back across the sea and remembered their fertile lands in Granada, and the gardens there, beautiful gardens, with fragrance all year round and carved arches and the most lovely fountains.'

Ásta, lost in the imagining of it, bristles to attention. The cheek of him to look wistful and drop his voice for some Spanish idyll he has never seen. Has this man not considered that his slaves do exactly the same from his own rooftops?

'My father came from another place altogether. He was not a Moor.'

'So I see,' Ásta murmurs, hoping this sounds worldly and flippant. Is this how a son of Egill might look one day, betraying his migrant stock with every blue glance? *Egill, Egill, where are you?*

'Am I boring you, Ásta?'

The evening shadows are beginning to soften the room, muting the wanton vibrancy of the bed, dulling the ceramic orange flowers fringed with trailing green leaves that frame the window. The air from outside is cool.

'Pray continue. Where did your father come from?'

'Here is a clue.' He leaps to his feet with a fluid unfurling of legs, an agile ascent from the floor that she can only admire, not having mastered it herself. On the other side of the room he taps a wall tiled to the height of his waist with pictures quite different from the blooming squares around the window. She has never paid these blue ships sailing across the far wall much heed. Now she sees that some lie placidly under a single sail; others are galleons, carried along with fluttering banners on stormy blue waves.

'My father brought these to the house. They were made in Holland in the Chinese style, Utrecht or Delft or some such place. I never learned whether he traded for them in Amsterdam or took them on the seas as booty, but he used to arrive home with more tiles than one mule could carry up the hill, until my mother had to point out that many of them had human figures in them, men on horseback or children playing, and could under no circumstances be displayed in an Islamic house. I suppose my father liked them because they had something of his old life in them, and he never was quite secure about what he might or might not be permitted to do as a Muslim. These lonely ships here have no people within them, so my mother relented.'

He runs an elegant finger along his blue and white fleet.

'So your father was a Dutchman?'

'He was. Johann Pitterling was his name.' Cilleby strolls back to the table and picks up his pipe. 'He was raised in the same seaport of Haarlem as the famous corsair admiral Murat Reis. You have heard of him?'

Of course she has heard of him. Does this obtuse man think she has forgotten who commanded the raid on Iceland?

'His name was Jan Janszoon, was it not?' she says coldly.

'Indeed,' he replies, oblivious or pretending to be.

He really is insufferable.

'My father was older than Janszoon, but they both took a path open to lively boys from poor families. They went to sea and were licensed as privateers by the Dutch government, which was fighting to become independent of the King of Spain. My father was busy ambushing a Spanish vessel for the loot it had itself stolen from the Americas, when he was captured by corsairs from Algiers. Just as happened to Janszoon later on. My father came to the conclusion quite quickly that it was no worse a fate for a Protestant Hollander to be captured by Algerine Muslims than by Spanish papists. He was soon back at sea on the other side.'

'And how did such a principled Christian manage to turn around his faith so easily?'

Caught up in his story, Cilleby ignores the sarcasm, which is annoying.

'I wasn't there at the time, obviously, but it never struck me that he had felt much enthusiasm one way or another. He used to say there was much that was similar to Christianity in the Muslim faith, much that was not and much that confused him either way. He took the view that it was power and greed and, often as not, revenge that drove men to fight in the name of making other men believe exactly as they did.

'It was my mother who was the truly religious one. My father did enough to court and marry her correctly, but she is the one who brought me up to honour the traditions of the Moors and the laws of Islam and to eschew the renegade preening that goes on in this city. She died when I was still a boy and it pains me how little I remember of her, except her beauty.' He smiles, looking past her. 'Perhaps a boy always remembers his mother as beautiful.'

Is that how Egill remembers her? Does he think of her face? What scenes does he see?

'I care for her two older sisters, as you know, and beautiful is not how I would describe either of them, so perhaps I delude myself. But I do know I was happy. My father was often at sea, but we wanted for nothing, and he would make my mother laugh with the presents he brought her. He kept producing golden slippers that never once fitted her.'

He trails off. Ásta too is somewhere else. She sees this Johann Pitterling playing as a boy among the ropes on the quayside at Haarlem and then sailing off to bequeath his Dutch eyes to the man who now holds her and her children in bondage. And then she sees that other boy of Haarlem, Jan Janszoon, also dreaming of going to sea to fight the Spanish. She imagines him being captured and led to Algiers, then turning his fate around to become such a great admiral that one day he will lead a fleet of ships all the way to Iceland. Here, then, is a question. If her family is in this place now by the will of the Almighty, must she suppose that God personally agitated the minds of kings to fight on the high seas and entice those Dutch boys to a life of piracy? Could he not have arranged for both of them to go and work in an Amsterdam counting house and leave her country in peace? Or was it all, as her uncle Jón believed, a divinely inspired plot, long in the hatching, to punish Icelanders for their sins?

For a while they are both quiet. Ásta, who has never learned when silence might serve her better, is the first to speak.

'But don't you blush with shame that your father's wealth, and your own riches, come from capturing your fellow men and enslaving them? It cannot be right to treat people like that.'

Cilleby removes his gaze from the window and turns to her with one of his most louring scowls.

'I have told you before, Ásta, that this is done the world over. There are some who believe themselves on a religious *jihad* to wreak revenge upon Christendom for the way it has treated Muslims in Spain and elsewhere, but for me, I can assure you, it is purely business. My father left me good things, as any father will if he can, and I have built on them. I have broken no law of this city and treated nobody in my possession in a way that would cause my mother to be ashamed of me.'

She could scream. 'Don't you see? If it wasn't for men like you buying us, there would be no trade at all.' Seething with frustration, she realises too late that she is shouting. 'You think yourself a good Muslim, but you're no better than a thief.'

She knows she has gone too far. You hear the thunder coming and the sky is suddenly crackling with danger. His hand rises and she flinches. Then it comes crashing down so hard that the table bounces.

'Get out,' he says, very slow and breathing hard. 'Get out this minute.'

THE SEALWOMAN'S GIFT

Ásta stalks to the door, shaken but holding her chin high. Differences so profound and visceral cannot be swept under a pleasant conversational rug the way Ólafur managed so handily with the captain. Still seething, she bursts into the roof garden in the middle of a story by the papery aunt and flings herself to the ground beside Marta, ignoring the curious glances. She is well aware of having overstepped a boundary with Cilleby, but she is not, she is emphatically not, going to allow herself to regret it. She cannot be true to the people she has loved – to Kristín, her uncle Jón, Margrét in her chains, Ólafur driven from his family, her precious, lost Egill – by staying silent. She cannot.

Marta lays a cool hand on her arm.

20

The balmy spring day is a good time to escape. The wives, gorgeously arrayed and teetering under golden headdresses it has taken Ásta hours to secure, have been despatched to a wedding. Cilleby has been silent for months and the effort not to regret that has proved rather more taxing than she expected. But today her thoughts are only on Egill. And on what she has learned from Anna.

By late afternoon a breeze is sneaking through the streets. She lets the door latch itself behind her and hurries off in full white-bird regalia towards the pasha's palace.

Anna has spoiled everything. The red apple, the black horse, the happily occupied boy – all the elements of a story painstakingly constructed to fend off the agony of not knowing – have been torn down and smashed, and she is left defenceless.

For Anna's husband has been telling her what he should not.

'Such horrors as I've heard, Ásta,' she blurted, barely pausing to unpin her veil. 'You won't guess what those powerful men like the pasha and the wealthier Turks do with the pretty European boys here. Well, it's got nothing to do with wealth really, I suppose. Between you and me, I didn't even know it was possible.'

Anna rarely thinks before she speaks. And as one who guards her own tongue less tightly than is wise, Ásta has never been inclined to blame her. But at those words she felt as if Anna had pushed her off a cliff. The low white walls of the roof garden span and every wisp of breath was sucked from her lungs.

Anna was immediately ashamed. After so many years in Algiers she rarely gives a thought to her old life. It is an effort sometimes to remember how unhappy Ásta still is or that she ever had another son.

'Oh, I'm sorry,' she said, her limpid eyes filling with tears. Her husband's stories had genuinely horrified her. 'There is nothing to say that Egill is one of these boys. Nothing at all. It's just the stories men tell.'

Today Ásta winds her way down through the city with a new pulse of panic. She knows too much; she doesn't know enough. The knowledge that is not knowledge but might be is clawing at her insides. She takes up her usual position on the other side of the street from the pasha's palace, hugging the corner shadows as she prepares to watch and wait. But as the hours pass there is nothing to see beyond the occasional janissary guard swaggering in or out. Where, then, can she try next? Where has she not looked? Instead of turning back for home she decides to walk further down the hill, around the back of the empty slave-market and on towards the seafront.

In the gathering dusk the harbour is a dim forest of gently swaying masts. The fishmarket by the quayside is silent. With a swoop of optimism it occurs to Ásta that she has never yet approached a fisherman about Egill. What could be more likely than that the pasha sends him to seek out the tastiest fish in the ocean for his plate, or that he has been sold on to help the

owner of one of these sleeping smacks to bring in the catch?
Egill would be good at it. Think how agile he is and quick to
learn, how the sea runs in his blood. Why has she not considered
this before? She should have been pacing the fishmarket. She
should have been asking around the alleys on the other side of
the mole. Can it be that she has allowed the memory of the last
time she was this far down the city to constrain her: the boat
nosing out of the waterfront villa, the chill sensation of being
wrapped to the eyes but utterly exposed? With the light dwin-
dling it would be well-nigh impossible for anyone at sea to make
her out this time. And there is hardly a thing to be seen on the
water in that direction in any case, except for a flaring of lights
much further out.

A small crowd has gathered nearby to watch this vessel, whatever it is, drawing closer. Among them she recognises the skinny
bare legs and threadbare tunic of the wiry man who drove
Ólafur's group around the slave-market with a stick all those
years ago. She also notices, with a faint prickling of alarm, that
there are no women in this crowd. Clearly this is not the time
to be asking strangers if they have seen a reddish-haired lad.
She will come earlier in the day next time.

She turns to make her way back. Behind her, a figure detaches
itself from the crowd.

Ásta has heard of people fainting with shock. Margrét used
to claim, improbably for a woman of her stern constitution, that
she had fainted clean away on discovering that a sock knitted
by Ásta actually fitted one of the children. But she has never,
until this moment when an unseen hand grabs her arm from
behind, had the slightest sensation of collapsing herself. As her
head swims and the world whirls around her, it is only the man's

implacable grip that holds her upright. That and the Icelandic voice.

'Ásta. It's Ásta, isn't it?'

He is big and wide-shouldered, with a flamboyant turban covering a head that she remembers thatched with fair hair. The face has coarsened. Difficult to say how at first glance, but he looks harder around the eyes. Perhaps it is only age. He must be twenty now at least, although his blond beard is still serving an earnest apprenticeship. He has a look of his father. If she were to imagine a young, muscular Jón Thorsteinsson, burnt brown and swinging with weapons, he would be something like this.

'Jón Jónsson,' she says delightedly, recovering at once. 'How did you recognise me?'

'I wasn't sure at first, but you don't see many Algerine women with fair hair peeping out of their *niqab*. It made me look twice. Then I thought I knew your eyes.' He laughs – a big, hearty sound that reminds her so exactly of her uncle that she has to stop herself flinging her arms around him in the middle of the quayside. 'If you remember, we spent that voyage squeezed very close.'

'But what are you doing now? Why are you here tonight? Have you news of your mother?'

The questions stream so fast that he laughs again. 'Come over here and we'll watch this barge coming in and I'll tell you everything.'

As the lights on the water draw nearer, Ásta can make out a flat-bottomed vessel manned by several oarsmen, with a figure reclining in the centre on what could pass for a throne. Even for this garish land the man is dressed to dazzle. His turban is even

more ostentatious than the pasha's, both in width and in the size
of the inset jewels, each one big as a gull's egg. His damson cloak
is so fabulously adorned with gold, shimmering and flaring in the
torchlight, that Ásta (ever grateful for the modesty of Cilleby's
sartorial tastes) spares a thought for the seamstresses. The oars
drip silver as they rise from the water, and plunge and rise, so that
the barge drifts in under the darkening sky like a floating palace,
all a-glitter. Smiling and waving to the waiting crowd, the man on
the throne looks as if he could not be more delighted to be here.
In the light of the flaming torches his huge beard seems to burn
with real gold. He looks – there is no other way to describe him
– magnificent.

'Who in the world is that?'

'Murat Reis,' breathes the young man at her side, with a
reverence his father reserved for the creator of the universe.
'The finest admiral in the world. The man I work for.'

Ghastly in the torch-shadow, the admirers on the quayside
cluster around the burnished barge to pay court to the pirate
chief of all the Barbary. A trumpeter offers a celebratory blast
or two from the prow, upon the conclusion of which the former
Jan Janszoon leaps to his feet, to the alarm of his oarsmen, and
launches into a regal speech with much waving of his gold-clad
arms.

Ásta pays the performance little heed. 'So you're a corsair
now?' she says dully. How many more shocks is life going to
bring?

'Yes,' he says, without a trace of embarrassment. 'I learned
my trade on the galleys and I captain a ship of my own now. I
follow that man there. These days they call me Jón Westman,
after our islands. I like the name, don't you?'

Ásta tries to keep her voice casual. 'Follow him where, Jón?'

'Oh, all over the place. Sometimes carrying freight to the eastern provinces – rugs, linen, animal hides and the like – and sometimes on, um, coastal raids.'

He pauses at the edge of difficult waters. A burst of cheering reaches them from the barge. She can no longer disguise her anger.

'Your father was murdered in a raid commanded by that man. And who knows how many other fathers, and mothers too. What were you thinking of?'

The air between them quivers with hostility.

'As a matter of fact, Ásta,' he says coldly, 'Murat Reis had nothing personally to do with the death of my father. The man who did is not someone I admire. But I won't pretend the admiral is other than he is, and I also won't stand here and tell you I regret the turn my own life took when I was brought here. What would I have been doing at home? Catching fish for Danish merchants to profit from? Hanging on a rope for a paltry egg? Freezing for half the year? Never seeing a tomato or a grape or a spice or so much as a grain of corn to eat with our endless bloody puffin meat?'

'And I suppose you're a Muslim now?'

'I am. It was necessary.'

'Necessary?' She could slap him for his smugness. 'How cheap did you sell the faith your father died for, then?' His eyes, piercingly blue in his sunburnt face, regard her icily. 'How could you, Jón? What would your mother say?'

He brings his face very close. It smells of musk. 'Let me tell you, Ásta, since you're so keen to preach to me about my family, exactly what my mother did say.'

'Margrét? You've seen Margrét?'

'I have.'

'And?'

'And she said thank you.'

'Thank you! Thank you for sailing off to abduct other people from their homes? Thank you, dear son, for putting others in fetters like mine? I don't think so, Jón.'

He looks now as if he would like to shake her. But there is pain as well as anger in the tightening of his eyes, and he won't speak. She says at last, 'I'm sorry. Tell me about your mother.'

'There's not much to tell.' He steps back from her and looks away, past the burnished barge and out into the dark. 'Perhaps you would find it useful to know that slaving on the galleys is the worst job on earth. Chained to your seat so you have to row for hour after hour, sometimes in your own mess. Your back flayed by the whip till it's nothing but blood and torn flesh. Your shoulders scorched by the sun. Your stomach aching for food. Your head screaming for shelter. I spent every second plotting how I would get away. I suppose my father would have died at that oar with a prayer on his lips: it's the kind of man he was and we both honour him for it. But in circumstances you haven't asked to be in, is it better to perish nobly at the oar or talk your way to the helm? That is what I asked myself.

'So I made myself indispensable. Strong, tough, full of ideas, good at navigation, skilled in getting men to do what he wants – that's Jón Westman. Before long I was being trusted to command others. I converted to the faith that would let me operate as a free man and then offered myself as a corsair. That way I could set about earning the money to ransom my mother.'

'Margrét is free?' It is Ásta's turn to clutch his arm.

'She was.' His bark of a laugh is wholly without mirth. 'For about a week. I took her to live with me but she was too damaged. She was always so tiny. My father used to say she could have fitted inside her own thimble.'

'I remember.'

'But when I found her, she was nothing. *Nothing*, Ásta. I carried her home easier than a sack of feathers. The weals from the chains were livid and weeping. I brought a woman to wash her and a doctor to dress her wounds. I had the softest lamb stew made for her, with zucchini in, and ripe tomatoes, and tiny onions, and I softened the *couscous* myself in milk. I tried to get her to sup from my hand, because every one of her teeth had been beaten out of her long before and she couldn't chew, nor tolerate a spoon. And I stroked her hair, which was nearly all gone, and spoke Icelandic to her, and tried to think of stories from my childhood that would bring her comfort. Day and night I rocked her in my arms. But she was too hurt. She couldn't survive being happy.'

The trumpet has begun again, singing over the water. Jón turns further so that his eyes are hidden. She gazes at his back. She cannot speak.

'And do you know all she ever said, that whole week? Do you want to know, Ásta?' Still he will not look at her. 'All my mother said to me was "*Takk*, my love".'

The streets are dark as she turns to make her way back. Jón Jónsson offers to accompany her home, but she can see he is done with talking and his attention is on the barge. It seems the refulgent Murat Reis is not disembarking here but, having received the obeisance of the people, is to be rowed to the sea-captain villas, one of which belongs to him. Jón means to meet him there.

'It is kind of you, but I'm used to walking alone. I even know my way these days,' she says, trying to strike a lighter note.

He nods her a curt farewell, and she walks quickly away, her thoughts in disarray. She is sick to hear of Margrét's end and dazed by the son's actions. How is she to look at this? Is there no judgement to be reached with ease any longer? Suppose she were to have the chance of freeing Egill into her own ravenous arms, would she not be tempted to capture a whole village herself to pay for it? Would she not utter any vow to make it happen, pausing only to append to her conscience a small note that repentance could be settled later, as she has no doubt Margrét's son has done?

She scurries along the street leading away from the mole, wishing she could ask Ólafur what he thinks and at the same time treacherously glad she can't, because does she not know already? It is as if a crack has been opening in the ground before her, one of those ancient clefts in Iceland's lava. Cilleby has done his share of enlarging it, Anna too, and the children with their innocent prayers. And here now is Jón Westman, the Icelandic corsair whose father was eaten by flies. Little starred flowers grow inside a cleft like this, and moss smoothes the hardest edges, but the crack is growing and tonight the sides feel too far apart for one woman to bestride.

Ásta turns a corner and puts a foot on the first of a bank of steps leading up to the steeper part of the city. The sandalled tread behind her makes no sound. The voice that tells her to be silent or this knife will be inserted into her neck does not come from Iceland.

21

'I've got her, Captain,' says the thin-legged man, poking his face around the door. 'Found her outside by herself again, down watching the return of Murat Reis.'

'Prick,' the captain grumbles, wiping olive oil from his lips with the back of his hand and waving for the plates to be collected. 'No, not you, Zafir. Bring her in. And make sure you remove the swaddling clothes. I want to see what you've brought me.'

Fleming heaves himself to his feet. A decent-sized table and chair will be at the top of his list when he gets to Rotterdam. The door opens again and a woman is thrust in.

Ásta finds herself in a severely furnished room lit by a couple of smoking bronze lamps. She takes in – just enough to recall them for the rest of her life – the mattress of blankets overlaid by a green coverlet, the low table from which one of the lamps is flinging a hulking shadow on the bare wall opposite, the high, dark window through which the faint lapping of water can be heard.

Or perhaps it is only later that she will notice the sound of the water. When the subdued swishing of the waves on the other

182

side of the wall takes her mind to the islands at home and she begins to count.

The chill that began at her neck is frosting its way down her spine. She knew it would be him. Knew as soon as she saw which of the sea-villas she was being pressed into.

'Why have I been brought here?'

She hears the tremble in her voice and despises herself for it, because there he goes, smiling to hear it too. There are traces of oil in his moustache, a scab gleaming on his scalp. His eyes look unwontedly dark in the light cast upwards from the lamp. His tongue is still moistening those dry lips.

'Oh, I think you know that.'

He begins to unwind his sash, in which there are tonight no weapons. Fear is thudding in her ears but she feels curiously detached, too, and able to think. Marta and Jón need her, and Egill will too when he is found. That means she can either resist and perish, or she can try to preserve for them a mother. Afterwards she will wonder at how obvious, as the interminable scarlet sash unwound, this choice appeared to her. By that time she will be drowning in shame. Shame that she allowed herself to be pushed to her knees before him. Shame that she looked straight up at his face when he commanded it. Shame that she did not bite with all her strength, as Margrét would have done.

'That's right,' he grunts. 'Fuck me, that's good.'

Those eyes, staring into his very soul. He could look at them until his dying day. Which, as it happens, he does.

183

It is recorded in the minutes of the ruling council, sitting in its judicial capacity as a court, that on the night in question the slave-woman A. Th. was brought home by her kinsman, the Algerine corsair Captain Jon Westman. He gave evidence that he had found her wandering near Captain Wahid Fleming's house in a confused and unbecoming manner, without the proper outdoor apparel. He had spent the evening with his employer, the honoured admiral Murat Reis, and they had heard no sign of disturbance from the neighbouring villa. He testified that, although the woman was dishevelled and appeared lost, there was nothing about her demeanour to suggest she had murdered anyone, nor could he imagine such a thing, as she was a slight woman and Captain Fleming had been a most powerful man. On returning the slave-woman to her home, he had informed her owner, Ali Pitterling Cilleby, an esteemed member of this council, of the circumstances in which he had found her.

Cilleby catches his breath at the sight of her. Her face in the partially moonlit courtyard is white as bone, except where a bruise has begun to bloom under one eye, and her hair is awry. She stands before him with her head lowered, flinching slightly at the clunk of the latch signalling her kinsman's brusque departure, but otherwise motionless. Most unlike Ásta, she is refusing to speak.

'I believe you were at the home of Captain Fleming,' he says, peering at what he can see of her face. 'Tell me at once what you were doing there. You are forbidden to enter the home of any man.'

She says nothing.

'Ásta, I require you to answer when you are spoken to. Why were you there?'

She mumbles something into her chest.

'Speak up, I pray you.'

'I was taken there at the point of a man's knife,' she says, louder, but with a quaver he has not heard before. 'I went to look for Egill and stayed out too late.'

'Folly, Ásta,' he says, with a click of irritation. If she were looking at his face, she would see a familiar storm gathering at the brows. 'That was asking for trouble. And what happened?'

What happened? She lay under the weight of him. She heard the lapping of the water outside and began to count her islands. That's what happened. She shut her eyes and went to another place. 'Sudurey, Brandur, Álsey, Hellisey,' she intoned inside her head. 'Ellidaey, Bjarnarey.' And when he smashed his hand into her face and told her to open her eyes, she took herself there anyway, staring right through his grimacing ecstasy to her beloved Small Isles, to Hrauney and Haena and dear old lumpy Hani that she used to call Oddrún. She made herself stay at Ofanleiti, the sun glistening on the water and the sky so clear she could see as far as Geldungur, and Súlnasker, and even little Geirfuglasker far to the south, trailing alone like a forgotten lamb.

'Ásta, answer me.'

Cilleby's voice is impatient. But there is another note in it she has not heard before, a soft thing under the irritation. And this, at last, is her undoing. She looks up, and in the pale moonlight streaming through the galleries to the courtyard he sees the glimmer of tears.

'It was my fault. I looked at him on the ship. I wanted to understand evil.' And she begins, without a sound, to weep.

Cilleby feels oddly and uncomfortably helpless. He doesn't know what to do with her. He doesn't know what to do about the flood of tenderness that has welled up in him. Nor does he know how to direct the anger that has burst into flame behind it.

Taking refuge in formality, he says stiffly, 'It is against the law for a man to abuse another man's property. I will ask you one final time. Were you improperly assaulted?'

Snuffling into her chest, she nods. Cilleby sweeps his cloak over one shoulder and strides from the house.

The ruling council of Algiers agreed that Captain Wahid Fleming had brought much glory to the regency since offering his services to the fleet some years ago, and expressed its dissatisfaction at the lack of evidence in the case. The council heard that he had been involved in a number of separate quarrels and had many established enemies, any of whom might have paid a thug to slip in by the sea entrance and surprise him in his bed. Captain Westman, himself a valorous servant of the state, accepted under questioning that Captain Fleming, while in pursuit of his legal activities on behalf of the regency of Algiers, had caused the death of his father in Iceland, but he protested strongly that merely being in possession of a motive and in the area at the time did not constitute proof of wrongdoing.

It was unfortunate, the council agreed, that there had been a noisy celebration on the same evening at the villa next door belonging to the celebrated admiral Murat Reis, who had earlier arrived from Salé in the sultanate of Morocco where he was ordinarily resident, leading to much coming and going all night.

The slave-woman A. Th., who, the court was informed, had admitted being in the victim's house earlier that night in wanton circumstances and without the permission of her owner, was nevertheless judged too weak to have plunged a knife into the ribs of such a large man with enough force to kill him in one stroke. One of the victim's servants, who gave his name as Zafir Chitour, said he was asleep in the house and heard nothing; however he wished to draw to the attention of the council a number of disparaging comments that the victim had made recently about Ramadan, which he personally had found upsetting; moreover he was unable to swear that Captain Fleming had at no time disrespected the Prophet himself, peace be upon him.

Admiral Murat Reis did not appear before the council in person, but sent a signed testimony to the effect that he had never trusted the victim and in his opinion the regency of Algiers was, as he put it in the somewhat indelicate idiom of the mariner, 'well rid of the bastard'.

At the conclusion of its deliberations, several members of the council expressed dismay that no perpetrator had been identified. It was felt that such a failure might cast doubt upon the reputation of Algiers as a well-ordered city, which depended for its smooth running on the rule of law and the well-judged harshness of the punishments that followed any transgression. However, after noting the views presented to the council and drawing attention to the absence of any witness to the crime, the Moor Ali Pitterling Cilleby moved that no further action be taken. The court duly accepted his recommendation.

When Cilleby calls Ásta to his room some days later, no mention is made of the events in the captain's villa. For this she is grateful – not only because she cannot speak of it, but because she has no curiosity, none at all, about the end her tormentor met after he fell at last into a noisy slumber and she ran from the room. Nobody more deserved to die: that is all. She survived and she will endure: that is all. Cilleby takes note of her pallor, the way she shrinks into her place across the table from him with eyes lowered. The swollen eye is a mottled green.

'I have news of your elder son,' he says, after observing her a while in silence. 'It was remiss of me not to make enquiries earlier.'

He checks himself. Has he just offered an apology? Amid the rumpus with the council the wish to bring her some cheer had come upon him quite suddenly. It was the work of minutes to instruct a scribe to peruse the records.

She does not look up, but the knuckle of the hand that is gripping the other on her lap whitens.

'He was sent to Tunis.'

Tunis? *Tunis?*

'It is not uncommon for boys to be sold among the different Ottoman regencies as the need arises.'

She will never see him again. Not ever.

He tries again. 'Ásta, I can see this is a shock to you, but—'

Her head shoots up. 'What did Egill do to deserve being sent there? Even I know Tunis is an even worse slave-hole than this one.' Then, in a long, hopeless wail, she clutches for her old story: 'He was helping the pasha with his accounts.'

With some effort Cilleby swallows a sharp retort. Surely she understands he has brought her good news? A word of gratitude might also be in order. He examines his nails briefly and decides to be direct. 'I will say only this to you, Ásta. You should welcome the knowledge that your son is gone from the pasha. He has been away between two and three years now, according to council records. I think in your place I might be thanking Allah.'

'What do you know of my place?' she snaps, roused at last. 'What can you ever know of me and my place?'

He holds up a hand, vaguely relieved to be argued with. 'Don't allow yourself to be diverted, Ásta. The pasha is not a good man. Any boy, any boy at all, does well to be out of his way. Do you understand what I am telling you?'

She does understand it. Only too well does she understand it. Cilleby has finally and terminally snatched away the story she made to protect her mind. She can endure what the captain did to her, but how will she endure what the pasha has done to Egill?

'And think of this,' Cilleby is saying, casting around for a way to comfort her while also being dimly aware of what an astonishing thing it is to be doing in his position. 'Your boy is older now, and if he has become a faithful Muslim he could be free and living a profitable life. I grant you that Tunis is not so . . . developed as Algiers, but there are opportunities everywhere for a lad with a sharp brain.'

He means well. She does see that.

'Thank you for finding out for me,' she says. Now that the trembling has ceased, there is a great heaviness upon her. 'I would consider it a boon if you would let me leave you now.'

When darkness comes seeping through the lattice window, it finds Cilleby in an aromatic cloud of hashish and tobacco smoke, still pacing up and down a chamber he can barely see. He is pondering why he should be missing, actually missing, the old, impudent Ásta. He is also experiencing again the disconcerting sensation of being uncertain what to do next. Somewhere in the base of his mind an idea is glimmering. But he is not sure. It would be, for many reasons, dangerous. And Cilleby, while he has courted danger somewhat recklessly of late in the public sphere, is not in the habit of inviting it home.

22

At a small wooden table in Skálholt, Bishop Gísli Oddsson lays down his quill and stretches his bony fingers with a sigh. A gale is thrumming outside the turf-house, sweeping rain across the flat plains between the Hvitá and Brúará rivers on which Iceland's southern bishopric sits, its wind-bashed wooden cathedral commanding the cluster of school and sleeping quarters, farms and smithy. It is still a sizeable community for Iceland, if no longer the powerhouse it was before the Reformation and the Danish state's seizure of church lands.

More to the point, Bishop Gísli reflects wryly, drawing his damp robe a little tighter, it is still among the wettest and breeziest places in the country. Summer. He permits himself a small groan. This is supposed to be summer. All things made by God are good so there must be a reason for rain, but to have quite so much of it when the rivers are swollen already and the hay is ruined . . . Well, it is not for men to work out the purposes of God. Which is all to the good, because there is much that is perplexing in the world, not least this matter of the Icelandic hostages in the Barbary.

There are serious problems with the new idea from Denmark, and listing them in a long letter to his brother Árni has not

presented an obvious solution. The bishop rubs his nose
thoughtfully. It is really very difficult to know what to do for
the best. At any minute Ólafur Egilsson is going to dash in that
door and there will be no stopping him when he hears about
the king's proposal. But he will have to understand that this is
not a simple matter. Ólafur has always been much too easily
carried away. Of course the poor fellow has suffered, God alone
knows how much. But from the moment he returned home,
nobody with any authority in the country has had a minute's
peace from his importunate requests for something to be done.
Of course, he has never quite recovered from the rebuff he
received from the Crown back in 1628 and feels responsible,
although everyone appreciates that he did all he could.

Gísli Oddsson's fellow bishop at Hólar has, of course, complicated the issue by approving the proposal right away. Those
thrawn northern Icelanders always insist on going their own
way, but that does leave the southern diocese with a difficult
decision.

The bishop lets his chin dip towards his chest. He'll have a
quick doze, and by the time he wakes up will hope to have a
better idea of what to say.

Ólafur sinks wearily onto the bench. It was a long ride from the
boat. His buttocks are aching and he is looking forward to his
bed. He can hardly wait to throw some clothes off: the wool
breeches are soaking into his legs and his wet feet are a riot of
itching. A chat with the bishop, even when he is a friend not
long in the job and a convivial companion, can surely wait till
morning. But Gísli seems to be in the mood to talk.

'I know you must be tired, Ólafur,' the bishop says, regarding him with shrewd eyes. He takes note of Ólafur's lank, white hair dripping miserably into his collar, the steaming coat hanging off him as if it belonged to someone else, the dark hollows around his eyes. The man doesn't look well. 'But before you retire, I thought I should tell you at once that the king wants to raise a ransom to bring the captives home.'

Ólafur ceases drooping at once.

'His majesty has proposed that churchmen and other leading Icelanders be consulted with a view to establishing a national fundraising effort.'

'What?' Ólafur eyes his superior hungrily.

'The proposal came in a letter to Governor Rosenkrantz, which I regret to say has taken a whole two years to be delivered. Churches and hospitals in Denmark are also being asked to collect money and I dare say the king will make a contribution himself, although it remains to be seen how much. The Crown has recovered some of its lost territories and does seem to be in better financial fettle than when you last, er, tried.' He raises a warning hand. 'But before you become too excited, Ólafur, I have to tell you I have profound reservations.'

Ólafur descends from his elated float around the rafters and stares at the bishop in disbelief. Reservations. After all the years of waiting to hear a word from the king – a word other than no – he is expected to sit here and listen to reservations.

And what a no that was. Not just 'No, there will not be a ransom' but 'No, a ransom is so far outside the realms of possibility, Reverend, that his majesty can't even see you.' Ólafur can still barely think of it without tears of shame and frustration. So full of hope he had been when he arrived in Copenhagen after those endless months of begging and walking in rags and sleeping under hedges, only to have it politely explained that King Christian had recently lost his long war with Germany and there was, most unfortunately, no money in the royal coffers for redeeming captive Icelanders such a long way from home. The guilt of that failure has weighed upon him night and day: that he should walk free under an Icelandic sky when his children cannot; that he should open his eyes to the islands slumbering in the morning mist when Ásta can only dream of it. He wakes to feel it pressing on his eyeballs. The hurt of it is the last thing he thinks about before sighing to sleep in his narrow bed at Ofanleiti. And now the bishop talks of reservations.

'Let me explain, Ólafur.'

Gísli Oddsson is alarmed by how fast the remaining dregs of colour have drained from his friend's face and chides himself for handling a matter of such personal importance so ineptly. However, Ólafur must realise that there are wider issues here than loyalty (laudable, of course) to his own family.

Leaning forward, he reminds his friend as gently as he can that the people of this country are desperately impoverished. It behoves every churchman to ask himself if it would not be more appropriate to feed the poor here in Iceland before trying to look after people so far away, when nobody has the slightest idea what has become of them. Indeed, might not many of those they would wish to redeem be already dead? And after so many years among the infidel, must not the Christian faith of others already have been corrupted? These are hard questions for Ólafur to face personally, as Gísli well understands, but as the superior here it is his duty to encourage him to think about them. What is more, to be more practical than Bishop Thorlákur at Hólar has shown any sign of being, what about the number of intermediaries who will all want a slice of the funds? Not just the governor's representative but the Lord himself only knows how many agents in Denmark, the Low Countries, Italy and Algiers.

'Do you understand my doubts, Ólafur?'

Ólafur has heard him out in silence, but a growing flush high on his cheeks betrays his agitation. 'You say Thorlákur Skúlason is in favour?'

'Yes,' Gísli concedes with a sigh. He might have known that Ólafur would make straight for this inconvenient point. 'The northern clergy have proposed that each household contribute one pair of mittens or the equivalent and Thorlákur has approved it.'

'Then let me beg you to still your doubts and listen to your northern colleague,' Ólafur says, leaning across and grabbing his friend's hand earnestly. 'Think of what we are instructed in the holy book of Hebrews: "Remember them that are in bonds, as bound with them; and them which suffer adversity, as being yourselves also in the body."'

The bishop feels suddenly very tired. He extricates his hand and pats Ólafur's in turn.

'We are also instructed to look after the poor – and there is great destitution in our land, as you well know. Forgive my scepticism, Ólafur, but if people give woollens or fish catches they can ill afford, and the money these are sold for disappears into the maws of middlemen along the way, as it surely will, how does that help anyone?'

Before Ólafur can answer, he clears his throat. 'And there is another important point to consider. As I'm sure you will agree as a man of Christ, those whose faith has been corrupted are no loss to Iceland anyway.'

Ólafur winces and withdraws his hand. *No loss.* A picture of Egill in the slave-market rises before him: his scared eyes, the promise wrung from him at their parting, the pasha's leering lips. Ólafur has never once allowed himself to consider that Egill might not have managed to hold to his promise to keep the faith. Sailing back from Copenhagen in that miserable summer of 1628, he made a ragged peace with the probability that he would never see his family again on this earth, but he has always refused to conjecture the possibility of not being reunited one day in heaven. He sees this now with a terrible clarity. No loss? No loss? *They would be a loss to me*, his love screams.

Rising slowly to his feet, Ólafur stops himself staggering with tiredness. With an immense effort he pushes his family from him and tries to control his voice, which he is afraid is going to let him down.

'Listen, my friend.' He speaks slowly and carefully but Gísli does not miss the quaver. 'We cannot know what has happened to our compatriots over so many years. We have no idea how many have abandoned their faith or how many have died. But I do know that there will still be some calling out to us for liberation. It is our duty – our godly *duty* – to try and save them.'

He flings himself on to the nearest empty bed and begins to peel off his trousers. 'You must do as you see fit, but Bishop Thorlákur is right and I believe we must take our lead from him. I can assure you that the people of the Westman Islands will contribute what they can from the little they yet have.'

His voice has steadied in the course of this speech. He drops his wet trousers on the floor and shoots his superior a rebellious look. 'I warn you that I won't rest until we've done it, Gísli, whether you approve it officially or not.'

He is asleep five minutes later. Gísli Oddsson sits watching him awhile in a storm of thinking. As bishop he should not allow his decisions to be swayed by one man's emotions. He has those at home to think about, and the wider health of society if people return to infect it with ungodly heresies. Ólafur clearly has no intention of giving this a moment's thought, but he himself must.

Nevertheless he is moved by his friend's tormented passion. Some time later, when the Bishop of Skálholt decides to set aside his misgivings and tacitly sanction fundraising in the south, it is Ólafur's gaunt face, reignited with hope and determination, that Gísli Oddsson will have before him.

On the ride back to the coast from Skálholt Ólafur is brimming with plans. He will walk the length and breadth of Heimaey, urging people to knit for the hostages. Socks and mittens will pile up in the new warehouses. Fishermen will contribute a catch. The Westman Islanders will lead Iceland with their selfless generosity, leaving the rest of the southern diocese no option but to follow suit.

Long before his horse has picked its way on to the beach below the Eyjafjalla glacier, crowned today with streamers of lightest grey cloud, Ólafur has the island repopulated and his family back at Ofanleiti.

The oarsmen prepare to push the fishing boat down the shingle. Humming to himself while he waits, Ólafur contemplates the dark humps and shadowy peaks that will resolve

themselves in the next hours into the green and silver hues of
Heimaey. How few of its secrets it reveals from a distance, this
island. You see nothing of the delicate colours, the gouged cliffs,
the wheeling birds. Nothing of the hurt people within.

Pondering this, Ólafur is suddenly struck by a set of difficulties quite different from those outlined by the bishop, and it is
enough to silence his tune in an instant. What he remembers
is that the Heimaey curled within those humps and shadows is
not the place the captives left behind. As the years have gone
on, the bruised community has attempted to heal itself. People
have adapted to their losses. Thoughts have turned to the need
for children to work the crofts and look after them when they
are old. And here is the chief source of Ólafur's new-spun
anxiety: many who were rent from spouses have sought comfort
in the arms of others.

The Church is not in a position to remarry people without
proof that the original spouse is dead or at least beyond all
possibility of coming home. Ólafur has explained this *ad nauseam*.

Ad nauseam. Into the very midst of the thought flits Ásta.
How she would enjoy that phrase. Ásta, Ásta. Ólafur sags under
the swift assault of grief, the air pressed from his chest by the
memory of her poring over Latin declensions in the lamplight
long ago, lips moving in solemn repetition while the meal cooked
itself dry.

With an effort he corrals his attention again. He must think
this through. Some people have gone ahead and made new families anyway, with infants born so flagrantly outside marriage that
the fisherman Eyjólfur Sölmundarson alone has fathered four
children by three different women. As Ólafur has spent much
of his priesthood reminding parishioners, adultery is a serious

matter. Not only is it one of the graver sins, but the ultimate penalty under the criminal law is execution by beheading.

Or it was until recently, when the king sent a letter to his representative on the Westman Islands, announcing that Icelanders whose spouses lay captured in the Barbary should be treated as a special case. 'We graciously feel that their crime should not be punished as hard as someone who has not been through the same difficulties,' Christian had written from his castle at Skanderborg. 'Therefore none of the people who have engaged themselves with other married people should be regarded as having committed a crime.'

That has certainly allowed Ólafur to sleep more easily of late. The sin remains, of course, but it is a relief to be rid of the worry that half your parishioners are going to lose their heads. And the truth is that even before the king's missive Ólafur was wearying of his own pulpit rebukes and perfunctory pleas for penitence. Every person on the island has been struggling to find a way to live again. These days the priest of Ofanleiti finds the taste for judging anyone bitter on his tongue.

Settling himself in the boat, he addresses himself to the thought that has so suddenly dashed his spirits. What are all these adulterers, safe in their legal impunity, going to think when they hear that a ransom is to be raised to bring home their spouses? Nobody is going to know how many will return, or when, or if, or who they will be – and it is bound to stir all kinds of uneasiness and anxiety. It is not hard to imagine the agony in some breasts, the fear in others, the remorse, the defensiveness. How much effort is a man like Eyjólfur going to put into bringing home his fiery wife Gudrídur, when he has been so deplorably free with his seed in her absence? There can be no doubt that in some homes on Heimaey the knitting may proceed with a degree of reluctance.

The boat dips and dives through the sullen waves. Ólafur, now thoroughly dejected, watches gloomily as the sleek back of a minke whale curves gracefully through the drizzle.

Think what happened when Jaspar suddenly arrived back years ago from Algiers and poor Jón Oddsson learned from him that his wife Anna had gone through a Muslim marriage ceremony and had no intention of coming home. That was an excruciating situation. Called upon to minister both to Jaspar, whose beloved daughter was quickly branded a whore by the scandalised island, and also to the bewildered and angrily wronged husband, Ólafur's chosen course of action was to urge them both to surrender to the will of God – advice that neither one nor the other considered helpful. Jón Oddsson had a woman moved into Stakkagerdi within weeks, and island gossip was as quick to insist that housekeeping was the least of her duties. At least, Ólafur reflects morosely, Jón Oddsson is one man who won't have to worry about his wife coming home.

The next day dawns sunny and warm on Heimaey, and Ólafur's optimism is back. When Magnús Birgisson's mother passes him on her way for water he is making for the Stórhöfdi headland, walking so fast and doffing his hat so blithely you would have thought the dear reverend had shed ten years since returning from the mainland.

'On a hot day like this too,' Agnes reports to her husband. 'I swear he was skipping like a boy.'

Ólafur, though with an unmistakeable jauntiness to his step, is actually as far from skipping to Stórhöfdi as Agnes is from telling a dull story. He has to stop many times to rest on the way up, especially on the steepest part where the puffins have staked out their burrows in the knobbly slopes above the sea. From there, panting heavily and bent double with the stitch in his side, he presses on to the top and looks out to sea. He has removed his hat, since even on a day as fine as this the winds up here are vicious, and his finely silvered hair is blowing across his eyes. Thorgerdur, more worried about her father being carried away than his hat, has instructed him to be sure and not venture too near the edge.

Ólafur stands like this for a long time, a frail figure under a vast, azure sky at the most southerly point of inhabited Iceland. It's the place he always feels closest to his wife: a mere ocean away, after all. Today the sun has woven a brilliant sash of jewels right through the sea and far to the horizon. In a flight of fancy he would once have left firmly to Ásta, Ólafur imagines himself walking along it all the way to Algiers.

He cups both hands around his mouth and shouts as hard as he can: 'Ásta! Egill! Marta! Jón! We're coming for you!'

Promise after promise he sends down that shimmering path to the south. Whatever the problems in raising a ransom, Iceland will do it. If some on the island are reluctant, others will knit more. If middlemen deplete one ransom, Icelanders will raise another. If that goes astray they will produce more gloves and catch more fish until they have another, until one day, may it please God, enough money will reach the Barbary to bring everyone home. He will take up the knitting needles himself, if he can only force his gnarled fingers around them. He will organise the island's effort by day and knit his own family home by night.

Tears are streaming down his face. It might be the wind. He is not sure himself.

'I will do it. Don't despair. I will do it.'

He stays on the headland for so long that Agnes sends her son up to see what has become of him. Magnús finds him asleep in the sunshine by the puffin burrows, his head resting on one hand and his hat clutched in the other, with such a look of contentment on his face that Magnús is loath to wake him and goes off to net a few birds instead.

Thorgerdur has already resigned herself to seeing her father washed up on the shore when Ólafur breezes back into the house and tells her to start knitting at once.

23

She has always liked to rise early and drink in the sea-dawn. Elbows resting on the limewashed sill of the roof garden, chin cupped in her palms, this is where Ásta used to feel closest to Iceland. Behind those pink cloud-mountains weighing down the horizon is Ofanleiti, she would say to herself. The same tides are pushing and pulling those same waters: only follow them and you are home.

And follow them she did, inside her head and wrapped in gilded fancy. There, pouting at her through a cloud of twirling puffin feathers, was Helga, returned to keep house for her father in an Ofanleiti rebuilt and snugly lined with polished wood from the dark forests of Norway. There was Ólafur, out for an evening stroll with the elfman she met on the afternoon they were betrothed, questioning him eagerly about how the hidden folk build their churches. A sleek grey head was bobbing just beyond the shallows. 'Oddrún,' Ásta would murmur to thin air and any passing seagull, 'keep an eye on him for me, won't you?'

At what point in all the years past – is it seven now? Eight? – did the fancies evaporate? Are time and continued disappointment by themselves enough to ravage a mind's capacity to imagine? She can easily believe it, just as she understands that the captain's assault on her self-respect has in a different way weakened her will to hope and to dream. But this morning, watching the sun rise over the white city, she knows there is more to the ebbing of her old imaginings

Bruises of the spirit do not heal quick and clean like a swollen eye; but they do respond to kindness. In the months since the sea-villa incident Cilleby, in his infuriating, self-justifying way, has been kind – as Alimah, who banned her at once from leaving the house and handed over most of her personal duties to Marta, has not. Kindness is hard to resist. Harder than anything in the world, Ásta sometimes feels. Except, perhaps, for the thing that is more than kindness.

'There has come no ransom,' he begins pleasantly. He is sitting cross-legged at the table, smoking.

It is an energising feature of their encounters that Ásta never knows whether his opening gambit will be to ask for a saga, enquire after an abstruse point of Icelandic genealogy ('Now, I've been puzzling over this daughter of Egill Skalla-whatever-it-is, the poet. Is she the one who married the Peacock fellow?'), or request enlightenment on a finer point of Danish maritime politics. About this last he well understands she knows nothing, but merely does it for the baiting and to observe her reaction. It has been some time, however, since mention was made of the ransom.

'No,' she concedes, wondering where he is going now and readying herself to resist.

'It is nearly eight years since we sent for it.'

What is there to say? She can hardly deny it.

'So I have decided it is time you adopted the faith of Islam. Then you may look ahead to the life of a free woman in Algiers.'

'I beg your pardon?' This she has not expected. 'Free? But you will receive no money for me.'

Another suck on the pipe, the smell of it sweet and heavy. Cilleby looking pleased with himself.

'It seems I will receive little enough money in any case. Not only is there no sign of payment from Denmark, but Alimah tells me your embroidery skills are also unlikely to command a fortune.'

He chuckles, and Ásta flushes to realise he is laughing at her. In fact, he has made the joke and forced the laugh to cover his unease about what Alimah actually said about Ásta's sewing, along with much else. In a rare but wide-ranging burst of temper his wife also drew attention to his continued reluctance to send the slut who had brought shame on the household by her brazen antics with the late Captain Fleming back to the slave-market.

'However, I will confess I have been forming an idea of my own,' he continues. 'I will explain myself at the proper time. But first I require you to convert.'

'I thank you for this offer,' Ásta replies carefully, 'which is generously meant.' She has no idea what he means but will give him the benefit of the doubt on generosity. The word *convert* she does understand, though. 'But I cannot possibly do what you ask of me.'

'Come now. You believe in God, don't you, whom we call Allah?'

He is settling back for a debate. Sagas, piracy, abduction, faith: they are all a talking game for him. She draws herself up straight and he in turn watches to see if the small chin, of which he has become bafflingly fond, will arrange itself for combat and the nostrils flare.

'I believe in *my* God, the creator of all things, who revealed himself in Christ Jesus and died upon the cross to save us all from sin.'

Yes, there goes the chin. 'Of course you do,' he replies airily. 'Your Jesus was a good Muslim and an important prophet. I hope you are aware that we pay him due honour.'

Heresy delivered in such a reasonable tone makes her head swim. In a city where men can be strung upside down and beaten on the soles of their feet to recant, here is a velvet tongue showing how it should really be done. Where are the beautiful certainties of the Lutheran catechism when she needs them? Where are the phrases that will stop the foundations of her life shaking? All those Sunday sermons and home prayers – near a lifetime of them and her mind is empty. She stares at him word-lessly for a moment, and then closes her eyes. She is at Mosfell, reciting to her father. She is bending over the darning at Ofanleiti, listening to Egill lisping the same words while Ólafur frowns at the stumbles.

'I believe . . . I believe that Jesus Christ, true God, begotten of the Father from eternity, and also true man, born of the Virgin Mary, is my Lord, who has redeemed me, a lost and condemned creature, purchased and won me from all sins, from death and from the power of the Devil, not with gold or silver, but with his holy, precious blood and with his innocent suffering and death, in order that I may be wholly his own and live under him in his kingdom, and serve him in everlasting righteousness, inno-cence and blessedness, even as he is risen from the dead, lives and reigns to all eternity.'

The words wash over her as she speaks them, bringing great balm. When she opens her eyes she finds Cilleby's own upon her. The softness of the look surprises her.

'Your language sings very prettily, Ásta, but I'm afraid I don't have the slightest idea what you were saying.'

She didn't realise she was speaking Icelandic, although she could not have recited the catechism in any other tongue. He nods as if she has spoken.

'I must tell you that a Muslim cannot accept that a human being can also be God and the creator of all things. It really is an outlandish belief. But when I bow to Allah and worship him as the one sovereign being, might it not be that my prayers ascend to the same place as yours?'

Her face burns. 'My prayers,' she says hotly, 'are said in the power of Jesus Christ, who came to redeem us. Holy scripture tells us he is the only way to God.'

'Well, we differ there,' he replies carelessly. 'But have you considered that all these religions, mine and yours and the Jews' and the others of which travellers tell, may be attempts to grasp a mystery so big that it can never be completely understood?'

He leans forward and she thinks how close to black at times are the eyes resting on hers. The blueberries that litter the hills at home in early autumn are that colour, and the sheen on a magpie's wing.

'This is not a question I would under any circumstances pose in the mosque,' he is saying. 'I will grant you that. But I invite you to consider it. Might there not be more on this earth and beyond it than any of us know?'

Here is another surprise. It is just the sort of question she used to pose to Ólafur. Other worlds, different ways of seeing.

Into her mind saunters the elfman, his neck hung about with fish, the rain on his lip.

'But if you are so sensitive to such things' – she gathers her courage for a leap into more dangerous seas – 'how can you live as you do, trading in human beings, taking women to your bed who are not your wife, having two wives . . . all of that?' She trails off, suddenly conscious of the actual bed behind him, its vibrancy subdued in the evening gloom. She has never dared so far before.

But he declines to rise to it, only saying with some stiffness, 'My religion allows me to keep slaves, and it is my understanding that your own leaves considerable latitude in this area. It also permits me to have a number of wives and concubines. We have discussed this before.'

'Does it allow you to chase a woman with child until she gives birth to it on the grass, dead?' The words are out before she thinks them, but she is glad to say it at last. 'Does it allow you to murder a priest who has harmed nobody and is only sheltering with his family in a cave?'

'I do no such thing.'

'Well, I invite you to consider that you as good as do it. You have carved and tiled and marbled this house with the blood of the innocent.'

He stands up and flings his pipe on the table. The back he turns to her is rigid with an emotion she expects to see flying from his fists at any moment. She clenches her jaw and glares at the soft folds of his tunic. Let him do it then.

When he turns back his brows are still mated, but there are no flying fists. Indeed the sight of her glowering at him makes him want to laugh a little. He must not let her disorder him like this.

'Ásta, women cannot be expected to understand how the world goes,' he says, sounding to himself near-miraculously reasonable. 'I realise this. Women are set apart and see little. I have talked to you more than any woman in my life before and shown more patience than I have ever had to command in my own house.'

'Yes, why is that?' She has been curious about this.

Cilleby has the familiar sensation of being disarranged on a wave of seaweed. *You may well ask.*

'Stand up.'

She scrambles inelegantly to her feet, and he comes round the table to place himself directly in front of her, so close that she can see dark stubble under the skin of his head and catch a whiff of scented oil. He raises a hand towards her face and pushes a strand of hair lightly from her forehead.

'What are these marks on your nose and cheeks?'

Dear God, the shock of these words. She is back in the slave-market, turned about like butcher meat and inspected for blemishes. The Moor is there in the white cloak assessing assets from the shadows. The captain whispering to him. The sea-villa. The sash. Unravelling.

She staggers backwards, panic snagging her breath. Her shoulders start to jerk. Her teeth are clattering in her mouth.

'Ásta, are you ill? Speak. You're shaking.' May Allah preserve him from irrational women. What is he supposed to have said now?

'Is it kohl?' she mutters, suffused with humiliation. 'I was helping Husna to adorn her eyes. Forgive me. I thought I had washed.'

He stares at her. Kohl? 'Your skin is very fair, Ásta, but these marks are like kisses of the sun. I like them. It is all I meant to say.'

She looks up sharply, and finds in his face neither judgement nor mockery, but only a bemused earnestness on the edge of taking offence.

'I don't know the name in this language,' she says with bad grace, making an effort to regain her composure. She is belatedly aware that he intended something in the nature of a compliment. 'In Icelandic we call them *freknur*.'

'Freckles,' he repeats. It sounds funny on his lips and despite herself she gives him a weak smile.

'Well, Ásta,' he says with a warmer smile in return than he intended, out of the relief of seeing hers. 'To answer your question, I don't know why I continue to seek out your company under the most severe provocation. The truth is I have not the faintest idea. You make me very angry and seem intent on misrepresenting me at every turn.'

He begins to pace the room.

'But here is my dilemma. The next minute, the very next minute, there I am studying these *freknur* of yours, and the way the shade of your eyes alters with the light in the room. And I start wondering what you are going to say next and find myself in the even more unlikely position of wanting to hear it.'

Up and down, past the bed with the satin quilt, over to the window, round the table, back again, acutely conscious of those steady grey eyes watching him all the way. He stops in front of her.

'And – very well, here is what I am trying to say. I find myself thinking that if I force you to do . . . anything . . . you will close up, just as you started to do there, and I will lose something I have not experienced before.'

He looks as if he is tempted to say more. But he only brushes her cheek once with his finger and concludes the audience abruptly, saying he will present the idea he mentioned once she has had time to consider the adjustment required to her adherence to Christianity.

The house is waking. From the roof garden Ásta can hear the slave-boys (perhaps Jón is among them) scuffling down to stoke the kitchen fires and fetch water from the courtyard well. Soon the aroma of baking bread will fill the house. Across the rooftops the city is being called to prayer: to prayer that is not her kind of prayer, in the name of a deity who is not her God. She strokes her cheek where Cilleby touched it. She cannot be sure what is behind this thing she will call to herself tenderness, but it is dangerous. It is tempting her from the faith on which her eternal future and her entire understanding of her place on earth is built.

Yet is she not halfway there already? She has long been able to watch Marta praying without being tortured by images of damnation. When Jón went off to be circumcised with his head held high, she hardly bothered deploring it. He was excited and happy, as he usually is when she can pin him long enough on the stair to assure herself of it. When he told her proudly that he was learning to read Arabic at the mosque, she was only glad for him. The truth is that it has become too wearying to imagine future consequences all the time, when there is nobody to remind her of them and nothing to be done. Ólafur cannot help. In fact, she no longer silently consults Ólafur over what to think about anything. Ásta is in truth rather tired of thinking.

But tenderness brings other hazards. This too she understands, looking out over the roofs of the waking city to the flushed sky. The sea may be flowing on like Bishop Gudbrandur's map to other places and other times, but her mind no longer attempts to follow. These days it strains only as far as a room with carved blossoms on the door and wonders what it might be like to wake up inside. Clearly it is not her soul alone that must look to its defences.

Once before in her life Ásta has been in this place. Not that being tempted to vanish in the arms of an elfman is *quite* the same as her present situation, but it was certainly another brink, and what she felt when she stood upon it is something she never experienced in all the loving of Ólafur.

It was the day she heard she was to marry him. She left the house that afternoon, telling him she would not be long. Glad of the biting air on her face, she walked far down to that part of the shore where enormous plates of light-coloured stone lie piled and broken amid tumbled black rocks and flaming beds of seaweed. She had once suggested to Ólafur (who told her not to be silly) that a bad-tempered troll must have spent an evening smashing dishes there after a disagreeable dinner. The light was draining so fast that the outlines of Sudurey and Álsey had already faded. She sat on a broken platter at the sea's edge, nudging the seaweed with her toes and wondering what was missing that made everything feel as grey as the islands when she was about to become mistress of Ofanleiti and ought to be happy.

It started to rain. Ólafur would be wondering where she was. She slid off the dinner plate, tied her shawl more tightly around her waist, turned to go back – and nearly yelped with fright.

There in front of her was a figure clad in rough-sewn fishskin waterproofs. A clump of wind-shredded grass had braved its roots in the black sand and the curly-haired young man was standing, legs stoutly apart, in the middle of it.

There could be no doubt he was one of the hidden people, although Ásta struggled afterwards to know why she was so certain. Collecting herself faster than he did (he looked as if he was already regretting his appearance), she asked who he was.

'A fisherman,' he replied, tapping the necklace of herring that glistened around his neck and looking awkward. 'I've just come from the boat. I live not far from you.'

Hands on hips she looked him over. She was confident of knowing every fisherman on the island, and his discomfited air suggested the point had not escaped him either. He could not have been much older than she was – nineteen or twenty perhaps – and still looked more boy than man, his cheeks downy fair, lips full and delicate as a child's.

'Then you must live in that grassy rock on the slope below the Ofanleiti farmhouse,' she said gleefully. 'Are you going to spirit me away?'

That, he said, recovering his confidence but still with an attractive gaucheness, would please him very much, since he had been drawn to her since she first arrived at Ofanleiti. He explained this with what she decided was a blush, although as the light was poor and the rain now pelting down, she might have imagined this detail. He told her he had observed the liveliness and the thinking in her. (Ásta was enormously flattered to hear this.) She had an air of being in touch with things that lie beyond what other people see. (Ásta swelled further.) Also, he went on gravely, he liked the gold in her hair. Feeling she

213

could listen to this all night, Ásta wondered if he also liked her eyes, which Ólafur said were . . . no, this was not the moment to be thinking about Ólafur. Such a longing had come upon him to meet her face to face, he added with a most endearing grin, that he had, well, he had sought her out and here he was. This too delighted her. He had a cheerful smile and spoke Icelandic with a pleasingly old-fashioned idiom ('A longing came upon me'), which she wanted to hear more of, especially about the longings. On the other hand, she had wit enough left to remember how these stories usually end and knew she must beware.

It was about then – she cannot recall the moment, although she went over it for years afterwards, only that it was sudden and overwhelming – that she realised she wanted him. It was so powerful, this feeling, so urgent, so entirely novel and pleasurable and achy and impossible to resist, that she really had to touch him. So she put her finger, just one finger, on his lips, which were so beautifully curved and appealingly moist with rain. And as she did she thought, *I could go with him now. I am ready. If he touches me in return, only so much as one nibble of this finger, one breath in my ear, I will go with him.*

He didn't move. Indeed she realised he was trying very hard not to move. She had a feeling that his fists were clenched and his head all but bolted into position so that he would not reach for her. The wind kept whipping her hair over her face and the glassy-eyed herring dripped with rain and they stood there motionless, her finger to his wet lips, until the light was almost gone and the rockpools were black as the sand and the boy's face was dimming and she shivered and suddenly thought of Ólafur waiting for her at home, Ólafur who made her feel loved.

And she lifted her finger. It was so heavy. It didn't want to come. She felt as if she were pulling out a living root.

Then she turned away and flew home without stopping once, though it was uphill most of the way. She ran and ran and did not look back.

She never saw the young man again. But sometimes she would spy a silver trail across the empty sea and think, *There he is, bringing home his catch*, and remember the glister of fish about his neck. From time to time she thought she could sense his presence at Ofanleiti. It was a slight change in the air, no more, but she was sure he was there, watching out for her.

And now, a million miles away and a girl no longer, it is as if she is standing on another blustery shore, bareheaded to the wind and exposed again. Only this time she is not dealing with a boy and Ólafur has not the power to draw her home. Wherever her husband is – floating in the ocean, his bones long ago washed white by the tides; under the mossy floor of some German forest; buried on Heimaey in a sanctified grave; or maybe, just possibly, still alive and seeking oblivion in the arms of some fat widow who will never make him laugh – in whichever of the situations she has ever imagined him, Ólafur is not here and she is at the sea's edge again.

24

Cilleby presents his plan with a reversion to the stiff-backed formality of the harem. He is wearing his red waistcoat over the big-sleeved linen shirt and has in Ásta's view rather overdone the rosewater. Instead of inviting her to sit down, he leaves her standing just inside the chamber door.

'Have you considered what I asked you?'

'I have,' she says, wishing she could go and sag to the floor as usual. It is unnerving to have him both so close and so distant.

'Yes?'

'It is difficult for me.'

So difficult that she has no idea how to tell it. One day she is almost able to convince herself that what is required is no more than a rearrangement of mental furniture: a prophet moved here, another one to the back, a few extra rituals. This is Cilleby's view of it, doubtless based on what he breezily imagines his father's conversion to have been (and let us see what he would say if it were the other way round). But for all that she may be halfway there, the other half is proving harder. Ásta has not listened since infanthood to three Lutheran priests, each aflame with certainty, without the horror of being banished from paradise and punished more severely than any hardship to be endured on earth carving itself deep. How can Cilleby imagine this is easy?

She opens her mouth to speak and closes it again. Cilleby, deciding that where Ásta is concerned silence may be taken as assent, stiffens his back further and launches forth.

'In the event of your conversion I have decided to make you my wife,' he says to her neck, pausing again for a response.

When she continues to say nothing he surges on, his delivery ever more portentous as it begins to dawn on him that she is neither stunned by the magnitude of this announcement (Ásta can be unpredictable but he did expect her to understand what it means for a man of his standing to make it), nor sinking to her knees with gratitude.

'As soon as you have adopted the Muslim faith we will be wed according to our laws and customs, and you will take an honoured place in my household beside Alimah and Husna. I trust you agree that I have always treated you with the respect due to a future wife.'

In her earlier years in Algiers the shock of receiving an offer of marriage from a Moorish slave-trader might well have robbed Ásta of the power of her legs. But she must be becoming inured to shocks, for this one, so solemnly delivered, only makes her want to laugh. His haughty air of bestowing an honour that any woman might collapse to receive does not help. To be sure, the sound that emerges from her is more of a nervous giggle, but the offence it delivers is so complete that Cilleby is at a loss. Since she has no menfolk to act for her and he is himself her legal owner, he has already placed himself in a most uncomfortable position, and mockery is so far from what he expected that a shadow of uncertainty passes across his face. Ásta, instantly penitent, assumes a grave air. Worse for Cilleby, who has a proud man's acute antennae for pity, she is now feeling sorry for him.

After an embarrassing period of silence, interminable to both and in which neither is sure how to proceed, Cilleby makes up his mind. He clenches the hands crossed behind his back as he feels his temper rising, but having learned over time where patience may take him with Ásta that command will not, succeeds in biting back his chagrin. His eyes revert to her face.

'Ásta, go and sit down, will you,' he says with an ostentatious weariness that is only partly acted. 'Why don't you tell me what happened when the most beautiful woman in all Iceland was let down by the most handsome man in all Iceland. Isn't that where we had got to?' He manages a dry smile. 'I thought I could contain my enthusiasm, but I find, after all, a pressing desire to learn what happened next. We will talk of the other matter when we next meet, by which time I hope your amusement will have abated.'

Ásta takes herself off to the table with the smallest suggestion of a flounce, obscurely nettled that he has not tried harder to persuade her. A damson cushion in embroidered silk, never seen before, is waiting in her usual place on the floor. Is this a token of the new status she was supposed to have assumed by now? Or has he merely noticed at last how she fidgets on the floor? As she sinks into the plump softness of it, the thought that placing this cushion here might have been a gesture of simple thoughtfulness by a man with more delicacy of feeling than she generally allows moves her. Indeed it moves her more than any stiff declaration of marital intent, and her eyes prickle with sudden tears. More prone to weeping since the captain's assault, she blinks them back fiercely. Cilleby wonders what he has done now, and if he will ever understand this woman and, for the hundredth time, why he bothers.

'You were telling me before about the heroine of your Laxdaela saga. You will forgive me if I don't attempt her name,' he says, picking up his pipe.

And Ásta drags her attention back to Iceland in the year 1000 and the doomed loves of the beautiful and imperious Gudrún Ósvífursdóttir.

'You will recall that Gudrún and Kjartan met at the hotspring baths and became very friendly. One day Kjartan announced that he was going to Norway. He asked Gudrún to wait for him for three years, but she refused to make any such promise. She was piqued that he wouldn't let her come along too. So Kjartan and his foster-brother Bolli sailed off to Norway.

'Bolli and Kjartan were the closest of friends, but Bolli resented Kjartan a little, handsome as he was and so good at everything. As the saga tells, Bolli arrived home from Norway before Kjartan and began to show an interest in Gudrún himself. He went out of his way to tell her that he had left Kjartan enjoying the company of the princess Ingibjörg (the King of Norway's sister and, I need hardly say, the loveliest woman in Norway). Having designs of his own, he also told her he had an idea the king would prefer to give his sister to Kjartan in marriage than let him return to Iceland. Gudrún appeared unmoved to hear this, but people noticed how deeply she flushed and the abrupt way she dropped the subject.'

'Why didn't Kjartan come home, then?' Cilleby's head is beginning to spin.

'Oh, did I not mention that he was being held hostage in

Norway? He was treated with great honour by the king, but he was a hostage none the less.'

Cilleby raises a theatrical eyebrow.

'Yes, all right, people were being used for bargaining. The king was trying to bring the Christian faith to Iceland in quite an, er, forcible way, and thought holding Kjartan would be the way to do it – with a little, you know, pressure. Oh, I don't know. It's a long story.'

This time both of Cilleby's eyebrows take flight. He is as relieved as she to return to the world of her stories and the old sparring game in which they are both at ease.

Ásta describes how the princess Ingibjörg presented Kjartan with an embroidered gold headdress to take home to Gudrún as a wedding gift, telling him she wanted everyone to see that the woman he had been keeping company with in Norway was not descended from slaves.

'You see,' Ásta cannot resist adding, 'even Kjartan, blessed with every favour a man could have, could not remove the stain of being the grandson of a slave. Melkorka, the Irish slave, remember? I told you about her a long time ago.'

'I could hardly not see, since you mention it so often,' Cilleby replies sleekly, his good humour thoroughly restored, 'but I hope you in turn will remember how many slaves there are in these great sagas of yours before you next choose to lecture me on the subject.'

'That is quite different. What you do is different in every possible way.'

'If you say so. Now before you become any more red in the face and your voice rises even higher, tell me what happened when the golden Kjartan came home at last. You see, I've been listening.'

'Oh, by the time the new faith was accepted in Iceland and Kjartan was allowed home, Gudrún had tired of waiting and married Bolli. She was reluctant at first, but her family persuaded her. And from this moment the saga is set for tragedy.

'It's said that Kjartan showed no emotion at the news that Gudrún had married his best friend, but people noticed he was rather moody that winter. In no time at all he went and married another woman – she was called Hrefna – and gave her the headdress he had meant for Gudrún. I need hardly tell you that the two couples did not get on well.'

Cilleby puffs thoughtfully while Ásta loses herself in the saga. She recounts the jealousies and petty humiliations that followed, and how the spite went too far until Gudrún finally goaded Bolli into killing Kjartan. Then Kjartan's family took their revenge by slaying Bolli. They ambushed him in his summer shieling when Gudrún was big with his child.

'It is said, you know, that Gudrún Ósvífursdóttir surpassed all women in courage and resolution. But to be honest I wouldn't say she came out of these killings well.'

Ásta has given Gudrún's character more thought since Oddrún spoke her strange warning on the slave-ship another life ago. She was an extraordinary woman, bestriding the saga with the force of her mind and the strength of her passions, but she could be cruel. After Kjartan's death, she gloated, 'What I like best is that Hrefna will not go laughing to bed tonight', which can only be described as nasty.

'Don't do as Gudrún did,' Oddrún whispered as she lay dying. Ásta can see the old woman now: the shadows on her face as the ship rolled and the lamps swung, the sour breath, the urgent grip of her fingers. *What was that all about, Oddrún?* Ásta is happy to affirm to herself that she has no more intention of arranging for the murder of anyone than she ever did. That someone was considerate enough to hasten the captain on his way was nothing to do with her. *Really, Oddrún, what did you mean?*

She has lost the thread of her story in the remembering. Ólafur is there again in the ship with Oddrún's head in his lap. But his face is smudged and lacks definition. With a slight catch of panic, Ásta realises that she cannot bring any of it properly back: the shape of his nose, the way his skin felt, the lines around his eyes when he smiled. And his voice – not a single thing can she remember about Ólafur's voice. Where has it gone? Where has *he* gone?

'Have we reached the end?' Cilleby asks politely. He likes to watch her eyes going to some faraway place in the middle of a story, the details of which frequently pass him by in a way that does not trouble him in the least. He would like to kiss those eyes. He has not waited so long for anything in his life.

'Not quite the end. There was blood still to be spilled.'

Ásta blinks away Ólafur's rubbed-out features to focus on a face that lacks no definition. She is acquainted (so she feels) with every variety of scowl in this one, the range of blue stares, the full set of bewildering emotional nuances that the black brows are so quick to convey.

'But remember I was telling you about the son whose father was killed while he lay in Gudrún's womb. The son's name was also Bolli. Many years later, a grown man, he went to visit his mother. She was a very old woman by that time. And it was then that he asked Gudrún the most famous question in all the sagas.'

'And what was that?'

'I'll tell you next time.'

He laughs, and so does she, and the earlier tension is quite gone.

But Ásta, darting out of the flowered door while Cilleby resumes his brooding, knows that next time will require an answer to a different question.

25

In all these years Ásta has not felt the lack of a friend more than now. Confined to the house from dawn to dusk, with the children always busy and Anna forgetting to visit, she ponders her answer to Cilleby on her own.

Is this what it is like for other captives in the city, too, loneliness furring their judgement as everything they thought they knew is challenged? Have they, too, discovered that their enemies cannot be demonised forever but begin to be regarded, in whatever guise, as human? Do they find themselves reluctantly understanding motives for actions they abhor? Are they waylaid by unexpected kindnesses? Are they tempted to grasp at whatever sliver of happiness offers itself because the reasons for doing otherwise become less and less obvious? She thinks of Jón Westman, the Muslim corsair; Anna, the contented wife of Jus Hamet; the lad Jón Ásbjarnarson running the Algiers civil service. How many other Icelanders must there be – and those of other nations, too – who have had to work out a new way of living for themselves, alone, and made choices with which those back home could not begin to sympathise?

No doubt Anna would put her finger on the nub of the question and force her to decide by saying something outrageous.

But Anna, with an expanding family and a slipping grasp on old allegiances, has not visited for a long time. Where else might she turn? To Flower, who last saw her own home when she was six? A thousand and one nights would not be enough to explain Ásta's scruples to Flower. To Husna, who shoots swift, questioning glances from whatever story she is in when Ásta returns to the roof garden of an evening? Ásta has no idea how much Husna knows of her relationship with Cilleby, only that she cocoons herself inside her own unhappiness and cannot be reached. As for Alimah, who with easygoing malice has removed all but the least pleasurable of the tasks that gave a focus to the day and would surely have her out of the house altogether if Cilleby let her, there will be no friendly advice from that quarter.

An Icelandic maidservant has lately joined the household. Sold on in the ebb and flow of the city's trade, young Gunnhildur Hermannsdóttir from the east fjords has had two different owners already and Ásta cannot think why she has fetched up here. With Marta now fully trained and impeccably assiduous in her duties, there hardly seems need of more help. Still, Gunnhildur is a welcome addition to Ásta's shrunken world, insouciant and talkative. She rarely returns from an errand to the market without a snippet of news from some compatriot she has bumped into, who has heard it from another through another. Ásta marvels at how the girl manages this, bundled to the eyes and supposed to be hidden from all men. She would no more confide in her than the muezzin on the corner.

Gunnhildur must have been barely out of childhood when

she was abducted and looks young still. She has an unusually flat face, on which all her features appear stretched and elongated, a pair of lively eyes pulled into a slant, a wide mouth that laughs easily and a squashed nose, which, as she explains with a shrug, was broken by her last mistress. Looking over the gallery from the harem, Ásta watches her ungainly progress across the courtyard under an armful of laundry and wonders if the way Gunnhildur looks is significant. What were Cilleby's purchasing instructions this time? Was he requested to scan the slave-market for the woman Alimah would find least objectionable? Ásta feels herself flushing as a new understanding dawns. Is this what Alimah instructed Cilleby to look for last time as well, when the ship from Iceland spilled its cargo into the white city? *Get me a seamstress, Cilleby, but make sure she's plain.* Was that it? *And not too young either.*

Well, it didn't work, did it? She thinks of the way he touched her cheek and said he liked her freckles, the way his eyes caress her sometimes, even when they are arguing. Especially when they are arguing. Resting her arms on the polished rim of the gallery, she wonders how it would feel to lean over the table and touch the hollow just below his cheekbones where there is no beard. How smooth and vulnerable the skin is under her stroking fingers. Like the breast of a young gull.

And in the elation of that imagining there comes a sudden rush of magnanimity for Alimah. How much household power can make up for having to share, over and over, the man who chose you first? Might thwarted loving also be what makes Husna so silently unhappy? Both have grown up expecting nothing less from a man, and nothing more, but a woman's heart is not always to be tamed by convention. Perhaps it is their attachment to the maddening Ali Pitterling Cilleby that gnaws at them both.

It takes a few moments for the damper thought to present itself that the prospects for Cilleby's third wife are, by the same token, not very encouraging.

It is from Gunnhildur that Ásta learns that Anna has given birth to a fourth child and that a Dutchman, boasting of money in his pocket to redeem hostages, is in town.

'To ransom Icelanders? You cannot mean this, Gunnhildur.'

'Oh, it's nothing. I nearly danced on the street to hear it myself, but the man who wrote the petition (he comes from Grindavík) says there is nothing to get excited about. He says this Dutchman is not the first to have come to Algiers chattering about ransoms for our people. The first one exchanged the money for animal skins and the second sailed away laden with chests of sugar. Not a single captive released.'

'And what petition are you talking about?' It is always hard to keep up with Gunnhildur.

'Oh, that's a different thing. Some men have sent another petition to the king. Such flowery language they used, I had to laugh. Our Grindavík man says they accused the lords of Copenhagen of "hardening their hearts against our mortal peril and anguish, the bloodstained birch of Christ on us, and the punishments hanging over us".' She declaimed the words in an exaggerated fashion. 'What's a birch, by the way?'

Gunnhildur has acquired a breezy resilience during her time in Algiers, along with immunity to religious torment of any kind. Ásta can imagine only too well what she would say about Cilleby's proposition. Live on in this city, cavernously lonely, traded down the ranks of household servitude and away from the children until one day you lose your teeth to an owner like Margrét's? Or sew yourself a prayer mat and marry Cilleby? Is this what you are calling a dilemma?

As the summer swelters on, Ásta weighs her decision and waits for the call upon which she must give her answer. Night after night she sits under the stars, drenched in the perfume of jasmine and grateful for the smallest puff of breeze from the sea, trying with only patchy success to concentrate on Sympathy the Learned, a slave-girl unequalled in beauty and learning who, courtesy of the wizened aunt, has been outwitting the sages of Baghdad for many, many nights. Sometimes she catches Marta's eye – Marta, the still centre of her life – and they smile at each other.

On the evenings when one woman or another slips from the roof garden and does not return, she tries not to notice. She knows her answer.

He receives her cross-legged on the rug, the red waistcoat replaced this time by his cream tunic with the orange stitching, open at the neck. The pipe is there on the table, but not lit. His greeting is tight, and from the set of his shoulders alone she can tell he is ill at ease. Ásta sinks on to the damson cushion and smiles encouragingly. Perhaps he is nervous to hear what she will say.

He holds up a peremptory hand, as if to stop her from venturing on to that ground until he has cleared another.

'Before we proceed further I have news for you, Ásta, and I am sure,' he begins in the tone of one who is not, 'that you will agree it is good news.'

'The ransom? Is the ransom come at last?'

He hesitates, but only briefly. 'No, there is no ransom. Please put that thought from you.'

'Then what?' Her smile recovers, unencumbered by any twinge of regret at the continued absence of the ransom. She will remember this later. 'What is your news?'

He takes a quick breath before speaking. 'I have secured a place for your daughter with the sultan in the city you know as Constantinople.'

There is a beat of silence, during which a tirade of cursing from a donkey driver wafts in from the street. Ásta stares at Cilleby, her smile draining. *The sultan?*

'It is the highest honour and the best position in the Ottoman Empire, the very best.'

Looking even more uncomfortable, he begins to fiddle with his pipe. This is proving as difficult as he feared. 'In al-Qustantiniyah she will have everything money can buy. Your daughter will live in luxury for the rest of her life.'

'She is to be . . . a concubine?' Ásta can hardly speak the word. 'Cilleby, she is not yet eleven years old.'

He makes an effort to lighten his voice. 'But remember it may be some time before she meets the sultan,' he says, over-doing the lightness and making it sound as if Marta will be calling into Constantinople on a social visit. 'And there are so many girls in the sultan's palace, so many hundreds, that she may never meet him in her life. But I cannot stress enough what an honour it is to live there. Even the Christian families of Venice vie to get their daughters in.'

Murad IV, ruler of the Ottoman Empire. Strong in battle and

cruel at home. A man of such violent, unpredictable rages that there is no one who has not heard of the corpses strung on street corners, the slaves impaled with a spear thrust between their legs and out through their head, while Murad watches.

'He's a brute,' she cries. 'Everyone knows it. How can you send my child to that man?'

Cilleby reaches across the table and tries to take her shaking hand in his. This is not going well. Alimah assured him that any woman would be honoured to have her daughter appointed to such a role. Taking in Ásta's white, angry face and remembering the pained scowl when he told Alimah he intended to marry again, it occurs to Cilleby that he might have missed something, and that there may be reasons other than lack of wealth why so many men in this city choose to confine themselves to one wife at a time. Ásta flings his hand away.

'And you'll get an excellent price for her, I suppose?'

Cilleby's patience is waning. 'There has been a transaction, of course, but I thought you would be pleased. Think of the size of the empire and how few girls receive this opportunity. Only the most beautiful and accomplished.'

'You dare to imagine you know what I feel,' she bursts out, trembling with fury. 'You thought I would be pleased to have my beloved girl shipped across the sea to be abused by that monstrous man?' She eyes his pipe with a view to throwing it at him. 'You don't know me at all, do you? You will never know me. And I don't know you.'

But you were nervous, Cilleby. You didn't want to tell me. You knew that much. Does that make it worse, or better?

He watches her inscrutably, only taking the modest precaution of placing his hand over his pipe.

'What a fool you've made of me to think I did, even in the smallest part.'

She lays her head on the table, flings her arms on either side and collapses into a storm of weeping. Not in all these eight years has she cried like this. Not when her uncle was murdered or Kristín harried to her death on the hill. Not when the ship sailed past the cliffs of Heimaklettur into exile. Not when Egill was taken. Not when Ólafur left. Not when the captain hurt her. Riven with groaning, gulping sobs, she howls like an animal for all that has been taken from her and everything she can no longer bear.

When she is done, shivering and snuffling into the wet table with her eyes stuck shut, she becomes aware of arms gripping her. She feels herself lifted, carried, laid down. Her clothes are expertly attended to – pantaloons loosened, bodice unbuttoned – in one fluid movement: even with her eyes closed she can tell he is good at this. But he is also whispering ragged endearments in Arabic as he undresses her, kissing every inch of revealed skin with a hungry tenderness that makes her open her sore eyes to search out his. And what she sees there, when he lifts them to her, she will never forget. Even after what follows in the morning and everything it will lead to, she will not forget.

There on the satin quilt, her body still shaken by after-sobs, Ásta finds her way to the place where his face is soft as a bird and strokes it with wondering fingers. Her mouth reaches for his. She licks tears from his eyes and tastes the salt in them and will never be sure, never as long as she lives, if they were her tears or his. He is holding back: that too she will remember with an inextinguishable flicker of the same grateful surprise. At the last it is Ásta who guides into herself the man who has sold her precious child to the sultan. And in the moment that he spends himself within her, she cries out that she loves him too.

26

Wilhelm Kifft is hot. This infernal city will be the death of him. He should be on the home strait to Amsterdam by now, the wind cooling his face, his fee in his pocket and the quiet satisfaction of a job accomplished bolstering his spirits, which, there is no need to remind himself, are currently much in need of bolstering.

'You'll be there and back before the northern weather turns,' Paul de Willem had assured him. 'Nothing to it, my dear sir.'

Well, the king's man had clearly never been in the Barbary. Nor can he have had the faintest notion of how business is done here or how extraordinarily difficult it might prove to find all those scores of people who were supposedly queuing up to be ransomed, never mind negotiate their release with a horde of slippery heathens. At this rate Kifft is going to be here for months more.

He settles himself creakily on to the stone floor of a small courtyard, in one corner of which a cheap table, so low it is hardly worthy of the name, and a few thin rugs have been placed for the convenience of an office. Smirking manservants have gestured that he would be cooler with his hat off, but Wilhelm Kifft is in no doubt that an atrium, whether in the shade or no, belongs to the outdoors and is on that account a place where a civilised Dutchman's hat must remain firmly upon his head. The plume, which parted company from the ostrich some time ago, has succumbed to a disconsolate droop exactly matching his mood.

The accommodation is even more basic than he had feared. ('There are no chairs,' he has written to his wife, still reeling. 'And nothing, my dear, that you would recognise as a bed.') In renting a place to house both himself and any freed Danish subjects awaiting transportation home to the northlands, Kifft had assumed he would require it for a matter of weeks. Now he is bleakly coming to terms with the realisation that it will be next spring or summer before he can envisage escape. The process is proving so slow that he has not yet a single ransomed hostage with whom to share it.

Two beads of sweat are making their way from his furrowed forehead, down his cheeks and into the grubby lace collar that was once white. Wearily he palms them off, wipes his hand on his heavy wool breeches, hoists the stained black cape over his left shoulder and with a sigh picks up his quill to resume the totting of the thus far paltry accounts of Wilhelm Kifft, King Christian IV of Denmark's much put-upon emissary to Algiers. The date is 5 September 1635.

27

In an agitation of haste Ásta flies down the airless streets. She pants through the gated arch that guards the entrance to the city from the sea and bursts on to the quayside. Fishermen have already landed the morning catch and are shouting their prices in a market so crammed with wares that she can hardly see across to the mole. Curses roar at her heels as she weaves a panicky path through them and brings a basket of giant crabs clattering to the cobbles.

At the far end of the mole a ship is being loaded with barrels. Janissary soldiers, their belted swords flashing in the sun, are already pushing people aboard.

Did he know?

Did Cilleby know, while the sun was spilling its latticed light over their wrapped bodies, that Marta was to go this very day? Did he know, as he nuzzled her awake with roaming tongue, that her daughter was at that moment running around the harem from room to room to find her?

A searing pain in her side is slowing her. It is like being in a dream where your legs are mired in mud and you cannot move them fast enough, you cannot get there in time.

He must have known. He knows every ship that arrives and

departs. He watches every investment and every sale. He told her Marta was going – she cannot pretend he was not clear on that point – but not that it was to be the very next morning. Not that. Even as she pleasured him he must have known her daughter was on her way to the harbour.

It was Flower who took her aside when she returned to the harem, longing only for an hour of peace over her sewing to think about the night – the shock of his news and the bewildering ecstasy of what followed – and to think what she should say to Marta. She had to prepare her adored child for the unimaginable life that awaited her. She had to begin arming herself to lose her.

'Ásta, Marta is gone,' Flower whispered. 'She looked for you to say farewell. Alimah told her last night that she would be sailing this morning. She was taken from the house an hour past.'

Ásta is nearly at the end of the mole, lungs bursting, her hand clutching her side. There she is. Surely it is her, standing a little apart from a group of veiled women waiting to embark, her hands folded in front of her. She is so very small. Ásta stumbles the last few steps towards her, trying to shout over the groaning of her breath.

Marta turns around. 'Mamma!'

A janissary looks over lazily but makes no move. Unable to speak, Ásta beckons her a few steps away, so that they are standing with their backs to the others, facing the sea.

'Slip . . . your veil . . . to one side. Nobody . . . paying us heed. Let me just catch my breath and I'll do the same. There, it's gone.'

'Poor Mamma,' Marta says, eyeing her mother's damp, fiery cheeks. 'Did you run all the way?'

'All the way, my darling. I'm so sorry I wasn't there when you left the house. I came as soon as I heard. It has happened so fast.'

'I know, Mamma.' Madame Alimah had said her mother was not in a position to say farewell because she preferred to laze around taking her pleasure, which didn't sound quite like Ásta. She is so glad to see her mother now that she feels a little like crying, although she thinks it will be better if she doesn't.

Even knowing her as she does, Ásta is amazed to see how calm her daughter is, how unruffled the rose-fair face with its spray of freckles that is her joy and her balm.

'But we knew this time would come, didn't we?' Marta is saying. 'I was thinking all the way down here of what you told me. Do you remember, Mamma? You said that if we were parted one day, we would be able to meet whenever we wanted inside our own heads, like you do with Egill and Helga and Pabbi.'

She reaches up to Ásta's face and strokes her damp cheeks. 'I was just practising when I saw you. It's like going into a room, isn't it? You're inside a story that isn't really true but it makes you feel nice while you're there.'

She puts her mother's hand to her lips and kisses it. 'This is better, though, Mamma. I'm glad you came.'

The beauty and the agony of her child bending so much thought, so much kindness and all the wisdom of her ten years upon making this parting easier for her: Ásta is near choked by it. But Marta's self-possession also calms her. Perhaps there was no need to prepare her daughter. Marta has had a whole childhood of preparation.

'Do you know where you're going?' she asks, trying so hard to match the level tone that she could be enquiring whether Marta needs directions to the carpenter's booth.

'Madame Alimah says I'm going to live in the palace of the sultan. He's an even bigger king than the one Pabbi went to see and kinder, Madame says, because he wanted to buy me when Pabbi's king didn't.'

'That's one way of looking at it, *mín kaera*,' Ásta murmurs, thinking that Alimah knows how to tell a story as well as anyone when she feels like it.

'Madame says the sultan's palace is three miles round and has four thousand people in it. How many people did you say used to live on our island?'

'Four hundred or so, I think. Maybe fewer.'

'So imagine the size of this palace, Mamma. I will meet there women from every country of the world and train with them in many skills. My job is called odalisk and I might learn to make sherbet or sing like a nightingale or tell stories as well as Madame Husna. Some odalisks are even taught to read out from the Koran. That's the task I'm hoping for, because once I can read I'll be able to write you letters, Mamma. Does that not sound perfect?'

'Did Alimah mention the sultan?' Ásta asks, light as a feather.

'She said that because I'm clever and pretty I might be specially chosen to serve the sultan, but that would depend on his mother, who's in charge of the harem. Madame said the queen mother used to be a slave-girl herself once upon a time, from the country of Greece, so I should understand it is possible for anyone to do well in the Topkapi Palace.'

Was Alimah being artless, or so cynical that Ásta is sick to think of it? Has she set out to hurt Ásta in the most effective way she could devise, even arranging for a replacement maid-servant in plenty of time, or is Ásta's head so full of sagas that she sees jealousy and vengeance everywhere?

Whatever the truth of it, Marta's eyes are shining – just as Helga's were on the day she left for Torfastadir. Two daughters, brimming with hopefulness. As she and Helga crunched along the shore to the fishing boat, it felt to Ásta as if her eldest child were leaving for the ends of the earth. How foolish that seems now. Helga was afire with the spirit of adventure and impatient of her mother's tears. 'It's only Torfastadir, Mamma. You can practically see it from Ofanleiti,' she said, ever one to exaggerate. But just as Helga was about to step on to the boat, the very moment she gathered her skirts and lifted a foot and gave a hand to the lead oarsman to steady her, she suddenly tore the hand away, rushed back and hurled herself into her mother's arms in a hurricane of weeping. Ásta still smiles to think how Helga could never have a single emotion without making a scene of it. They stood there on the black shore, embracing as if they would never see each other again. She often thinks of this.

But little Marta does not cry, and for her sake Ásta will not either. When they hear the shout for the women to embark, she tugs the veil back across Marta's face and quickly sets her own. For a few seconds more they stand with their hands entwined and gaze mutely into each other's eyes, making the picture they will see for the rest of their lives.

'She has the same eyes as yours,' Ólafur used to say when Marta climbed on his knee and took to inspecting his own. He joked that he would have to keep a watch on her one day, for she would beguile any man who saw her.

My God or yours, may he protect you, my little one.

Marta rests her head one last time on her mother's breast. Ásta buries her face in her hair and breathes in the smell of her. Then, with quick, neat steps, the child runs to the ship.

All afternoon Ásta finds reasons to be about the courtyard. She collects a heap of onions and toys with their skins. She tweaks a herb or two from the pots. Running out of excuses she even offers, to Gunnhildur's astonishment, to pull water from the well.

'Have you no embroidery today, Ásta?'

'My fingers are stiff,' she says, very brightly and in Gunnhildur's opinion suspiciously, making a show of stretching them. 'Let me help you instead.'

When Cilleby's warning cough is heard in the vestibule, Gunnhildur grabs her jug and makes the customary exit up the stairs. Ásta stands up and flicks a speck of mint from her tunic.

When he sees she is not moving and determined to speak, his smile is replaced by a heavy-browed frown. 'What is this, Ásta?' he mutters, his voice low and tight. 'Be so kind as to await my call. It is not fitting that we talk in public.'

'Why did you not tell me Marta was being sent away this very day? Why was I not even alerted to say goodbye?'

'I am not obliged to tell you anything,' he replies with a brusqueness which, if she were less angry herself, she might recognise as defensive. 'As a matter of fact, I had forgotten she was to go so soon, but this is not the place to discuss it.'

He makes to move past her and she reaches out to restrain him. He throws her hand furiously from his arm. 'Never touch me like that. You know it is forbidden.'

'Reveal then why you didn't tell me.' More intent on drawing blood than answers, there being no answer from him she can ever forgive, she hurls the questions anyway. 'Am I really to believe the time of her sailing merely slipped your mind while you were' – this with a sneer – 'otherwise engaged?'

It is a pleasure to take the rake to his face. She watches the harrowing coldly.

'Or must I believe, Ali Pitterling Cilleby, that you didn't tell me because it is all just sport to you and you are as much a monster in your way as the sultan?'

He stares at her in disbelief. If he had remembered when the girl was to sail, would he have mentioned it? He has no idea. He was near out of his mind with happiness. But for such insults to be hurled at him in a place where the smallest slave-boy can hear, after everything he has done for her, everything he has said to her and to no woman before . . . He has no words.

Then, in the hush of the courtyard and to the satisfaction of at least a dozen hidden ears, he does have words. They come hard as a Damascus blade and crafted to kill. 'What you, a slave-woman in my house, wish to believe or require to know are of no concern to me.'

And whipping his burnous about him, he strides straight back out of the house.

Long after the latch has settled, Ásta still has not moved. As Gunnhildur, peeling herself away from the harem gallery, rushes off to tell Flower, she has never in her life seen someone look more lost.

28

The winter of 1635 and the spring of 1636 are as dry as anyone can remember. There is barely enough rain to fill wells and fountains and to water the thirsty fields. Crops perish in the countryside and the market stalls of the city are often bare. What food can be obtained rises in price, and although Wilhelm Kifft is grateful for a royal purse fat enough to attend to his personal needs, he could have wished for a more auspicious time to keep a growing group of liberated hostages in *couscous*.

The free house is filling now but it has been slow, frustrating work. Even in this teeming slave-city, he had imagined that Denmark's captive subjects would hear of his mission and simply flock to him at once, leaving him only to negotiate the ransom deals, a task for which he flatters himself well equipped: you merely have to keep in mind that all Turks, Moors, Berbers, Jews and the rest are scoundrels and liars and will invent any story to push the price up. But he has to confess – and he will have to find a careful way of making this point to the king's commissioner when he presents his invoice and explains why it has taken so long – that he arrived with little idea of the delicacy of many situations.

Despite his best efforts he can find no owner willing to part with a slave-child. The children all seem to have been brought up as Muslims, so they are no loss to the civilised world, but there are a number of mothers who appear reluctant to leave without them. Kifft is not a man without heart, as he frequently assures himself, but he would need the wisdom of Solomon to sort out some of these cases. There is also proving to be a quite staggering number of adults who have embraced the infidel faith, may the Almighty God forgive them, although some do claim it was forced upon them. Of course he has had to tell a number of them that they have thereby forfeited their right to be citizens of the Christian realm of Denmark, which was upsetting for some. But, really, how can an Amsterdam merchant who dabbles in diplomacy ('Never again, my dear, I promise you') be expected to interrogate a man's soul? Others, once hunted down, have pronounced themselves perfectly content to stew in their infidel practices and remain in Algiers, settled in a skilled occupation with a new family and no desire to be anywhere else.

Kifft mops his brow with a soiled lace handkerchief. It goes on and on. Some captives have retained the true faith but become so valuable to their owners that tempting inducements are being offered for them to stay on with their skills, which also raises the price demanded if they decide they prefer to go. There are more captives again who simply cannot be found, some gone to Tunis, some to Tripoli, some who were taken to Salé at first and are now rumoured to be here (but where exactly, God only knows). And with scores of Icelanders in the cemetery, and some suspected not to have received a Christian burial at all, it has been the work of months to arrive at a reasonable deduction of who among the original four hundred Icelandic captives remains alive in the first place.

Kifft struggles even to understand their names. He writes down the nonsense he hears, yet when he repeats the name to another of their kind he is looked at as if such a person has never been heard of and he is the one who is touched by the sun. Oh, the wild geese he has chased hither and yon as the weeks have mounted in this accursed city. He will leave soon, no matter what.

Seated with uncomfortably crossed legs at his wobbly bamboo table in the courtyard, where he is expecting a visit from – he checks his paper – a Mr Aille Pitterlingk, Kifft shakes his head to swat away the buzz of problems. The feather in his broad-rimmed black hat sways sadly. This Pitterlingk sounds Dutch, which means he might be more amenable to reason than the natives, but he has proved most evasive over the months, sending messages, refusing to meet, keeping him guessing at every turn. Kifft recognises the tactics. If it were not that the fellow owns half the city and holds a particular hostage for whom Kifft might later find himself answerable, he would ignore him altogether and he could sing for his ransom money. Today Kifft intends to look him in the eye and demand an answer.

There was a farmhand at Ofanleiti once whose hand was cut off in an accident with an axe. Ásta has never forgotten him. For all the blood, pools of it, lakes of it, he was still surprised to find the hand gone. He had not felt its parting from his wrist. But when the scar began to form, then the hand that was no longer there started to madden him with pain. It burned him in the night and he woke the room with his cries. He was only a young lad. Ásta saw him once making to lift with it, and when he realised afresh that it was not there, he cried again.

Such has it been to lose Marta. At first Ásta went through the actions of living numbed of feeling. She rose and washed, she shelled chickpeas and stitched. She must have eaten. She sat through evening stories of which she heard not one word. And then the pain came. Now she feels her daughter every moment of the day, from waking to sleep. She smells her hair in the flowers, she hears her singing to herself as she sews at her side and sees her sitting among them in the rooftop garden, her face silver in the dusklight. But when she reaches out to stroke the sweet face, it is gone.

She has received neither word nor gesture from Cilleby: no summons, no acknowledgement of her presence in the harem, not so much as a glower over the coffee pot. And she is glad of it. So she tells herself when the remembrance comes unawares of the times she swam in sagas behind a carved door and let herself begin to love. Alimah has her attending to her face and hair again (having discovered, no doubt, that Gunnhildur's stubby fingers lack Marta's dexterity) and Ásta is once again treated to her languorous watchfulness in the looking glass. From Husna she has sometimes received from beneath lowered lashes a glance that might be construed as sympathy.

Months have passed since Marta left, months as arid as the seasons, when she has cared for nothing and for nobody but little Jón, who skips about the house on his errands and dances away laughing when she reaches for him.

'Pray be seated, *mijnheer* Pitterlingk.'
    'Cilleby.'
    'I beg your pardon?'

'Cilleby. Ali Pitterling Cilleby.'

'Ah yes, forgive me.'

This is certainly no Dutchman. Taking in the dark looks under the creamy cloak and generous turban, Kifft reverts regretfully to the common tongue.

'As you know, I have attempted to speak to you many times since I arrived last summer, hoping to conclude a ransom for a priest's wife by the name of, let me see, Asta Tors . . . er-something and a lesser Icelandic woman called, um, now where was it, ah yes, Gnudele Somebody's-daughter.'

Kifft is annoyed at himself for getting flustered. Really, nobody could manage these names and this man has no right to sit there with his arms crossed looking down his not inconsiderable Moorish nose at him as if it's Kifft who has been stalling for months on end.

'Well, now I am here. Perhaps you could explain yourself.'

Explain myself! Kifft breathes in deeply. The man has been well apprised all along of his mission. This house is rented from him, *in Godsnaam*.

'Very well, then. *As you know,*' – the emphasis is as sarcastic as he dares – 'the Danish-Norwegian realm, which includes Iceland, has no direct relations with the Ottoman regency states of North Africa and has had to bring in other nations. King Christian instructed an agent by the name of Paul de Willem to arrange the redemption of as many of his people in Algiers as could be found and transport them to Christian territory. *Mijnheer* de Willem made the arrangements through Amsterdam and Marseilles, and I, your humble and obedient servant, was engaged to lead the mission. You are aware that the Low Countries have a consulate in this city?'

'Naturally.'

Kifft fishes among the heap of documents on the table, while Cilleby looks on coolly. 'I received a message in, hmm, let me consult my papers, yes, August of last year, to say that you were not – emphatically not, according to my note – interested in discussing a ransom of the principal hostage, but would throw in the other with one or two who were eligible for release in your other houses. Am I correct?'

Cilleby inclines his head a fraction. Kifft sighs. The fellow is most unhelpful.

'Then an agent of yours came to me the very next month, claiming you had changed your mind and were now prepared to release both women for, in the case of the first, a considerable amount of money. A figure was finally agreed, or so I was led to believe. I have it here in my notes somewhere. But when I attempted to bring the transaction to a conclusion over the winter I was told that you were "still considering" the matter.' Kifft's voice rises irritably. 'Really, Mr Pitter . . . um, Cilleby, it is most unsatisfactory. I know you people are out to squeeze as much money out of me as possible, but I have had enough of the game and would ask you to understand that I will allow the price to go no higher. Proceed at once, I beg you, or I will spend the money elsewhere. Goodness knows, I have expenses enough.'

Without a word Cilleby rises gracefully to his feet. Courtesy obliges Kifft to follow suit, but he is so annoyed that he remembers his knees and declines to bother. All the delays, obfuscations, bargaining tricks, difficult captives and obdurate owners he has had to deal with in the last year seem to have risen as one to mock him in the person of this haughty individual, and Kifft has had enough of them all.

'Mr Cilleby, what are you going to do, sir?' he calls up peevishly, as the man whisks his cloak over his shoulder and turns to leave. 'I am sailing soon and require an answer.'

'You will have it,' Cilleby says curtly. 'There are certain matters to be resolved and then you will have your answer.'

He begins to walk across the courtyard. Kifft glares after him. Not so much as a 'good morning'. These Algerines are quite the rudest people on earth, with the possible exception of the French.

He raises his voice. 'Pray remember that I must see this woman in person, to ascertain that she is not being held against her will. Or if she is to go, I must satisfy myself that she still adheres to the faith of Jesus Christ. This is absolutely required.'

Cilleby does not break his stride – only snorts as he raises the latch.

29

When she steps inside his chamber for the first time since she tumbled, laughing, from the satin mattress on an August morning a lifetime ago, Ásta receives no greeting. He is standing in the middle of the room, his posture at its most self-consciously erect and formal.

'I have something to tell you.'

It's Jón, she thinks dully and without surprise. Perhaps he has a maharajah of India in mind for her last child. Perhaps Jón is to be traded for a sack of gems from an African princeling. She is ready. This time her heart comes armed.

For his part, Cilleby finds his sternness under immediate attack. These pale, pinched cheeks and the hurt, grey eyes: she has suffered in the months since he last looked at her properly. The jolt of compassion strikes him almost as hard as on the night she staggered in from that damned sea-captain's villa. He must never forget where that led him and how narrowly he escaped suspicion. This woman plays havoc with everything that is ordered and predictable in his life, but she makes him feel . . . She makes him *feel*. He will have to be careful. The conclusion he has reached, after months of indecision, must be conveyed without emotion. May it please Allah it is the correct one.

'Please be seated, Ásta.'

She stalks to the table and arranges herself on the silken cushion. He joins her on the other side and folds his hands.

'There has come to the city an envoy from the King of Denmark,' he begins again. 'He has been here for some weeks. Some months in fact.'

He pauses for a reaction. She gives him none, but continues to inspect a golden thread on his robe, just below the neck, from which she assures herself she will on no account remove her eyes. She will not ask why he did not tell her before. This is only the news some slave-woman in his house has been waiting nearly nine years to hear.

'I made it known to this emissary that I had not decided whether or not you were available for ransom. A price was agreed, but I declined to finalise it.'

What?

'I kept abreast of his mission, having other interests, as you will understand, while I have continued to ponder the matter that is of some private moment, for all that your previous behaviour should have settled it. However, now he tells me he will sail soon and the question of your ransom must be settled at once.'

The thud of Ásta's heart is loud in her ears. Not one emotion in the tumult of feelings this news unleashes is uncontested by its opposite, except the anger. And this she is determined to control better than before. She does not move her eyes from the thread, not by so much as one blink.

Cilleby's irritation is on the rise, too. 'Ásta, I would have you engage with me. This is important.'

She takes her time to reply. 'In what way does it concern you

what I think on this or any other matter?' she says at last, proud
to sound neither annoyed nor sulky but, as she fancies, offhand
in a dignified sort of way. She is gratified that he is becoming
ruffled. She can imagine the black brows drawing closer, the
rain-blue eyes hardening. She could go on like this for hours,
staring at his chest and maintaining this cool dignity.

'Ásta, I am not requesting to know what you think. I'm telling
you what I have been thinking and I wish you to pay attention,
since it clearly has a bearing on your—'

'It's always about what you think and what you want, isn't
it?' She raises her eyes furiously to his, laying instant waste to
her stratagem. 'My fate and that of my children – my place is
only to be told about it.'

Even to her own ears this sounds petulant and silly. As if it
could be otherwise, slave or not, Christian or Muslim, Algiers
or Iceland. She is a woman.

It is exactly what Cilleby is thinking.

'Ásta.' He says her name softly and smiles. Oh God, his smile
has always undermined her. It makes her insides shift so that
she can't think straight. 'Ásta, you are a woman,' he says patiently,
confident that this is all the answer required to silence her. As,
indeed, it is.

'And as a woman in a culture in which you were not brought
up' – Cilleby has reflected much on this and is proud of the
magnanimity he has permitted to bloom in himself, despite the
stinging provocation – 'you have made some unfortunate mistakes,
as I'm sure you have realised yourself since we last spoke. And
"monster" was an unfair judgement on one who had secured the
most prestigious position in the empire for a slave-girl.'

She is awed, truly awed, by how little he understands.

'But no matter. I was angry, Ásta, that you should cast a successful negotiation in my face and make such outrageous accusations in public, especially after . . . However I have convinced myself – pray do not prove me wrong – that, with Alimah and Husna as your guides, you can be taught to behave appropriately. It is for this reason that I have decided we will enter, after all, into a formal betrothal and tell Mr Kifft to spend his money elsewhere.'

Cilleby sits back and grins, so relaxed now in his own munificence that Ásta almost forgets herself and grins back.

'Why?'

'Why what?'

'Why do you want to marry me still? Why don't you want the money?'

He hesitates. She lets her eyes bore into his. Let him answer this one.

'Very well, I will be honest if you don't throw it back at me.' Another hesitation. 'I have missed your company, Ásta. I have wanted . . .' No. He shakes his head. Nothing in his experience has given him the words, or the humility, for this kind of explanation. 'I can only say that these last months have seemed in every way dry.'

He drops his eyes to the table and inspects the grain of the wood.

Ásta is trying to work out what she thinks. She ought to be laughing scornfully and demanding to be ransomed this instant. But is that what she wants? Is it? She looks at his polished head, his eyes lowered in the embarrassment of being unable to express whatever it is he wants to convey. She does not understand this man. But so unmade is she by sorrow and desire, all mixed up and sapping her strength and insight, that she has long since ceased to understand herself either.

'Do I have any say in what you will tell this man Kifft?'

'You do.' He rallies at once. 'I will not force you to stay here. Force is not a proper basis for marriage. But I cannot see why you would wish to avail yourself of the belated bounty of the Danish state. The old man who left you here nine years ago is surely no longer alive. You know that as well as I do. After all this time you will be a stranger in your homeland, and quite alone, for of course your son will remain here.'

'My son?' He is using Jón to bribe her. 'In the name of all you worship, Cilleby, in the name of all mercy, surely you would let Jón come with me?'

'He will stay.' Of course the boy will stay. After all this time, does she have no idea how matters are arranged here?

She stares at him, fighting the tears she has sworn he will never see again.

'Come now,' he says soothingly, 'the lad will go far in Algiers. What kind of life would a circumcised Muslim boy have in your Iceland?'

'A free life.'

'Really, Ásta? Really? Free to rise to the top of society? Free from the freezing poverty you have told me of? Free to eat an orange? Free to worship Allah? Jón will earn his freedom here soon enough. It's a well-governed city and you know already how far an intelligent boy can advance.'

Cilleby is playing with her mind. Little Jón dances through it, beaming at her from the stair.

'And one day,' he is saying, emboldened to a flight of fancy by having arrived at an argument she cannot refute, 'you will visit your son in his own house and sew in his roof garden as your grandchildren play at your feet. Is that not a picture for you? You will be able to tell them about the man who made poetry and buried the treasure, the one whose name I can never pronounce. And your grandchildren will pass those sagas on to their children, and they to theirs, so that within the white walls of Algiers the deeds of their Icelandic ancestors will live on through the generations. Surely that pleases you?'

It does please her. Oh, it delights her. Too much it delights her.

'It would be a pleasing story if I didn't know you might at any moment take it into your head to sell Jón to Tunis, Salé or Constantinople if the price is right, and never even think to tell me his ship is about to sail.'

He stands up – abruptly but, as ever, beautifully. How she has missed the elegant uncurling of limbs, the animal gracefulness of him.

'Please don't start again, Ásta. I am offering you honour in my house and in my bed, where, since we are in a private place and your position still provides some latitude, I may say my recollection is that you fit very well.'

She feels her face reddening, and his look softens. 'We will make a bed of stories, Ásta, you and I. I will take care of you and you will tell me sagas until we're old.'

'That too is a fairy-tale,' she mumbles. He has always understood how to seduce her. 'Well, then. What must I do?'

He smiles comfortably. 'This Kifft fellow has rented a house, from me, in fact, where those whose purchase has been completed are awaiting departure. Be so kind as to tell him my decision. He insists on seeing you personally. I assure you he will be glad to find himself many hundreds of Danish dollars the richer.'

It is a shock to see the men and women seated around the plain courtyard talking openly to one another. They are free now, but still, a shock. Making her way tentatively past them, Ásta assumes she must know many of these people of old, but they are not easy to recognise, the women still veiled and the men worn to leather and bone by years of hard labour. The tall, cloaked man with a hood pulled close to his head and his eyes burning above a black hole in his face must be Einar Loftsson. Unrecognised behind her own veil, she makes no move to greet him. She cannot risk being tugged back into that world. She is here to speak to one person alone.

'Is your name Kifft?' she asks the man with an ostrich-feather hat presiding over a sea of papers in the corner.

He hauls himself to his feet and she glances over the dark breeches, the grimy cape and the long hose that might once have been yellow. Merchants strutting the port in European dress are not a rarity, but the dirty socks and the hair straggling from beneath the wide-brimmed black hat on to a collar of soiled lace are obscurely comforting none the less.

'I am Ásta Thorsteinsdóttir.' How strange to speak her father's name after all this time. 'Thorsteinsdóttir,' she repeats, both for her own pleasure and for the benefit of Mr Kifft, who is looking blank.

'Ah, yes, yes.' He gestures to a spot on the floor and descends ponderously himself. 'I have been expecting you, madame. Let me just find the document I need.'

He scrabbles among the papers with one hand, holding a pair of round eye-glasses to the bridge of his nose with the other.

'Apologies for the disarray, *mevrouw*.' Kifft pushes aside a closely written list of figures and launches tetchily into his latest gripe. 'I have been calculating the year's expenses in preparation for departure. I must say I did not expect to have to spend so much money on having dresses made for women who only possess, er, well . . . And shoes too. Does no slave in this city have a pair of shoes?'

He glances at Ásta over his spectacles, which are on the slide, and rests his gaze on her feet. 'Although I am not referring to you, of course, *mevrouw*. Mind you, those pretty lambskin slippers are hardly up to the rigours ahead and you may be glad of a sturdier pair. Now, here we are.'

Kifft taps the paper with a knobbly finger. His nails, she notes with distaste, are long and dirty.

'Now Mrs, er, Torstiens, I have here the amount of your ransom. As I intimated to your master, a most objectionable man, it is time we sorted this out. And I'm sure it is an understatement to suggest that you will be as relieved as I to do so, hmm?'

He picks up an elegant swan's feather. 'Your master also talked of throwing in an Icelandic maid for a paltry sum, so you should know we settled some time ago on 500 Danish dollars for both of you. However, I have not thus far been able to get him to finalise the sale. I'm delighted you are here at last to end the prevarication.'

'Five hundred dollars,' Ásta says softly. So much money he is prepared to sacrifice. She will never understand that man if she lives to be sixty.

'You may well repeat the sum. The ransom is higher than

anyone else's.' Kifft makes a preparatory flourish with the quill at the top of a fresh page. 'Now, madame, I only need to hear from your own lips that you still adhere to the faith of our Lord Jesus Christ and then we shall be done. A mere formality in your case, of course, as the wife of a notable priest.'

Ásta's head is beginning to swim in the heavy afternoon air. A man in yellow socks is talking to her of Jesus Christ, to whom she has not given a thought in aeons. He jabs her conscience like a janissary knife by speaking the word *wife* in a context quite other than the one that has been so intensely occupying her. Snatches of Icelandic drift drowsily across the atrium. Ásta, feeling as if she has wandered into another life, tries to gather her wits.

'You mistake the situation, sir. I have decided to stay.'

Kifft's mouth opens and then closes again. While not the first, she is certainly the most prestigious hostage to have uttered to him these profoundly inexplicable words.

'That is what I am here to tell you. I have a son, and . . . and, you know, ties here. I was under the impression I merely had to appear in person as evidence that I am not being held against my will.'

'Yes indeed, yes indeed, quite correct.' Kifft blinks. 'Well, I must say this is a surprise. I can't pretend I won't be glad to hold on to the money. As I was saying, my expenses are far in excess of what I expected and I have not been able to afford everyone. But I confess I am somewhat taken aback to hear it, *mevrouw*, when it's your own husband who organised the ransom.'

'My husband? You must be mistaken. He . . . surely he . . . years ago . . .'

Kifft pounces on his papers again. 'Let me see, let me see.' He picks out a crinkly sheet, looks it over and taps near the foot of the page with a grubby fingernail.

'Yes, here we are. "Asta Torstiens, *dess Presters frouwe*." The husband is, hmm, the Reverend Olaf, er, Olaf Egg, who first alerted the Danish monarch to the fate of his suffering people in the Barbary. Known to have been tireless in pressing the bishops of Iceland for action and organising the raising of exceptionally large funds, relative to the size of population, in Vest . . . Vestmanna – good grief, this language – somewhere in Iceland.'

Ásta's eyes blur with tears. 'He's still alive then?'

'Oh, that I could not say. I believe he was rather old.'

Kifft is becoming restless again. '*Mevrouw* Torstiens, I see you are upset. These are emotional times for any captive. But for the avoidance of doubt I would be grateful if you could confirm your position without ambiguity. Do you wish to be ransomed or not?'

'I don't know,' she says, closing her eyes. 'I don't know.'

The Dutchman swipes his spectacles from his nose and deposits them on the table with an irritated clunk. No fee on earth will be enough to compensate him for the trials of this year.

'Then perhaps, madame, you will be good enough to send word when you have an answer. I sail in one week.'

Pinching his eyes between his thumbs, Wilhelm Kifft sighs long and deep. Only seven more days to go.

30

The thing about thinking, Ásta reflects, crouched over her sewing near the stairwell of the harem gallery in the hope of catching Jón on his way past, is that when every possibility of choice is taken from you, when the children who are your very limbs can be torn off on a whim, there comes to be little point in it. You tire. You get out of the way of it. That kind of captivity is as much about the mind as the shackle. The only kindness you can offer yourself is to forget, and forgetting becomes easier as thinking gets harder.

Then, all of a sudden, choice arrives: a gate appears at your hand. Yet still you cannot think. Helga is gone, and Egill, and Marta. Ólafur, deep in a grave you have dug for him yourself, piling on the clods as the seasons turn, is in no position to beckon you through. All you can see, all that fills your mind, is your boy, your last dancing boy, and the need to be near him. And all the time your limbless body is aching to be distracted from the gate by a man who, one way or another, is responsible for every loss you have had to bear.

Then – see what happens – an irritable Dutchman in yellow hose appears, shuffling his papers and peering through his eye-glasses into a world you used to know. He shakes you into

SALLY MAGNUSSON

remembering. He shocks you, painfully, so terribly painfully, into
thinking about the gate and what might lie on the other side.

She can tell Jón is on his way down from the second floor
before she sees him. She knows the way he jumps from step to
step when nobody is looking, testing himself with two at a time,
trying not to land on a pink streak in the marble.

'Jón *minn*,' she calls as he emerges from the stairwell at a trot.

'Mamma, I have to work,' he says in Arabic, affectionate but
anxious to be off.

'I have something to tell you. Listen. A man has come with
a ransom.'

His eyes open wide.

'I've been given leave to go home. But not you, *minn kaeri*.'

'This is my home, Mamma.' He says it in Arabic, but using
the Icelandic *mamma* with a slight accent she adores. 'But I like
you to be near me.'

'I like to be near you too. But you'll be a man soon, with a
life of your own to live here. Your father needs me in Iceland.'

She has not the slightest idea if this is true.

'And Helga – remember the sister I used to tell you about –
she'll be there somewhere too. So I hope. But my heart is being
torn down the middle. I don't want to leave you.'

Jón takes her hand and solemnly rests on her Ólafur's brown
eyes. Another of her children trying to comfort her. How can
she bear this?

'Then don't worry about me, Mamma. I have plans. I'm going
to be rich one day and I'll sail to visit you. The master says it's
quite possible that I'll own my own ship.'

'He has spoken to you?'

'I wait at his table. He speaks to me often. He says I'm quick with numbers and will make a good merchant.'

Dear God, what kind of merchant? 'You won't take captives, Jón *minn*, will you? You must never make of other people slaves. Promise me this.'

But he is hopping from foot to foot. 'I must go, Mamma. I was to fetch the water at once.'

And on he skips down the stairs, without jumping.

This is what comes of thinking. It shreds your heart.

It is a risk, but time is short. She has watched Cilleby go into his chamber and assured herself that he is alone. Seeing her walk in without having received a summons will tell him at once what he needs to know.

He whirls around as she enters, the outrage at a social indiscretion more egregious than anything she has yet perpetrated flushing across his face, tightening his eyes – and just as quickly fading in the second it takes him to grasp why she has come. She nerves herself to walk forward and join him in the centre of the room, where the evening sunshine is throwing the final criss-cross shadows across the flowered rug.

'I see you've changed your mind,' he remarks casually.

Cilleby has always had an instinct for the moment when a deal is about to break down: that split second when you sense the upper hand slipping and know the time has come to pull out. This with Ásta, his wayward, grey-eyed weaver of tales, has strayed far from business, but he knows the signs. He will not demean himself.

Ásta, armed to resist argument and combat coercion, is at a loss to meet what appears to her not as pride but humility. The formal speech she has prepared flies from her head, and she reaches over and seizes Cilleby's two hands in hers. It is another breach of etiquette, but this time there is no outrage. His smooth thumb starts to rub her palm, gently, round and round. So sad and stern he looks, she wonders if he even knows he is doing it.

'It's Jón,' she blurts out. 'There are other things I meant to tell you too, because I started, you know, thinking. But it's mainly Jón.'

'But he'll be with you here,' Cilleby protests, startled out of the dignified aloofness he had determined on.

'You wouldn't understand.' Is she supposed to explain what it is like to listen for Jón's thump-thump on the stair, waiting in an agony of dread in case this is the day that a happy business opportunity, or a wife's spite, or a pasha's desire means he is gone as suddenly as the others? 'What can you, who breathe power like the air, know of having someone you love snatched from you?'

He says nothing, only continuing the rhythmic rubbing inside their clasped hands.

'Let me try to explain, then. My son is happy as he grows away from me in the life he was born into. I see that. But what I must face is that if anything were to happen to stop him being happy, I could not prevent it or protect him in the smallest degree by being here.'

Cilleby flinches. The stroking stops abruptly, though he does not remove his hands.

'You see, I don't think I could bear to have him torn from me one day and to languish here after that, fatally wounded, my imagination full of horrors. Better – this is what I've been thinking – to store my child forever in my mind as he is now, skipping up and down the stairs and dreaming of owning his ship. I can visit him in that place. It's my story. I can protect him inside it and he will never be taken from me.'

Cilleby is looking into her eyes, his expression unreadable. Ásta gazes back, discomfited to realise that, even while thinking about Jón, she is itching to reach up to his face and dribble her fingers down his cheek. The thought is even growing upon her of how lovely it would be, and how restful, and how exciting at the same time, if he were just to lay a finger, one scented finger with its beautifully pared nail, against her lips to silence her, and if he were then to scoop her on to the satin quilt and lay her down on it and instruct her, very softly, to stop thinking, that no good ever came from thinking.

But he does not, and she does not. She battles instead to recover the image of Ólafur that Wilhelm Kifft placed before her.

'And something else,' she says, gripping his hands the tighter to secure her own. 'Ólafur Egilsson knew me. That's what I had forgotten. He made me feel known. He made me feel beloved.'

A fugitive sob escapes her. Although nothing has equipped Cilleby to sense which man she is weeping for, he feels his own eyes moistening. He could have her in his arms in a second, on the quilt in two: they are both ready and he knows it. Later, when he is dreaming Ásta's face on to that of every woman he beds, he will look back on his conduct today as the finest thing he has ever done, only excepting having a man killed for her. Already, with the detachment he has been at pains to cultivate since she came into the room and he felt the direction of the wind, he is conscious of a glow of nobility at what he is giving up, even as some distant flicker of a thought is toying with how he might invest the windfall and the noisiest part of his mind is screaming that this is going to hurt.

He resumes the rhythmic rubbing of her palms, while Ásta falters on.

'Ólafur wanted an old sealwoman to die with a hand stroking her head. He owed her nothing and received nothing from her. Or *for* her, Cilleby. Do you see?'

Argue with me. Please argue with me. 'She was the lowest, most ridiculed of people. I don't expect you to understand why that matters to me – I'm not sure I know myself – but when I went to see the Dutchman I remembered. I began to think about it.' *Don't let me do this, Cilleby.* 'And it's why I am going home to him, whether I find him there or not.'

Cilleby swallows. 'In that case you must go,' he says equably.

That lone swallow is all that betrays the effort it is costing him not to say what he is suddenly, wildly, thinking: *Come to me instead, Ásta. Let me make everything right. I'll treat your son as my own. I want none but you. Come to the bed of stories where you belong.*

For all her long life afterwards Ásta will remember that fragment of time when she thought he was going to plead with her to stay. She will see again the faint quiver in his throat that at the very last seemed to speak of something for which he had never found the words or the right thing to do. She will wonder then what she would have done if he had found them. No, that's not true. She will never doubt what she would have done. But she will wonder often, being to her very last days more prone to wondering than she would wish, what her life would have become.

'I will make the arrangements with Kifft,' he says, and the moment passes.

He raises both her hands briefly to his lips and lets them fall, then reaches past her to open the door.

'Let me wish you a pleasant journey home.'

On the thirteenth day of June 1636, as the wind fills the sails of a merchant ship bearing thirty-four Icelanders away from the busy port of Algiers, Ali Pitterling Cilleby is at the end of the mole in his cream-white burnous with the hood up to watch it leave. He is alone.

ORANGE

June 1636 – May 1639

I would like to comfort and strengthen the people with my words, but I cannot.

Reverend Ólafur Egilsson

31

Not a word is spoken among the Icelanders strung along the side of the ship bound for Marseilles, as the white city shrinks before them. After all his efforts, Wilhelm Kifft has been able to gather and afford to ransom just thirty-four of the four hundred or so who drooped upon decks much like this one nine summers before. To these he has added another sixteen Danish and Norwegian men, captured on different occasions at sea, giving Kifft a group of fifty to harry back to the northern lands like a gruff shepherd who has tarried at the shieling too long.

All but six of the Icelanders are women, and every arm is empty. Next to Ásta stands Gudrídur Símonardóttir, a sallow, dark-eyed woman in her thirties who in their old island life lived near Anna Jasparsdóttir's croft at Stakkagerdi. She is clutching the side of the ship as hard as Ásta, for Gudda too has just said farewell to a son.

All who came with children, or had them after, have left them behind. Two women have only lately given birth to the bastard infants of their owners and are in particular agony over what will happen to those babies now. When she hears their stories in the months of journeying to come, Ásta will think of how she ran from the sea-villa with the captain's unholy seed streaming down her own thighs. She will remember how she imagined for a while, in the numb grieving for Marta when her body's rhythms went awry, that Cilleby's child might be growing within her own belly. She will think then, listening to the glazed-eyed laments of the other bereft women, that you can always find sorrows worse than your own.

Staring out at the retreating city with his fierce eyes is Einar Loftsson. He has paid his own ransom by selling his *brennivín* and the caps he knitted himself. He leaves two grown children, a wife in the cemetery and, as cannot fail to be remarked by anyone who encounters him, his nose and the greater part of his ears. It seems to Ásta that Einar's mutilated face tells all their stories without the need for words, for they have all left scraps of their torn selves in Algiers. Only Gunnhildur's spirits have recovered enough to permit a light flirtation with the swarthy French seaman who directed them aboard, there being many ways to survive.

When the coast can be seen no longer, Ásta casts about for a space on deck to fight the familiar nausea. She slumps near the black-clad figure of Mr Kifft, who has organised his papers on the surface of a barrel, precariously secured from the wind by a purloined piece of rigging and one elbow. Perched on a mountain of coiled ropes, he is attempting to mark off names on lists. His testy glance softens to see her head flopping into her knees.

'Excuse me, *mevrouw*, are you quite well?'

She looks up. With the sea breeze on his face and the Barbary behind him, the Dutchman looks liberated himself: even the ostrich feather has assumed a perkier posture.

'Yes, thank you. A little sea-sickness, that's all. I've never been a good sailor.'

Kifft lays down his pen and regards her closely. '*Mevrouw*, this is a hard time for you. I am not so stony of heart that I don't see what it is for a mother to leave her child. But every day will bring you closer to home. You must dwell on that, as I do.'

Heavens, the woman has a flinty eye. 'Er, not that I am suggesting I'm in the same position as you at all, of course not.'

He picks up the quill again with some haste and bends over his papers. This Mistress Torstiens is a shrewish character. She snapped at him most rudely yesterday in the free house when he tried – out of a courtesy bearing signs of wear – to congratulate her on making the correct decision.

'Here, look at this,' he says before she can think up a retort, happening gratefully on the entry at the top of the ledger. 'See, here is your name. You read, I believe, madame?'

She pulls herself to her feet, laying a hand on the rim of the barrel to steady herself in the swell. 'What is it?'

'It is my statement of accounts. Every penny I have spent is noted here. And believe me, there will be much to be added. Heaven knows how many ships I have yet to buy passage on and how many inns will require me to pay for bed and board for fifty people. It brings me out in a sweat to think of it. But where was I? Yes, you will like to see this – the proof that you are bought and safely out of captivity. There!'

She peers around the feather and reads, in Kifft's close, businesslike hand, the words: '*Gekofft von Aille Pitterlingk Cilleby: 2 frouwen tho weiter Asta Torstiens dess Presters frouwe vnd Gnudele Hermanns. Costen alle beyde – Rd. 500. Portgellt – Rd. 134.*'

Ásta is no scholar of Dutch, but it is not difficult to spot the erratically spelled names of Ásta Thorsteinsdóttir, the priest's wife, and Gunnhildur Hermannsdóttir. Nor is she long in ascertaining that they have been purchased together, from one Ali Pitterling Cilleby, for 500 Danish rix-dollars plus harbour dues, like a pair of prime cattle.

'It is quite a sum,' Kifft says, recalling the thunderous face of the Moor as he more or less snatched the money from his hand. You would think the scoundrel would at least have looked happy to receive his ill-gotten gains.

Kifft reapplies himself to his accounts. 'Barbarians, every one of them,' he mutters under his breath.

Kifft shepherds his group northwards. From the port of Marseilles he arranges a boat to carry them up the river Aude to the French town of Narbonne nine miles inland. Then they are jolted as far as Toulouse in ancient, rickety wagons pulled by mules, sleeping in the open air wherever they can find shelter. From Toulouse they sail along the canalways of the Garonne to join the Atlantic at the port of Bordeaux, where a ship with fifteen cannons bears them around the northern tip of France to the south coast of England. There they clamber into an even bigger ship boasting twenty-eight cannons. It is always the first thing the men count, the number of cannons; the women tally the rats. From the island of Texel in the north of Holland, they sail or walk along the river from one village to another, until they arrive at the great trading city of Amsterdam.

The journey is arduous. The effect of long walks in wet clothes, of chill nights, poor fare and the strains of constant danger from piracy prove too much for some who are already weakened by the conditions of their captivity; as the weeks pass, the thin band of Icelanders becomes further depleted. But those with the strength to survive the rigours do occasionally find their experiences exhilarating. In the days when she and Ólafur sat in an Icelandic turf-house trying to imagine a bigger world, Ásta would have been stunned to think she might one day encounter sights like these. She wonders if Ólafur, on the journey he made all those years ago himself, was also awed by the immense cathedrals, heady with incense and lush with relics and gilt, which are so different from the diminutive starkness of any church in Iceland. Did he too sail past baleful fortresses guarding the coasts of a Europe always at war and observe to himself, as she has, that they are no match for the Algerine pirates who sniff out bare inlets and empty bays like dogs a bone? Perhaps he also marvelled at all the neatly tilled fields of waving grain, with never an elf-mound or lava stone among them, and admired (he who always had an eye for the way people dress) the costly clothing that women wear in the grander towns, their bodices inset with gold and silver buttons, their dresses so gaudily different from the grey weaves of home. Ásta feels her mind enlarging as her heart shrivels.

There are no women wearing veils in the lands they pass through, but it takes Ásta weeks not to feel undressed outdoors without one. Every woman confesses to feeling the same. Nor will all the years of life left to her be enough to set aside fond thoughts of her baggy harem pantaloons, tied at the ankle, in which she could run up stairs as easy as a man. She will find herself remembering the freedoms of captivity: the freedom to withdraw from the gaze of men under a veil, the freedom from skirts that trip you in the rain and soak up the mud.

But memory is like that, always so eager to aid you in missing what you can no longer have and forgetting the rest. It is not Cilleby's scowl she sees when she thinks of him (as she does most of the time, no matter how often she instructs her thoughts towards Ólafur), nor the invincible arrogance, nor his refusal to acknowledge the iniquity of his trade and the many ways it has hurt her. No, memory parades a man patting his small daughters and sipping a civilised coffee. It insists she hears the note of irritated tenderness in the moonlit courtyard the night Jón Westman brought her home. It invites her to smile with him over the complexities of saga plots and names that end in *dóttir*. It bids her remember his renegade eyes and his warrior brows and his rumble of a laugh and his scented baldness and the endearments wrung from him in the satin bed.

She dreams sometimes on her travels, although not about him. Fitfully asleep among the scurrying rats in the hold of yet another merchant ship, she is visited by Marta, crying out to her from a bed of flowers while hairy hands grope her smooth young body. Another night it is Egill who comes to her, backed against a white wall, his eyes wide with terror as the thick lips of the pasha pout towards him. Only Jón dances and laughs for her still. In her dreams she is joyful in his company, although there is always the growling of danger in the background, a sense she cannot pin down that there is a reason why she is surprised to be with him. When she wakes, the absence of him aches and burns like the stump of another lost limb.

When they arrive in Amsterdam on the eighth day of August, Kifft, having chased his flock purposefully to the docks, announces – hat in hand and with a bow that sends his plume sweeping through the dust – that he is to accompany them no further. It has been a singular honour to arrange the freedom of the Danish majesty's most lamentably detained subjects and to guide them thus far, but he hopes they will be kind enough to recall that it is considerably more than a year since he left Amsterdam. It being the case that the time stipulated in his contract has been much exceeded, they will understand, good people as they are, that, much though he would wish it otherwise and inconsolable as he is that they should be departing without him, he really ought to be getting home. A ship awaits to carry them to the realm of Denmark. He can assure them they will be amply taken care of in Glückstadt, where King Christian is currently in residence and is minded – so his most gracious majesty has intimated to his most humble servant – to receive his subjects personally. From there they will be conveyed by sea to Copenhagen, where those who are to journey onwards to Iceland will be given passage home.

Then Wilhelm Kifft clamps his hat back on his head and almost runs from the quayside, in such manifest relief to be rid of his charges that, watching him fly, they enjoy their heartiest laugh for a long time.

Christian IV, King of Denmark, Norway and Iceland together with the Westman Islands (although not, to his profound regret, and certainly not for want of trying, of Sweden) has scarcely laid eyes on a more dreary band of travellers than the group who straggle ashore at Glückstadt on the nineteenth of August. They are women mostly, as far as he can see, although much too drab to set the royal pulse racing.

A man who inclines to joviality himself, Christian has tended to regard the Icelanders, when he has spared them a thought at all, as the dourest of his subjects. Not that he has ever been to Iceland, or (come to that) the Westman Islands, although the fishing revenue is of course excellent, but there are always a few of them hanging around Copenhagen. They have a preposterous air of intellectual superiority (solely based, as far as he can gather, on their distant ancestors having written sagas and histories) and are forever grumbling about unfair pricing, making no allowance for the way his monopoly for Danish merchants has secured the only business Iceland's poorest trading harbours enjoy. Hardly the people he would seek out for a party.

However, he does concede, stroking his pigtail and wondering about lunch, that these unfortunates trailing up to the palace have had a hard time of it. That man at the front – is it possible he doesn't possess a nose? Hideous sight, poor fellow. Yes, a good feast should cheer everyone up, himself included, and if any of the men have wits left after their ordeal, he might be able to get some useful naval intelligence out of them.

Christian is proud of Glückstadt. He has had it reclaimed from marshland to compete for trade with Hamburg further up the Elbe and is particularly fond of his new palace, designed with the combination of pink brick walls and twirly gables to which he is most joyously attached. Approaching it from the heavily fortified pier, the Icelanders peer curiously around. Their sovereign is a legendary builder of palaces, towns, fortifications, castles and naval ports the length and breadth of Denmark, all at the ready (so Kifft never tired of complaining) for whatever misguided war Christian might take it upon himself to dabble in next. In Kifft's gloomy opinion as a man of business, all this construction could only be impoverishing the Danish state and making it less likely that he would see payment of his expenses.

Christian is awaiting them in front of the palace in a scarlet riding jacket and black boots, looking, as Ásta whispers to Gunnhildur, as if he has just leaped from his horse. 'Pity the horse,' Gunnhildur giggles. Einar, who is gazing at his stout sovereign with loyal awe, shoots her a warning frown.

The king offers brandy-breathed enquiries after their health, and is soon showering them with copious ale and the finest fare the Glückstadt kitchens can provide. The food unsettles many a stomach unused to being so richly filled. There were days when Kifft had claimed his purse would not stretch to any food at all, and the privations of the journey are plainly written on every face around the king's table. The latest to succumb was old Halldóra Jónsdóttir, who survived abduction from Heimaey, nine years in an Algiers kitchen (afterwards declaring roundly that she would die happy if she never had to sieve another grain of *couscous* again) and every rigour of the homeward trek, only to return to her maker on a ship within sight of Glückstadt with frost in her hair. At least she never did see *couscous* again and may be presumed to have departed happily.

Christian presides genially over the feast, giving no sign that his capacity for carousing has diminished with advancing years. His drinking prowess has been the talk of Europe ever since a riotous state banquet in England in 1606, at which the young Danish king drank the famously incontinent court of his brother-in-law King James under the table: rumour has it that upon his finally falling at the feet of a tipsy young woman playing the Queen of Sheba, it was necessary to carry the insensible monarch out of the hall to sleep it off. In Iceland news of their sovereign's antics had spread with surly mirth. Einar knows the stories, but he is impressed all the same. The king is a lively host, friendly and curious and able to hold his drink quite well enough to pose a string of keen questions about their life in Algiers. Einar struggles manfully in his limited Danish with some pointed enquiries about the number of ships the Turks had and the position of their defences.

Much restored by pork and ale, the king's affability reasserts itself further when he sees how grateful his poor subjects are to be ransomed. As he listens, he strokes the beard that flows down the middle of his chin like a tidy grey waterfall and occasionally lets a finger rest on his pigtail. This confection – quite astonishing, Ásta thinks, unable to keep her eyes off it – reaches to his shoulder, where it is prettily tied with a scarlet ribbon.

Well, Oddrún, you missed that pigtail.

Ásta is a little shaken to realise that Oddrún was more or less correct in her dying description of the king. True, the gold medallions on a chain hanging beneath the voluminous lace collar are not buttons exactly, but they could pass for them at a distance. And the jacket is undoubtedly very red. If Ásta ever manages to puzzle out the sealwoman's final riddle and work out what she is on no account to do, Oddrún's occasionally being right will have to be borne in mind.

Some days later the king sends them onwards to Copenhagen with hearty wishes for the future. Merchant ships will be put at their disposal there to take them to Iceland. While awaiting these, might he suggest they admire the many wonders of Copenhagen? They will assuredly gasp at his new Børsen trading exchange, its spire coiled with the sculpted tails of four mighty dragons. Beyond the city walls they will spy his delightful summer palace of Rosenborg, built (he confides) to escape the dank old castle by the sea. And his new ring of bastioned defences around the city – a wonder to behold.

As it transpires, Iceland's weary hostages will have more than enough time to study the architecture of Copenhagen, and much besides. Disembarking there on a whey-faced afternoon at the end of August, they learn that the last ship of the summer has already left for Iceland and there will not be another until spring. It will be many months yet before they can sail for home.

32

The cathedral known as Vor Frue Kirke is set on what the residents of Copenhagen, who have plainly never visited Algiers, are pleased to call a hill. It does lie high enough to see across to the town's many islets and canals, taking in the numerous small-bricked buildings that the king has been so energetically constructing, all of which throw into sorry relief the miserably dark streets and ramshackle dwellings in which the Icelanders are obliged to see out their first northern winter for a long time.

The Church of Our Lady is much more austere than the cathedrals Ásta admired in France, which had not been smashed and stripped of their Catholic adornment in the name of Martin Luther's Reformation. She likes the bare, vaulted airiness of it, although in truth it is not the building that draws her attention so much as the young man who is leading them through it. He has big, sloping shoulders and long, wavy hair, and he holds himself somewhat self-consciously as he walks. She wonders, because she always does, if Egill would look anything like this now with twenty years upon him.

She will learn that Hallgrímur Pétursson is from Skagafjördur in the north of Iceland and had been studying at the Latin school in Hólar when a chance meeting with a couple of German merchants took him to Denmark. While labouring as a blacksmith's apprentice, he was spotted by the provost of Roskilde University, an Icelandic scholar by the name of Brynjólfur Sveinsson, who sensed intellectual talent in the boy and persuaded him to train for the Lutheran ministry. Now in his final year in the seminar attached to Vor Frue Kirke, Hallgrímur has been tasked with 'refreshing', as his superior put it to him, the faith of those who have been separated from wholesome Christian influence for an alarming number of years. In what better way might Iceland's redeemed hostages fill the hours of enforced winter idleness in Copenhagen than by re-learning the doctrines of the Lutheran church?

The young man has been explaining this somewhat diffidently to his compatriots, their number down to twenty-seven, as he leads them through the cathedral for their first religious class.

No, Egill would look nothing like this man, his bones so big and his features dark and heavyset. Ásta thinks of Egill's thin white arms and is cuffed by the usual wave of longing. But there is something about this awkward lad all the same. Something in the sensitive eyes, the long arms he looks as if he doesn't know what to do with either, with the youth of him and the earnestness of him, that reminds Ásta of her firstborn son.

Hallgrímur himself is wondering nervously what he is going to do with all these people who have seen more than he can begin to imagine and endangered their souls in a multitude of ways it is incumbent on him to correct. Halting by the plain altar, he glances around the group from beneath a tongue of dark hair. Old, young (but no children – how strange) and for the most part as poor-looking and unkempt as he, they are regarding him with a range of expressions. Tired resignation is what he mostly discerns, along with varying shades of wariness. He also takes note of an encouraging beam from a flat-faced girl with a large mouth; a fond, maternal smile from a grey-eyed woman in her forties who is gazing at him with a faraway expression; open hostility from a fiery-looking man with a grotesquely mutilated visage; and from a striking woman with a sad, hunted face and eyes black as an anvil, a look of frank interest that makes him blush to the roots of his hair.

All in all, it may be said that his preliminary survey of the first pastoral flock of his ministry makes Hallgrímur Pétursson long fervently to be back with his books in the draughty library on the other side of the quadrangle. He is charged with reforming these people, and it is soon clear there is much work to be done. He is not to know that by the end of the winter the life to have altered most will be his.

For a part of each day, as these grow ever shorter and more wet, Hallgrímur addresses his class from the front of a chilly inner room of the cathedral. The stone walls are glossy with damp and he has no means of providing a fire. In minute detail he leads them through Luther's catechism and every one of the ten commandments of Moses. Sometimes he also listens, leaning his cheek against a hand like a sheep's haunch as one person or another makes a stumbling attempt to explain the agonies and temptations they met in another world.

By the following spring he has heard things he will not forget in a lifetime. Here are people who were preserved from going mad by convincing themselves that their children could pray the wrong way and still go to heaven. People who have come close themselves to surrendering to a different creed. People who have asked whether churchmen are always right about everything. People who wonder yet if there might be more to heaven and earth than even Martin Luther knew.

Hallgrímur Pétursson has his answers, but never again will they arrive in his mouth, or grace the poetry to which he is beginning to turn a hand, quite as glibly after the winter of 1636.

Hallgrímur also has other matters on his mind. It is Gunnhildur, beside herself with excitement, who first reports a suspicious overnight visit to the house where black-eyed Gudrídur Símonardóttir is boarding. The attraction between the two is plain to see (so Gunnhildur declares) and as romantic as anything in the stories of Scheherazade, although for her personal taste she could have wished Hallgrímur better looking and a shade less intense. And of course Gudda is old enough to be his mother.

Everyone keeps an eye open for stolen looks and the casual brushing of hands, and everyone is amply rewarded. Some among the group are angry and others merely amused to observe their appointed religious mentor in such poorly disguised combat with one of the very commandments in which he is so earnestly instructing them. Ásta goes so far as to wonder whether the Almighty himself might be displaying a sense of humour in this regard. But all are alert to the dangers of this improbable coupling. It is well known that Gudda is returning to a husband on Heimaey.

The days are beginning to lengthen again when Gudda whispers to Ásta that she is expecting a child. They are sitting on a bench in the dank cathedral room, rubbing their cold hands as they wait for the day's class to begin.

Ásta blows out a long breath, which lingers white in the gloom. 'You must know this is serious?' The penalties for adultery are severe and there will be no hiding it now.

'I do, but I can't be sorry. That's the worst of it, Ásta. I was content enough being married to Eyjólfur. At least I think I was. It was so long ago, so far away, I can barely remember what I felt then.'

Hallgrímur enters the room in a flurry of threadbare black robe and settles his books on the table, still with that pleasing shyness about him and the thinking behind the eyes that remind Ásta so much of Egill. Gudda's dark eyes follow him.

'He has come to me like a kind of blessing,' she whispers. 'Can you understand that, Ásta? I've been with many men these last years, sometimes forced to it, sometimes enjoying what I should not. What does a commandment of Moses have to say to such as me in the life we have been made to live?'

'Have you mentioned this question to Hallgrímur?' Ásta enquires drily, seeing his eyes search out Gudda as he clears his throat to bring the class to attention. She has no enthusiasm for condemning the young man's ill-disciplined ardour. Hypocrisy is not a crime, else there would scarce be a priest left standing, and he must take his chance with the actual law. Rather it is another emotion that floors Ásta as she observes the couple's darting smiles. This woman has a son not much older than Jón left behind in the Barbary, a husband at home, a bastard in her belly and a capital charge hanging over both her and her passionate young lover. Yet here she sits in the Church of Our Lady, smiling. *She is happier than I am.*

Gudda leans close. 'Let's say,' she murmurs out of the corner of her mouth, 'that he was quick to realise his studies have not prepared him for everything.'

A small flower, white with a tiny yellow heart, has sprung up in the woods beyond the walls of the town. Ásta nearly shouts with gladness to spy this frail promise of spring guzzling the light through the bare trees. Soon a canopy of sticky young leaves is stealing the rays. Warmth is returning to the air and each day lingers a little longer. Sunshine is beginning to split the leaden skies of Copenhagen.

The harbour, too, is returning to life, with much hammering, provisioning and hauling upon sails. The winds and waves of the North Sea are ready to receive ships again and the Icelanders will be sailing soon.

There will, however, be one fewer of them embarking for the Westman Islands. Gudda has learned that her husband is likely to have drowned with tens of other fishermen in a dreadful storm at sea. It happened more than a year ago, but news travels slow when, like everyone, it has to wait a long time for a ship. Eyjólfur's presumed fate has rescued Gudda from a dangerous situation.

Hallgrímur Pétursson has not shared with the class his view on whether adultery is still adultery if the husband is dead but the lovers were not aware of it at the time, but this delicate theological question is of keen interest to those who must determine the couple's fate. Ásta is more inclined than ever to fancy a heaving of divine shoulders in the firmament. It is decided that the lovers will be charged with the lesser crime of concubinage. Hallgrímur will not complete his studies, but return to Iceland in disgrace and Gudrídur with him. They are to make for the trading station of Keflavík, and will marry if Eyjólfur's drowning is confirmed.

At the beginning of May merchant ships begin to depart Copenhagen for the twenty or so Danish trading posts around the coast of Iceland. Gunnhildur is heading back east to Djúpivogur, bursting with stories and gossip. If she stops talking within a week of arriving, she will not be the girl Ásta takes her for.

Ásta's own wait is also over. She gathers up her skirts and steps into the boat behind the bristling bulk of Einar Loftsson. Then they are rowed out to the ship bound for Heimaey.

33

The first Danish ship of the early summer is always a joyous sight on the island. People whoop and shout to see those big square sails tacking ever nearer, bringing news, letters, animals, nails, grain, perhaps some wood: whatever treasure they have dreamed of the winter long.

The wind chivvying the distant ship is also sweeping across the stony face of Helgafell, from where Ólafur Egilsson is watching the white speck on the horizon growing bigger. The climb took him a good deal longer than it used to, but he would be nowhere else today. There is a possibility – just a possibility – that his family is aboard that ship.

He has found himself a sheltered vantage point below a circle of misshapen rocks: frozen trolls, as Ásta would describe them, with their knees and jutting elbows. Ólafur shakes his head. See what she has done to him. Once he would have seen a volcano's ancient spewings; now he imagines trolls. Soon, God willing, he'll tell her, and she will laugh to hear it.

But he must not let himself be carried away. He must not hope too hard. Let him hold only to the facts and what is known for sure. An envoy was sent to Algiers. That much the knitting did accomplish, although the money it raised went twice astray and they had to set to again and again. The latest envoy is reported to have arrived in the Barbary some two years ago. Is that time enough for the ransom to have been paid, the captives released, the journey home completed? Surely it is. That ship inching ever closer really could be carrying his family.

To think that Marta will be twelve by now, a young woman, and the baby nearly as old as Egill was. Ólafur has often wondered what he is like, their little Jón. He has been in the habit of envisaging him as another Egill, imagining Egill's face under the cap of dark hair that is all he can recall of the baby. He must prepare himself for a surprise, because they are always different, children. Marta is bound to be nothing like Helga – even at two she was her own person. And might Egill, might even Egill come too? He'll be a man now, surely able to be ransomed like any other. In any event, Ólafur must be a patient father to them all. Iceland will be a foreign land to them, and cold. He can't expect everything to go smoothly after nearly ten years away. And Ásta, dearest Ásta, is likely to chafe under Thorgerdur's iron rule. He will have to bring his diplomatic skills out of storage there. Ásta will have suffered. Ólafur has never attempted to put flesh on the ways in which she might have suffered, because if imagining cannot make you feel better there is no point to it that he has ever seen. But he will bend his strength to helping her and he will love her. He will love them all.

The ship, dipping and rising across the sea, is making good progress. It will be here within the hour. Ólafur begins a gingerly scramble down the mountain scree and hurries to the harbour.

Heimaey's guardian cliffs are busy with summer birds and Ásta's heart swoops to see them. Funny to think that they too have been all the way to warm climes and back. It's a relief to feel her spirits lifting a little. The noisy cliffs, the sleepy green island, the blustery sky: they are just as she has always pictured them. It is only she who is not as she was.

A thin young man bends to help her out of the landing boat, grabbing her by the elbow as a gust of wind nearly topples her back in.

She stares, struggling to place him.

'Magnús Birgisson,' he says, courteous and excited. Most of the island has gathered around the harbour, craning to see who might step on shore next. 'Let me help you, Ásta.'

Magnús takes her by the arm and guides her away from the crowd. People are beginning to point and jostle. He tries to steer her in the direction of an old man watching quietly from the side. But Ásta is tired: it has been a long voyage, she was sick the whole way and she needs to get home.

'Ásta,' says the old man, 'do you not recognise me?'

As Magnús is obliged to report later to his mother, who refuses to put broth on the table until every detail of the meeting between husband and wife has been divulged, it was all very uncomfortable. The Reverend Ólafur seemed upset to discover his wife was alone and Ásta was very quiet.

'What did they say?' Agnes asks, poised avidly above him with the bowl.

'Not much.' Magnús fiddles with his spoon. 'He wanted to know where the children were and she said she would tell him on the way home, and they stared at each other for a while and then turned to walk.'

'How did she look?'

'Not much changed, I suppose.'

Agnes waits for more. 'Distant,' he says grudgingly. Magnús had found the couple's encounter sad in a way he is not going to try and express to anyone. 'She seemed a bit distant.'

'And what happened?'

'Nothing.'

'Did they embrace?' his mother persists. Why the Almighty did not see fit to bless the male of the species with an eye for important detail has always been beyond her.

'Not that I noticed. I think maybe he held her hands for a while. Can't remember.'

'And what news of the children?'

'Couldn't hear very well. I didn't like to go too close.' Tramping across the heath behind them with his arms around a sack of meal for Thorgerdur, Magnús had wished himself miles away.

Agnes keeps a tight hold of the bowl and glares at her son.

'All right, then. She mentioned that Egill had gone away some-where and Marta somewhere else and the young one – Jón, they call him – I think she said he was a servant in Algiers. But Mamma, the reverend looked terrible. He stopped walking and every bit of colour went from his face. And before you ask – he didn't say a word. Just turned away to the sea and bent his head.'

'Poor man,' Agnes sighs. 'And there'll be more than him in shock tonight with so few returned. And what of Ásta?'

'Ásta?'

'Yes, Ásta. What's wrong with your ears?'

'She was crying, I think. Is that what you mean? She turned

and asked what I was doing standing there and didn't I have a delivery to make? A bit sharp, you know. And then she seemed to notice the house for the first time – we were nearly at Ofanleiti by then – and she said, "Is that it?" And she made a sort of sobbing noise. Mamma, I'm hungry.'

His mother bangs the broth on the table and stalks to the kitchen. Nothing for it but to waylay the Ofanleiti serving girl tomorrow morning.

34

The morning after the return of the captives, so many fewer than hoped for, a passing fisherman spots Ásta and Ólafur standing outside the Ofanleiti crofthouse. They are staring out to sea and don't see him. The sky is a soft blue; yesterday's grey clouds have been chased away and the air is dawn-fresh. The man is struck by how miserable Ólafur looks, his hands hanging by his sides and his eyes registering no interest in the scene that a watcher may discern, only glancing now and then at his wife and then quickly ahead again.

Ásta, on the contrary, is drinking it in. Or rather, the man thinks (he being used of old to noting Ásta's demeanour with some exactitude), she is less drinking than sucking into herself the sight of the small islands tickled by waves, the faint whiff of seaweed mixed with the smell of the springtime earth, the piping and fluting of birds and the sea rumbling in that contented way that fills everyone with pleasure on such a day.

Her form still appears beautiful to the fisherman, although he will admit he has never been the most detached observer. What surprises him most is the bloom of health about her. Even after what he must suppose was a testing journey home, she looks younger now than Thorgerdur, who is worn so haggard by outdoor work and the struggle to feed the family. Ásta's hair remains thick, its fairness only slightly darkened and silvered, and her skin appears less gouged by the weather than any woman here who has passed five and forty years in rain and wind and a little sun.

In the days to come it will also occur to the fisherman that she is carrying herself differently. From what he used to observe, Ásta always had nerve, saying out loud what others would not, laughing at what nobody else would dare to find funny. But she was also impractical and dreamy, and drew much of her strength, it seemed to him, from Ólafur. The woman who has come back seems more knowing, less compliant. She has a confidence that holds itself tight and aloof. Thinking it over, it will appear to him extraordinary that someone who was dragged from her home a captive should return with such a sense of owning herself. She has felt much: that he can tell here and now. It is there in her eyes, grave as they always were but without the spark of mischief that used to lighten her face in an instant. Indeed her eyes are furrowed around with such pain that it frightens him a little. Her eyes are at odds with the girlishness of her form and they age her in a different way altogether.

Ólafur must sense it too, this unfathomable suffering, this air that clings to Ásta of being apart and dangerously strong. Perhaps that is why he droops so at her side.

Watching Ásta drench her senses in an Icelandic springtime, it comes to the fisherman that she is unreachable. And it is not his business to reach her, he reminds himself. There must be no more of that.

He adjusts the rope on his shoulder and turns away.

Neither husband nor wife can bring the other succour: they have not the language to share their pain. Ásta has not found a way of telling Ólafur about her life in the white city, for fear of where it might lead and all the different ways in which it would wound him and torture her. And he, struggling to swallow his questions, alert to how difficult he found these himself when he returned, does not know where to start in understanding what she has become or how to bare his own heart.

They have scarcely touched since the first clumsy grasping of hands at the harbour. In the moment of meeting it came to her in a panic that she did not know this man: Ólafur's nose was never so large, or his neck so thin; his back was not this stooped, or his hair so white. Nor could Ólafur's joy at catching sight of that dear, familiar face in the approaching boat long withstand the ice in her eyes or the terrible absence of his children. *Why am I here? Why have I left my child?* Ásta shrieked to herself that night, while he, facing the other way, wept in silent agony for the family he would not see again in this world or the next.

Out of delicacy for feelings he suspects border on revulsion, Ólafur makes no request of Thorgerdur and his son-in-law to surrender the married compartment behind the curtain at the back of the *badstofa*. Instead, he and Ásta sleep in narrow beds set into the wall on opposite sides of the room, among children who are not theirs. Ásta lies near enough her husband to count the spidery veins in his cheek and the hairs in his nose, but too far to reach a hand to him in the night.

She does have word of Helga. She does have that in which to wrap herself. Their daughter has married a lawman and settled in Skammbeinsstadir in the south of Iceland. She has children. Three already, Ólafur tells her, with another on the way. And for that moment they draw together, smiling to think of their mischievous Helga in a nest of infants. Her husband, Finnur Gudmundsson, writes to say there is no question of her travelling in her condition, but that she sends by his hand her most fond and respectful wishes to her parents and thanks God day and night for the safe return of her beloved mother to Iceland. Ásta stores the news with the rest of her disappointments and tries to rejoice that Helga has made in these ten years a fruitful life that is complete without a mother.

Ólafur spends most of his time ministering to the distressed island. With two hundred and fifty taken and only a handful come back, he encounters hurt behind almost every door. Some of the women have returned to confirmation that husbands or sons were among the fifty fishermen who drowned the previous year, while others were shocked to find another woman in their husband's bed and nowhere to sleep but alongside them. Families whose loved ones never did emerge from the spring ship have had to bear the final shattering of hope. Ásta cannot conceive of what Ólafur finds to say to them all. She has not asked. Once she would have run to meet him as he plodded home from such a doleful mission, back stooped and eyes on the path, and taken his arm and thought of something to cheer him. Now she makes sure to be busy with an urgent task elsewhere. It is Thorgerdur who is left to pull the shoes from her father's feet and hang up his socks to dry.

As the summer draws to a close, Thorgerdur chooses her moment. The two women are making *skyr* in the dairy, a dark, shivery place that Ásta hates with a passion, though she never minded it before.

'There have been strains on my father that a man half his age might have buckled under,' Thorgerdur begins, stirring vigorously and not looking at Ásta. 'He is well past seventy. Nothing else has tied him to life but the hope of your return. Don't you see that?'

It is so unlike Thorgerdur to start a conversation about anything other than the time the milk and rennet are taking to curdle that Ásta forgets to bridle.

'I do,' she replies quietly in the dimness. Why deny it? Of course she sees.

'Then why are you not warmer with him? We all know you have suffered, but so has he.'

'I treat him with due respect,' Ásta says tightly.

'Pray leave the respect to me,' Thorgerdur snaps. 'You're his wife, not his daughter.'

With a visible effort to speak more temperately, she tries again: 'No marriage is without its trials, as no one need tell me, but you must surely know that you alone can make my father happy.'

Ásta is silent. What is she to say? That a daughter is exactly what she feels herself to be? That happiness is a luxury we are all well used to living without?

Thorgerdur pauses in her stirring. She hesitates a moment, inspects the spoon, then bursts forth with, 'Look, Ásta, would you like our bed? My father has not requested it, but it ought to be yours.'

'No.' The answer comes too fast, and she tries to soften it: 'Thank you, Thorgerdur. That is a generous offer, but it is not necessary.'

Thorgerdur is not an easy person to talk to. Her stiffness repels intimacy and her eyes, rather than draw you out, tend to dart hither and thither, looking, as Ásta always fancies, for dirt, which is so plentiful they are rarely still. But now she raises her head, looks straight across and speaks almost gently.

'Ásta, what is wrong?'

Blinking back a rush of tears, Ásta turns away. How is she to answer, when so much, so very much, is wrong? The dark, cramped, smoke-ridden house. The greasy mutton soups, with never a vegetable or a herb for taste. The back-breaking plucking of a thousand feathers. The dresses grey as dried mud. The reek of fish and the cold summer's damp. Thorgerdur's children, who sleep in beds where Marta should be lying with a hand tucked under her cheek and Jón bouncing in the puffin-feather duvet she never had the chance to make for him. Ólafur, whose touch she cannot bear, whose sympathy only adds to her furious guilt, whose limp silver hair makes her wish for a head that bore none at all and yearn for the scent of rosewater.

She runs an eye over the previous batch of *skyr* drying on the rack, checks that it has stopped its dripping and lifts the pail of whey from beneath it. Dare she confess any of this to a brisk woman whose answer to all that is hard in her own life has been to clamp her mouth in a line and set her arms to work and never think to dream of what cannot be?

She puts the pail down again.

'Do you remember the wife of Njáll in the saga? When their sons' enemies set the house ablaze, they offered the old couple the chance to leave and save their lives. Njáll refused, and so then did Bergthóra. "I was given to Njáll in marriage young," she said (do you remember?), "and I promised him then that we would share the same fate." And then she and Njáll went back inside, lay down on their bed with an oxhide to cover them and died together in the fire.'

Thorgerdur makes no comment, only beats the milk harder.

'When I was a young wife to Ólafur and he was fit and handsome and full of such life and energy that I could barely keep up, we lay in bed side by side and I told him that was how I wanted to die too. We would go together, he and I. "Ásta *mín*," he said – you can imagine how he would say it, very dry – "could you not provide for us a less painful way to meet our maker?" And I said, "It's not the burning I want, as well you know". I was probably giggling by then, because Ólafur could always make me laugh, "I just like to imagine us together to the end." And he said, "Well, naturally", or some such phrase, "and with you playing the role of heroine to the end, of course." I could tell he was smiling in the darkness. "I'm touched, dearest," he said. "But you must remember that Bergthóra was an old woman herself by then and you are much younger than me. You will find better things to do when I'm old than lie down and die with me under a smelly old hide." And I laughed and said I would be with him to the end, whatever befell us, and what was wrong with a good oxhide? "Whatever is to come, Ólafur, we will share it," I said to him. Those very words.

'But Thorgerdur, we were not given the same fate to share. We were not allowed to keep growing together in the same earth. I turned my face to a different sun and put my roots into a different soil, and he – I know it sounds harsh, Thorgerdur, but he has begun to wither. Far from wanting to lie down and burn with Ólafur, I find I cannot bring myself to lie beside him at all.'

She looks at Thorgerdur in the shadows, challenging her to slap her down. 'There, I've said it. Now you know the wickedness you are dealing with.'

Thorgerdur has listened without expression. There is none now as she rests her spoon and says sourly, 'You think Gísli's stale breath and thrusting haunches bring me to heaven on earth? You were always one to live in a saga, Ásta. It is nothing to do with age or a change of soil, but a matter only of the will. My father will not see many more summers. He needs you. It is all I wanted to say.'

35

The winter seems never to end. Sometimes Ásta thinks she will scream to wake one more day in darkness. Sometimes she does. She hurls herself out of the house and feels her way down the slope and across the lava field to the cliff edge and there she howls louder than the wind itself into the black sea. Ólafur watches her go with the troubled look that drives her to fury these days, a fury no more easily contained for having no focus and no excuse.

How could she have forgotten, how could she possibly not have remembered, what it is like to live for month after month with only a few watery hours of light a day, with cold that seeps into your bones and feet that are always wet? Is it conceivable that she never noticed before how foul the habits are here? Even Thorgerdur, waging doughty war on the dust as she may, stokes the fire with decayed puffin corpses and handfuls of dried sheep shit, using fingers she thinks nothing of sliding into the mouth of her babe to soothe him. Ólafur kneels to pray without a thought of washing. And what should he wash in anyway? What should she wash in herself, when there is no tiled fountain, no copper jug spilling water from a courtyard reservoir, no shiny brass tap in a scented bathhouse, but only a reeking well into which some fool has chucked a pile of rotting orange flippers?

Can she not have noticed how the turf walls bend in on you and bear down on you until you are desperate to break out and breathe again? Only there is no roof to escape to here but just gabled grass, and the wind would toss you off it anyway if it did not freeze you first. To think she spent more than thirty winters in a house like this, yet only now is oppressed by the way the stinking fulmar oil in the lamp mingles with the stench of the animals and the meat smoking over the kitchen fire and the ripe sealskin jackets on their hook, making her sick with longing for the tang of mint and cumin and an atrium open to the sky.

When the sun returns in the spring of 1638 Ásta feels like a small, hibernating creature rubbing a nightmare from its lids. The morning radiance sometimes blasts her eyes. Even when the sky is dull she can smell the earth in the drizzly air and it overwhelms her with nameless yearnings.

One April afternoon she pulls her shawl around her shoulders and slips from the house before Thorgerdur can raise a protest. Fleeing clouds are bringing spits of rain, but it is a joy to be outside. Gulls scream overhead to their nests in the crags, and she wonders if the puffins, too, are back. Such an ache she has to see these small birds again.

By the seafront she watches kittiwakes delivering stalks of grass and tangled wool to rocky crevices. Some, settled in their pairs, have already turned their pert backsides to the world. She would be content to do that. Alone and perhaps not so pert, let her only sit for the rest of her life staring at glistening black rock and shiny green moss, her back to the storms and the wind.

More kittiwakes are riding the waves on folded grey wings and inky tails. She searches for a black head among them, but can see none. Back she walks past the Há, where the sea comes crashing in on boulders emerald with slime. The cliff there is where young Erlendur Runólfsson fell when he was shot, the day the pirates came. Ásta looks up at it for a long time. Was the boy still alive to see the jagged waters rushing to meet him? Is there time to repent as death hurtles towards you, or is every last prayer snatched away as you fly?

The wind comes in spurts, lifting her skirts and spinning her about as she makes her way home. Go there, it commands, shoving her aside. No, I've changed my mind. Go there. Now rest awhile, but not for long, because I'll be back – so it warns – and then I will remove you from the ground altogether and thrust you in a different direction, after which you will stagger to your feet and set your skirts straight and point your chin to the future, and then, of course, I might just come and knock you down again. You know how it is, the wind will say. You know how life is.

Nearing Ofanleiti she spots Magnús Birgisson on the summit of Helgafell, keeping a watch for the return of the pirate ships that every islander still dreads. She is sure it's him building the cairn up there, tall as a rake. Why is Egill not with him? How can it be that one mother's child is here piling stones on a mountain and another is lost, so deeply, darkly lost that, try though she might, there is no place to imagine him.

She finds Ólafur in the *badstofa* with the little table drawn up to the side of his bed and a book open on it. He looks up with a wary smile of greeting, before returning his concentration to the page. She is so irritated to find him reading calmly, careless of the storms beating in her own breast, that she has to fight the impulse to toss the book to the floor.

Hurling herself on to the bed opposite, she begins to tug off her damp socks. She thought it would ease in time, this irascible reaction to the very sight of him. But Ólafur is responsible for drawing her back to everything she is finding hard to live with and away from all she cannot be reconciled to living without. Nothing can change that. Nothing is easing.

Yet Ásta is not so lacking in insight as to believe it is Ólafur's fault that a marriage between two hurt people after ten years apart has proved to be beyond redemption. He would have tried, no doubt, if she could have brought herself to let him. Nor can she blame him for not understanding what it is to wake each morning to the stink of mouldering bird and feel yourself to be not only in the wrong place but, may God forgive her, the wrong marriage.

In her fairer moments, Ásta will concede that Ólafur is slower to judge than of old and takes care not to smoke out those sadnesses she would keep hidden. But the same cannot be said of the rest of the island.

Like those who arrived with her, she has returned to find herself a stranger. Ten years of island memories have been made without them, forged in a different kind of trauma from their own, causing a different kind of damage. The place even looks different from the one they remember. A new Landakirkja stands on the hill, the costs of the timber and furnishings borne mainly by the merchants. New trading houses have sprouted where the old people burned. The rebuilt crofts seem, like Ofanleiti, shabbier than they recall and the poverty drearier. Some homes are still empty, with roofs caved in and the wind weeping between the stones. New walls have been erected around the remaining ones such as would deter no janissary that Ásta ever laid eyes upon but which make people feel safer in their beds. New people have moved in from the mainland. There are new insecurities, new suspicions, hurtful whispers that began as soon as the rejoicing – muted from the start when it was realised how few were returned – had begun to ebb. Surely, people started to say, it will take more than a few classes in Denmark for folk who lived so long among the heathen to become pure of mind again? What practices have they condoned, what heresies do they harbour, what dangers are posed to Christian minds by their very presence among decent men and women?

Gudrídur Símonardóttir, whose reason for not returning to the island remained a secret for about half an hour after the return of her fellow hostages, is now derided as Turkish Gudda. It is the settled wisdom of the community that she was never any better than she should be anyway, and it is hardly more than she deserved that her poor drowned husband Eyjólfur, may God rest his soul, should have taken so many women into the croft at Stakkagerdi after she left and fathered those bairns of his by the various mothers. Nobody could be surprised that Gudda went bad, leading God's anointed priest (well, near enough) into sin like that, blighting his prospects, and old enough to be his mother at that. Well, she has received her just deserts all right: a pauper in Keflavík and a lesson to every fallen woman.

Gudda's salacious story has stirred up old memories of Anna

Jasparsdóttir, whose father is forced once again to defend her Muslim marriage.

'Do not blame her,' Ásta hears Jaspar shout at the crone who spits at his feet on the path to the harbour. 'How can you know what it was like unless you have walked in her shoes?'

Few are much inclined to spend time in the shoes of those who have come back. The island senses something different about the returned, as if they have been subtly re-formed while they were away and emerged in a shape that keeps slipping through the hands of their families and neighbours. The women especially have returned not as victims inviting sympathy but as people in command of themselves who stand in some indefinable way taller. They carry themselves as if, ludicrously, they know better than those who have nursed their own wounds on this island for ten years without questioning the true faith and going romping in heathen beds, as everyone knows those folk must have done. Even, whisper it, the Reverend Ólafur's wife, who was caught (did you hear?) in a man's bedroom at midnight. Caused a terrible fuss apparently. Mind you, Ásta has always been strong-willed and difficult for the reverend to handle. And doesn't he look ill these days and no wonder? Look at her wandering aimlessly around the island, just the way old Oddrún Pálsdóttir used to but nowhere near as friendly. Barely gives you the time of day now, eyes burning as hot as that Einar Loftsson, who has been striding about as if he owns the place since the day he came back. Terrible what those savages did to his face, of course. You could push your whole fist into that hole, and not much left of his ears either if you ever see him without his cap on. Just goes to show, though. If you spend all those years among barbarians who can do a thing like that, one way or another you're not going to come home unsullied, are you? Stands to reason.

Even Magnús's mother Agnes, uncomfortable with the more vicious slurs on people who never asked to be taken captive, thinks they should at least make more of an effort to join in. As she mentions to her husband, who is trying to get to sleep and would rather she didn't, 'Ásta and Ólafur are not even, you know, *living as husband and wife*. That's what Inga up at Ofanleiti says anyway. I know he's getting on a bit, old Ólafur, but you have to ask why?

'Do you really, my dear?' her husband replies, patting her ample thigh and heaving himself on to his other side with a sigh.

Ásta tosses the first sock on to the earthen floor and sets to work peeling off the second. The moisture has dimpled her feet.

'The air has brought colour to your cheeks, Ásta *mín*,' Ólafur hazards, laying down his book and choosing a tone he judges neither too light nor too hearty, as one might select for a skittish horse. 'Are you feeling better for the walk?'

'I'm feeling perfectly well, thank you,' she replies, picking bits of wool from between her toes. Why must she always sound like this? She tries again. 'I was only looking to see if I could spy my first puffin. It's early yet. I'll look again in a few days.'

Taking encouragement from this expansive reply, Ólafur brightens. 'Did you miss the birds when you were away?'

'I did. At first.' She has no desire to go there and gives her feet an ostentatious rub in the hope that he will take the hint.

He does not take the hint. Ólafur has been gathering his courage for just such a propitious moment and is not inclined to let it pass.

'You have suffered much, Ásta,' he begins carefully, 'and I know there is nothing I can say that will suffice.' When he rehearsed this speech in his head, it had been with Ásta looking straight at him, her gaze becoming ever softer, not picking stubbornly at her toes. 'But', he takes a breath and a rush at it, 'can you find no solace in prayer? God has promised always to hear us.'

Ólafur, please, not this.

She scratches the rash between the smallest and the second smallest toe of her left foot with tense concentration. Ólafur's speech is doomed. He knows it. But he continues to address her bent head, because he has started now and it is time.

'This afternoon when you were out I was reviewing some examples from scripture.' His hand falls on the book and his fingers begin a nervous thrumming. 'Think of Moses, Ásta. His prayer was so strong that it parted the Red Sea. Or' – tap, tap – 'think of the three men, Shadrach, Meshach and Abednego, told of in the holy book of Daniel. Their prayers in the fiery furnace took the power from the flames themselves, did they not? And of course' – tap – 'one might consider—'

'Ólafur,' she interrupts, looking up at last and making an effort to keep her voice low, 'it is very good to hear about the Red Sea, but you should know that God has not answered one of my prayers, not a single one, in nearly eleven years.'

The tapping stops. 'God's answer may not always be what we look for, but he does promise to hear us and console us,' Ólafur says, very earnestly. He has said it before. He has said it on Sundays. God knows he has said it often enough to himself. It is the best he can do. His eyes are trying to seek her out, trying to know her, pleading to be known.

'What is the point of being heard and not answered?' she whips back with more passion than she intended. 'Why does God make us suffer so? What are we punished for, exactly? And if I may mention another question that occurred when I was away, why does he give a mother a heart to love and then empty her arms child by child by child by child?'

Ólafur presses his forehead with two long fingers. 'Children die all the time, Ásta. You know that as well as I do. We lost an infant ourselves only a few days old. We live in a world of suffering. And it's why we look with such longing to the next one.'

He knows he sounds like a priest. That's what she is thinking, isn't it: that they used to be able to talk in a different way?

'Let me ask you one thing in return,' he says, trying again. 'Do you imagine that this father here does not also think of his children every day? Especially the son he was never allowed to know. I can't explain, even to myself, why that loss should hurt so much, but it does. Does it ever occur to you that it might be something to be grateful for, Ásta, that you had nine years to get to know our Jón Ólafsson and I but two weeks in the hold of a ship?'

Do not touch that nerve, Ólafur.

'Grateful?' *I left him. I left my child. I left him alone. I left him forever.* 'Grateful for God's great mercy in keeping me enslaved so much longer than you? Is that what you mean?'

Ólafur shakes his head slowly and looks at his hands.

'Anyway you make my point for me. Why are we both made to suffer?'

'He lays suffering upon us all,' Ólafur begins, clambering back to the pulpit for safety, 'so that his blessed name might be praised.'

Enough. She kicks her sodden socks out of the way and stands up. 'Ólafur, just tell me this. Why should God's name be praised for taking the birch to us?'

Ólafur looks anguished. 'Ásta, this is blasphemy. Pray lower your voice.'

'I don't care who hears. Is it a crime to ask a question? Yes, I suppose it is. Didn't you ever ask a question yourself, Ólafur? Not one? Then here is another from me. Report me for it, if you will. Why must I believe that a child who lisps innocent prayers to Allah is bound for hell? Why is my mind required to accept this?'

'You go too far, Ásta.' Ólafur's voice is trembling. He stands up to face her, staggering a little, so that he has to lay a hand on the table.

'Yes, I have gone too far. Too far to come back to you, old man.'

He makes to lay a hand on her arm and she casts it away. 'I wish I had never come back. There's the truth of it, Ólafur. I should have stayed away with my infidel son forever.'

He crumples back on to the edge of his bed, winded. She rushes out of the house and runs without stopping.

36

The fisherman has taken his time laying out the cod on the high ledge. No need to hurry. It's pleasant to be out on an April evening like this, when the afternoon rains have cleared and you can feel the sun on your face and hear the new-returned birds fussing in the hummocks. It is gusty still – good drying weather for the fish. He wipes his hands on his trousers and slithers down the crag, taking care over some of the sharper outcrops. He is not as fast at this as he used to be, though he likes to think he could still put a younger man to shame. Then he lopes homewards over the lava heath.

In the distance a full-skirted figure is running headlong down the Ofanleiti slope as if she had a pack of dogs behind her. She crosses the heath well ahead of him and is soon stumbling across the pitted grass towards the sea. She loses her footing often among the lava stones, but is quickly up and off again. Lengthening his stride, the fisherman alters direction.

By the time he reaches her, treading softly on the grass, Ásta has arrived at the cliff edge. The hem of her skirt is lifting a little in the gusts and her hair, which has thoroughly escaped its cap, is trailing in wind-blown tendrils down her back. There is less gold in it than there used to be, although her neck is still shapely. She has neither a shawl about her shoulders nor – he has just noticed – shoes. Above him a male snipe is practising its dives. Down it goes, long bill pointed earthwards, its wings humming in the wind, then up again, and off on another fluttering circuit of the sky. The fisherman wonders whether, for all his good intentions, he should let Ásta see him, or just pass on.

She takes a step nearer the edge and his heart misses a beat. What on earth is she thinking? One big flurry of wind and she'll be over. She can't . . . Surely she can't . . .

Without another thought he lunges forward, thrusting out an arm to seize her. At exactly the same moment, she turns around.

'Oh,' she says. 'It's you.'

Well, he might have hoped for a better welcome.

She doesn't look as wild as he would have expected in a woman about to throw herself off a cliff. Drained more than anything. Empty. Perhaps he had her intentions wrong: he really is not very good in these situations. But this dull look she is giving him – no surprise, no interest – is not flattering. Surely he has not changed that much? A trifle less hair perhaps, and more of it on his chin – but she might at least offer a spark of recognition.

'Yes, Ásta, it is I,' he smiles. 'It's a long time since I met you before. I was dripping with fish, as I recall.' He was hoping to raise a smile in return, but her expression remains indifferent. 'You placed a finger on my lips. Do you remember?'

'I remember,' she says, still in that tepid tone, but not removing her eyes from his face. Her blank scrutiny is becoming uncomfortable.

'We were both young then,' he ventures, for something to say, feeling as awkward in this moment as he ever did then. He is like a man who has stepped boldly into the shallows and finds the water up to his neck.

Ásta does not shift her gaze. *How ill at ease he is still. How warm and cheerful his eyes are.*

'I was thinking when I saw you,' she says, as if he had asked, 'that I would just take another step. It's a dreadful sin, isn't it? But I have committed so many that one more should be of little account. Everyone would think the wind had carried me. And then, you see, I just wanted to look at a bird in the sky one more time.'

His stomach plunges straight to his feet to realise he was right the first time. 'Ásta, Ásta,' he says softly, 'is it so bad to be back?'

'I am lost,' she says, still in the dull voice that seems to be talking to itself, but gazing the while at his face with a gathering intensity much more reassuring to his vanity. 'I belong nowhere and there is no one who knows me. Forgive me. I sound as if I'm pitying myself.'

The light from the late sun shining across the water is rimming her hair with gold of its own. He cannot stop looking at it.

She shrugs. 'It seemed important somehow. To be known. More important than . . . anything.'

'I know you, Ásta,' he says, startling himself. Why on earth did he say that?

'Why do you say that?' The first glimmer of interest has sparked in her eyes. He even detects – he knows her face so well – a tiny glint of amusement.

'I don't have the faintest idea.'

She smiles then, and it reaches her eyes, and the lines around them crease most beautifully. And he relaxes. Just like that, the fisherman relaxes. The nerves vanish and in that instant he knows why he is here and what he must do.

'Perhaps what I mean to say is that I have been near you for a long time over the years, before you left and again this last year since your return. I have seen you around the place – you know, here and there – and seen your unhappiness and given much thought to who you are. Who you, as it were, really are.'

She nods slowly, thinking about this.

'I was a little bit in love with you once, you know,' she says.

'And I with you. Still am. Madly.'

At this he laughs in such a merry, open-faced way that she is amazed to find herself relaxing too. He can hardly believe he has said this, but continues to feel wonderfully at ease. Gazing at each other fondly, they stand not a foot from the cliff she had meant to step over and chuckle.

'Do you really?' she says.

'Do I really what?'

'Still love me?'

'Yes. But not, perhaps, madly. That's the wrong word, because I have not lost my wits. In fact, I find my wits to be at this moment more than usually present.'

She is listening. Funny, how hearing him speak soothes her jagged spirits like a mother's song. She takes a small step towards him and he responds with an equally small and, he hopes, barely perceptible step back: she is too close to the edge yet. The snipe is still whirring above them and there is a plover whistling in the grass close by. Ásta cannot take her eyes off this man. The evening sun has cast a mellow glow on his face, which is rough and wind-creased. His beard is a tangle of flame and there is no sign of the youthful curls; in fact, she would be surprised if there is much hair at all under the tatty woollen cap.

'Which is why,' he continues, easing backwards a fraction again, as if trying to tempt a wary beast to follow, 'it seems right to remind us both that there are different kinds of love and different ways of loving. The deepest ones bring pain, always, and it cannot be otherwise. Love and suffering, as you may recall from your catechism, are what all worlds are founded upon.'

It is not precisely how she remembers the catechism.

'But I am more sure today than ever, Ásta – and you may be certain I have given a great deal of consideration to this – that we cannot live in two worlds. And in lamenting too long what belongs in the other we will bring upon ourselves and others only destruction.'

She gives him a scouring look. 'Of what worlds are you speaking exactly?'

'That is as much for you as for me to say,' he replies, hoping this sounds wise without requiring him to commit himself. There are worlds aplenty in her story, and in Ólafur's, and at least a couple in his own. And so many realms of being that even she, who is more sensitive to them than most, would not believe it.

She is studying him now with the half-serious, half-amused appraisal he remembers from the last time they talked. For a while they stand so still and silent that a second plover, breast splashed black with summer plumage, is emboldened to join the other on a rock behind them. Half hidden in the encircling grass, the birds regard them politely.

Ásta, as she did all those years ago, reaches a hand to his face.

'I see you have a beard now,' she smiles, running a finger

through it. 'It reminds me of the seaweed on the shore that time, all fiery reds and oranges. Do you remember?'

'And white. You will notice how much there is of that, too.'

'Of course. It's been a long time.'

'Yes, I have grown older. As have you, Ásta, lovely as you still are. And you will become older yet, if death spares you as long as I think it will.'

'I know what you're saying,' she says, tensing again.

'I am saying that you are known, Ásta. You are deeply and at every age and for all time known. And you have it in you to know also.'

He lets her ponder that. Going over the encounter later in a cold bed, rubbing her frozen feet against each other in a frenzied attempt to bring some feeling back to her toes, she will wonder (being alert to her own propensities) how much of all this she imagined. Yet it does feel most profoundly real. It feels like having a prayer truly heard, like being embraced and held fast by some deep, ancient goodness.

'Now' – he has never felt so masterful – 'I want you to let me kiss you.'

She looks immediately wary, but he leans towards her, strokes away a greasy clump of soft-lit hair and presses his lips gently to her forehead, which feels like ice. It is the most feathery of kisses, light as a snowflake, if also one he allows to lie a while. When he stands back, her eyes are closed.

'Now go and put some socks on,' he orders cheerily, and her eyes spring open. 'If your feet are as cold as your forehead, it's going to take you hours to thaw out. It is time I went home for my dinner.'

She looks at him carefully to make sure she has understood.

Then she grabs his two hands in hers, brings them to her lips and kisses them.

'Thank you,' she says.

When she reaches the bottom of the Ofanleiti hill, Ásta turns and looks back. There is nobody there to see, but she raises an arm in salute all the same. She climbs the slope, picking her way between stones and wondering what possessed her to run out without shoes.

Ólafur is already in bed. He is lying on his side, turned to the wall. As Inga, the serving girl, informs her in hushed, scandalised tones, he did not even say the household prayers. Just pulled the covers around himself without a word.

'He looked terrible after you went out,' she whispers with relish. 'I've never seen him so pale. He hasn't moved since.'

Ásta creeps into her own bed, where she spends most of the night testing her toes and mulling over the tumultuous emotions of the day. It is the strangest thing to have come upon the elfman like that when she was so out of herself, so nearly at the end of everything. And then to have felt none of the old stirrings of youthful desire but only safe and comfortable and – he was right, he was right – profoundly known. She wonders, as sleep arrives to muddle her senses, if it might feel something like this to be understood and restored by your maker, the maker of all things, whom for this lovely moment, shivering in a damp bed with cold feet, she has the fleeting notion of understanding in turn.

With a meal in him and a hard day's work behind, the fisherman is long asleep. In the morning he will lie awake, listening to the sounds of his family getting up around him, and be glad he did not do anything silly. To know with complete certainty that you have said and done exactly the right thing for the person you love most in any world, with no consideration of the cost, does not come to a man often in life. His heart will feel uncommonly light all day.

37

Ásta wakes to the rustle of paper at her ear. A pale light from the membrane window has mottled the room grey. Pulling herself blearily on to one elbow, she looks across to Ólafur's bed. Empty. Beside her head on the pillow lies a neat pile of unbound papers.

'Did Ólafur leave this, Thorgerdur?'

Thorgerdur is hauling children out of bed with determined verve. 'No,' she snaps, with unconcealed hostility. There is no such thing as a secret quarrel between husband and wife in a *badstofa*.

Still propped on her elbow, Ásta picks up the first page and looks curiously at Ólafur's careful scrawl: *The Travels of Reverend Ólafur Egilsson*. Below the title he has inscribed: 'Captured by pirates in 1627'. Ásta has noticed the work on his shelf. In fact, she spotted it the day she arrived home, her eyes ranging hither and thither in the gloom, heart sinking. She could not bring herself to read it. He has not asked it of her.

'Well, then' – she pursues Thorgerdur's implacable back – 'how did these papers come to be on my pillow?'

Her stepdaughter has thrust an infant on to Ólafur's bed and is stripping off a fruity overnight cloth. Children are milling about the room, bickering over socks. Behind the curtain at the back Gísli's snores rumble on.

'Did you put them here, Thorgerdur?'

Lifting up the baby, Thorgerdur wheels around with a glare. 'The shelf required dusting. Perhaps you would be so kind as to do that and then replace the book. Assuming you can fit in some work between walks today.'

Placing the papers on Ásta's pillow was an impulse Thorgerdur would normally have scorned. The gesture feels like weakness when Ásta deserves to be straightforwardly throttled for the way she spoke to her father yesterday. Thorgerdur was shocked at how he looked when he left the house at first light, refusing to wait until the fire was lit in the kitchen, his face ashen and his hand shaking on the latch. If Ásta does not read the book now, Thorgerdur may feel obliged to hit her with it.

Ásta smoothes down her dress, pushes aside the duvet and eases her torn feet to the floor. She thinks wistfully of washing and a change of clothes, but no more than usual and perhaps with a shade less resentment, since she has woken refreshed and is feeling rather mellow. The Reverend Gísli Thorvardsson staggers out in time, scratching his backside and ruffling her hair affectionately as he passes. Once the children have been hustled outside to work and Thorgerdur can be heard safely thumping about the dairy, she pulls Ólafur's battered table to the side of her bed, places his travel papers upon it and begins to turn over the pages.

The island is still muffled in morning mist when Ásta leaves the house. She walks with little thought of direction, her own mind occupied by what she has just learned of Ólafur's, her heart still strangely expanded by yesterday's experience at the cliff edge, which felt like an epiphany. She is surprised when she realises she has wandered as far as the shore. Keeping an eye out for rockpools bloated with yesterday's rain, she picks her way along the black shingle. The mist has shrouded the islands, hiding everything but a few feet of sea. Across the water a seal is calling. *Woo-ooo-ooo*, it cries above the whoosh and suck of the waves from a rock she can't see.

Why did Ólafur not tell her? Why is it only in words written for others that she is permitted to glimpse her husband's soul?

She stops walking to listen to the call of the seal sounding mournfully through the mist. Shakes her head. Sighs to herself. *All right, Oddrún. You too. What is it you have for me?*

Oddrún was right about the king. Christian did say no. Or at least, according to Ólafur's agonised memoir, he did not say yes. Carried by nothing but hope through the perils of the journey home, Ólafur was near felled by his failure. This Ásta has only this morning understood. His writing made her weep for him. As one calamity followed another, Ólafur had tried to convince himself that all that had happened must be as God wished it, because it could not be otherwise: the pirates ravaging the island, the pasha choosing Egill, the soldiers hauling him from his family without time for farewell, the king saying no. Over and over he writes that eternal life will repair all separations, even as he surely suspects it may not mend the ones that matter most to him. Ever more painfully he tries to reconcile his own lived experience with what the Church teaches. Only he never quite succeeds. Ásta sees that. She sees how his sorrow kept getting in the way of the strong word he longed to preach to others.

Yes, Ólafur did ask a question. His whole book is an argument with himself. She has known as little of what he has become as he has known of her.

He writes of the swan (this is what most moved her most), which is said to sing most beautifully when it is sick and close to death. 'But my nature is not that way. I let myself get distressed.' Ólafur, Ólafur. Always so easily made happy and so quickly brought low. 'In this I imitate not the swan but the raven, which cries the same way when he is crushed and dying as when he lives.' These were the words she could not read for tears.

But perhaps it is not a song that Ólafur lacks. Has he not better needed someone to make him laugh? Someone to tell him he should forget swans and ravens, since they belong to the mythmakers, and remember the kind of bird he really is. Someone to remind him of the time long ago when they were out together with the fowling net, the grassy cliff-top heaving with puffins, and she grabbed his sleeve and made him lay down his net.

'See them strutting in their priestly black coats, so busy with important concerns,' she had said. 'Yet when they turn around, what do we see but a soft white breast and a striped orange beak that nobody observing that sober, upright back would expect. Orange, Ólafur. You keep trying to be black, but I saw from the very first day I came to Ofanleiti that your colour is orange.'

'You and your fancies, Ásta,' he said, shaking his head. 'This is a fine thing to be telling me when I am about to pull a dozen little priests from the sky and break their necks.'

'And the voice, Ólafur,' she teased. 'They have your voice exactly.'

'Nonsense. You'll have to do better than that.' He was laughing now. 'The puffin makes hardly any noise at all. I think we can both agree that has never been my problem.'

'No, but they do growl, Ólafur. Just place your ear to the burrow and you will hear yourself in the pulpit. Pray try it sometime and learn what the rest of us suffer.'

He threw a handful of grass at her. Then he grabbed her and swung her in the air, round and round with her hair streaming and her skirts flying until she shrieked for mercy. It is a long time since she has thought of it.

A silver sky is beginning to emerge from the mist, and islands and skerries are recovering their shape. Closer to shore a group of seals is starting to flop back into the sea from a ledge so nearly the same muddy grey as themselves that only the movement gives them away. One remains alone on the rock, gazing straight across the water.

'Speak to me, then, Oddrún,' Ásta shouts, cupping her hands over her mouth. 'You always had a mind to speak when I wasn't listening. Well, I'm listening now.'

The seal regards her levelly out of big wet eyes.

'Come on, Oddrún, you told me a riddle once. You told me not to do what Gudrún did. Not do what, Oddrún? There won't be a better moment for me to know.'

They stare at each other, Ásta and the seal, until the last wisps of vapour have trailed to nothing. Then the seal turns its back, lumbers wetly over the lip of the rock and disappears into the waves. By which time it has come to Ásta how the saga ends.

The mist leaves behind a sparkling April day. The sky is the colour of the polished ceramic beakers in which she used to serve Cilleby his coffee, an intense, eye-watering blue stippled with a few lazy clouds that the breeze has not the energy to shift. The grass is still dimpled with snow, but the air is scented with spring.

Walking back across the heath she catches sight of Ólafur in the distance, making for Ofanleiti from the direction of the harbour. Shrunk into himself with his head down, he doesn't notice her until she is almost upon him. His smile of greeting is so bleak that it forgets to be wary.

'May I walk with you?' she says and, without waiting for a reply, turns about and settles into his tired step. They walk side by side in silence until Ólafur, continuing to look straight ahead, says, 'Do you really think I haven't known the soul's anguish?'

She says nothing.

'In the years without you I pored through the holy texts. I brought to mind example after example from the prophets, the apostles, the martyrs, every saint I could think of and, of course, our Lord himself. And still there was no peace. Every day I had to find words of comfort and explanation for others, but could find none for myself.'

The headland of Stórhöfdi can be seen to the south now, and the further islands, slumbering in the sunshine. Ólafur looks over at them, speaking so quietly she has to lean in to hear.

'I tried to be like Jón Thorsteinsson, always so steadfast in his convictions. You observed once – do you remember? – that he had no mountains to climb in the mind. Well, it's true. And that is because he knew the truth and proclaimed it without a waver.'

Ásta ponders this. 'Did you hear, Ólafur,' she says carefully, 'that the Reverend Jón's son has become a renegade corsair? They call him the Westman.'

Ólafur inclines his head. He has heard about a lot of things since the hostages returned. More than she knows.

'Then you will know that licensed piracy – exactly what robbed him of his father – is how he earned the money to ransom his mother from her chains. Our dear Margrét breathed her last in the arms of her Muslim son, grateful to be there. Now, let me ask you this: would that not have presented mountains, and ravines too, for Jón Thorsteinsson the husband, Jón Thorsteinsson the father? What poem might he have written about that? What dream would serve to make sense of it?'

Ólafur stops walking and turns to look at her directly.

'I don't mean to make light of this, Ólafur,' she adds quickly. 'You know I loved my uncle dearly.' Then, carefully again, the way being strewn with eggshells: 'I only wonder if it may sometimes be easier to die a visionary and a martyr than to live a feeling man and an honest priest.'

Ólafur gives a short, mirthless laugh. 'You know, I have even been jealous that he died the way he did – passing into eternal life from an infidel blow with the name of Jesus Christ on his lips, ripe for legend before he was even in the grave. Now when people suffer on this island, they remember Jón Thorsteinsson and feel themselves stronger. While I . . .'

He hesitates and looks down again. His clasped fingers are working restively.

'Go on, Ólafur. I'm listening.'

'I failed.'

He looks up again, but not quite into her eyes. Ólafur has told himself he will speak to her only the truth, will hold back nothing of his own weakness, whether she despises him for it or not. But this unexpectedly gentle encouragement is threatening to unman him more than her scorn.

'I could not bring my family back. That was the biggest failure. But I also failed to bring comfort to others, although God knows I tried. My preaching sounded hollow in my own ears. I filled nearly every page of my book with the sacred promises on which we rest our hope and they were words, words, words, because what I really felt was despair.'

She takes his arm in silence and they go on a little way.

'You will recall hearing that when I and the others were in Copenhagen on the way home last year, we received classes from a priest in training by the name of Hallgrímur Pétursson.'

Ólafur nods. 'I hear he lives a hard life now for a man with such a fine mind. He and Gudrídur received permission to marry in the end, I am told.'

For a priest she recalls being stern about adultery, he too is taking trouble with the eggshells.

'You would like him, Ólafur. He was rather wet behind the ears and extremely rash in his ardour, but he reminded me of our Egill as he might be as a young man – a thinker, you know, seeing more than he says.'

Ólafur smiles to himself, imagining Egill as the priest he thought he would be by now, climbing the pulpit of Landakirkja in a black robe with a white ruff at his neck. Ásta sees the thought passing across his eyes and hurries on before it can lead him into shadow.

'It was a lot to expect of this young man that he would be able to draw us easily into the fold again, as if we had just wandered off to crop on the wrong kind of grass for a few years.

But he did have a knack of saying simple things that struck deep. He told us that God in the person of Jesus Christ had himself been where we were, abandoned and in despair, and that there is where he would meet us. I have a feeling Hallgrímur would say something of the kind to you. He might even suggest that it is in your very weakness that you manifest your God most truly to others, not in the unassailable strength of the martyr.'

She shrugs and casts down her eyes. Humility is not Ásta's strongest feature but she is trying very hard. 'Of course, that might just be me speaking.'

Ólafur gives her one of the mild but searching looks she has been finding so irritating of late. She puts up with it meekly enough and is congratulating herself on her forbearance when he says, not mildly at all but with some asperity, 'It's good to hear you speaking at all, Ásta. After yesterday I thought you might not address another word to me again.'

A wan smile accompanies this, which softens the accusation and makes her think twice about pointing out how very annoying it is to be preached at when you long only to be understood.

'I was at fault, Ólafur,' she says instead. 'You have done nothing to deserve the way I've treated you, and I don't have the words to explain it. Except to say that I used to belong in this place, I used to know who I was. And then I went away.'

They continue meandering home under her lapis lazuli sky. It is Ólafur who breaks the silence.

'Sometimes, when you were away, I would walk to Stórhöfdi. People thought I had taken leave of my senses to labour all the way up there for nothing, but I had such a longing to get as close as physically possible to where you were. I would pray then for you and the children, that you might be treated well. My prayers seemed to flow easier up there in the wind, and they were invaded less often by the man who bought us.

'He came to me over and over again, the Moor in the shadows. There he would be, in my prayers and in my sleep, standing before me in the white cloak he had on when he sent me to the king. But he never had a face. Always that white hood and no face.'

Ásta keeps her gaze on the sea, glad he cannot see her own face.

'The name of Ali Pitterling Cilleby was not known for cruelty. I learned that much when I was there. Jaspar and I were fed well and never beaten, and I tried not to let myself forget that. Over the years of our separation Cilleby's name rang in my head like a forge hammer, but I held on to that – that he was not cruel.'

'Ólafur, I must tell you . . . I have to tell you something.'

His eyes stay fast to the islands. She does not know how to say it. It was another world.

Ólafur turns towards her and lays his two hands on her shoulders to bring her round to face him. Then he gently tips up her chin until she is forced to look at him.

'*Mín kaera* Ásta, do you think I have lived all these years on this island, watching forbidden love filling one empty hearth after another, without wondering about you?'

Wondering all that time? Fearing? Had he really? She has never thought about it.

'And what about you, Ólafur?' she asks with studied airiness. Although she knows fine there has been no fat widow squeezed into Ofanleiti, it is a relief to be diverted from what she is going to have to tell him. 'May I be permitted to wonder also?'

'As you rightly observed yesterday, I am some small way past my prime,' he replies, very dry. 'And two wives are enough for any man, don't you think?'

Goodness, she is going to laugh. She can feel it on its way, the old bubble rising at the wrong time. He sees it and doesn't know what to do, and the laughter dies in her throat as fast as it arrived.

'Yes, Ólafur, on reflection I do think two wives are probably quite enough for any man,' she says soberly. 'But I do need to tell you something.'

'Tell me nothing.'

He begins to walk again. His step is so much quicker than before that she has to run a little to catch him and cannot see his eyes.

'You came home, Ásta. That is enough.'

38

Something in the air around them has shifted. To be sure, nothing happens that garrulous young Inga judges worthy of reporting to the rest of the island. The passage between their beds remains too wide for an arm to reach across in the night. Nor do they say much, cleansed of words as both feel themselves to be. But something has changed. It reminds Ásta of the fugitive breeze that used to escape the sea on a stifling afternoon and creep through the white city to refresh the roof garden; somehow, from somewhere, it has stolen into Ofanleiti. Ólafur, dazed with thankfulness, feels it as the breath of life in Ezekiel's vison, arriving to revive a valley of dry bones.

A few days after their walk, he comes hurrying home and whispers that there is something he wants to show her.

'What – now?'

'Exactly now. The light will be with us a while yet this evening. Come on. I promise you'll be glad of it.'

He sets off at once and Ásta trips across the springy heathland behind him. Spring is blooming among the grass and stones, although you would have to look closely to see the tendrils of snowy pearlwort and the furled pink buds no bigger than a newborn's fingernail.

'Ólafur, slow down. Where are we going?'

'You'll see.'

He leads her along the cliff path to a stout rock hollowed on one side and cushioned with greenery. 'Here, this will do. Make yourself comfortable, and look over there.'

Two diminutive puffins are standing side by side on a grassy ledge just below the cliff-top, their heads twisting this way and that, as if unable to contain their curiosity about the world to which they have returned. As Ásta watches, one flies off and the other potters alone, making space on the ledge again when the mate returns. Far below, the sea is pimpled with black heads.

Ólafur smiles to see her smile. 'There, I thought you would like to see them back.'

They sit watching the birds in silence, while Sudurey, Álsey and Brandur doze to the west and the setting sun lays down its path on the water. Then they stroll home together.

Seeing how she struggles with so much that never ruffled her before, Ólafur does his best all summer to show her other things. He points out the tiny green sandwort roses blooming white out of black gravel. He makes her look more closely at the lava they walk on every day, so deep buried under roots and crumbly earth in places that the rocks themselves seem to have feelers in the land. One day he even gives her a turn by patting the big stone at the foot of the Ofanleiti slope and suggesting, with barely an eyebrow disturbed, that she should take a look, for if ever there were a rock that looks like an elf-home it is surely this one. 'Ólafur, are you being serious?' she gasps, wondering if anyone else is fainting clean away to hear this too. He revels in her pleasure. He is much restored.

When a letter makes its way across the water from Finnur Gudmundsson, they pore over it together for news of Helga, and when Ásta's eyes fill with tears to read it, he strokes the back of her hand with one careful finger. Helga's latest born infant lived only weeks; she is already confined with another.

In the autumn he hustles her off to pick blueberries. 'Try this,' he says, shattering a spider's web to pluck one and rolling it for her in the palm of his hand. 'See how perfectly round it is. Look at the shine on it. So dark you think it's black, but tip it in the light like this and, see, it's a dusky blue.'

That colour. She puts the berry in her mouth and bursts the smooth skin between her teeth, savouring the flesh, remembering his taste.

Ólafur is watching her a little sadly. He always knows when she leaves.

She catches herself and smiles to him. 'It's all right. I'm back.'

'I know,' he says, so gently she could weep.

'I always come back.'

'I know.'

She puts her hand to his worn cheek and strokes it. Then they begin to fill their basket with fruit.

Sometimes there is no simple answer to a question: not one that will serve the truth at any rate. That is what Gudrún tries to tell her son at the end of the Laxdaela saga. She is a very old lady by then, having outlived her lovers and withdrawn into, of all things, religious seclusion. Her son Bolli Bollason, by the husband she goaded into murdering Kjartan Ólafsson, comes to visit her and asks a question that has obviously been much on his mind: which man of them all did his mother love the most?

Evasively, the old woman mentions her four husbands and their qualities or the lack of them, hoping this will suffice. But her son is persistent. 'You still haven't told me which *man* you loved the most. There is no need to conceal it any longer.'

Then Gudrún gives her answer. 'I was worst,' she says, 'to him I loved the most.'

And was that Kjartan, the man she wanted but could not have? Or was it Bolli, the father of her son? The saga does not tell.

Do not treat worst the one you love best. *I hear you, Oddrún.* But that still leaves a question the saga does not ask. It may be that the sealwoman had it in mind that an answer should be sought to this, too. Is it by the wanting that we measure love, or by something else?

The summer of 1638 is followed by an especially tough winter. Usually the sea-wind sweeps the worst of Heimaey's snow away before it has time to pile against doors and block out what light is left. But this winter it has stayed.

Ólafur has developed a cough he cannot shake. In January his legs nearly fail him as they trail back through the snow from Landakirkja. He keeps having to stop to catch his breath and spit.

'Lean on me a moment,' Ásta says.

He puts his hand to her shoulder and she an arm around his waist and they rest like that on the heath, she bearing the frailness of him as the last of the afternoon light sinks over the mainland.

'I think it is time to ask my son-in-law to take over.' His face is pale as bone and his forehead speckled with sweat.

'Come, Ólafur,' she says playfully, her heart the while thudding with alarm. 'Remember what Gunnlaugur Adder Tongue said: "a man shall not limp while both his legs are the same length." Our Jón loved to hear that story.'

Ólafur manages a wry smile. 'My legs are the length they always were, but I'm afraid they are not going to carry me much longer.'

Since then he has barely left the house. Day by day the winter saps his strength, the snow seeming to smother the life in him, the wind sneaking through the walls to steal the warmth from his blood. His chest heaves with coughing and his eye is too bright.

'He should be in the master bed,' Thorgerdur says to Ásta. 'I have spoken to Gísli and he agrees. It really is time.'

Ásta draws aside the grey wool curtain that droops across the far end of the *badstofa* and helps Ólafur into the bed. His head sinks gratefully on to the pillow and he shuts his eyes. She pulls the curtain across.

'Move over,' she says, and his lids fly open.

Obediently he shuffles towards the wall and she clambers in beside him, primly arranging the covers around them both. The duvet smells of Gísli. After a moment or two Ólafur stretches out a tentative arm and she lets her head fall into its crook. She turns her body towards him. Their feet embrace, sock to sock.

'You're lovely and warm, dearest,' he murmurs.

After that Ásta sets the curtain aside by day, so that Ólafur

333

can feel part of the winter activity of the household, the making and the mending, weaving cloth and weaving stories, while children with stomachs becoming emptier as the stores go down squabble over fishbones. When the room becomes so dark that nobody can see their hands any longer, Thorgerdur lights a grudging lamp with the oil she guards like a troll in case it too should run out before spring. And then the tales begin.

Ásta and Ólafur have taken to holding their own private *kvöldvaka* behind the curtain, while Gísli drones at the other end. One evening Ólafur asks if she ever heard any stories in 'that place'.

'None that you won't find immoral and dangerously heretical,' she whispers, wondering if there is a single tale from the harem that would not put her on course for re-education.

'I am warned and my spirit is on guard,' Ólafur says, very solemnly, and squeezes her hand.

Hoping that Gísli isn't listening, she chooses Sympathy the Learned, since they might as well begin with an impossibly clever slave-girl routing the men. She is careful to remove all mention of Allah, the Koran, the ruling Caliph, Sympathy's breasts (which, as the papery aunt told it, were like pomegranates separated by a valley of delights) and her navel (carved so deep it would have held an ounce of nutmeg butter – a picture nobody else in the harem ever seemed to find astonishing).

'Young Abu al-Husn was his father's joy and the light of his eyes,' she begins, lying back against the cold wall with her hand still inside Ólafur's. 'When the old man felt that his debt was about to be paid to, er, God, he called his son to him, saying: "My child, I must prepare myself to stand before the Master. I leave you great riches, fields and farms, which should last your lifetime and the lifetime of your children's children. Enjoy it without excess, thanking the great giver and being mindful of him all your days."

'With that the merchant died, and his son shut himself away with his grief. But all too soon his friends led him away from his sorrow. "Have done with tears," they said. "Make the most of your riches and your youth."

'So Abu al-Husn forgot the counsels of his father. He satisfied every caprice of his nature, frequenting singers and musicians, eating enormous quantities of chicken every day, unsealing old jars of strong wine, and hearing ever about him the chinking of goblets. He exhausted all he could exhaust and spent all he could spend, until he awoke one morning to find that there remained of his possessions only a single slave-girl.'

Ólafur is listening. Sometimes she has to stop while he coughs and then she strokes his forehead until he has breath again and nods for her to go on. This one remaining slave, she tells him, was the supreme marvel of all women.

'She was called Sympathy. She was as upright as the letter alif. That's the first letter in the Arabic alphabet, Ólafur, and it stands straight as a blade of grass. And her figure was so slim that she might defy the sun to cast a shadow by her. The colouring of her face was a wonder and its expression was filled with blessing.'

'Just like yours, my love,' wheezes Ólafur, who has recovered the knack of laughing at her.

'"When I dance and sing," Sympathy told Harun al-Rashid, the (shall we say) leading official, "those who see and hear me are damned by my beauty. When I walk in my perfumed clothing, balanced upon my feet, I kill. When I wink, I pierce. When I shake my bracelets, I make blind. When I move my bottom, I overthrow.'"

'Ásta, stop.' Ólafur clutches his chest. 'If you make me laugh I'll only cough. Come closer. I am not too old, nor too ill, to be overthrown a little myself.'

Night after night, lying by Ólafur's side, Ásta recounts the tales she learned from Husna and the papery aunt. One evening his breathing is so sore and anxious that she takes him right into the roof garden itself.

'You should not be up here, Ólafur, when the women are telling their stories under the stars but, see, they don't notice you. Close your eyes and just breathe in that jasmine. Breathe it deep. That's right, my dearest, that's the way to do it, nice and slow. Can you smell the perfume? Now let the velvet night caress your cheek. Do you feel it on your skin, soft and warm? And look about you. There are women you won't recognise here, but see who sits beside me with her legs crossed, rapt in the story. It's your little Marta, grown since you saw her last. Can you see her pearly skin and those freckles on her nose and the calm, serious eyes? She doesn't move in the slightest, but only listens. Just imagine how our Helga would be shuffling and looking everywhere. Marta's stillness draws you to her. Look. She has seen you now. Do you see? And she's smiling.'

When Ásta looks at Ólafur next he has fallen asleep, his breathing sweet and steady, his cheek wet.

Thus does Ásta Thorsteinsdóttir discover there is more than one way to make a bed of stories.

Ólafur no longer has the strength to cough, and his chest rattles so loud it is setting the whole room on edge. Even the children are subdued. Inga has taken to loud bursts of sobbing, the latest of which prompted Thorgerdur to give her a good shake and hiss in her ear that he wasn't dead yet and could she not try a hymn instead? Gísli has been to sit on Ólafur's bed to pray aloud, emerging a little red about the eyes himself.

Ólafur lies still and mute as a statue behind the sagging curtain. His eyes are shut, but Ásta has a feeling he can still hear. She takes Gísli's place on the edge of the bed and envelops his right hand in both of hers.

'Ólafur *minn*, I want to tell you about a . . . well, I was going to say a vision of mine.'

It is so dim behind the curtain that she can't be sure, but it seems to her that his lips twitched.

'Oh, all right, then. I don't know what to call it. Maybe I'll just say a story. Anyway, it's a picture that has come to me as clear as an Oddrún dream – and I fancy more reliable.'

Another shadow of a twitch.

'You are in it, Ólafur, and in such a beautiful place. Perhaps it's Torfastadir. Remember how you described it to me in the pasha's prison, with Hekla dusted in snow? Only this is summer. The grass around you is vivid green and it's studded all over with tiny white flowers, and the clear, Icelandic light has washed everything clean and fresh. There are horses grazing in the meadow, and you are walking past them towards the far river. You stop to let the dark brown one nuzzle your hand – his name is Skími – but you mustn't linger long, because you have someone to meet beyond the river.

'"Welcome," says the man when you reach him at last. He is

wearing a long cloak. Not a white cloak, Ólafur. I hope you are taking in this point. There is nothing white in the slightest about this man. His cloak is orange as the sun. "I have been waiting for you, Ólafur Egilsson," he says.

'You know him at once, although you can't remember when you met. You feel as if you have always known him. Together you begin to walk towards the distant sea.

'After you have gone a while in silence, the man turns to you and says, "Why do you sorrow still, Ólafur Egilsson? Your pain is over now. I am taking you home."

'"I fear I will miss my children," you say, hanging your head. "I am not even sure I'll see my wife again in the place we are going."'

There is a faint quiver within her cupped hands, a leaf stirred by the lightest breath of wind. She knew Ólafur was listening.

'"I see," says the man. "Then let me show you something."

'He leads you along a small path and you arrive soon at a gate. Are you listening, Ólafur? "Don't go in," says the man in orange, putting a hand on your arm as you reach for the latch (which is a clever one that pulls the gate shut again by itself – you'll love it, Ólafur, when you get a chance to practise). "It is not time to meet them yet," says the man, "but you may look."

'You peer over the gate into a garden. It has clouds of starred jasmine trailing over the walls, and vines with plump purple grapes twined around the archways, and from somewhere nearby you catch a whiff of mint. And then you see him, standing by a knobbly palm tree. He is older than you remember and his hair is burned fair with the sun and he's tall as you are, his body nicely caught up with his arms. He looks up from his book and smiles and waves.

'Then a girl catches your attention. She is sitting on the grass sewing, deep in concentration, until she feels your gaze upon her. "Pabbi," she cries, "look who is with me."

'And you notice beside her a laughing young woman with curly red hair, surrounded by little children. Their attention is occupied by a boy with a wide smile whom you recognise at once, though you knew him only as a baby. He is capering about on the grass to make the children laugh. "Pabbi," he shouts when he sees you, "I'm going to sea."

'You look at them one by one. Then you look back at the man and he shrugs – as if to say, all that worrying, what was it about?

'Then you look again, for someone is missing. And that is when you see me. Yes, Ólafur, even I am there in the garden, sitting quietly in the corner with my hands around my knees, watching them all proudly. "I will be with you later," I shout over. "Keep the bed warm."

'You turn back to the man in orange, feeling that your heart will burst with happiness.

'"Come now and rest, Ólafur Egilsson, in the place where you are known," he says, putting an arm around you. "The others will join you later."

'Then the pair of you set off back down the path towards the sea.'

On the other side of the curtain the room has fallen quiet. Honestly, if she had realised how well a vision goes down, she would have thought to have one sooner.

Ólafur's eyes flicker open. They find her and they thank her. To die known, to die beloved, to die certain: no man can ask for more. Perhaps, she thinks, raising his bunched fingers to her lips and kissing them one by one, this was Oddrún Pálsdóttir's gift to them both.

Ásta slips into the bed beside him. As the hours pass, she listens to each slow breath and the empty air between. When she wakes next morning, her face pressed to his cold cheek, she is alone.

39

The woman steps cautiously from the boat, holding her skirts away from the creeping tide and thanking the fisherman for his trouble.

'It was none,' he replies. 'I am only glad I was able to persuade you. I'll be here again tomorrow to row you back, as long as the weather holds. The sea can be chancy at this time of year. Do not, I pray you, return alone.'

The woman takes a moment to press her boisterous hair back under the wool cap. It blows straight out again. 'How is she?'

'More peaceful now that Ólafur is buried, I would say. A winter death is always difficult. His body lay wrapped in the storeroom for weeks, resting between one sack of meal and one of salt, until the earth was soft enough to lay him to rest. She worried that he was lonely.'

The woman bows her head for a moment and he looks at her fondly. It was brave of her to come with him. It is not every woman who will follow a big-bearded stranger when he turns up at her door saying he has a horse to spare and a boat waiting. But even as a young girl she never feared adventure, this one. She left her children with her husband (as shocked and protesting as any man would be) and set off on the journey to her mother.

'We don't have much time,' she says, gathering herself. 'I must go to Ofanleiti at once. I hope I can remember the way.'

'You'll remember the way, Helga,' says the fisherman.

There is a moment, one delirious moment just after her daughter has erupted into the room and is flinging herself towards her, when Ásta is convinced that Helga has flown straight from Ólafur's garden to meet her in heaven. Obviously her own arrival there is another pleasant surprise and it is most gratifying to have got at least one story right.

Then Helga is in her arms.

'Mamma,' she cries, hot-faced from the hill, hair as exuberantly awry as ever, 'I've come to fetch you home.'

When it is time for the household to settle to sleep for the night, mother and daughter squeeze together into Ásta's slim bed. There they lie looking at each other in the sunlight still filtering late in the evening through the cloudy pane.

Then Ásta has to devour her all over again. Nose and cheeks, forehead and ears, the finger Helga sliced the top of with a forbidden knife when she was small, the soft place on her neck where she always squealed to be touched, the thick red curls that are darker now than they used to be and smell of rank smoke. Twelve years of kisses, twelve years of hunger.

And when Helga asks her mother, giggling, if she remembers how old she is, Ásta says, 'But you're still my child. I can't tell you what it is to have a child.'

Then Helga lays a cheek against her mother's and Ásta wraps an arm around her waist. And both of them are glad to be no stouter or they would be on the floor.

'By the way, Helga,' Ásta murmurs in her ear, 'can I ask when you last washed your hair? There's no need to flare your nostrils like that, my darling. I just wondered.'

And together they drift to sleep.

1669

From Snjallsteinshöfdi in the district of Landsveit you can see right out to the islands on a fine day. The grass grows flat for miles towards the sea, which is further away than it seems. Ásta never tires of watching the horses running there in the wind: dark brown and grey, piebald and fawn, one near as white as a Moor's burnous.

She has lived more years than even Ólafur managed and would not object now to a long sleep. She knows where she will lie. Helga has shown her the place, at the foot of a quiet slope within sight of the farmhouse, with icy Eyjafjallajökull to the east. The graveyard faces south, south to where Egill is, south to where Marta went, south to where Jón will be breasting the waves at the helm of his ship. Unless, of course, one or other of them has made it to heaven before her, which is always possible and will be lovely.

But Helga is here. Darling Helga, who has put up with her for thirty years and never sat through a story yet. She is quick and impatient, with an exhaustingly restless eye on the work to be done next. True heir of Margrét, Ásta smiles to think: however did she produce her?

She has not told Helga all that happened in the years she

spent far from Iceland. Helga is warm and loving, but she has neither Ólafur's curiosity nor Marta's delicate understanding. Perhaps it has been for the best, since there are griefs that lie too deep for stories. For those who want to know what it is for human beings to be stolen and traded and lose their children, there is always Ólafur's book, which has been much copied and passed around. By now others may have written their own accounts of captivity. Men, of course. They will all be men. Does it matter that nobody will know how it was to be a woman?

Once she lies in the quiet earth, Ásta Thorsteinsdóttir, the woman who came back, will become the wife of a pastor again. Nobody will know she had a mind as interesting as his and experiences no man would think to record. Nobody will know how she questioned and puzzled and wondered about what lies around and beyond the lives we so agonisingly lead. Nobody will know that she longed to make a poem like Egill Skallagrímsson and compose a saga that would lose people in their imagination four centuries hence. Nobody will know how she put her lips just below the cheekbone of a slave-trading Moor, where his skin was smooth as the breast of a young gull, and told him that she loved him.

She does occasionally mention that she knew a sealwoman once, who left her a gift that helped her to see. 'And I don't mean spectacles,' she will laugh when her great-grandchildren stare. They like to hear how Oddrún Pálsdóttir lost her skin under the midnight sun and lived on Heimaey telling dreams until she was an old woman. 'That was before the pirates came,' Ásta will say. Then the youngsters clutch each other and shiver, because every child knows about the pirates and every adult worries that the sails of an Algerine galleon will appear again one day off the shores of Iceland.

As age has loosened her tongue, Ásta has lost any qualms about telling people she was once kissed by an elfman. 'Just here,' she will say, 'light as a snowflake,' and tap a forehead more papery than the old aunt's ever was. The elfman lived in a rock near Ofanleiti, she tells them with a dreamy look, and he knew her better than she knew herself.

Poor old Ásta, people say, exchanging a significant glance. She was always one to see things.

Author's Note

Tyrkjaránið

The Turkish Raid, or *Tyrkjaránið* was one of the most traumatic events in the history of Iceland. Within a matter of days in the summer of 1627, corsairs from Algiers and from Salé in Morocco raided a number of coastal regions, killing dozens and carrying at least four hundred people back to North Africa, where they were sold into slavery.

Iceland's experience was far from unique: several Mediterranean states (no slouches in the piracy business themselves) lost many thousands of their citizens to the thriving slave-economy of Algiers. It was a time when slavery was being practised across the world and the mass transport of Africans to the New World was just beginning: the first African slaves were brought to Jamestown, Virginia, in 1619. In Algiers there were captives from all over England (four hundred listed in 1669), from Wales, Scotland and Ireland. Most of those were snatched at sea, although a raid on Baltimore in West Cork in 1631, also led by the corsair admiral Murat Reis, carried off one hundred and seven men, women and children from their homes in an attack very similar to the one on Iceland. Ransoms were being raised for hostages right across Europe, with religious orders in Italy, Spain and France doing much of the fundraising and negotiating, while English governments preferred to explore military options.

But relative to its size, Iceland, the furthest north the corsairs reached, was hit particularly hard. To lose four hundred people out of a population of around forty thousand – including most of the island of Heimaey – is by any standards a stupendous national tragedy, particularly for what was at the time the poorest country in Europe. That may be one reason why Iceland has kept painfully in its collective psyche what has largely faded from the memory of other affected nations. It may also be down to the Icelandic compulsion to write. Voluminous historical narratives were written afterwards and copied by hand. It was felt important that the nation's great trauma should be understood and never forgotten.

I came upon *The Travels of Reverend Ólafur Egilsson* in the English translation by Karl Smári Hreinsson and Adam Nichols some years ago. The original manuscript is lost, but nearly forty somewhat differentiated copies survive. Confusingly narrated in places and packed with biblical references, it describes the raid on the Westman Islands, the four weeks the author spent captive in Algiers and his journey to Denmark in pursuit of a ransom from the king. Under the dense religious language (wholly of its time but laborious for a modern reader) can be glimpsed a man who loved his family and was distressed at losing them, a scrupulous reporter, a clergyman who found his own sorrows near intolerable and the effort to contextualise them within his faith agonising. He mentions an eleven-year-old son, a younger un-named child, and a boy born on the ship who was named after Ólafur's murdered fellow priest. Other than Egill being the first choice of the pasha and perhaps subsequently going to Tunis, the children's fates are not known. There was also a wife. 'My dear wife,' Ólafur calls her. She occasionally floats into focus in his account and that of others – a detail here, a line there – and then away again.

But who was she, this woman who gave birth on a slave-ship and returned ten years later without her children? With the help of Helga Hallbergsdóttir, curator of the Sagnheimar Folk Museum on Heimaey and indefatigable genealogist, I was able to establish that Ásta Þorsteinsdóttir, born in Mosfell, was the niece of the island's slaughtered poet-priest, Jón Þorsteinsson, and was the second wife of Ólafur Egilsson. He already had a daughter, Þorgerður, whose husband Gísli returned to Heimaey to take over the priestly duties after the raid. Ásta and Ólafur had an elder daughter, Helga, who was not captured with them. The couple had two years together on Ásta's return, before Ólafur died on 1 March 1639. Ásta herself died in 1669 in Snjallsteinshöfði on the mainland, where Helga was living with her husband Finnur Guðmundsson. A fragment of inscribed stone, all that remains of Ásta's gravestone, has been moved to a museum in Skógar on the south coast.

But what happened to Ásta in Algiers and after she returned to Iceland? What was she like, this woman who grew up among educated men? What did she think, what did she dream about, what made her laugh, how did the mind of a woman from a small, homogeneous society react to finding herself in one of the most heterogeneous societies on earth, how was the stern religious faith she grew up with affected, how did she deal with the mental agony over her children, why did she return without them, what happened to her marriage? History can tell us no more than it does about almost any woman of the time in Iceland or anywhere else, unless she happened to be a queen.

SALLY MAGNUSSON

Joyfully, I appropriated the freedoms of fiction to feel my way into these long-ago lives, and in doing so to explore the role of story itself in helping us all to find ways to survive. While I have done my best to make it historically authentic, this remains emphatically a work of imagination, coloured by the present as well as the past.

Ásta and Ólafur did live in Iceland in the places described in this novel, as did Jón Þorsteinsson and his wife Margrét, whose son Jón did become a corsair nicknamed Jón Vestmann and ransomed his mother, described in at least one source as being in chains. Jón Vestmann himself had an eventful life as a pirate captain and leader of many raids. He returned at last to Copenhagen, where he had to make public atonement for abandoning his faith and undergoing circumcision, and died there in 1649. Anna Jasparsdóttir, the wife of wealthy Jón Oddsson, did indeed convert to Islam and marry the Moor Jus Hamet, and was vilified for it back home. Young Jón Ásbjarnarson did rise in the Algiers civil service. An envoy by the name of Wilhelm Kifft did organise the ransom of thirty-four Icelanders, and the Dutch entry in his accounts concerning Ásta's purchase is exactly as quoted in his gamely spelled ledger. This is the only unequivocal mention I have been able to unearth of Ásta's owner. I have drawn for some aspects of Cilleby on reports about the fantastically wealthy corsair leader Ali Pichilin, owner of six or seven hundred slaves, two palaces, his own mosque and a fleet of galleys, a man noted for his intelligence and his taste for debating with Christians. Einar Loftsson did lose his wife, and indeed his nose and ears, according to an autobiographical account referred to in other sources, and managed to purchase his own ransom. Guðríður Símonardóttir, from whom has survived a tantalising fragment of a letter sent home from Algiers to her husband Eyjólfur, did fall for Hallgrímur Pétursson when the trainee priest was refreshing the faith of the returning hostages in the winter of 1636–7, and Eyjólfur, who had a number of illegitimate children by then, was among those drowned in a terrible accident at sea, just in time to save the lovers from harsh punishment. Hallgrímur went on to become Iceland's most revered hymnwriter, his name remembered in Reykjavík's fine Hallgrímskirkja cathedral. Their love story has been re-imagined by Steinunn Jóhannesdóttir in her novel, *Reisubók Guðríðar Símonardóttur*, also available in Norwegian, German and French. I am delighted to record here Steinunn's generosity in sharing her own considerable research and patiently answering my questions.

Ólafur Egilsson tells us that on his return to Iceland he did visit the Bishop of Skálholt, who at that time was Oddur Einarsson. I have imagined Ólafur's subsequent visit to Skálholt at a time when the new bishop, Gísli Oddsson, is known to have been struggling with the implications of carrying out the king's wish to begin raising a ransom. There is no historical evidence that Ólafur threw himself into the fundraising efforts, but it seems to me most likely.

Murat Reis *aka* Jan Janszoon from Haarlem had a long career as a corsair admiral, moving freely between bases in Salé and Algiers, and is thought to have masterminded the raid on Iceland.

This is a fascinating period in European and North African history, which deserves more attention. I am grateful to Professor Þorsteinn Helgason, who has been a most encouraging historical mentor, and commend his forthcoming book, *The Extreme Point: The Turkish Raid in Iceland 1627*, which he kindly made available to me in manuscript form.

As well as being little known in Europe, this is a period in Algerian history to which that nation's own scholars are only just beginning to turn their attention. I am grateful to academic and author Dr Linda Belabdelouahab Fernini of the University of M'Sila for her time and insights, and to writer Med Megani. Special thanks to Said Chitour, personal guide *par excellence*, who led me patiently around what remains of Algiers' precipitous Casbah area, where the captive people of so many nations lived, died, suffered, made shift, used their ingenuity, recanted their faith or held on to it, waited for ransoms that sometimes came and sometimes did not, and in a not insignificant number of cases made interesting new lives for themselves.

Heimaey, only inhabited island of the volcanic Vestmannaeyjar archipelago (which has expanded since the seventeenth century and now boasts a fifteenth island, Surtsey, which exploded out of the sea in 1963) is the most welcoming of islands. Huge thanks to Magnús and Adda, who put me up at the wonderful Hótel Vestmannaeyjar and kept me right on puffins. And to the afore-mentioned Helga Hallbergsdóttir in the folk museum, who devoted many hours to sharing her own insights with me. Also to Kristín Jóhannsdóttir at the island's Eldheimar Museum up the road, which is dedicated to the dramatic volcanic eruption of 1973 (when, it might be noted, the sealwoman's dream came true at last).

Thanks also to Páll Zóphóníasson and Páll Magnússon, to Ragnheiður Erla Bjarnadóttir, who advised me on early seventeenth-century church life and buildings in Iceland, and to my willing translators of ancient papers: Jan Zuidema in Holland, Joakim Pitt-Winther in Denmark and Sigurjón Jóhannsson in Reykjavík. Also to my old friends, Marta Guðjónsdóttir, Ragnheidur

Guðjónsdóttir and Kjartan Gunnar Kjartansson, who accompanied me all over south Iceland hunting down historical locations.

To Two Roads publisher Lisa Highton, who patiently encouraged a novice novelist to find her feet and her voice, Federico Andornino, editors Helen Coyle and Amber Burlinson, cover artist Joe Wilson and designer Sara Marafini, the great team at Two Roads and John Murray Press, and Jenny Brown, most encouraging and indefatigable of agents – thank you all. I've been awed by your skills and support.

Most of all I want to thank former Icelandic president Vigdís Finnbogadóttir, who once upon a time drove a young woman around Iceland in a blue Volvo and helped her to see trolls in the lava and hidden people in the rocks and sealfolk dancing on the beach at midnight. And my late father, Magnus Magnusson, who introduced me to the sagas and told me about the most famous question of them all.

Acknowledgements

The quotations from Reverend Ólafur Egilsson's memoir preceding each section are taken, with thanks, from *The Travels of Reverend Ólafur Egilsson: Captured by Pirates in 1627*, translated and edited by Karl Smári Hreinsson and Adam Nichols, Fjölvi, Reykjavík, 2008. An updated edition was published in 2016.

The tales about the origins of the hidden people in the unwashed children of Eve and the Girl at the Shieling can be found in *Ísklenzkar Þjóðsögur og Æfintýri* (Icelandic Folklore and Legends), a large body of traditional tales collected by Jón Árnason and Magnús Grímsson, first published by Jón Árnason in Leipzig in 1862 and 1864. I have made free with a number of different English translations, notably by Jacqueline Simpson, J.M. Bedell and May and Hallberg Hallmundsson.

The version of *Laxdæla Saga* I relied on was the 1969 Penguin translation by Magnus Magnusson and Hermann Pálsson. The four lines from the tenth-century *Sonatorrek* of Egill Skallagrímsson, a skaldic poem lamenting the deaths of two of his sons, is from the translation of *Egil's Saga* by Hermann Pálsson and Paul Edwards, 1976, also Penguin. For the story of

Sympathy the Learned I am indebted to an English version by Powys Mathers of *The Book of the Thousand Nights and One* from the French translation by Joseph Charles Mardrus, London, 1923.

Broadcaster and journalist Sally Magnusson has written 10 books, most famously her *Sunday Times* bestseller *Where Memories Go* (Two Roads, 2014) about her mother's dementia.

Half-Icelandic, half-Scottish, Sally has inherited a rich storytelling tradition.

The Sealwoman's Gift is her first novel.

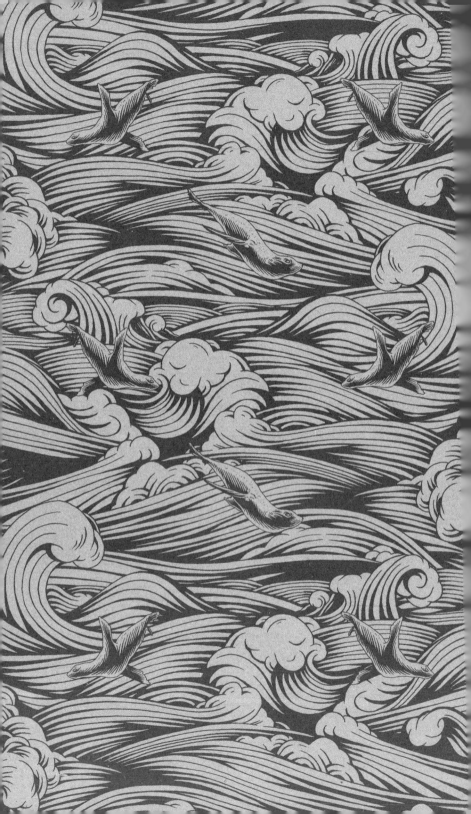